THE BODY OUTSIDE THE Kremlin

THE BODY OUTSIDE THE KREMLIN

A NOVEL BY

JAMES L. MAY

DELPHINIUM BOOKS

THE BODY OUTSIDE THE KREMLIN

Printed in the United States of America

For information, address DELPHINIUM BOOKS, INC.,
16350 Ventura Boulevard, Suite D
PO Box 803
Encino, CA 91436

Library of Congress Cataloging-in-Publication Data is available on request.
ISBN 978-1-883285-84-5
20 21 22 LSC 10 9 8 7 6 5 4 3 2 1

First Edition

Jacket and interior design by Colin Dockrill

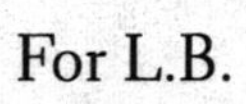
For L.B.

Part One

NATIVITY CATHEDRAL

1

Someone must have been telling the Information and Investigation Section about me and Gennady Antonov, for I was summoned from roll call for questioning the morning they discovered the body.

I picture myself in the moments before the summons came. A freezing and sickly young man—a prisoner, waiting for the count of prisoners to finish so he could move and force a little heat into his arms and legs. From where I stood, I could look up from the ragged coats and hats worn by my fellow *zeks* to a pair of snow-swept churches, which hemmed us in on either side.

In the dark they were heaps of shapes. The towers of the larger Transfiguration Cathedral, were blackened, stunted, out of proportion: their cupolas had been lost in a fire. Men who'd been here longer than I said it had happened two years before, shortly after the Bolsheviks took the place over from the monks. What remained was all arches, boarded windows, dirty whitewash slapped on brick and stone. Without the cupolas to anchor its shapes in the air, the whole structure floated off into abstraction—flat in the light from the arc lamp, like geometry on gridded paper.

"Seven."

"Eight."

"Nine."

"The thirty-fourth group of ten."

That was concrete enough. I could hear the count taking place somewhere to my right. We were waiting to be tallied before they split us into our work detachments and gave us our assignments. In my customary spot, I'd be part of the sixty-fifth or sixty-sixth group of ten. Between me and the tally's progress hung three hundred prisoners' worth of fogged white breath.

This was October, 1926, on the island of Solovetsky, in the White Sea. I was twenty years old.

Being hungry enough for a long enough time can produce a sensation like moving backward very slowly while staring straight ahead. That morning, the objects before me—the churches' arcs and angles, the coats, the hats, the swollen features of my neighbors—seemed to have receded a little more every time I looked at them, without my ever quite catching them in motion.

The counting stopped. When, after a minute or two, it hadn't resumed, the men around me began to murmur.

Then a new voice, shouting a name instead of counting: "Bogomolov! Prisoner Anatoly Pavelovich Bogomolov!"

The name was mine. It had never sounded quite so alarming. I couldn't think of any rule I'd broken, but on Solovetsky the wheels of justice ground erratically. You could have a bad day and for an imaginary crime get a real bullet in your real head.

"Better go quick, Tolya," my friend Foma muttered behind me, giving me a light push. "Don't forget about yelling."

Faces turned to look as I hurried to the front of the column. Some pitied, others were resentful. Being singled out by name promised nothing good for the named *zek*: that was the pity. But a delay at roll meant a slow start on today's quota, less time before call of roll tomorrow for food and rest. Of that there was little enough already—hence the resentment.

Wind sluiced through the alley between the churches. I'd felt it already, but stepping out from the sheltering mass of bodies made it worse. The company commander, a man named Graski, was waiting.

It was famous, Graski's sadism. When your work platoon was shaken out of bed at midnight to toil squelchingly at shoring up the walls of a canal, his name certified the orders. Our boots were thin and full of holes because of him. Weevils in your bread?

Graski laughed about it somewhere. So, yes, sadism—but not of a very inventive kind. Too much work, too little food, noxious living conditions, the occasional beating to death of a prisoner by the guards, another prisoner being made to stand naked in the cold during winter or among clouds of mosquitoes in the summer: most of his monstrosities simply arose from his position. Even the most personal of his abuses towards us—he would require us to yell "Good morning, Commander," more and more loudly in response to his "Good morning, prisoners," until he grew bored—was tedious. But it was that we hated him for. That was what made us spit when we said his name.

Thus when he nodded at me, I bellowed, "Good morning, Citizen Commander," back at him as loudly, short of shrieking, as I could.

The commandant was an image of grimy virility. Unshaven jaw, barrel chest, face like a plough blade. One hand was tucked between the buttons of his coat. He stood with a man I didn't recognize, a few guards lined up behind them.

"Enthusiastic, aren't you?" he said with a frown.

"Is this Bogomolov, Comrade Graski?" asked the other man.

Graski shrugged. "I suppose so. You Bogomolov?"

"Yes, sir," I said.

"He says yes," said Graski.

The other man was highly ranked. I could tell because his leather jacket hung down to his thighs. In our present era the *apparatchiks* dress up in suits to go to the office and relax at their dachas in peasant tunics. But at that time the Party was close enough to its underground roots to favor the severe manliness of leather—let less fervent revolutionaries make accommodations with freezing temperatures. With that coat, he might even have been one of the few assigned, rather than sentenced, to his position.

That would have been a mark of true distinction. In fact, most of our jailers, the men like Graski who guaranteed Solovetsky's continued functioning as a prison, were themselves serving sentences. The difference was, they were not only *zeks*, but also members of the Cheka, the Bolshevik secret police agency under whose authority the camp was administered. Or, rather, they were members of whatever acronym designated that agency at a given moment. During the time of my imprisonment I believe it was OGPU, for *Obyedinyonnoye gosudarstvennoye politicheskoye upravleniye*, the Joint State Political Directorate. At other times during the sorry term of my affiliation with the organization, its letters have been NKVD, or MVD, or most recently KGB – but never mind what they stand for. To me they will always mean simply "Cheka," with all of that name's dread and menace. And all of us on Solovetsky knew it was the Cheka that kept us there, whatever its official title.

The laws of demography decreed that the Cheka would have its share of the country's rapists and mean drunks, all of whom had to be sent to jail like other criminals. The genius of the organization, in those days as today, lay in its adaptation to those laws. It recognized that such operatives don't lose their political suitability when the State is forced to lock them up: most still make good Communists, effective spies and bosses. And this realization solved yet another problem: a camp with a population like Solovetsky's—some 10,000 souls in 1926, a big-enough number, if nowhere near what it would grow to in time—needs administrators, while a Party as progressive as the Bolsheviks has few personnel to spare for the care and feeding of wrecking workers and reactionary class enemies. Did it take some archbureaucrat to untangle the dilemma, or did such a rational piece of political economy slap even the freshest Party member in the face? Whichever, the solution was elegant: let the prisoners run the prison, with the ideologically correct ones ministering to the incorrect.

The idea that the man in the leather jacket might fill a role important enough that it had not been assigned to a prisoner flooded my back teeth with sour spit. No *zek*, unless he is an informant, benefits much from conversation with a Chekist. And the more highly placed they are, the more dangerous.

"You know Gennady Mikhailovich Antonov?" asked the man in the leather jacket.

Tucked into the inner pocket of my coat was a monograph on the *raskolniki*, the Old Believers, which Antonov had lent to me just the week before. At that time I still tried to improve myself by reading, and the material on mathematics or logic that I would have preferred did not present itself every day.

"I know him to speak to," I said.

Blond hair parted on one side gave this Chekist a boyish look, somehow intensified by heavy features in a lean face. He'd taken off his cap, a leather one like the jacket, and was tapping it lightly against his right leg. I must have gone through the same motions a thousand times on the streets of Saint Petersburg. But in that courtyard the gesture looked alien, outlandish, as if he'd casually pulled a tooth from his mouth to see if it needed cleaning. You wouldn't uncover your head that way unless you had a room with a stove to go back to, and soon.

"This is the one, then," he said. "Come with me."

He waved over one of the guards, over whose shoulder a rifle was slung on a strap, and we marched away from Company Thirteen. Behind us the count resumed.

Solovetsky. Then, as now, people called it Solovki for short, as if they were mentioning a friend. Solovetsky, Solovki: new words of the Soviet state, which like so many others were old words with new meanings attached. Before 1917 they'd been names for an island monastery, the oldest in the north: you imagined sanctified cassocks and beards, snow-covered shrines among the evergreens, rocky shores, the pealing of bells over empty distances. Separated from civilization by Karelia's undeveloped wilderness, the holy place lay almost on the arctic circle. Five hundred miles of forest and swamp to Saint Petersburg, a thousand to Moscow, two hundred by storm-rocked boat to Arkhangelsk. For five centuries, monks drank kvass there, upholding Orthodoxy against the Antichrist's advances. If you were devout, you might once have made a pilgrimage during your summer holiday, sent back a postcard showing white spires and a shining bay. Even if you weren't, you might still have seen the postcard.

And after? After the revolution, Solovki was no longer a spot to visit. Its name meant inaccessibility and cold. It meant disappearance. It was the space between two parentheses, where certain elements were to be isolated from the rest of the social equation until, at some uncertain, later moment, the time would come to evaluate them. Solovetsky was for embezzlers, wreckers, Mensheviks, and anyone who did not sufficiently repudiate the bourgeois conventions of the past. Such types were sent for three-, five-, or ten-year sentences, and who knew what might be waiting for them when they got out? The state itself had not yet existed for quite ten years. I suppose there was general consensus that Solovki was an icy hell. But remoteness is one of hell's properties. We like to believe that hell is somewhere else.

Those of us confined there naturally acquired still another perspective. Solovetsky was a prison-labor camp, its main product lumber. Remote as the place was, all its other needs had to be supplied locally as well. And so Solovki also raised vegetables, manufactured bricks, operated a power plant, washed clothing, administered programs for the edification of its inmates, buried them when they starved or had to be shot. Operations centered on the former monastery kremlin, a citadel of lichen-covered stone walls and thick towers. It stood with its outbuildings on the main island of Solovetsky itself, but needful outposts scattered themselves all throughout the archipelago's islands.

You were told when you arrived that you'd stepped out of the sphere of Soviet power, onto a shore where only Solovki Power mattered. Every new group of prisoners had this shouted at them the moment they were unloaded from the boat. "No more Soviet power! The only power here is Solovki Power! Solovki Power!" Bewildering distinction, for an audience still blinking in the sunlight after the suffocation and dark of the hold. But it was certainly a threat. "Soviet power," if an increasingly empty phrase, was at that time still a comforting one. It recalled the old worker's councils, which the Bolsheviks had claimed to be representing when they seized control of government. There were echoes in it of self-reliance, egalitarianism, democracy. Though the soviets themselves were for radical laborers and soldiers, in the tumultuous year before the Revolution everyone had seemed to be ready to form representative organizations at the slightest provocation. My father had once been a member of a temporary council formed to represent the interests of the train car my family rode in on the way to visit relatives in Nizhny Novgorod. He'd spent the whole of the fifteen-hour ride strategizing with his fellow members over how to ensure that our luggage was properly looked after and that the refreshment cart did not pass us by.

In that case, what was Solovki Power?

It proved to be an angry guard's boot grinding your face after he'd knocked you down with no warning. Or it was an old man being forced to carry railroad ties, one after another, until he collapsed and died of exhaustion. Some other week, it might be your work platoon being forgotten, so that for two days you had no work assignment and worried someone might take it as an excuse to forbid you collecting your rations. The regime on Solovetsky, cruel and deadly, was also haphazard, clumsy, random. We *zeks* sawed, chopped, and dug. We lifted. We dragged and hauled. In winter, we wore poor clothes and shivered in the winds that tore among the trees. Insects swarmed us when it was hot. We ate—never enough. We thought about eating: how little we had eaten, what we might eat, when we might eat, where we might get something else to eat. Feet swelled. Hands callused. Faces chapped. Solovetsky's ancient stones moved about from place to place in wheelbarrows.

The official name for all of this was *SLON: Severnye Lagery Osobogo Naznacheniya*, the Northern Camps of Special Significance. The word *slon* means "elephant," of course. Another new meaning for an old word.

The Chekist walked ahead while the guard followed along at my side. Out of the corner of my eye, I watched him put a dirty glove into his mouth. He pulled it off with his teeth, then reached underneath his coat to scratch his belly.

I couldn't blame him. I had lice as well.

Passing beneath a low arch brought us out into the main courtyard, where *zeks* from other companies already hurried back and forth along paths tramped in the snow. The man had asked about Antonov. Across the yard I could see the Holy Gates, shut tight as normal. Beside them, a narrow door led up a flight of stairs to the museum, where Antonov worked.

That did not seem to be where we were going. Instead, we passed through a white series of alleys and yards, eventually arriving at the Nikolski Gate, beneath the kremlin's northeast tower.

Already there was a line. Regular traffic in and out of the walls was required to pass here, even though the Holy Gates had been designed originally as the kremlin's main entrance. Presumably this was because Nikolski was smaller, making our passages in and out easier to monitor. If it meant long lines, well, that was simply the price of being a *zek*. You were lucky even to be able to stand on those lines. Most only left the kremlin en masse, under guard with their work groups.

The Chekist, however, passed immediately to the front, pausing only to show a set of documents to the men on guard. They wore the standard uniform of gray coat, high boots, and military cap. A goiter swelled the neck of one, and the other smacked his lips nervously. They handed the documents back and forth beneath their guttering lamp, then quickly waved us through.

Outside we stopped. The wind was blowing snow across the lake that lay behind the kremlin, and off to my left I could see the broken stalks that marked the turnip fields. Now that the walls were behind us there was a faint lightening on the eastern horizon. It was frigid.

The Chekist stretched his arms above his head and inhaled deeply, then interrupted himself with a hooting cough. When he had finished, he turned to me.

"So, Bogomolov. You must be curious where we're going."

"Yes," I said. The air froze everything it touched. Even gloved and in the pockets of my coat, my hands felt raw.

"Well then, why not ask?"

I hesitated. It would not do to tell too much. "Is this about Gennady Mikhailovich's . . . devotional propensities?"

"Devotional propensities? I know nothing about it. You must tell me: *is* this about Antonov's devotional propensities?"

So, he was playing with me. Fine. "I only know he was religious. I don't know what you've called me here for."

"And you don't know where we're going either. Why not ask?"

I was to follow his lead. Trying to outtalk him would do no good. "Where are we going, Citizen Chief?"

"We're going down to the wharf. Now I have answered two questions, and you owe me at least one. So: how do you come to know Gennady Mikhailovich Antonov?"

"We met at the museum. A few weeks ago."

The Chekist laughed. "Yes, I see you're a student." He gestured at my cap. "What do you think of this cap, Razdolski?" he asked the guard. "Perhaps you have never seen such a thing before. In the cities, young men wear them to show that they're educated."

Razdolski scratched the back of his neck halfheartedly. He

did not have much attention to spare for my hat. Beneath its layer of filthiness, it was white, with a short visor and a blue band. I'd received it upon graduation from my gymnasium in Petersburg. Too light for the weather, somehow it was all I'd managed to pack during my hurried preparations after my arrest. I'd stuffed it with rags, but they didn't make it much warmer.

"Guard Razdolski is not a man of much culture," said the Chekist, "but his silences are eloquent. They invited you to the museum on the basis of your hat, then? And you met Antonov there?"

"That's right," I said.

"Quarantine Company leaves you plenty of time for intellectual pursuits, does it?" It didn't, of course. It was Quarantine's roll call he and Razdolski had just retrieved me from. Its official name was Company Thirteen, "Quarantine" being a kind of joke—whether or not we were sick was of no concern to anyone involved. Every new prisoner served there for three or four months, until its regimen had treated any moral contagion—insubordination, undisciplined behavior, excessive appetite, expectation of warmth or kindness—you brought with you from outside. In the meantime you slept in Nativity Cathedral, the next church over from Transfiguration and its burned towers. You lined up for abuse by Commander Graski, toiled at the most brutal assignments, and starved. Only once a *zek* had suffered enough to receive a clean bill of behavioral health could he hope to escape to something more permanent—a day we all looked forward to with anticipation and apprehension. Some companies were better than Thirteen, but others were just as bad, or even worse. We watched everywhere for ways to improve our chances.

"I'd heard students could make connections," I said. "I went when I could. Not often."

"Of course. Everyone knows you can't get anywhere without connections. I don't blame you." The Chekist shivered and rubbed his arms. "Brrr. Come on. Too cold to stand still."

He took a place at my side, hands clasped behind his back. "And so you and Antonov struck up a little acquaintance, got to know each other," said the Chekist. "You became friendly. Where did you have your little talks?"

"Sometimes I stopped by the museum to watch him work in

the evenings. If I had the time after supper."

"And those were the only times you saw him?"

I swallowed. "The only times."

"Hmmm. Antonov did something with those icons, isn't that it?" He paused for me to nod. "Some members of the Party object to that kind of thing. Why spend effort on the paraphernalia of the religious delusion? It's like putting lamps and opium pipes on display."

He shrugged. "But that's not what I think. It's all part of the study of history. Of anthropology, even. Marx is clear about this. We're the results of a historical process, so why not keep in mind what came before?"

He began kicking his boots through the snow now, throwing puffs of it up into the wind and moving a little ahead. "For instance, there's a monograph to be written by someone—not me—on the miracles icons were supposed to work. If religion is a delusion, a miracle must be a hallucination, eh?"

He continued kicking for a moment, then spun around so abruptly that I nearly walked into him. He placed a hand on my chest, giving me a sharp push. Stepping backwards to regain my balance, I bumped into Razdolski's hard body.

"You lied to me just now," said the Chekist.

"What do you mean?"

"You met Antonov in the Company Ten dormitories. The other week."

"That—it was only for a moment," I said. "I barely—"

He cut me off. "You didn't want to mention that you'd gone into a building off-limits to you."

The kremlin wall stood to my left, its giant stones cold and crusted with snow. My teeth had begun to chatter. Clenching my jaw only moved the trembling to my throat.

All the friendliness had gone out of the Chekist's voice. "What were you doing in the Company Ten dormitories?" he said.

It all would have been better if I'd been wearing a warm scarf. A former cellmate of mine, a housebreaker from Rostov, had once given me this advice: always wear your coat when they interrogate you. If you're cold, he'd said, you'll be paying attention to that instead of what you're saying; you'll lose track of your story.

It almost made me laugh, this man's having waited for me to

get chilled through before asking his difficult questions. Didn't he know how much I was in his power? The cat-and-mouse routine was ludicrous, unnecessary. For the first time that morning I felt angry. Less at the injustice of it, perhaps, than at the extravagance.

"I might be able to tell you what you want to know if I had the faintest idea of what this is about. What's Gennady Antonov done? Why bring me here?"

Like that, the breath exploded from my lungs. My knees fluttered out of existence. It feels like you'll die, being punched in the solar plexus.

"Shut up," the Chekist said quickly. "I am asking questions now. What else are you keeping to yourself? What did you talk about with Antonov?"

The snow burned against my cheek. It was a minute before I could push myself up, much less wheeze out an answer. "Nothing," I finally said. "Food—he gave me a little food. That's all."

"Why?"

"I don't—I don't know. Pity, maybe."

"What did you talk about?"

"Icons. That's all—all he ever talked about."

"Tell me about the food he gave you."

"Porridge. A bowl of porridge, and a strip of haddock. And a quarter of an onion. I stayed long enough to eat the porridge, then I left. You can—" I took too deep a breath and started to cough. "You can hit me again, but that's all I can tell you."

The Chekist crossed his arms. "Well, Guard Razdolski. He invites me to hit him again. Is this backbone, or stupidity? He sounds sincere. Shall I hit him again?"

I managed to look back at Razdolski, who shrugged. He was scratching the back of his left leg.

"Come on," said the Chekist, "both of you."

For the rest of the way he was silent. The path took us around the corner of the kremlin, then down a gentle hill to the bay, where the quay began about forty yards from the walls. The dirty white facade of the main administration building loomed over us, set back from the water and parallel to the wharf. At the far end, a group of men stood in a group around something on the ground. We made our way towards them.

Closer to the water, logs were stacked in pyramids. The whole camp had mobilized to produce lumber during October, in anticipation of the sea's finally freezing at the end of the month; it was the last chance for Administration to bring up the year's production levels. In quaratine we'd done hard labor among the trees for the past three weeks.

Some of the waiting logs might even have been ones I cut myself, arranged into these monuments along the water. They would have to be loaded onto a ship soon, but for now the quay was empty.

It hadn't been easy to meet the quotas. Even the invalids ranked Class 2 Fit, who weren't normally approved for heavy work, had had to cut wood. When I'd arrived, I'd wondered whether it would be a good idea to get myself sorted into Class 2. Now I was glad I hadn't. Their rations hadn't increased to match their assignment. We watched them waste away before our eyes.

The crowd of men parted as we drew near. Before I'd had time to take in what lay before us, the Chekist said: "At any rate, here we are. To answer the question you posed a minute ago: I've brought you here to look at this corpse. A drowning. Found floating in the bay last night."

It was, of course, Gennady Antonov.

2

There. The body signals that things have begun, doesn't it, in a mystery story? What I'm writing down is a mystery, then, a *detektiv*. Here is the body, at the beginning.

My new neighbor, Vasily-the-tank-commander, was the one who suggested I might write something about my time in the camps, those thirty years ago. A memoir, he called it. "A record of what you witnessed. We know next to nothing about what it was like in the early years."

But Vasily is an idiot. Vasily-the-tank-commander thinks commanding tanks in the war against the Germans taught him something about our national character—about human desires. "Russians are burning to hear the truth, Anatoly Pavelovich," he says. "Humankind burns for the truth!" Vasily is a Party member. He has had read to him a speech of Khrushchev's that says Stalin was less than great, and thinks things will be different. What happened to me back then matters now, according to him.

Idiocy, worthy of an idiot. Humankind doesn't want truth. If it did, mystery novels would end as soon as they began. "Citizen X was killed by Criminal Y for reason Z. The End." Why withhold it, if the truth mattered at all? The writer knows the answer, doesn't he? Just as I know, now, who killed Gennady Antonov.

No, what humankind wants is not truth. Humankind wants a body.

And this is the lesson of my experiences in the camps as well.

Antonov's body lay curled up on the wharf like an ear. The legs with their knees drawn up to the belly, the bowed spine connected to the bent neck: they made the lobe and the outer volute, while the hands crabbed before his chest suggested ridges spiraling inward. His clothing and long hair, wet after being fished out of the water, had frozen to the stones of the quay.

It was now past sunrise, turning into what in October we called a fine morning on Solovki: gray clouds with the sun showing through at moments, a strong wind blowing in off the freezing sea to the west. On the south side of the bay, a shelf of ice had begun to creep out from the shore. The deeper water here by the quay was only cloudy. The wavelets lapped slow and slippery against the stone.

The Chekist had been gone for an hour or more. After a few cursory questions about whether I recognized the body (I did) and whether I knew how it had come to be floating in the bay (I didn't), he'd left me and Guard Razdolski behind with strict instructions that I was neither to go anywhere nor to interfere with anything. Gradually the little crowd had moved away as well, casting dubious looks in my direction. Now Razdolski stood a short distance from Antonov's corpse, arms crossed and the gun dangling off his shoulder, only unbending from time to time in order to scratch his chest or beard and sniff his dirty fingernails.

Antonov wore trousers, boots, and a sweater, but no coat or hat. The posture was rigor mortis—that much I knew from having had, in the Lubyanka, an elderly cellmate whose expiration we only noticed when he failed to rouse himself to claim his share of soup.

No, what shocked me about Antonov's corpse wasn't the posture, but the face. It was pink, bright as if painted. Only the week before, he'd been explaining the polychrome technique to me. The medieval artists who used it were not, he said, bound to slavishly imitate the colors they found in nature. Instead they chose pigments in obedience to whatever laws of sacred beauty tradition had revealed. Skin might be green or light blue, the sky ocher, the ocean black, the leaves of a tree gray or gold.

Now, with a magenta face, Antonov might as well have fallen

victim to the technique himself.

Where I stood at the end of the wharf, the bay lay between me and the southern portion of the kremlin; you could have drawn a secant line across the irregular curve of the water's edge and connected me with the Holy Gates. Their portico was overlooked by a collection of windows in different shapes: a big demilune, the squares of casements. Each opened into what had been the Annunciation Chapel—now the museum.

Gennady Antonov wouldn't be returning to his workbench there. He'd remain on the quay, stuck to the ground with frozen hair and cloth, until someone moved his body somewhere else.

It always struck me that Antonov was the only person on Solovetsky who really belonged where he'd been placed, among the venerable paintings and pots of glaze. His quiet speaking voice came out of a tufted beard full of crooked teeth; he wore, always, an astrakhan hat and an expression of extreme mildness. Massings connected by thinnesses defined his body and face: thick fingertips and knuckles on slender hands, bulbous nostrils on a long, narrow nose, bulging eyes beneath a fine brow. He'd moved smoothly but unexpectedly, as though the air around him had a different consistency than it did for everyone else.

I'd pinned certain hopes on Antonov. And now, here he was. Drowned, frozen, and magenta. The wind pulled at my cap and stung my ears. I yanked it back down onto my head as best I could, and stomped my feet to keep warm.

Sledges laden with timber had begun to arrive at the landing. The men dragged them in teams, uniform and small at this distance, but assuming odd angles as they strained forward over the muddy road. There was still no ship to receive their loads. Presumably one of the camp's boats —the *Gleb Boky*, named after one of the bosses of the OGPU, was used to transport both prisoners and goods, and there were several smaller steamers as well—would be arriving later in the day to take the wood on board.

By now Razdolski and I were the only ones standing at the end of the wharf with Antonov's body. Some of the sledge-pullers stopped to look out at us before they unloaded at the other end.

I had started to worry about my next meal. If I was still here when the time came for my platoon to line up at the steaming pot at the edge of the trees, Foma and the rest would simply divide my portion between them. That was still hours away, but the Chekist had departed for who knew where, to return who knew when. Some provision might be made for Razdolski, who'd been posted over the body as part of his work assignment, but I doubted he'd share with me.

At least I'd saved a hunk of last night's bread in the lining of my jacket. I broke it in two, putting one of the pieces in my mouth. It lost its flavor almost immediately, but I chewed until the stuff mashed to paste between my teeth. Then I swallowed, slowly.

You learn to make bread last.

I'd started on the second piece when the tall shape of the Chekist separated itself from the unloading activity at the other end of the quay. Next to him someone propelled himself along with a cane. As they drew closer, this figure resolved into an old man with a large gray mustache. Though I couldn't place him, he looked familiar.

"Here he is," said the Chekist as they came to the body.

"Yes." With his cane, the old man gave Gennady Antonov a light, sad prod. "Here he is."

"The identity, you see, is not the issue." The Chekist pulled a cigarette from a cheap northern-manufactured packet and tapped it against one palm. "But we have no coroner. Can you confirm drowning as the cause of death?"

"Perhaps," said the old man. "Once I've examined him."

"Examine, then." The Chekist lit his cigarette and threw the wooden match away. "You aren't bothered by its being an acquaintance, are you, Yakov Petrovich? I assumed this would be a professional matter for you."

That was who the old man was, then. Antonov's cellmate, another denizen of the relatively privileged Company Ten.

Such relative differences were important. Even today, with the Gulag governed by the famous principles of "economic rationalization," which declare that every prisoner shall be fed only in proportion to his contribution to the NKVD's yearly production plan, successful *zeks* learn to ferret out inefficiencies, find ways to be rewarded with a full portion of calories for less than a full measure of work. The man who parlays his friendliness with the doctor into a position as a medic, or his schoolboy lessons in arithmetic into a job keeping the accounts: he is the one who lives.

And you must understand: SLON was not yet the Gulag. It was not rational, economically or otherwise. How much more plentiful, then, were the opportunities to find an advantageous arrangement? With the prisoners running and, indeed, systemizing their own prison, administrative positions that could be distributed as the spoils of patronage proliferated. Clerical obligations multiplied as men found ways for themselves and their friends to avoid being murdered by hard labor. The production plan still ruled the island—I suppose that during October of 1926, seven internees out of ten coughed in Solovetsky's forests and fumbled dangerously with its frozen tools—but its reign was less complete than it would become in even five years' time. After all, the idea of operating an internment camp on such a large scale was quite new. Our jailers were still working out how best to exploit us.

Hence the companies like Ten, which consisted in the main of prisoners taken up into Solovetsky's (bloated) bureaucratic or (slimmer) professional layers. To receive such a transfer was what all of us in Quarantine's splintered cots dreamed of—all of us with any acumen or hope of making the necessary connections, anyway. If, by dint of demonstrated competence, ruthlessness, or willingness to butter up those with influence, you got the assignment, your ration would only be a little better than in the labor companies, and you would enjoy no more freedom of movement. But at least your work could be done indoors, without the risk of its leaving you sick or crippled.

I couldn't recall where this Petrovich worked, but I'd met him once before—on the occasion the Chekist had been interrogating me about, in fact, when Antonov had brought me to their cell to collect the haddock and fragment of onion.

It had been a brief encounter. I'd remembered his name only because it was slightly odd. Yakov Petrovich Petrovich: the surname was the same as the patronymic. He was the oldest man I'd seen in the camp, above seventy, at least. The mustache occupied a thin, wrinkled face. In the same way, certain dilapidated squares are dominated by statues from before the Revolution.

"I am observing the scene," said Petrovich. "I am thinking. This is how a detective works. Basic investigative method."

The Chekist laughed. "My organ has its own investigative methods." He picked a flake of tobacco from his mouth. "And anyway, the body was found in the water. I doubt you'll learn much from its present situation."

"When was he found?"

"This morning, early. Between 4:00 and 4:30. The prisoner assigned to clean the administration building's third floor saw him floating. At first we thought he was a swimmer—he'd drifted into the middle of the bay. A rowboat had to be sent."

Petrovich nudged Gennady Antonov with his boot, then turned and registered Razdolski and me. The eyes above his mustache were sunken, yes, red-rimmed and watery, certainly—but their blue irises scraped you bare. I nearly looked away when he turned them on me.

"What's he doing here?" he said to the Chekist.

"He knew your cellmate."

"Yes, and?"

"Someone had to identify the body."

"I know you," the old man said to me. "I've seen you before. What are you called? Bogdanov? Bogolyubov?"

"Bogomolov," I said. "Anatoly Bogomolov."

Petrovich looked unsatisfied, but he shuffled back towards Antonov's corpse. At its side he bent slowly down on one knee, leaning heavily on his cane and clicking his tongue. "So. Livor mortis present in the hands and face." He brushed a piece of hair back over Antonov's ear, breaking ice from it in the process. "He was like this when they pulled him out? Stiff like this? Good." He muttered, half to the Chekist, half to himself. "A submerged body floats curled up like so, head downward—same as a baby in Mama's belly, so they tell me. You always find lividity in the hands and face. Cold water keeps the blood pink, you see? Otherwise he'd look bruised."

He shoved at Antonov's shoulder for a moment, then got his other hand underneath the knee, but the body's position gave him trouble. He let it go. "I need him on his back."

"Help him, Bogomolov," said the Chekist.

"Me?" I asked. The prospect of touching the corpse worsened the ache in my sternum where he'd hit me. My lungs fluttered.

"Yes." He'd wedged the stub of his cigarette between two fingers, and without appearing to be actively smoking it, he was holding it up to his lips. The hand in front of his mouth hid his expression.

I looked at Antonov. With the legs bent and stiff as they were, he would not be easy to lay flat.

"Go on," said the Chekist. "Turn him."

Antonov's ankles felt strange through my gloves, but I could at least tell his knees were locked. Holding him that way, it didn't take much effort to swing the body over onto its back and hold it steady. Some of the hair frozen to the dock ripped with a dry sound.

The grating noise in the old man's throat was a chuckle. "You look like you are deciding whether to buy a pair of boots from the rack."

Antonov's ankles were delicate, but with great bone lumps in them. He had always seemed like a collection of knobs held together by wire. I tried to think of anything he had ever said to me, and couldn't. Death made him something basic as a line.

"It's a lever of the second class," I said.

Petrovich barked—that was his laugh, as I would learn—and looked up at me again. "What was that?"

Those blue eyes. This time I did look away, only to find myself staring into Antonov's face. Along with turning pink, it had grown bloated, sponge-like, with the eyes flat and dull beneath their half-drawn lids. "I'm sorry. It was nothing."

"Nonsense," said Petrovich. "A lever, you said."

The Chekist's expression was readable now. He looked pained, I thought, suffering from the ludicrous turn things had taken. I said hurriedly: "It was a pointless remark. I only meant I get leverage by holding the feet this way. Turning him on his back makes the ground a fulcrum. Since his center of gravity stays close to the ground while the feet go in the air . . . It doesn't matter."

Petrovich shook his head, still amused. "Suppose it doesn't. Now then."

He pushed at the legs, then pulled on an arm. He tried to turn the head on the neck. "Rigor mortis is pretty well advanced. He would have died at least five or six hours before they fished him out of the water."

The old man pried open Antonov's mouth with two gloved fingers and looked in. While I continued to hold the ankles, he got down painfully onto both knees and pumped Antonov's chest—

once, twice, three times—and after that opened the mouth again, still not removing his gloves. This time he nodded slowly.

"You're wrong," he said to the Chekist. "He didn't drown."

"You're sure?"

"No foaming at the mouth. A man inhales fluid, his lungs force it out again when they collapse, even if he's long gone. With the air and slime in him, it comes out a mess of white bubbles."

"Dead before he went in the water, then," mused the Chekist.

"So I conclude."

"What killed him?"

Petrovich bristled his mustache. "Not drowning. I'm not done examining."

While we watched, he ran his hands over Antonov's chest, then lifted up the collar of his sweater to peer beneath it. Evidently not finding what he was looking for, he pulled the sweater up, revealing the pale belly and breast. He ran his fingers over a streak of pink, the same color as Antonov's face and hands, that ran laterally along the dead man's ribs.

Every time he nudged the body, I felt the vibration through Antonov's legs.

"No obvious wounds," he muttered. "Use that leverage of yours to lay him on his side, Bogomolov. No, the other way, with his back to me."

Petrovich removed his gloves now and ran his fingers through Antonov's icy hair, pressing it apart and spreading it out while he looked closely at the back of the neck. "There. That bruising, you see?" he said. "Spinal cord enters his brain just there. Skull and vertebrae crushed with minimal fuss. Very economical use of blunt trauma, done by someone who knew the best way to crack heads. Afterward they let him lie somewhere for an hour or two. Face down, I think. Long enough for the blood to start pooling there at the side of the chest."

The Chekist was quiet. "He was certainly killed, then?" he said finally. "No chance of an accident?"

"Put whatever you like in your file," said Petrovich. "I won't argue."

"That's not why I brought you here."

Petrovich planted his cane on the snowy stone and began pushing himself up. When he'd finally struggled to his feet, he took a moment to catch his breath. "In that case, it's no accident," he said. "It's murder."

Razdolski chose that moment to clear his throat and spit, then lapsed back into his natural silence. For a long time, no one said anything. The Chekist had taken off his cap and was tapping it against his thigh again, looking out at the water. I began to feel hopeful I'd be allowed to return to the platoon in time for our meal.

"You want to find out who did this," said Petrovich at last.

"Yes," said the Chekist.

"You'll need someone who knows how to do real detective work, then."

The Chekist's lip twitched. "You might be surprised, Yakov Petrovich, how effective our techniques can be."

Petrovich shrugged. "Your way is good when you already know what you're after. When you're nosing after clues, not so much."

"Why offer me this?"

"I get bored sitting behind a desk with those eggheads at Krim-Kab. And I wouldn't mind being owed a favor." He smoothed his mustache. "Besides, Gennady Mikhailovich was my cellmate. I liked him."

"I would have to write you an authorization under my stamp. A free-movement permit as well."

"Little enough to ask for, isn't it, if I'm doing your job for you?" The old man straightened his back and grimaced. "I'd need a helper. There are things I can't do anymore."

The Chekist's eyes narrowed. "Who do you have in mind?"

"What about Bogomolov here? He held Antonov's boots admirably just now. Seems to have a brain in his head."

"Out of the question," said the Chekist quickly.

"Wasn't me that brought him," said Petrovich. "Now that you have, he might as well make himself useful. What do you think, Bogomolov?"

The idea was baffling. Two hours before, the Chekist had been treating me like a suspect.

I stammered. "What would I—? That is to say, I doubt I could be useful. I really know nothing about—about any of this."

"You don't need to know anything. Someone needs to help me move around. Maybe lift the odd rock so I can look under. And if you know more than you realize, so much the better. I'll get it out of you."

The Chekist started to say something, then stopped. He looked at me, then at the old man. "There are matters you might be able to help with, Yakov Petrovich. We'll need to discuss it. For now, come with me. You too, Bogomolov. Razdolski, stay with the body."

The ear-like shape Antonov had made when we arrived had been unsettled: the hair deranged, the limbs disturbed, the face turned away. He looked like nothing but a dead body now. We left him on the quay and walked back in the direction of the kremlin's stone walls.

3

The face of the detective, his dramatic appearance onto the scene of murder: these are elements of the genre almost as crucial as the body, so critical that they give the *detektiv* its name. Petrovich, the old man with the mustache and the striking eyes, the strange name—he answers the demand, surely?

It was when I was a boy in Saint Petersburg that I read mystery stories. Obsessively I read them, passionately. For a few kopeks begged from my mother I could get a new one at the newsstand on the corner. The adventures of the famous detectives were sold then in installments. Nick Carter, Sherlock Holmes, Nat Pinkerton. My school friends and I traded the back issues between us as well. There was always another *detektiv* to read, and if the quality varied wildly, at that time my taste was not particularly discriminating.

Father was driven crazy by the lurid covers, with their revolvers and Chinamen in bright colors. "Trash!" he would cry, seizing them from me. "Rot!" The weekly magazine we took was *Niva*, that bastion of the middlebrow and virtuous, and he was convinced I could find all I needed of reading material in the children's supplement (for which we paid a ruble per year in addition to the normal subscription price). But the incidence of millionaires killed by poisonous snakes in those pages was too low for me. I acquired new mysteries as fast as Father could throw them away.

Knowing what was to come—that was part of the appeal. The best editions came with a red band along the top of the cover, with a sort of medallion embedded in it showing the face of the detective. If you saw Sherlock Holmes's pipe and long nose, you knew the story would be cerebral, a head-scratcher. Nat Pinkerton, King of Detectives, had a lower brow and a squarer jaw. He was American, and his cases always included good doses of fist-fighting and gunplay. Naturally we liked him best.

But there was more to knowing-what-was-to-come than knowing what to expect from the heroes. You knew there would be a puzzle—a murder. You knew that it would be solved. In some cases this happened via deduction, in others through chases and conveniently timed confessions, but either way the effect was the same. Crime and its sources would be hidden, then brought to light.

You do know what is to come, don't you? My story ends, like all mysteries, with the crime solved, the guilty punished. Only the details are to be determined. Maybe all writing is like that now. We have censors and a writer's union to make sure that the outcome of all stories in the Soviet Union lead to the same approved ends.

At least with mysteries, the outcome has always been determined in advance.

Last night, Vasily-the-tank-commander appeared in my basement with a bottle of vodka and a jar of pickles, as he sometimes condescends to do. He saw I had been writing before I was able to cover the papers on the table.

I explained that I was writing a mystery story, not the memoir he'd wanted. No, I told him, he could not read it.

How satisfying, that disappointed look of his.

The road was icy.

"Give me your arm, will you?" Petrovich said as we negotiated a slippery spot. The hand on my elbow was surprisingly light.

Viewed on a map, or from the vantage point of an angel sitting in the low gray clouds that so often hang over it, Solovetsky's kremlin is bordered to the west by the bay, and to the east by a body of water the monks called the Holy Lake. In between, its walls define an elongated pentagon, three hundred yards north to south, a hundred east to west. A tower rises at each vertex, with a sixth in the middle of the long western wall. The monks gave these towers names as well, but I find I can barely recall them. Which was White, which Spinning Mill? At the northeast corner, Nikolski Tower shared its name with Nikolski Gate. Of that I'm certain.

Centuries of abbots had filled the body of the pentagon with all the dormitories, chapels, refectories, brewhouses, and basilicas that had seemed needful to them, but from where we walked in the cold shadow of the western wall, all you saw were the towers, a few spires, and the huge stones that made up the sloped walls. The chill wind still blew in from off the bay. As we passed the Holy Gates, with the museum above, I looked up. Up close, you noticed how the portico's bulbous pillars were splintered, their paint peeling.

At the southwest corner, the road continued on, while the complex angled east, off towards the pentagon's point. Here the Chekist stopped. "Wait here," he said to me. "Petrovich, you come."

A rough wooden structure stood a short distance away, up against the kremlin's stones. A chimney pipe gave out wisps of smoke. It was with vague envy of the heat they represented that I watched them enter—first the Chekist, then the old man.

The wind pierced my coat. All I could calculate about being singled out the way I had been was that its effect on my food prospects was equivocal at best. In just a few hours I'd gone from standing to be counted with a thousand others to blinking like a stunned horse by the side of the road, alone. This was change, a delta—though in which direction or along what axes was hard to tell.

On the one hand, working with Petrovich could have its rewards. It would at least mean a short reprieve from work in the Quarantine Company—maybe more, if my work impressed the right parties. And I knew the *zeks* in Ten received a dry ration, two weeks' worth of food all at once. But could the old man be relied on to share? Exchanging today's certain lunch for the unreliable yield on his future generosity sounded like a bad deal.

It occurred to me that my friend Foma, at the work site with our platoon, might think to claim my kasha for himself, on the understanding he would pay me back for it in bread later in the evening. It was the kind of thing we did for each other, when we could.

Foma and I had met on the prison-train from Moscow. "Hey, schoolboy," were his first words to me. He'd recognized my cap, or more likely had it pointed out to him. "I want something to pass the time. Tell us a story, why don't you?"

I had just woken from one of the cramped periods of dozing that were all that was possible during that ride. It was late afternoon. Somewhere up the tracks, the slow-moving engine that dragged our car could be heard puffing away. Forty-five men, even fifty, were in that car. Foma and I had been packed next to each other on a narrow bunk that ran around its perimeter. These were the first words we'd spoken to each other. We had been traveling for three days.

"What makes you think I know any good stories?"

"The times I was sent to school, they always tried to get us to read out stories from the books."

I explained that I studied mathematics, not literature, but Foma said that he didn't mind what kind of story I told, as long as it didn't have trains in it. As I would learn, Foma was from Ukrainian peasant stock; all academic fields were much the same to him.

All I could think of was "The Animals in the Pit," a tale I used to read to my sister Dinka, from a big gilt-edged volume called *Stories for Children*. It was one of her favorites. A fox tricked a hare, a wolf, and a bear, ate them, then ended by being devoured by dogs himself. She always liked the violent ones.

My neighbor on the other side, an old man with a walleye, propped himself up on his elbow to listen. Foma stared at me skeptically throughout the telling. "That's a story for kids," he said after I'd finished and he'd thought about it for a minute. "That's not so good, for someone who's been to school in the city."

"Well, all the stories I know for adults have trains in them. Anna Karenina throws herself in front of a train."

We rode for ten more days before we reached Kem, where the prisoner-transport ferry embarked for Solovetsky. The walleyed old man died on the way, and the train guards took him out and dumped him in the woods when we stopped to take on water. At a different stop, when they let us out to empty the piss bucket, I was able to buy three hard-boiled eggs from a farmer by the side of the tracks, using the last of the money from a package my parents had managed to get to me while I was in Kresty. I shared the eggs with Foma—by then we were friends.

"Better for us, probably," he'd said to me around a mouthful of egg, "not to get split up when we get there. I'll keep an eye out for you. You can do the same for me."

We'd done it, so far, as much as we had been able. Claiming my kasha and giving me credit for it in bread—that would be in the spirit of the arrangement. It was possible. As I dwelt on it, it even came to seem likely, though whether it was reasoning or simple hunger that made me think so would have been hard to say.

At last the old man emerged from the wooden building, alone. In his hands he held several loose papers.

"That's settled, then," he said, coming over. "You're going to assist me while I find out who's killed Gennady Mikhailovich."

Hardly looking at me, he set off down the path, jabbing with his cane."But what does it involve?" I said, catching up. "I told you, I don't know anything about it."

"You don't have to know anything about it. Just do as I say." He lowered his brows. Stray hairs shot off from his mustache in every direction. "You're a little cold-blooded. You'll do fine. 'Lever of the second class.' Ha!"

His laugh was a bark again, abrupt and harsh. I hadn't thought I was being cold-blooded. "Is that why you wanted me?"

"Why do you care?" He looked at me shrewdly. An odd look—since what did he have to be shrewd with me about? It shifted the balance of his face back from his mustache to the rheumy blue spike of his eyes. When I didn't say anything, he shrugged. "Well, it was that, and that Razdolski, whom I'd have gotten otherwise, is a block of wood. Working with stupid people makes me stupid, too. You, at least, look at what's in front of you. You use your brain in the presence of a dead body. If you can do that, and you don't have to walk with a cane, we'll get along." He thrust the bundle of papers he'd emerged from the cabin with at me. "I do have to walk with a cane. You carry these."

The documents looked official. They were printed orders, signed, initialed, and stamped in two different colors, with Petrovich's name and mine filling the blanks.

There were three. One was simply a pass for Nikolski Gate, authorizing both of us to enter or exit. The next, the most elaborate, identified Petrovich as conducting an investigation on behalf of the Information and Investigation Section. There was no form for that, so the Chekist had written a set of instructions onto a standard work-assignment order, stamping it four times to verify its authenticity.

What held my attention was the order transferring me from Company Thirteen to Company Ten. It was what I had been hoping for from my acquaintance with Antonov, if delivered in an unexpected way. The Chekist had written "TEMPORARY" at the top in capital letters, true, but I didn't think I would be transferred to Ten, even temporarily, without being allowed to eat there as well.

That changed things. Any doubts I'd had about reassignment sank away into my stomach with a gurgle.

We were going back the way we'd come, towards Nikolski. Without the Chekist to keep up with, Petrovich set a slower pace. "Maybe I *can* be helpful," I said. "I've read quite a lot of *detektivy*."

The old man snorted. "That will make you less of a help, not more. You mean you spent your pennies on them as a boy? Or you still choose to read trash? "

"They aren't all so stupid."

"No? All right, then, expert. Since you have read so many reliable accounts of criminal cases, tell me: what should our first step here be?"

I thought about it. My fictional detectives were invariably keen on examining the scene of the crime. Sherlock Holmes, indeed, was a scientist of forensics; he'd written a monograph on footprints and could often wrap up his cases after applying his mind to a stretch of apparently featureless ground. In one of the stories about his visits to Russia, he identified an Indian hunting baboon as the culprit on the basis of the tracks it left in a second-story room after climbing in its window.

"If they found him in the bay," I said, "he must have been killed nearby. Maybe we could look for signs of a body being dragged along the bank, or thrown into the water."

"Ah, you're an expert tracker?"

"No."

"Of course not. Me neither. Do you think it's going to do us any good to go around staring at the ground for footprints? Between the wind and the snow and everyone in this camp dragging something somewhere, what's going to be left? How would we ever know if we found something?"

He had a point. "All right. What do we do instead, then?"

"No, I want to see what you've learned from these stories. You tell me."

The only other answer I could think up seemed feeble, but I'd prove myself altogether spiritless if I said nothing. "I suppose we question the victim's acquaintances or associates. We'll see if that turns up anything suspicious or strange."

The old man shrugged. "That's not terrible. Of course, you're an acquaintance and associate of his yourself."

His glance had, again, that combination of bleariness and intensity. I supposed it meant I was being given the opportunity to start showing I was not a block of wood like Razdolski. "Yes, of course. Let me see, what do I know about him? He was from Yaroslavl. I believe he'd grown up there and did most of his work there. He told me once about the bombardment during the civil war—what was destroyed, how much work there was repairing what was left. Of the art in the churches, I mean."

"Yaroslavl. White city, wasn't it?"

"I believe so," I said. During the war I'd been eleven years old. I knew only that Red victories filled the streets with celebrating workers, while at home my parents grieved in secret over the defeats of any army that claimed to represent the Constituent Assembly.

"The two of you talk politics much?"

"No. I have no idea of his—his loyalties during the war. I don't suppose he approved of the Bolsheviks' attitude towards the Church. But he never seemed very worldly. He talked about Christ more than politics."

Petrovich grunted recognition. "That's true. I told him once he should have been a priest, but he said his calling was different. Gave you the feeling he expected God to pop his head in the window at any minute. Unsettling. Doesn't mean he had no ideas about the world of men, though."

"No. But he never told them to me." There was a pause while I cast about for more to say. Called on to produce an intelligent or helpful idea about what circumstances of Antonov's life might have led to his death, I felt my mind empty itself. "You were his cellmate."

"For a year and a half, or close to it. I've been here two years. Antonov moved in after the Azerbaijani I bunked with at first died. I suppose I knew him well enough."

That didn't help me much, and no more was forthcoming. Now the old man seemed lost in thought. The round holes his cane made in the snow measured our progress. "He never told me what he was charged with to be sent here," I volunteered after a dozen holes. "That would be helpful to know, wouldn't it?"

Petrovich stopped to clear his throat, a rattle of phlegm that turned into a cough. When it was over he said: "That I do know already. It was when they arrested the bishop in Yaroslavl. Antonov wrote the OGPU a letter, saying no ruler who committed outrages against the princes of the Church could hope to rule Russia legitimately. With the predictable result: they came for him right after the bishop." He rubbed his chest. "He had the strength of his convictions, anyway."

"It's hard to picture him being involved in violence," I said, lamely again. "Or—or doing something that made someone violent. It hardly seems real."

"We always say, you never know a man well enough until he's dead. Usually not even then."

I mulled that over. "You seem experienced with this kind of thing."

"Ha! You could say that. Thirty years as an investigator with the Odessa police department is one kind of experience."

"I suppose that's what makes you skeptical about *detektivy*."

Petrovich laughed again. "Because I know what solving a crime is really like. In those things they always find just the right clue at just the right time, so that no one ever has to do any real work and the detectives are free to apply their fists to whomever the crowd wants to see punched. Then people like you think my job is all footprints and brawling. I can tell you, when you search for footprints, nine times out of ten you only end up with a crick in your neck. Either there's nothing, or so many pairs of feet have walked through the site of the murder that it comes to the same thing. I can count on two fingers the number of murders I've solved by knowing the killer's shoe size."

"What is your first step, then?"

"Need to see what he was doing outside the kremlin. Always a good start to retrace your victim's movements, figure out what sort of business he was into. There's always something."

We'd passed most of the water. Out on the quay, Razdolski was still standing where we'd left him. We stopped for a moment to look. I'd thought we might be able to make out Antonov's body, but at this distance you couldn't see it.

"I asked our friend back there to leave the corpse somewhere foxes won't get at it," said Petrovich. "No point burying it yet. We might need it another time. It's cold enough—he'll keep in a shed."

As we continued around the wall, another road split off from ours, heading north. It passed through vegetable fields and outbuildings, then a stretch of logged stubble before it disappeared behind a hill of uncut evergreens. To the east the Holy Lake was frozen over, the mouths of its canals white.

"Now, here at SLON we are surrounded by desperate types, any one of whom could be a murderer," Petrovich was saying. "What you might call an embarrassment of suspects. But carrying out your investigation in a prison has it benefits as well. If Antonov left under his own power, they should have a record of it at the gate. Could bring us closer to the time of death. Maybe it will say who wrote him a pass."

From the outside, Nikolski Gate looked tiny, out of all proportion with the massive tower hunched over it—a hole gnawed through the kremlin wall by mice. Built out from the wall to its left was a small lean-to, the guards' shelter. The shack stood open where it faced the path, its roof bowed under a burden of snow.

A short queue of prisoners waited to pass through on our side. Petrovich insisted that we cut to the front. "Never get anywhere being shy," he said. "These papers mean we're important men." I'd expected grumbling as we passed, but there was none. Most of the men in the line seemed to be trying not to look at us.

The passage through the wall was dark, but with the doors thrown open at this hour, I could look through and see the walls of whitewashed buildings inside. On duty were the same pair of guards who'd waved me through with the Chekist earlier. The one with the goiter sat behind a table with a clock on it, his rifle close to hand.

Goiter's eyes bulged in his head, sizing us up. "End of the line's back there," he said.

"Not for us," said Petrovich. "We have business with your records before we pass through."

It was breathtaking, frankly, the old man's audacity in talking this way. Prison life has so many lessons for the *zek* that it is hard to tell which is the first, but to avoid provoking the guards is certainly a very early one. I felt my heart beat faster, but all the other man said was, "Need to see your papers."

Petrovich gestured impatiently for me to hand him the documents from the Chekist. When I did, he showed both the gate pass and the investigation order. "We're interested in someone who left the kremlin last night. Probably by himself."

"Still have to check it all," said Goiter. He read slowly, beckoning his partner over before he had finished his examination.

"It's from Infosec," said the second guard dully. The two men exchanged a look.

"Yes," said Petrovich. "'Cooperate with any of the bearers' inquiries.' I believe it also says something about an investigation of serious importance."

"You two aren't regular agents," said Goiter. His eyes bulged at my hat.

Petrovich's eyes narrowed. I hoped he wouldn't say anything rash. "We wouldn't need the authorization if we were, would we?"

"Wait a minute," said Goiter.

The guards withdrew into the shack, taking our documents with them. They stood by a rusted stove, backs to us. I could hear them murmuring but couldn't make out what they were saying.

"Is there a problem?" called Petrovich.

The two men came back. The second one stood behind with his arms crossed as Goiter put the authorization on the table.

"The pass is fine," said Goiter, handing it back. "You can go through. But the logs, they're limited access. All you have here is a work order. I can't show them to you with just this."

"You read the order, didn't you?" said Petrovich. "You saw the signature?"

"I saw."

"So?"

"I told you. Limited access."

"Do you think that will matter to our friend who signed this order? You think he'll appreciate having to come here to explain how things stand?"

Goiter pressed his lips together for a moment, then turned and went back into the shack. Returning, he slapped a new-looking ledger in front of us on the table. "You can look at it here."

The log proved to be a converted account book with "Unaccompanied Individuals" written on the spine. While we examined it, Goiter resumed processing the entrants at the other end of the table. His partner, however, hurried off through Nikolski—in response, I thought, to some signal exchanged between the two.

"Let's see," said Petrovich. "When I returned to the cell from work last night, he was already gone. That was 5:30, and gate curfew's 6:00, so perhaps before then . . ."

At the top of each left-hand page, the words "Payments Received" had been crossed out and replaced with "Entrance," while on the right-hand pages, "Expenses" had been replaced by "Exit." Each entry spread across both pages; anyone who went out was expected to come in again, and vice versa. The columns reserved for rubles and kopeks were used for hours and minutes: times of entrance on the left, times of exit on the right.

Antonov's entry, when we located it, had him leaving the kremlin at 5:18. There was no record of reentry. Every row had a place for the prisoner's name, the reason he'd left or entered, and the authority under which he'd done it. Antonov had either not been asked or refused to explain his reasons for passing through the gate. But the name that had issued his pass was familiar.

"Vinogradov," I said. "The museum director. That's Antonov's boss."

"Good," said Petrovich. "We'd have been visiting the museum today in any case."

I glanced at Goiter, who seemed to be watching us out of the corner of his eye. "Shall we go, then?"

Petrovich shook his head. "No, as long as we're here, I want to see what else is suspicious in this book. Who knows? Some of these names around his may be important. Any others without an explanation for leaving?"

We searched for another minute, me looking over the old man's shoulder, but we were soon interrupted by the return of the other guard. He trailed behind a third man, who also wore the guards' long gray coat and high boots. In place of a rifle, this one had a pistol on his belt and carried a baton.

The man strode up to the table and tapped the ledger, the tip of his baton beneath our noses. "Put this back where it belongs, Vlacic," he said to Goiter.

"We're not quite finished," said Petrovich.

He'd gripped the book, but Goiter—Vlacic—snatched it out of his hands. When I objected—"Hey!"—the baton tapped me on the shoulder, hard.

"So," said the new man, "you two are the ones who I'm told are prying into our business here. You don't look much like Infosec."

"I don't give a damn about your business," said Petrovich. "We are investigating a matter, yes. For Infosec. It doesn't concern you and you have no authority to interfere."

"Doesn't concern me, eh?" He looked at me. "And what about you? Do you give a damn about reporting our business to Infosec? About stirring up trouble for me and my men? Making us look bad?"

Again the baton hit my shoulder—harder this time, a numbing shock to joint and clavicle. I stepped back, putting my hand to the spot. The blow would bruise. It raised reverberations where the Chekist had hit me earlier in the morning. "Yes, I mean—no. I—"

"Tolya is my assistant," said Petrovich. "Hit him again, someone will hear about it."

The old man sounded steely, but the men in the queue had all edged away from the table. Vlacic and his partner had both picked up their guns. For a long moment, the guards' boss stared into my face as though into a gutter whose clogging filth he might need to unblock with his stick.

"All right," he said at last. "You've seen the log. Now go through the gate. Your papers are good. We only need to know your names. That, and where you bunk."

"I didn't see a place for that information in your log," said Petrovich.

The other man smirked. "Special circumstances."

It was a threat. He was asking where to send his men in case our investigation took a direction he didn't like. But there didn't seem to be any way to avoid answering. Petrovich's cell was on the fourth floor of the Company Ten dormitories. For my part, I was relieved to be able to say that I normally stayed in the cathedral with Company Thirteen, but had just been transferred. I didn't know yet where I would be assigned a bunk. The commander seemed to accept that; his attention by now had turned to Petrovich anyway. He gave his men the signal to let us go.

Halfway through the tunnel under the walls, I couldn't keep myself from glancing back at the lean-to. The commander had turned away and was talking to the other guard. Goitered Vlacic, however, had opened up the day's ledger, and his pen was poised, but it wasn't moving. The bulging eyes watched us coldly.

4

Passing from the courtyard into the museum jarred me, the way it always did. The bitter wallscape of the kremlin, its soot and sawdust and filth, above all its uniformity: all of that followed you up the dark staircase, then gave way abruptly to detail and color when you opened the door. Enameled tiles shone from the lintels, gold adorned the walls. Christ stared down from the corners with His saints and angels. The chapel's iconostasis and altars were gone, but none of its decoration had been stripped. Nothing had been painted over.

In the space the walls enclosed, where a congregation would normally have stood, three large casement windows illuminated two short banks of desks. Conveyed from some zone of bureaucracy and file keeping, the desks looked shabby and out of place in the elaborate surroundings. Men sat at them quietly, working. The effect was uncomfortably intimate, like fingers on the back of your neck.

The museum. Nineteen seventeen had taught us to reimagine what our institutions could be in Russia. Was there anything inconsistent about maintaining a collection of the monks' relics and miscellanea—officially, the Solovetsky Anti-Religious Exhibit—in the middle of a prison camp? Not in the Northern Camps of Special Signficance's world of randomness and disorder.

At SLON, certain inmates starved or were worked to death; others wrote monographs and restored paintings with tiny brushes. Why not? We questioned everything. Could the work of culture be done with forced labor? There was only one way to find out.

Elsewhere the latitude granted on Solovki to explore new forms of carceral life gave rise to other endeavors. Signs were everywhere on Solovki, telling you where to go, where not to, instilling principles important for prison life. They were almost always regulatory. Yet one of the first I noticed simply read "THEATER," in large black capitals. For the edification of the *zeks* and the entertainment of the camp bosses, a whole troupe of actors, most professionals before their arrests, was maintained. They staged plays by Chekhov, Gogol. I remember a production of *The Inspector General* I once saw, sometime after the events I am describing. Done with sumptuous sets, its splendor was necessary to show that the satire targeted the imperial system, not the Communist one. It was permitted for all of us to laugh.

There was a library, too, and several magazines published on the monks' old printing equipment. The stories circulated in our literary journal, *Solovetsky Islands*, were surprisingly good, not the sort of cant one would have expected from an official outlet at all.

If some Moscow Bolshevik had inquired why such extravagances were to be afforded to social malcontents and enemies of the state, the answer would have been that they were crucial to our reeducation and ideological development. There were even still elements of the Party, then, who would have believed that was important—who believed Solovetsky was an experiment in reform, rather than extermination. Because these liberal types existed to be flattered, our bosses even put us to work analyzing the camp's social problems. Every so often a report would be issued by a prisoner committee with recommendations for increasing the rehabilitative value of a stay on Solovki, or addressing "the housing crisis among juvenile inmates." They weren't even always ignored.

But of course the true function of such intellectual or cultural groupings was never really to improve the life of the camp as a whole. The men who commissioned them did so to aggrandize themselves, to gratify their superiors, or to solidify their own power by handing out good posts. As for those who worked in them—

well, finding a place among the camp's artists or "scientific administrators" meant entering one of only a few little bubbles of culture and comfort that existed for imprisoned intellectuals—habitats where delicate creatures could uncurl their antennae and flounce their gills in the flow of one another's conversation.

Gennady Antonov's role at the museum had been to restore the Solovki's collection of icons. On the four or five evenings when I had been able to come to the workroom, we would have our conversations while he worked beneath his lamp. To watch him manipulate the tiny scrapers and brushes of his trade was a kind of luxury. Beneath his fingers, soot-stained varnish peeled away, tempera glowed, gold leaf reappeared. He insisted artificial light was best for his task: "The faithful will revere the icon in lamp- and candlelight, Tolya. I must work by the same light."

A short man rose from the desk nearest the door, beneath the big middle window. "You two look like you're in the wrong place," he said.

"My name is Petrovich.This is my assistant, Tolya. We're here to see Director Vinogradov."

"Lots of people want to see the director," said the man. He barely moved his jaw when he talked. You could see his nose had been broken at some point in the past. One hand held a book, shut on his finger to keep his place.

"He'll want to speak with us," said Petrovich.

"Not possible."

"Why not?"

"He's not here."

"We'll wait."

"Fine. He'll be back in a week. Find somewhere else to wait in the meantime."

The little man took a step towards us, gesturing at the door, but Petrovich didn't budge. "What do you mean, he'll be back in a week? Where's he gone?"

A deep breath might have raised the other man an inch above five feet. His chin jutted at us like a weapon. "Not sure I see how that's any of your business, friend."

Petrovich crossed his hands on his cane. "And who are you?"

"I'm the assistant director of this museum. Name's Ivanov."

"All right," said Petorivch. "Show him the papers, Tolya."

After skimming the Chekist's order, the man—Ivanov—glared up at us, first Petrovich, then me.

"We've been deputized," I said.

"Infosec's fallen on hard times," said the little man. "But all right. What's this investigation you're conducting?"

"Something we need to talk to your director about," said Petrovich. "Where is he?"

"Cape Kostrihe."

"Kostrihe?" said Petrovich. "What on earth is he doing there?" The cape lay four or five miles south of the kremlin by road. There was nothing there. You might expect to find a lumbering team, but not the director of the museum.

Ivanov sniffed. "You're not familiar with what we do here, maybe. It's not just the collection. Publish a journal, too. Research. The director's training is in archeology. There are sites that interest him on Kostrihe."

"Archeology?" I repeated.

"That's what I said."

"When did he leave?" said Petrovich.

"Yesterday afternoon."

"Why now? It would be easier in the spring. No snow."

"It's an expedition. Sledges, tents, men, blankets. Food for a week. The director's a resourceful man. He wouldn't be one to let weather stop him."

That didn't satisfy him, but after a moment of staring at the head of his cane Petrovich said: "All right, leave that for now. We're also interested in one of your colleagues here. Gennady Antonov. We'll need to see his desk."

"Antonov? He didn't come today. It's my headache to write him up." Ivanov narrowed his eyes. "What's this all about?"

Petrovich didn't answer, only met the little man's gaze. They were both silent for a minute, each trying to work his stubbornness on the other. When Ivanov turned to look at me, it surprised me.

"They found him floating in the bay this morning," I said. I had to clench my teeth to stop a yelp after that. Petrovich's cane had rapped me sharply on the shin.

"Floating?" said Ivanov. He looked surprised. "You mean dead?"

The old man shot me a look out of the corner of one blue

eye. “Just show us Antonov’s desk,” he said.

The blood hadn’t quite drained from Ivanov’s face, but for the first time he looked unsure. “I’ll have to tell the director what happened.”

“He can find out from us, when we see him,” said Petrovich. “Now you know what this is about, and you saw who we’re working for. Show us the desk.”

Men raised their eyes as we passed. The little noises they made in their work—the scratching of pens, the rustle and snap of pages turning, chairs creaking—were like the noise that passes for silence in the forest.

At the end of its row, Antonov’s desk looked the same as always, both messy and exact. Sealed jars of paint, brushes, scraping tools, and a lamp crowded around the edges of the piece he’d been working on. The painting would leave an image of itself after it was removed, a silhouette of clutter.

What struck you first was the way the panel’s composition divided it. On the left, the background showed a tawny waste of rock, textured with vigorous strokes of black and white; in a different painting it could have been a choppy, burnt-orange sea. To the right stood a confection of pink battlements and bulging domes, with an emerald palace rising out of the center. Without perspective, the city’s walls were crazed, each segment straining off towards its own vanishing point. Citizens thronged to gaze down at the action in the foreground from towers and windows. The people, overgrown and too detailed, loomed larger than their buildings. On the plain below, the spear of a mounted knight—Saint George—pierced a tendril of smoke with a scarlet pig’s head and scarlet talons, which must have been a dragon. All of this was intact. It was a third figure that Antonov seemed to have been at work on: a princess, identifiable by her crown. A pair of golden slippers bore her towards the city. She led the dragon by a cord, slender and red. Paint could be seen flaking away from her golden-green gown.

“Listen,” Petrovich said to me in a low voice as we stood looking. “Don’t go blabbing the details of the investigation every chance you get. Don’t give out information without getting some back in return. Sometimes you want to see what they say to you before they know you’re investigating a murder.”

"Yes," I said. "I'm sorry. I'll be more careful."

"Nothing for it now. Mention something like that in a place like this, everyone knows the story before you can turn around." He pulled open a drawer. "Help me go through this desk."

"What should I be looking for?" I asked.

"If I knew that, we wouldn't have to look. Find whatever doesn't belong. If it tells you something we didn't already know about him, that's what we want."

The two uppermost drawers were filled with brushes and paint. Most of what we found beneath that was notes on restoration projects. *Annunciation No. 34 (2.68): Modulus = length of nose. Head's radius slightly less than two moduli, two full moduli at chin. Three-quarter profile; center pupil of left eye. Plaster separating from linen about mouth and chin. Careful of proportions in repair!* On some pages Antonov had sketched outlines of the figures he was concerned with. Some he'd daubed with paint, others not. I couldn't say I understood his working methods, but that was to be expected. None of it seemed out of place.

One thing about imprisonment: it turns quite ordinary objects strange. I had not, I suppose, performed the simple act of opening a desk drawer for more than eighteen months.

When they came to arrest me, I was still studying nightly at the desk that had once supported my schoolboy exercises. It had been moved into the sitting room as a consequence of our flat being broken up into a communal apartment, but it remained mine to use. The forbidden books seized for evidence against me were lined up neatly on it, along with five or six others, between two brass bookends.

As a boy, under the influence of spy fiction, I'd written "confidential dispatches" for the purpose of hiding them from my parents. The space behind the drawers became accessible when they were pulled out, and would accept a few sheets. Into that chamber, tangible but invisible, I filed imaginary plots, intelligence on fictive but critical troop movements. None of it was ever discovered.

Antonov's desk had the same space, with the same gaps at the back of the drawers. Papers rustled against my fingertips when

I reached through. With adult hands it was difficult, but after a moment I pulled out several creased and flattened documents.

Smoothed flat on the table, they were disappointing. Of a piece with the rest of Antonov's notes, they'd clearly fallen into the space behind the drawer accidentally, after it had been pushed closed too full. Still, I reached back in. This time I had to lean down and contort my shoulder.

Out came three more sheets. Two were the same mashed scrap, but one had clearly been dealt with more carefully. It had been leaning, folded, against the back of the drawer, as if placed.

Unfolded, it was a note in a feminine hand: *A package has come from my mother with a few rubles. I will be inside, visiting the commissary store before nightly roll. This Thursday. Please meet me.—V.* Beneath the signed initial another sentence had been hurriedly scribbled. *The thought of your goodness is all that enables me to continue as I have.*

Petrovich sucked his teeth when I showed him the note. "That tells us something we didn't know."

"What do you think?" I said.

He glanced around the room. "We'll talk about it later. For now, hold on to it."

I considered explaining how my spy stories had led to my making the find, but thought better of it. I'd already made the mistake of mentioning Antonov's death—attributing the discovery to frivolous reading would hardly make Petrovich reevaluate my expertise.

We hadn't been working much longer when one of the men from the other bank of desks stopped at my elbow.

"I say, did I hear what you said to old Ivanov over there? Has Gennady Mikhailovich really been . . . ?"

"What did you hear?" said Petrovich.

Without quite answering, the man introduced himself as Johan Sewick, explaining that he was in charge of maintaining the museum's catalog. He was sure he knew Antonov rather well, and hoped all was well with his friend. He would be happy to help us with anything, anything at all . . . He was tall, and wore a sports coat over his sweater. Beneath wavy hair, the earpiece of his glasses had been repaired with wire. My shin still smarted—a reminder to take my cues from Petrovich, who seemed distinctly reserved. Even so, I thought the man in charge of the museum's catalog might be worth knowing.

The old man did at least seem willing to involve him in our investigation to the extent of asking him several questions. Sewick had last spoken to Antonov on Monday, when they'd discussed the price of pipe tobacco in the commissary. No, he hadn't seemed different than normal, or worried. He had no enemies or debts. Sewick wasn't aware of any arguments he'd recently been involved in. He laughed when Petrovich asked whether Antonov might have been involved with a woman, then grimaced.

"Antonov? No, no. He isn't that type at all." He cleared his throat. "But, I say, I'm afraid these would be the kind of questions you would be asking if—if something horrible had happened."

"You heard what we said to the assistant director," said Petrovich.

"Yes, yes. Well—a tragedy, of course. Very sad indeed." Sewick leaned forward. "But just a word of advice. There may be more reliable guides to the affairs of the museum than our Anti-Religious Bug."

"Your what?" said Petrovich.

"He means Ivanov," I said. Antonov had mentioned the nickname to me once.

"Just so. Director Vinogradov has left Ivanov in charge, this time. But, you know, the role of assistant director does not necessarily invest great authority in the man who fills it. You might say he's no more than a glorified secretary for the director."

Petrovich said: "You call him a bug?"

"Ah," began Sewick. "Yes. Well, that—"

"It's because he's so small," I said. We were speaking quietly enough not to be heard at the front of the room, I hoped.

"Correct," Sewick continued. "The assistant director is diminutive, and his strain of atheism is, so to speak, virulent. We joke that you must be careful not to contract him, like a microbe." Petrovich didn't laugh, and Sewick looked uncomfortable. "Ah—well, the assistant director is, shall we say, a self-made man. He did not have some of the advantages of education others have. In fact, he was formerly a servant in the household of the Metropolitan of Novgorod. You will understand, of course, that certain members of the serving classes—that is, the former serving classes—can bear grudges against their masters' creed. Hence, 'anti-religious.'"

The old man's eyes had taken on their flat, sharp, intensely blue look. "Huh."

"Officially, of course, our museum *is* anti-religious. But a collection like this one naturally requires a certain sophistication of outlook. Ivanov, by contrast, talks incessantly about the great God-deception and the science of atheism. To be blunt, he did not like Antonov or Antonov's work. He found his approach 'unscientific.' And, in general, the assistant director's thinking can be . . . unbalanced."

Petrovich leaned back in his chair. "You think you would be better at helping us with them than Ivanov."

"Well . . ." He took on a significant expression. "You can find me here until curfew most evenings. I would be only too happy to help."

"All right," said Petrovich. "Tell me. Why did Vinogradov choose yesterday to depart on this expedition of his? Why not wait until spring?"

Behind his thick glasses, Sewick looked surprised. "Well . . . yes, the director's expedition. Hmmm. I can't say I know his mind on that matter."

"You're not surprised at his leaving in October?"

After thinking for a moment, Sewick said: "You know, perhaps it is odd. I can't think of a reason he would have had to go now, instead of some easier time. I'll inquire for you, if you like. Discreetly, of course."

"Do that."

After the other man had gone, Petrovich went back to perusing the stack of things he'd taken from Antonov's desk.

"He could be a useful contact, couldn't he?" I whispered.

"He might," said Petrovich.

"You don't seem enthusiastic."

"Listen, do my job for long enough, and you learn to spot a certain type." He turned a page. "Man like that can't be relied on. He wants to use us to beat his rival, maybe score points with Vinogradov. Maybe score against Vinogradov. That's fine as far as it goes, if he ends up knowing anything useful. Just don't let him pilot your investigation."

"Oh," I said.

"At least you didn't mention the bay again."

Another ten minutes turned up nothing for me but a sketch of the bay from the museum's windows and, tucked away at the bottom of a drawer, a brush with a broken handle. Petrovich, however, had found something to read intently. "I need to ask Ivanov about this," he said.

Outside the windows behind the assistant director's desk, the sky was filling with gray clouds. Ivanov was bent over the book he'd been holding earlier, making notes in a little pad that lay open beside him. With the broken nose, the way he raised his head and narrowed his eyes at us looked off-center.

Petrovich laid the papers he'd been looking at on the desk. "What can you tell me about these?"

Ivanov hesitated, as though he'd have liked to refuse to look, but after a moment he did. "Looks like the list of pieces for that requisition the other week. A lumber order, they called it. Came with approval from on high."

"What do you mean?" said Petrovich. "What requisition?"

I'd craned my neck to get a look as well. Together the pages seemed to make a list, with perhaps a hundred items drawn up in columns across all three. I thought I recognized the format used to reference icons in Antonov's notes: an accession number, followed by the name of a place and a year.

"Wood's in demand this time of year," Ivanov was saying. "They're trying to ship every splinter they can from timbering to the mainland before the sea freezes up. Hard to get so much as a board for any other purpose, apparently. And if you look at it the right way, your religious iconography only amounts to some old planks that happen to have paint on them."

"Planks?" I said.

"That's right, planks. You've looked at an icon before? It's painted on wood."

It gave me that old, hungry feeling of moving slowly backward away from the world. He couldn't be saying what he seemed to be. I glanced at Petrovich. "But what do they do with them?"

"What do you usually do with a plank? Hammer nails into it and attach it to something else."

"What, they use it to—to repair floors with? Is it a joke?"

Ivanov shrugged. "A joke for some. Certain kind of Party member finds it funny to show his disdain for the Church with that kind of thing. The priestly class's disfranchisement has been accomplished, but they can still be told to go screw." The little man did not look amused. He looked hard. "Not that I can't see what they mean by it. Something right about putting them to use, isn't there? Don't have to be a Communist to see that. Why not fix your floor with an icon? Maintaining the wealth of the Church meant the people slept in hovels without proper floors or walls for six centuries." He relented slightly. "But that approach is too crude. The director and I have talked about it again and again. The whole purpose of an anti-religious museum is preservation, so we can see what the religious delusion was really like. It would be one thing if what they were taking was the trash that used to be sold to backward congregants on festival days. I could have gotten behind that. That sort of mass-produced stuff has no artistic or historical value—it only meant money for the priestly mountebanks. But our pieces here are important artifacts."

Still I was having trouble believing. "They can't be coming to you whenever they need a board."

"Not whenever," said Ivanov. "This requisition's the second. First was last year, around the same time. Like I said, it goes through because of the push to overfulfill the lumber plan before the last boat goes. In the administration offices, filling a carpentry quota without using up what's logged means a lot, come October. They send them to the cabinetry workshop. Usually the director's connections can keep greedy hands off our collection. He tried this time, too—went off to meet with Commandant Nogtev himself about it, then came stomping back in a foul mood. Nogtev turned him down. Normally he's an ally, but the wind blows differently when the last load of the season's about to leave."

"All right," said Petrovich before I could ask anything else. "Let's grant that it's strange. But what I'm interested in is, would have been Antonov in charge of choosing what went? He compiled this list?" When Ivanov nodded, he went on: "But look, there are a dozen places where someone's crossed out his selection and written another in. Who'd have done that?"

There were three columns on the page Petrovich indicated, labeled 40 × 24in, 15 × 12in, and 15 × 15-24in. The last of these was much the longest, and continued on the page that followed. The corrections Petrovich was asking about appeared in all three columns, with no discernible pattern.

"It's the director's hand," said Ivanov.

"You said you have important pieces here. Things with artistic, historical value? Their goal would have been to choose the least important to sacrifice, then, wouldn't it?"

"That's right. That's what the director wanted."

"Well then, what I don't understand is what Antonov needed to be corrected about. He was the expert: he should have known what the collection could bear to part with, shouldn't he? What could they have disagreed on?"

"No idea," said Ivanov. "Sometimes people see these things differently. But it's not my area."

Petrovich nodded slowly at that. "All right. You said they took them for cabinetry. Which department did the order come from?"

"Anzer Division. Cabinetry workshop's up there." Solovetsky was in fact only the largest body of land in the archipelago named after it. Anzer Island was to the north, across a small channel. The encampments there, like those on the other outlying islands, were administered separately from the numbered companies based in the kremlin. Hence Anzer had its own division, and a degree of autonomy from the rest of the camp apparatus. "They have a supply warehouse down here, though. Sent some men to pick it all up."

"I'll need the name of the man who signed the order."

"I don't have it."

"There must be a record."

"Records like that are locked up in the director's office."

Petrovich maintained a level gaze. "But you have a key."

Ivanov leaned back in his chair and crossed his arms. "Not sure I can help you with that. The director doesn't like having his office opened when he's not here."

"You saw our investigation order," said Petrovich.

"I saw. I saw you were talking to Sewick, too."

"Ah," said Petrovich. The way his mustache bristled gave me the impression he was amused. "I'd say he was talking to us, really."

"Oh yes? And what did he say?"

"Your colleague couldn't think of a reason for Director Vinogradov to have left on his expedition now instead of in the spring. He seemed to me to be suggesting there was something suspicious about it."

"Damn Sewick! Damn him!" Ivanov had been all implacable stubbornness, but now he seemed ready to fly into a frenzy. He'd kept his voice low, but the look he directed at the manager of the card catalog was murderous. The other man, oblivious, continued to file records into the two large cabinets at the other end of the chapel.

"I thought you might be able to offer a more complete explanation," said Petrovich.

It cost the little man a visible effort to tear his attention from Sewick and screw down his anger. "Yes. Of course I am. The director's study of the sites on Kostrihe is to be finished in time for the next meeting of the Society for Local Lore. That's January. If he doesn't have a piece ready to read to the body by then, the next one's not until June, and then the Proceedings won't come out until August. That's why he had to go now. Otherwise it's too long to wait."

Petrovich was mild. "That sounds plausible enough."

"What did you tell Sewick about this business with Antonov?"

The old man shrugged. "Nothing more than I've told you."

"You think he was murdered? That's why you're investigating?"

"Yes."

The little man looked once more at his rival, then opened his desk and took out a key. "All right. Come with me."

The office he led us to must once have been the chapel's sacristy. A short hall separated it from the sanctuary. Ivanov had us wait outside while he went in to consult Vinogradov's records.

Petrovich had gestured for me to bring the list of requisitioned icons along with us, and now I took the opportunity to look over it again. Every peasant household had a few icons in a corner, and most weren't particularly valuable. No one worried if a few drops of wax spattered when the candles in front were blown out, or if the stove got them a bit sooty. But no one hammered nails through them either.

And Antonov had called the paintings in the collection remarkable. Several were attributed to Simon Ushakov, whose figures bore a certain fleshy resemblance to those of Rembrandt, his contemporary. There was even one he believed to be the unacknowledged work of Andrei Rublev, worn down by the years since the fourteenth century until it resembled, to me, a much-handled door on which there happened to be painted an image of the Prophet Elijah. Antonov was honored, he said, to restore the work of such wonderful workers in the sight of God.

That was how he expressed it: "such wonderful workers in the sight of God." He'd meant it, too. That talent he had for uttering phrases from a medieval chronicle as if they were the most natural way to talk about our very modern situation—it surprised me every time. I hadn't felt grief looking at his body on the quay. But the image of him slowly reading over a list of icons to be destroyed, then filing it away in the welter of his desk—that felt like sorrow.

"The name you want is Zhenov," said Ivanov, shutting and locking the office door behind him. "Manager of the Anzer warehouse, down on the south side of the bay. Wrote it all down for you." He handed a slip of paper over to Petrovich, who examined it and handed it on to me, to be added to our growing stack.

"Listen," Ivanov went on, "you come to me, not Sewick, when you've got questions about our business here. He'll say anything about anyone if he thinks he'll benefit. Doesn't have the interests of this museum at heart, or of your inquiry, either, even if he does have the director's ear." He shook his head. "There'd be no reason for Vinogradov to be on Kostrihe in October, if he'd only listen to me. I am his true colleague and the best friend he has."

Petrovich leaned forward, gripping his cane. "You mean there is something wrong about this expedition?"

Ivanov's voice was growing hoarse, excited. "Oh yes. Not the way you're thinking, maybe. But you seem like an intelligent man, Petrovich. The excavation with true value would be here, within the kremlin. Only the director must be convinced. You see? It would provide material of crucial interest for years to come. The monks squatted over this island for hundreds of years. You don't think they have more hidden than we've discovered so far? Gold, jewels, their texts—the secret, perverse ones. You know the tsars would send nobles to Solovetsky when they didn't want to hear from them again?

When the Communists first arrived, the place was littered with chains and hooks—every kind of torture device."

Petrovich sat back, nonplussed."You're right, it wasn't what I thought you meant," he said. "No one ever described Solovetsky to me as a Gehenna. Not until I arrived here as a prisoner, at any rate. Didn't families use to visit on their holidays, before the Bolsheviks took it over?"I asked.

"Well, yes, but such acts weren't performed openly. A man can buy his children an iced bun while the Church conducts monstrosities behind closed doors. But it's all part of the record. Look it up! Peter the Great sent his own court dwarf here to be imprisoned when he mocked him. My piece in the last volume of the Society's Proceedings describes it. But Sewick and the others laugh, tell the director it's worthless."

The Anti-Religious Bug. I could see now how he got his nickname. From under his carapace, angry legs had emerged to scrabble at the topic. Antonov had once mentioned the tsars' tendency to exile their political foes into the Solovetsky monks' custody, but I thought tortures and hidden treasures sounded farfetched. The intensity on the man's crooked face was transfixing, hypnotic, in the manner of the insane.

"If it's part of the record," I said, "what do you hope to discover with an excavation?"

"Simple. If the worst offenses were hidden, they need to be uncovered, don't they? The best way to do so is with a careful examination of the architecture and the material record."

"But the monks are still on the island. Why not ask them?"

The little man scoffed. "You haven't heard of the blood rituals? Every monk commits a murder or a rape when he takes his vows, to bind him to the Archimandrite. Records of what each man has done are kept with the most precious treasures. So no, they'll keep their secrets. They won't be telling the location of the stash to you or me. An investigation is the only way."

I glanced at Petrovich, who appeared to find the idea of pacts sealed in blood even less plausible than I did. But I could tell he was making an effort not to alienate Ivanov, in case we needed him again. "You're telling us you believe Vinogradov's research priorities are misplaced," he said evenly. "That's unfortunate, but for our case what matters is the research he *is* conducting. What's he looking for on Kostrihe?"

Ivanov waved a hand dismissively. "Labyrinths. Spiral sort of mazes. Stone Age. They're patterns of rocks laid out on the ground, not full-fledged structures. Found on Kostrihe, some other places, too. Well preserved. Interesting-enough subject—you wouldn't expect anything else from a scholar like the director—but not nearly so important as what's here, under our noses." He shook his head. "Damn Sewick!"

"Fine," said Petrovich. "But another question about our case: can you think of a reason Antonov might have been outside the kremlin? An errand for Vinogradov, maybe?"

Ivanov shook his head quickly. "No, no. There'd be a record at the gate, wouldn't there, if the director had sent him out? Now, my current project starts with old account books. That's where to find the truth of history, isn't it? Rubles and kopeks tell the story. Every time they built—"

Petrovich interrupted: "Could it have had something to do with these icons that were requisitioned?"

"Doubt that. Those were collected three days ago. All that business is done, long done." Ivanov was speaking quickly, undeterred from his subject. "But listen. The accounts show that every time they built, they spent more than needed. So they were diverting supplies to something, eh? And the proportions of these churches: the interior dimensions don't match the exterior. I don't have to tell a savvy fellow like you. It means hidden chambers. Rooms they didn't want to leave a record of building, rooms no outsider was meant to find. Now what do you think we'd find in those rooms?"

The old man couldn't stand it any longer. "Thanks for your help, Assistant Director," he said. "We'll let you know if there's anything else."

Out in the stairwell, the cold began to seep back through my clothing. Petrovich needed help descending. He went down the stairs a step behind me, leaning on my shoulder. "It would make a good story," I said as we reached the lower door. "Labyrinths, secret depravity, and treasures hidden in the walls."

He grunted what he thought of that. Outside the clouds had grown darker, and flurries of snow had begun to fall.

5

The chest at the end of Antonov's bed held three potatoes, an onion, a shriveled beet, a tin cup with a hinged lid containing a half-pint of sunflower oil, a tiny amount of sticky molasses-sugar in a twist of wax paper, buckwheat groats in a paper bag, three pieces of salt cod amounting to perhaps a half pound, some dried turnip greens wrapped in a dish towel, and salt. It had to be almost a full dried ration, ten days' worth out of twelve—minus bread, of course. That would have to be distributed daily.

Folded up to one side of the food were two sweaters, one a gray pullover, the other a dark green cardigan with horn buttons. Beneath these: a thin, checked scarf; a white dress shirt with attached collar; an undershirt; and a rolled-up tie. A well-thumbed black Bible lay on top, along with two identical spoons, a metal bowl, a safety razor with a Bakelite handle, a brush, and a small lump of black soap.

It was a small box. The contents had been packed together so tightly you could see where a small kettle with a wooden handle had been removed. Petrovich had taken it to the stove down the hall to make tea.

I'd waited until I couldn't hear the thump of the old man's cane before raising the lid. Two of the potatoes went directly into the pockets of my coat, but it was hard to tell how much more could be taken without his noticing. Had he registered what was there when he pulled out the kettle?

It did not occur to me to wait and ask what would happen to Antonov's ration. To take as much as I could get away with was a reflex, the same as blinking when a bright light shines in your eyes.

From out in the hall, the sound of the cane returning surprised me. The lid banged shut, but I'd managed to take a seat on Antonov's bed by the time Petrovich appeared in the doorway.

"Everything all right here?" he asked.

"I'm fine," I said.

The cell must have been a monk's, before. There was no door in the doorway for Petrovich to close as he came through. The space, perhaps nine feet long and six wide, was for the most part occupied by two narrow pallets. These left just enough room to walk to a recessed window set into the wall. Flaking plaster covered the walls and the low ceiling. The gray floorboards showed signs of long scrubbing.

He set the kettle and the teapot on the windowsill, where a cheaply made wooden chess set was stored. Then he limped to his own chest, at the foot of the other bed.

"My daughter can sometimes send a little money for the commissary." He pulled the tin of tea from the pocket of his coat, shaking it gently before putting it away in the box. "Not much. It's weak stuff, what I make."

The note I'd found in Antonov's desk had referred to the commissary as well. The general rates at the camp store were known to be extortionate, and even the special rates available to well-placed *zeks* were high, but if you had the money, luxuries like tea could be had. Indeed, almost anything could be had on Solovki with enough ready currency. Rumor circulated of an imprisoned Mexican count who, in spite of whatever he'd done to get himself on the wrong side of the Party, had bought with five thousand rubles the right to live in the camp commandant's own house. How true that story was, I don't know. But the trouble was to have the money reach you. Anyone whose funds remained in his package after the examiners had checked it over for contraband was probably well connected already.

"I haven't smelled tea since leaving Petersburg," I said.

He grunted and came up with a heavy mug and a tin cup. These he placed on the sill as well, then stood waiting for the brew to finish.

"What's the next step now?" I said. I was afraid my anxiety would sound in my voice, but it was better than waiting silently. Had he heard the bang of the lid? "The note I found must be a good clue, mustn't it?"

He turned to look at me. "Might be." The blue eyes considered. "Had you ever heard of him talk about a woman before?"

"No, never. My impression was the same as Sewick's. He didn't seem like the type."

"Why not?"

I gathered my thoughts. "It's that he seemed more like a monk than a prisoner here. Not just because he was devout. He had a kind of higher calling, didn't he?"

Petrovich nodded, then turned back to the window. I watched while he poured the tea into the two cups and brought them over. Handing me the tin one, he sat down and said: "Tell me how the two of you met."

"Ah," I said, surprised. "It was a lecture. At the museum."

The evening's program, conducted under the auspices of the Society for Local Lore, had been open to any *zek* who was interested. I hoped to make connections. I'd heard of it from a philologist from the University of Kazan, who slept in the next row of beds over from mine in Quarantine, and who I suppose had been moved to share the opportunity by my schoolboy mien and obvious wretchedness. Before my arrest, I myself had studied briefly at the University of Saint Petersburg. Higher education was more common on Solovetsky than in the general population—the Cheka targeted the academies particularly—but still rare enough that men like him could be motivated by scholarly solidarity.

On the appointed evening, however, his work platoon was late returning: they must have missed their quota. After bolting the ration my own platoon was issued, I went to the lecture alone, arriving late and taking a seat in the back.

At the podium, a botanist read from his notes about the ghost orchid, a rare flower that grew among the roots of firs and larches. It had been discovered to be surprisingly common on Solovetsky. He apologized for the lack of illustrations or specimens: the camp lacked the resources for both scientific drawing and cultivation. But the ghost orchid possessed a tiny, fleshy, white-and-purple blossom, with a pale stem. The stem was colorless, he said, because the plant lacked chlorophyll of any kind, performing no photosynthesis. Instead it was a saprophyte, a member of that class of plants which draw nutrition from the decaying matter in which they grow. He speculated that the flower's rarity might stem from its dependence on certain types of fungus to predigest the dead things it consumed.

There was much more, but my attention wandered. In fact, I dozed.

I only jerked back to consciousness when the audience began to scrape its chairs and disperse. By the time I knew what was going on, the room was nearly empty; even the botanist folded his notes, tucked them into his jacket, and headed to the door without waiting to be asked questions. The few who stayed spoke to each other in low voices, grouped by the windows or the door.

I was staring at a painting intently—actually gathering courage to introduce myself to someone, anyone, so that the evening would not be entirely wasted—when Antonov appeared at my side. "You enjoyed the lecture?" he asked.

His bad teeth were the first thing I noticed, followed by the Astrakhan hat, which looked warm. I ventured something about Botanist Fedyaeev's breadth of knowledge and evident eminence in his field.

"Difficult to concentrate on spring flowers at the start of September," he said. "But a useful habit to cultivate. I mean considering Creation in its unity. The flowers of the field hold their place in Christ's plan, even after the frost is on the ground."

What can you say to something like that? Whatever conversational sally I'd been planning, already less than brilliant, was completely defeated by his turn to the metaphysical. Even later, when I knew him better, he never lost that ability to put me at a loss for words. But I must have managed to come out with something. It was clear he was being kind.

"He took you up," mused Petrovich.

"I think he felt sorry for me."

The old man nodded. He slurped at his tea, thin lips moving

under his mustache. "You had no idea he would be at the museum?"

"No, of course not. That is, I'd hoped to make connections at the lecture. But Antonov was a complete stranger to me. I only hoped to meet someone who might think I was worth helping."

"And you did. Lucky." Petrovich had been staring at me while I told the story, and I'd had to stop myself from fidgeting. I was sure it would look suspicious. "You didn't have any source of connections on the island? Sometimes fellows who knew each other in a remand prison before their sentencing find themselves reunited here."

"At Kresty I only met the men in my cell. If any of them are here, I haven't heard of it."

"You're young. Don't you have a family worried about you?"

"I do," I said. "They are. But I doubt they know anyone on Solovki." Even if they had, I wasn't sure they knew where I was. I hadn't had a letter in more than a year.

Petrovich grunted. "That's good. After you mentioned those damned detective stories, I wondered whether you'd grown up one of those orphan hooligans, always reading Pinkertons on the boulevard and watching for something to steal."

It took a special effort not to jerk my guilty hands away from the potatoes. He was making a joke, if not a very kind one. It was true that the *besprizorniki*, gangs of orphaned children that seemed to accumulate on every street corner during those years, often whiled away their time over kopek-beer and *detektivy*. But I had always considered their enthusiasm for the genre slightly incongruous. I could understand what they liked about the exotic settings and wild plots; I myself appreciated the way the stories let you escape the mire of everyday life. But that members of a group known for criminality should love stories that inevitably ended with the punishment of criminals—that was perplexing.

And anyway, I could never have passed for a *besprizornik*. My student cap should have been good for that, if nothing else.

"My father held the rank of collegiate assessor. A supervising engineer in the Saint Petersburg water bureau."

"Ah, respectable. That's as bourgeois as they come. All right, then. If you're so respectable, what did you do to end up here on Solovetsky?"

Another joke. He knew as well as I did that bourgeois respectability made it more likely to find oneself a *zek*, not less.

"My sentence is three years," I said, "for reactionary political association. I was a member of—well, of a student group. Truly, though, there was nothing political about it."

We had called ourselves the Academy of the Uncertain Arts and Ephemeral Sciences—the AUAES. The name seemed amusing at one time, though the joke eludes me now. My old schoolmate Arnold Palvo, a Russo-Finn who'd joined the University's classics department, sponsored my admission. It was a gas, he told me; the fellows were clever but not stuck up. Based on papers they read to the group, "Academicians" received "Chairs" with gag titles. Apart from that, they mostly arranged hiking and rowing expeditions outside Petersburg.

At my first meeting, nine of us crammed into Palvo's attic garret in a narrow building by the Neva. He held the Chair of Portentous Languages, having lectured on some Latin text about divination and omens. I spoke on Lobachevsky's non-Euclidean geometry, then sat in the stairwell while inside they debated what title to bestow.

In the end they settled on Chair of Imaginary Geometry. Evidently this sounded fanciful enough to nonmathematicians, but it was disappointing, even a little embarrassing, to me. Lobachevsky intended the term "imaginary" to suggest an analogy with the imaginary numbers, already well known when he described his strange spaces. At any rate, there was nothing funny about the term. "Imaginary geometry" was a real term, and to be called chair of it implied a degree of expertise I did not possess. Moreover, it meant the others had missed the point of my lecture. I needed to develop a better sense of humor about the whole thing, said Palvo.

We were infiltrated as a matter of course. Sergei Manilusky was a medical student, a year younger than I, new to the university. He'd met one of our members at a political lecture, and was shortly voted the Chair of Transcendent Digestion.

I was the first of the group to be arrested, though I presume the others followed. Manilusky claimed to be interested in certain questions about the origins of mathematics —whether mathematical truths were discovered or merely remembered or revealed as things we already knew. I made the mistake of showing him a used German copy of the *Meno* I'd picked up in the market. Plato was never my specialty, and my German was poor, but there had been something about geometry in it.

"A week later the Cheka appeared in the family dining room to seize it and take me away," I said.

We had been eating dinner. Father had just finished scolding my little sister Dinka for slurping her soup, and her eyes were blazing in that furious way she had. I remember her anger being replaced by fear when we heard the knock and the police announced themselves.

Of the five rooms we'd had before the war, the housing council had allowed us to keep a bedroom and the dining room. The latter being the only room large enough for our two best rugs, my mother had laid them, one atop the other, under the big table. I remember one of the men who came for me looking at the floor, noticing. I had the presence of mind to hope he would not arrest Mother as well, for hoarding.

The other tenants made themselves scarce. Neither of the Vsevolovs, whom I had liked, had the courage to emerge from their room to wish me good luck. I heard the Alinskys shushing their children behind their door. Mother followed us out into the stairwell, but the officers told her to return to her room.

The memory ached in my chest, a lungful of warm clay. Something else, along with the potatoes, that I didn't care to be seen hiding.

"Evidently the import of foreign philosophy is illegal," I concluded, swallowing.

Petrovich gave his barking laugh. "I was right, then. There is something wicked about your reading habits."

"Only if you consider that there is something wicked about Plato." Anger flared in me. Before I could stop myself, I said: "And what did they arrest you for, Yakov Petrovich?"

The old man continued to chuckle, but I thought his tone changed. "I told you I was a policeman, didn't I? I belonged to the local branch, not *okhrana* or militia, but inevitably you end up doing certain favors for the security forces." He grimaced. "In fact, they were our bosses, at least when it came to anything they took an interest in. Mostly I could track down robberies and murders without interference, but let there be whiff of subversive activity in a case, the rumor of a threat to state security, and I am taking orders from Major Krikov in the name of the tsar himself.

"Well, the Bolsheviks aren't forgiving about such things. There were records of my having assisted in the arrest and prosecution of people they considered allies. Never mind whether it was my having passed on something a stick-up artist I'd arrested said about the way a batch of anarchists funded their bombing operation, or for my putting handcuffs on a revolutionary fellow who'd assassinated the others in his cell on orders from above. Even if all I'd ever done was lock up killers, I was an agent of the Imperial State—I can't deny it—and so here I am."

What he'd said made me remember my nervousness. My anger evaporated as quickly as it had bubbled up. I was conscious of sitting unnaturally still, but adjusting my seat might have emphasized the bulges in my pockets.

"We were talking about Antonov," I said.

"So we were." He sighed. "All right. Tell me, do you know how much longer he had on his sentence?"

"They gave him five years, didn't they? And you said he moved into your cell a year ago. He must have had four to go."

The room was dim. Outside the window, it was snowing harder than before. While we'd been talking, the hallway had begun to fill with the sounds of men returning to the dormitory for their midday meal. Most of the inmates in Company Ten worked in offices around the kremlin, and could come back to prepare their rations at midday.

Petrovich rattled the phlegm in his chest. "Ever hear him mention plans for when they let him go?"

"No," I said.

"No, neither did I." He thought, then went on in a gravelly voice: "Still, four years is a long time. Maybe he would have liked to get off the island a bit early. That something he talked to you about?"

"Do you mean an escape?" The idea alarmed me. I'd heard whispers of men who'd escaped, or tried to. In the winters the White Sea froze hard enough to walk over, and if you made it to shore, the border with Finland was not much more than a hundred miles away. It would be a grueling hundred miles, however. We were as far north again from Saint Petersburg as Petersburg was from Moscow. In that snowbound, subarctic wilderness, it would be a lucky five days' walk that brought you into sight of another human being, much less presented an opportunity for shelter or supplies. If, instead of Finland, you hoped to reach the parts of Russia where you might lose yourself in a town sufficiently large and anonymous, your walk south would be much further, to the tune of four or five hundred miles. Either way you faced extremes of frostbite, hypothermia, exhaustion, and starvation even worse than what we endured in the camp. And that was not to mention pursuit by the Cheka, or what they would do to you if they caught you.

Antonov had simply not seemed like the type. "No, never. He wouldn't have wanted to abandon the collection."

"A good point. Maybe I'm being too susceptible to suggestion. The Cheka gets nervous when a *zek* is found in the water. Last barrier before freedom. No one's encouraged to go swimming. But that doesn't mean it has to be our theory of the investigation."

"And Antonov didn't drown. You said so yourself."

"True." Petrovich looked at his mug, then leaned carefully down to place it on the floor. His hand shook a little as he lowered it, as though the mug were heavy for him, but he moved deliberately. Then, just as slowly, he stood up from the bed, went to the corner of the room, retrieved his cane, and sat back down.

He looked at the simple wooden handle for a long moment before he raised his narrowed eyes to me. In a quiet voice he said: "You wouldn't be keeping anything from me, would you?"

"I—"

I did not want to be sent back to Company Thirteen. Not so quickly. The dry ration, the privacy and quiet of the two-man cell, the break from hard labor—everything about Company Ten was better. But if Petrovich knew I'd taken something from Antonov's chest—

"I'm sorry, Yakov Petrovich. I shouldn't have done it. It's just that I hadn't seen so much food together in one place in such a long time." I pulled the potatoes from my pockets and held them out. "Here. Please forgive me. I promise, from now on I can be trustworthy."

"What?" The old man cocked his head at the spuds, blinking. "Did you take those from my chest?"

"No. From Antonov's."

Petrovich frowned, then chuckled. It sounded like rocks grinding together in his throat. "I see. This is what's been making you squirrelly. Well, not to worry. Probably best you have what's left of that ration anyway. There should be a good deal there. They don't like handing food out unless it's at the appointed time, so I can't say when you'll be issued your own."

One of the potatoes went along with a few flakes of fish from Petrovich's ration and groats from mine and his together. The old man retrieved a bowl from his own chest, while I used the metal one from Antonov's.

We sat and ate across from each other on the pallets, the soup hot and not too thin with groats. I had been right earlier, after all: this business would not be costing me the day's lunch.

The blue eyes were watching me whenever I looked up from my meal.

6

It has been five days since I wrote the words at the end of the last chapter. The notebook creaks open with the soreness of a disused muscle. I was not sure I wanted to continue writing. I am still not sure.

It was an unpleasant surprise to find myself putting down what I did about Mother, about Dinka. To include such matters runs counter to my plan; I aimed to show the reader a murder and set him a puzzle, not relive family disasters. What could be more pointless, more unpleasant? As I said to Vasily-the-tank-commander, this is a *detektiv*, not a memoir.

Yet since Thursday I have not been able to put the apartment of my childhood out of my mind. At work, I walk about the factory floor and feel that I am creeping through my old family halls like a ghost. That marble bust of Pushkin with the crack in the neck. All of the gory drawings of soldiers machine-gunning each other that Dinka tacked up above her bed.

Why should I want to return to that past, since returning only means living through its loss all over again? Why subject myself to it, in writing or otherwise?

I live now in a city on the other side of the Urals from Saint Petersburg—even if no one calls it that anymore, in these pages I do not have to refer to it as Leningrad—but the flats in this building are not unlike the one I grew up in. Run down, imperial, split into rooms that house a family each. In the foyer, wallpaper peels beneath high ceilings. Furniture the residents have no room for is stored at the foot of the staircase, or on the landings, and in winter, to keep their sausages and pats of butter from spoiling, they push them into the space between the inner and outer windows in net bags.

It is not the same for me. I take no more part in the lives of the families on those floors above than I do in that of my own family. My place is in the basement, my closest neighbor the building's boiler. My bedchamber started life as a utility closet. There is one window, high up in the wall, with only one pane. The released *zek*, it seems, is never quite allowed to reenter the mainstream of the great Soviet project. Who would want an enemy of the people in a communal apartment?

And this is exactly how I would prefer to have things. When the housing committee presented my assignment, I was glad. Not only because it was a better situation, though it was. (For the three years prior, I'd lived in factory barracks. No running water, no place to cook. Anyone would be glad not to have to do his eating in the cafeteria, his necessaries in the outhouse. As it is, I have only to go upstairs for these things. And the new home came with a permanent residency permit. It is possible to hope that I will not be moved on again, further east.) No, I was glad, because to live apart from my fellow citizens, in accommodations no one will envy, is desirable. Men in my situation have been denounced for less, much less, than a decent room.

Even basement living comes with social complications, of course. My-neighbor-the-boiler I have to thank for the visits of my other neighbor, Vasily-the-tank-commander. Last December it failed, and he, descending in the evening with the building's useless superintendent to see if it could be got going again, knocked on my door and asked if I'd come turn a wrench. When at length the thing gurgled back to life, he clapped us on the shoulder, first the superintendent, then me. "There you are! That pump has years left in it."

Two nights after that, he knocked again, this time after one in the morning. He'd been returning from work that kept him very late at the factory, he explained. He'd seen my light was on. "You work the second shift, don't you?" he said. "I didn't realize anyone had the room down here." Later he said: "Lots of people have something in their past. Doesn't mean they're not good workers." He meant he found me acceptable. Perhaps I did not act as inhospitable as I felt. Ten days later he came again.

It is six months since I moved into the building. Since I arrived in this city, four years. Vasily is the first person I have seen socially in that time—longer, even.

I have not been back to Petersburg since the time of my release. By then, my parents' and sister's situation was no longer secure. The regime's tolerance for "bourgeois experts," Father's social category, had diminished. His position had grown uncertain. Worse, because of his background, whenever the department's payroll was short, which was often, instead of being paid in rubles he was issued a warrant—a promise of later payment, which, as he explained to me in one of the few letters I ever received from him, in fact proved nearly valueless due to the difficulty of collecting on it. He, Mother, and Dinka could not possibly have afforded to visit me in Ekaterinburg, where I found myself shortly after my release. Nor would it have been safe for them to declare their attachment to a politically unsuitable son.

There was a letter from Dinka when Father died, but that was before the war and I've heard nothing since. I do not know whether she and Mother are still there. I do not know whether they survived the siege of the city.

Those rugs with the dining table on them. Mother was proud of her furniture.

Here there is no rug, and only the one chair, the one I sit in now. When Vasily Feodorovich was here the other night, I gave it to him. We put the glasses on my little table and I sat on the bed to drink. I did not show him what I've written.

Shall I continue writing? I think I will. Perhaps being reminded of our old apartment is not intolerable. And the pleasure of having something to hide from idiot-Vasily is too much to give up.

Outside the quarters of Company Ten, the snowstorm was worsening. Flakes hung in the air and plunged about the yard in masses like schools of fish. I was wearing the gray jumper from Antonov's chest, and had wrapped the scarf around my head beneath my cap to cover my ears. It cut the wind a little.

The old man and I had examined the chest for clues after our soup, without finding anything more than I'd already turned up. He'd suggested I take anything I wanted from it—anything but the teakettle, which he claimed for himself. It amounted to quite a haul, even with that exclusion. I thought with satisfaction of how being the possessor of a razor and brush would improve my status with Panko and Genkin, bunkmates of mine back at Company Thirteen. Even Foma would be impressed by the new warm clothes.

"Our first task for the afternoon is to visit the address given us by Ivanov," Petrovich had said. "The warehouse where they took the icons."

"You don't think the note I found is a good lead?"

"It may be. But so far the most unusual thing about Antonov's death is his turning up outside the kremlin walls. Any business he had out there is worth looking into." The old man had thought for a moment. "And the icons-into-lumber arrangement is strange as well. The sea's about to freeze, so the bosses are trying to ship every last scrap of cut wood off the island before it becomes impossible. So much I understand. And because of that, cabinetmakers have an easier time getting icons than new boards—especially since it gives certain Bolsheviks an opportunity to bedevil the monks. It makes sense, I suppose. But it's still an odd business. Couldn't hurt to grasp the details a little better."

Along with the name "Valery Zhenov," Ivanov had written down "Warehouse Number Three." The warehouses were out on the rocky finger of land that separated the southern end of the bay from the open water. Getting there meant showing our pass to a new pair of guards at Nikolski. This time we passed through without incident, though I worried the man who wrote down our names looked at our faces longer than he had to.

Ivanov had mentioned that the warehouse belonged to Anzer Division. SLON had filled the forests with its ventures the same way the monks had salted them with shrines, and each administrative unit took its name from the island whose activity it oversaw. Big Muksalma, Little Muksalma, the Big and Little Zayatskys. Furthest to the north, last and most distant, was Anzer.

You reached Anzer by following the road north. You would pass the church on Sekirnaya Hill, home to the camp's dreaded penal division, then take a ferry. By all accounts, discipline was harsher still on Anzer, food harder to come by. Stories circulated. I'd heard of a pile of severed hands, displayed by an overseer who called them his "pearls." How credible the story was, I don't know. It wasn't unheard of for tired prisoners to cut off a finger or toe to get a few days' rest. A boss might plausibly be proud of how many he'd been driven to self-mutilation by his quotas. Whatever the truth of it, the tale gave Anzer Division an ominous sound to my ears.

We circled the kremlin again, then negotiated a small, decrepit dry dock the monks had once used. From there a path led out to the point. A strong wind blew in from the ocean; twice I had to rewrap my new scarf after it had been tugged away from my ears. Across the water, where they'd pulled Gennady Antonov's body out, falling snow whipped along the edge of the quay.

The warehouses were a series of wooden, two-story boxes. In the one that had a numeral 3 painted on it, the doors to an upper loading bay were thrown open.

Several prisoners were busy lowering a container down onto a sledge with the aid of a small crane that jutted from below the roof. One of them stood on the sledge to direct the crate into place, while two others strained to hold the rope regulating its descent. With each length they paid out, the block at the end of the crane's arm squealed sharply.

A fourth man had his back turned to us and was observing the others with his arms crossed. Petrovich cleared his throat at his shoulder.

"Valery Zhenov's place, isn't it?"

"Eh?" The man turned, showing us small features cramped together beneath a beetling brow. His shoulders could have been built to measure out doorframes.

"The warehouse. Valery Zhenov's office is inside?"

"That's right."

Petrovich stood for a moment, gloved hands on his cane, watching the crate descend. "What kind of man is Zhenov? Good boss?"

Taller than I was, the other man towered over Petrovich. He

wore a heavy black coat that hung open, revealing a blue shirt buttoned up to neck. "Who're you?" He took a second, slower look, first at the old man, then at me.

"We need to speak with him. On behalf of camp administration," said Petrovich.

The man shrugged, accepting the answer. "The boss isn't as bad as some of the White Army fucks around here. Funny one, though. He's there now. You can go in."

The White Armies—Denikin's and Kolchak's, as well as the Volunteer Army—had famously been regiments of officers. You never met a veteran willing to admit a rank lower than lieutenant. Partly this was down to such enlisted men as they'd commanded being less enlisted than conscripted, and happy to have their service forgotten if they ever made it home. But even so, officers were said to have outnumbered the regular soldiers two to one. After the First World War, only those with some rank in the old system at stake were willing to shoot or be shot in the name of the tsar.

That put Whites in an equivocal position at SLON. "Class enemy" had rarely been a more accurate term. These were men who'd machine-gunned the crowded socialist vanguard. But punishing them for it would have been too straightforward for Solovki.

I've said that any position of authority needing to be filled would go, first, to a Chekist. Yet with the camp constantly expanding, there were simply not enough Chekists to go around. After membership in the secret police, the best qualification was previous managerial experience. Thus one increasingly found bosses in the camp who were less than ardent Communists. In their former lives, these new members of the administration were likely to have been principals in some manufacturing concern—or officers of the White Army. Where else was managerial experience to be found?

With authority came privilege, naturally—and the opportunity to feather one's own nest. And so, despite the Whites having enacted their enmity towards State and Party in a manner more deliberate and positive than most could claim, many of them enjoyed better rations, softer beds, and warmer lodgings than the rest of us.

The crane squeaked again, loud enough to set my teeth on edge. "Get it centered, Luka," the big man called to the one on the sledge. "You won't want to push that fucking thing if it's not balanced."

Inside the warehouse, crates and barrels ordered the dim space. A second rope-and-pulley apparatus hung down in the center of the big room, with a wide mezzanine running around all four sides. We reached the second level via a set of stairs along the back wall, at the top finding a small office, walled off from the rest. Pasted to the door was a strip of paper, on which "Division Five Subcommandant for Supply Administration Valery Viktorovich Zhenov" had been written in large letters.

"Enter," said a voice in response to my knock.

Inside, a man staring intently into the head of a hairbrush held out a hand, gesturing for us to wait. While we watched, he teased a single hair out from among the bristles and placed it on the page of a book that lay open on the desk next to him.

The squealing of the crane could still be heard outside, fainter now. Petrovich cleared his throat.

The man—surely Zhenov—turned. "Ah, forgive me. I mistook you for men from my platoon. What can I do for you?"

"You're in the middle of something?" said Petrovich.

"No, no, quite all right. Busy as we are, I'm used to fitting in health and hygiene around the rest."

Petrovich introduced us, and he and Zhenov sat down while I took Petrovich's coat and hat and hung them up on pegs Zhenov pointed out by the door. It might have been polite to remove my own cap, but the office was chilly. I settled for taking off my coat and unwrapping the scarf from around my ears.

Zhenov smiled thinly as I took my seat next to Petrovich. "You are not a Gruenewaldian."

"A what?" I said.

"I only mean that if you understood modern thinking concerning the effects of pressure and torsion of the hair on men's health, you might prefer to be free of your hat band. Don't think that I am immoderate. Out of doors, the benefits to thermoregulation of covering the scalp more than outweigh any drawbacks. But when you have the benefit of a roof and four walls. . .however, you must suit yourself. Most Russians are like you, particularly our young men. I do not hesitate to call Dr. Burkhard Gruenewald a genius, but his theories enjoy a greater popularity in his native land." He put the brush aside, penciled a short note in the book next to the hair, and closed it. His hair was fine, frizzy, and receding, leaving him with a high forehead and a surprised expression. Beneath it, his face was mustachioed, with heavy cheeks. "There you can find clubs devoted to follicular health. I am a patriot, of course, in spite of everything. But in certain matters the Teutons are more advanced."

Ignoring the look I shot him, Petrovich explained that we were investigating a certain matter for Infosec. The recent requisition of icons from the museum by Anzer Division had come to our attention.

I couldn't tell whether this alarmed Zhenov or it was simply his natural expression. "Is there anything the matter about that order?" he asked.

"That's something we're trying to find out," said Petrovich.

"Well, it was all approved at the highest levels. Normally a request for wood would go through the timbering office, I know, but, because of its unusual nature, this one went to Commandant Nogtev himself. It was he who sent it on as an order to the museum."

"You'd made a similar requisition before, I think."

Zhenov chuckled uneasily. "Well, no, not I. To tell the truth, I would never have thought of it. A bit blasphemous for my taste, perhaps. It was something they came up with last year, under the man here before me. Normally it would never be approved—I understand there are elements in Nogtev's inner circle who are protective of the museum. But at this time of year, with the sea about to freeze and the year's final calculation of lumber-plan fulfillment to be made, I daresay nothing is as important as maximizing lumber shipments. One of my men suggested we try it again, and the request was approved. They were only too happy to assign us material that wouldn't reduce output. And of course I was pleased not to have to wait for the wood."

The crane, which had stopped for a moment, resumed, louder than ever.

"Maybe you could describe your normal operations for us,"

said Petrovich.

The other man was eager to do so; here he was on firmer ground. Warehouse Number Three, it transpired, stood at the crossroads of Anzer Division's supply chains. Foodstuffs, tools and building supplies, clothing, a certain amount of fuel: anything that had to be shipped to Anzer passed through these doors. Barring lumber, which was administered centrally, anything produced on the northern island came back to Zhenov's warehouse, too. Such shipments consisted of finished goods from Anzer's workshops, along with a little fur from its limited trapping operations and, increasingly, salt from its boiling houses, which had been allowed to sit idle after the monks were displaced but were now beginning to see use again.

In fact, despite being based here at the kremlin, Zhenov and his men were members not of the Main Division like Petrovich and me, but of Anzer Division. His subordinates had their own small dormitory in a former kvass brewery not far from the warehouse, while Zhenov himself stayed with several other highly placed prisoners in a cabin along the northern road.

While Zhenov talked, I could sense Petrovich's blue eyes moving around the room, taking in whatever its details might tell him. The room was sparsely furnished. Two filing cabinets, several sets of bookshelves, the desk Zhenov sat behind. The chairs he'd directed us to were hard and straight-backed. A small window, high in the wall behind the desk, let in gray light. Apart from a broken piece of mirror nailed to the wall where Zhenov had been standing when we came in, there didn't seem to me to be anything out of the ordinary. Only the crane's tortured screech gave the place any atmosphere at all.

"How did the icons reach the workshop on the other island?" the old man asked.

Zhenov explained. The requisition had been loaded onto a train car bound for the dock at the island's northeastern tip. From there it was transferred to the ferry, the same one that transported prisoners to and from Anzer.

There had been no need to store the icons in the warehouse: the whole undertaking was planned with enough notice that he was able to arrange a spot for them on that day's train in advance. He had not personally overseen their collection from the museum, but had checked that all was in order before they were loaded. As Zhenov described it, this was standard procedure. He went daily to the wireless telegraph station, where he was able to communicate with the small station on Anzer, as well as to the kremlin telephone office, where he could talk to those of his men who were stationed at the end of the line, responsible for loading and unloading the train and ferry. In this way shipments to and from the island were coordinated, and any requests from units based there could be relayed. He took steps, of course, to make sure that no materials were lost or misappropriated along the way; for the icons, which might be particularly valuable, he had devised a special system of accounting.

"I make the trip myself on a weekly basis. There is no substitute for personal inspection when it comes to confirming that your orders have been carried out correctly." He looked searchingly at Petrovich. "You and I are kindred spirits in this attitude, are we not? Don't be surprised, I can read it in your hair. A characteristic denudation in the lobes of Struhl. Yes, care and scrupulousness produce a predictable pattern of baldness, in men of a certain age. As Dr. Gruenewald says, 'The concerns of a lifetime etch themselves onto our scalps, the way the eroded landscape records the ancient river's history.' For the young, of course, the character has not had as much time to act on the fibrillose field. Early baldness is typically the result of serious psychological disorder, or of sickness as a child." He glanced at the hat I was still wearing. "Or perhaps of careless mistreatment."

It was ridiculous, of course. Some *zeks* reacted to prison this way—transforming themselves into grotesques by adherence to some fixed idea. Better that, maybe, than to remain who you had been before. In one way or another, we were all changed.

Petrovich said something about his scrupulousness requiring him to ask why the requisition had included specific dimensions for the requested icons. How had the dimensions been determined? How had it been known that icons would be available in those sizes?

"Ah, yes," said Zhenov. "The measurements. We simply passed along what had been requested by the cabinetry workshop, as I recall. It amounted to just a few square yards of board, but of a desirable quality. They'd had last year's shipment to give them an idea of what was available, I suppose. And they coordinated with Ivan, my foreman."

"What were they going to build?"

Zhenov seemed to hesitate before he said: "The cabinetry workshop's production schedule isn't set here. I only find out what the workshops do with the supplies we've sent when they've finished their work and are ready to ship it back. You'd have to ask them."

Petrovich pinched his mustache, considering. At last he said: "Fine. Tell me, Subcommandant Zhenov. Are you acquainted with a man named Gennady Antonov?"

"I can't say that I am."

"Antonov worked with the icons at the camp museum. He was the one responsible for deciding which of them they'd give to you, and which they'd keep. He hasn't visited this warehouse recently?"

"Not to my knowledge. Why do you ask?"

"Last night he was murdered."

Zhenov pursed his lips at the word. Two fingers rose to his hairline, just brushing the hairs there.

Petrovich went on: "You can see why we'd be interested in his involvement with something as out of the ordinary as your icon requisition."

You could see Zhenov gathering himself, putting on a military attitude. "In truth, I can't say that I can. Just why is it you believe our department here is connected to the—the murder?"

"There's no connection," said Petrovich. "Not yet. At this point we're only trying to reconstruct where Antonov went yesterday, what he did last week. Anything unusual interests us."

Zhenov stammered. "Ah. Well—yes. But if I had met the man, I assure you, I would remember. I keep careful records of all my affairs. Indeed, the main thing in maintaining a Gruenewaldian regimen is to keep a careful journal. Close observation of your own scalp condition is the key to health. Variations among the hairs of the Herr-Professor-Doktor's nine regions are subtle, but with the help of his guides, and careful record keeping, even someone as inexpert as myself can tell the difference. For instance, under normal circumstances, over fifty percent of the hairs I lose in a day come from the left-anterior and left-supra-auricular zones. However, in a period of sickness this summer, I observed a distinct spike in my crown's rate of denudation. In fact, the spike began before I'd even begun to feel other symptoms. If I'd been more knowledgeable, perhaps having been forewarned I could have done something to fend off the episode. No man is immortal, of course, as Dr. Gruenewald rightly notes. The loss of a certain number of hairs each day is merely the sign of natural human decay—which, in a situation like ours in this camp, is inevitably accelerated. The important thing is to minimize the loss, and also to ensure that it occurs evenly, at a similar rate across the entire scalp."

Petrovich was not willing to be distracted by follicular health. "Your men might have met Antonov when they collected the pieces from the museum."

It had been nervousness, clearly, that launched Zhenov's new recitation of Gruenewaldian pieties. But you could hear the Subcommandant gaining confidence as he touched his topic's familiar points, until by the end he'd made himself aware of the affront to his dignity and office that our investigation represented. Now he sounded angry.

"I must say, Petrovich. I consider it distinctly ungentlemanly of you not to have explained the seriousness of your investigation immediately. A fellow feels rather caught out, describing the details of his business without knowing there's been a murder. I have nothing to hide, of course, but you must know as well as I that even the appearance of involvement in such a case can be, well, quite dangerous!"

Before Petrovich could reply, the block outside gave a squeal that made us all pause. Louder still than it had been before, the sound warped nauseously, a change in pitch drawn out over a period that must only have been several seconds but felt longer. Then a metallic snap, a cry, and the noise of men shouting.

"Dear lord," said Zhenov. "Excuse me."

Petrovich motioned for me to follow. He would come along behind.

Out on the stairs, Zhenov fumbled with a cap he'd taken from one of the pegs in his office. Even as he raced ahead of me, I could see him making gingerly adjustments to its band.

The man bled into the snow, still pinned where one end of the container had crushed his leg and hip. He sprawled, moaning, half on the sledge and half off. The crate's other end, still attached to a set of straps like the ones that had come loose, remained suspended, perhaps two feet in the air. If the crate fell, what was left of the wounded man below the waist would be pulped.

The big overseer we'd seen before struggled to keep it from slipping free. "Don't let it go, you prick-fingered cunts!" he yelled to the men working the crane above. He'd squatted to get a grip, and the muscles bulged hugely beneath the fabric of his coat as he strained against the weight. Wind strummed at the rope that ran from the pulley, freezing and wild. "No! Fuck, don't pull. Just hold it there!"

Zhenov and I were the first to reach them, taking up positions on either side. Even with three of us and the support of the straps, the weight was incredible. I could hardly believe the big man had been able to support it by himself.

"Lift," he said hoarsely. We heaved. Dizziness came over me, but the crate began to move. The tendons stood out in the overseer's neck. You could smell him—like an engine, he radiated heat and fumes into the cold air.

The pinned man screamed.

"Shut your fucking mouth, Luka," the big man roared. "Lift!"

By this time, others had run to join us. Inch by inch, the box rose. At last someone dragged Luka free of the sledge. On a signal from the big man, the crate crashed to the ground.

"A stretcher," cried Zhenov. "A stretcher, quickly!"

There was a bustle of activity as something suitable was searched for. Strangled sounds of pain came from the wounded man's white face. His trousers were sodden with blood.

At length someone returned with two wide boards, and they carried him off in the direction of the hospital. Before hurrying after the makeshift litter, Zhenov grabbed his overseer's sleeve. "That block should have been checked, Ivan. We could hear the sound it made from my office."

"It was checked," said the other man sullenly, rubbing one shoulder. "Greased it like I was going to stick my prick in. It always squealed. They give us bad equipment, sometimes bad things happen."

Petrovich had made his way outside at some point during the commotion. "You all right?" he said to me.

I must have looked shocked. "I'm fine," I said.

It didn't look as though we would be able to finish our interview with Zhenov. Before we could depart, the overseer came over, offering his hand.

"Thanks for the help," he said to me. "Name's Kologriev. Fuck your mother, ugly business, eh? Maybe Luka'll be all right."

"Anatoly Bogomolov," I said. It was like shaking hands with a brick.

I hadn't quite met his eye. He looked at me appraisingly. "The pulleys—one of the little bitches must've snapped off inside the block."

"Yes."

Petrovich barked his laugh that might as well have been a cough. "Tolya's not quite used to the blood, and has had a full day already. You see he's good in a pinch, though."

Kologriev nodded. "You found the boss. What'd you want to talk to him for, anyway?"

"Something you can help us with, maybe. You the foreman here?"

"That's right."

Kologriev admitted to having been in charge of collecting the icons for the lumber requisition. The pickup had gone smoothly; with five men and two sledges, the only inconvenient part had been going up and down the museum's stairs. "All of that came from Anzer," he said when Petrovich asked about the requested dimensions. "Didn't pay much attention to it, to tell the truth. Just counted up big, small, and medium-sized. Made sure we had the right number of each."

"Remember meeting a man named Antonov? He might have shown you which lots to take."

"That the little one with a chip on his shoulder?"

Petrovich's mouth twisted a little. No, that's Ivanov, the assistant director. Antonov would have been taller and quieter, with a beard." He indicated its length on his own chin.

Kologriev shook his head. "No one like that."

"Anything that struck you about the pickup at all, at the time?"

"Only that fucking museum being there to start with. Monks must have had it good here once, if it was all like that. Can't believe the pricks in Administration let them keep on that way." He looked back and forth between us. "'Scuse me. Maybe you two are working for the center."

"Infosec. Don't worry, temporary basis only." The old man tried again: "But Antonov—you don't remember him? Long beard, quiet voice. About Tolya's size. His work was restoring the icons. A painter."

Kologriev shook his head. "Nah. But every son of a bitch looks the same to me in this camp. He might have been there. Why're you looking for him?"

"He was murdered," said Petrovich.

At this, finally, the big man looked modestly impressed. "Murdered? Fucking bad luck." He reached up to massage his shoulder. The fabric of his shirt strained over his chest. "But then, we all have bad luck. *Zeks* get killed every day. Every son of a bitch looks the same to me, and fuck your mother, they all have different versions of the same bad luck."

Without the noise of the crane, our walk back was much quieter than the approach had been. For all his foul language, Kologriev had had a point. What had happened to Antonov was sad, but not really so different from what befell others every day. Starved, murdered, or smashed by a box of saws: dead was dead.

7

We'd passed back over the dry dock by the time Petrovich spoke again. The wind was blowing snow into our faces.

"How did they meet?" he said.

The question took me by surprise. I'd just noticed a red stippling of blood on the path in front of us: we were following along the way Luka's litter had come. Remembering the noises he'd made still brought about a sympathetic clenching in my throat.

"Who?" I said.

Petrovich stopped and looked at me. "Thought you'd be able to handle something like this, after your self-possession with Antonov's body. You're not going to be in a cloud all afternoon over an accident, are you?"

"No." I shook my head. "No. You're talking about Antonov and the woman who wrote that note, aren't you? That's the next clue we need to follow."

"Ah!" The old man shook his cane at me. "And what makes you think it's a woman? Why couldn't V stand for Viktor, or Valery?"

"You said it was a woman before."

"Maybe I did. I am asking what you think."

I shrugged. "It would be an odd note for a Valery to have written. And the handwriting looked like a woman's."

He started off down the path again. "That's what I think, too. I want to know who she is, what they were up to. So, how did they meet?"

I was aware of Solovetsky's women as a distant presence. Several hundred lived outside the kremlin, in a separate dormitory behind the main administration building, north of the bay. You would pass them sometimes, walking in groups to their work. Not long after I'd arrived, my platoon had been assigned to remove stones from a field out by the power substation, near the little brick building that housed the telephone system's switchboards. Every day, the half-dozen girls who operated them would go by in skirts. I remember the sound of their conversations, their voices reaching us over the waving grass. The summer was fading, the sky blue. By then I'd lived for a year and a half without hearing a female voice.

Telephone operator was a plum assignment, of course. Most of the women labored like the rest of us, sawing timber the men had felled, or working the vegetable fields. What it took for a girl to get something better was spoken of in sniggering tones. Often it meant she'd entered into what *zeks* termed, with their characteristic combination of coarseness and delicacy, "a calculated marriage." They took pull, these marriages, an amount of pull most could never hope to muster. You had to have something to offer the woman in the first place. Then you had to be able to arrange to live together, or at least provide for regular private visits. But the arrangement was respected, if not quite respectable. Most men would leave a "married" woman alone.

Could that have been what Antonov's acquaintance with the mysterious V consisted of? It seemed unlikely. But under what other auspices did men and women come together on Solovki?

"Some women work in the kremlin," I said to Petrovich. "They could have known each other that way."

"Not likely. What did the note say? 'I will be inside this Thursday.' If she had a regular way into the kremlin, she wouldn't have cared about the day."

I fished the note out from the interior coat pocket where I was keeping our papers. The slip fluttered in the wind as I read. *A package has come from my mother with a few rubles. I will be inside, visiting the commissary store before nightly roll. This Thurs-*

day. Please meet me.—V. Beneath that: *The thought of your goodness is all that enables me to continue as I have.*

"I don't know," I said, catching up to Petrovich. "It could be that. But from the way it's written, it's possible she's often inside, only doesn't have much opportunity to meet." He grimaced, but didn't deny it. I went on. "And wherever she works, it doesn't necessarily tell us how they knew each other, does it? It could have been a simple chance encounter. Those happen anywhere, by definition."

We'd turned and were heading north on the road along the bay again. Petrovich's voice creaked irritably. "Grasping after certainties is an amateur's mistake. Too many Pinkertons: you think you'll go on from excitement to excitement, without false starts, because that's the way it works in your stories. No. Investigating crimes is mostly boredom and asking questions whose answers turn out not to matter. If you thought you were guaranteed an adventure when I took you on, you're wrong."

"I was only trying to be logical. I don't want an adventure."

"Logic! Another fantasy. How many cases do you think have been solved with logic? Not many. Working a murder means looking at things and talking to people. Maybe then you think, a little. After that you look and talk some more, see who has secrets that might be squeezed out of them."

"All right," I said. "I only want to help. You must guide me about what sort of thing is useful."

Petrovich huffed, ruffling his mustache. "What are we going to do if we only follow necessary and logical leads, eh? Sit practicing deduction in our cells? This is like the footprints. You think there will be a thread, and if you can just think along it, it will lead you from the beginning to the end."

I was learning to take the old man's badgering in stride, I thought. And what he'd said was interesting. In fact I had had Sherlock Holmes in mind again, with my remarks about what was necessary and true by definition. There was a line that I'd always remembered from *The Sign of the Four*, to the effect that detection ought to be as dispassionate and unromantic as the fifth postulate of Euclid. What intrigued me was precisely that this postulate, the parallel postulate, was the one Lobachevsky's imaginary geometry had shown not to be necessary for a coherent account of lines and shapes in the plane. It had occurred to me to wonder whether there wasn't something romantic, something arbitrary and passionate, about the fifth postulate itself. In that case, why shouldn't the logic of detection prove to be a fantasy, just as Petrovich had said?

"I have to make reasonable assumptions," he continued, a little mollified by my acquiescence. "Lucky for us, your average *zek*, man or woman, can't move freely around the camp. We saw Antonov needed a pass from Vinogradov to go out through Nikolski. He can't have been having those written for him all the time. Whereas the girl couldn't—probably couldn't—come into the kremlin regularly. So, where does that leave them to bump into each other?"

"It sounds like you have an idea."

"I do. In July, Antonov was in the hospital for over a week."

There was a small surgery within the kremlin used for treating emergencies and brief illnesses, or sometimes for isolating the infected during epidemics, but anyone sick enough for long convalescence was transferred to a larger facility outside the walls. That would be where they were taking Luka, in fact. It treated both men and women.

The hospital was something *zeks* talked about. On the whole, it was not considered a bad place in which to find yourself; the place had served as the monks' infirmary for decades, and in general the arrangements there were less haphazard and makeshift than in the rest of the camp. If you managed to get yourself admitted, you could lie in bed for days, safe from your work quota and receiving an invalid ration that wasn't too bad. The trouble was how sick you had to be to get in—almost to the point of death if your bosses were unsympathetic—and the risk you ran of catching something else from your fellow patients once you had.

"I suppose they have records," I said.

We needed to look at things; the files would be things to look at. So far, so good. But notwithstanding what Petrovich had said about deduction, I still didn't feel certain he'd hit on the answer.

The old man must have seen me thinking. After we'd gone along in silence for a minute, he said: "You have something to add?"

I tried to run through every possibility in my mind. "Maybe

they knew each other in Yaroslavl. You were saying it earlier, sometimes people run into old friends here."

"That's a possibility. There are ways of finding out. There might be a list of known associates in Antonov's file. In fact, reading that file might fill in some background we're missing. We report back to our friend in the Cheka tomorrow morning. We can ask then."

The hospital was northeast of the kremlin, within view of the administration building. As we approached the door, I noticed more blood on the ground. I'd kept noticing traces of it in the snow, all the way from Warehouse Three.

Petrovich had warned me there would be no thread to lead us. And Luka's track of blood hadn't, after all, been what led to the hospital. Even so, we'd followed it. What did that mean—following a thread not because it was a clue, but only by accident, despite its unrelatedness to your case? Sherlock Holmes would not have liked it. I doubted Petrovich would appreciate my pointing it out either.

The hospital's main door opened onto the front hall and a stale smell. There was no one there. In one corner, unlaundered gowns and blankets had been gathered up in several baskets.

"No use our wandering the halls," said Petrovich. "Probably they're busy with the fellow Zhenov just brought in. Someone will show up." There was a desk in the corner opposite the gowns, with a chair behind it. The old man lowered himself into it with a pained exhalation. He seemed glad for the chance to sit down.

"This woman we're looking for," I said after we'd been waiting a few minutes. "Do you think she was Antonov's lover?"

"It was that kind of note."

"It just doesn't seem like him," I said.

"Like him? What's like him?" Petrovich pulled a long face. "If he had a woman to bump up and down in bed with, that's what he was like, and what we thought he was like before was wrong. What he was like is what we're trying to find out."

"I only mean the note surprised me."

"To me it would make some sense for there to be a woman in it. That's one of the things you look for, when a man's been killed. Money, women, or drink. Mostly drink—those are easy to solve.

Next is money, of course. But women are pretty common."

I wasn't sure what to say to that. Somewhere deeper in the hospital, someone had begun calling piteously for a doctor. The old man thought about it for a minute, then continued: "There would have to be another man, as well. She wouldn't have killed him herself."

"Why not?"

"Women who murder don't do what was done to Antonov. Blow to the back of the head—I've arrested a few who were strong enough, maybe, but it's not what they choose. Your lady murderer does it with poison, occasionally a gun. Men are the ones who strangle you or beat you to death." He mused. "Both sexes like a knife. Ladies are used to it from cooking, maybe."

At length an orderly appeared, expressing surprise at finding Petrovich in his seat. Once the old man had explained what we were looking for and shown our papers, he led us upstairs.

The hospital had three floors, each organized around a central hallway with wards on either side. Men and women slept in separate wards, the orderly explained, but as long as they could move under their own power, nothing prevented them walking across the hall to meet a member of the opposite sex.

At the top he unlocked the door to the records room, an unheated garret. We spent the next several hours in our coats, searching through intake-and-discharge ledgers for the letter V. Slow work: the hospital's files were all written by hand, some so sloppily that, in the dim light coming from the single small window, they were hard to make out. As often as actual admittance records, I found myself reading outdated diagnoses, or orders for more medicine. The latter had mostly been stamped "DENIED." Making the job even more time-consuming was the hospital's practice of recording admissions not in a master list organized by date, but in logs devoted to different illnesses and injuries. By the time Petrovich was convinced we'd been through everything that might help us, my eyes ached and I'd started to shiver. But the search was successful. In the typhus log we discovered one Varvara Grishkina, a Veronika Fitneva in bruising-and-broken-bones. Their stays overlapped with Antonov's.

Our questions were directed to a doctor who, queried in his examination room, could say nothing about Grishkina. He thought he recognized the name "Fitneva," however. It took being reminded of her injury—she'd been admitted with broken ribs and internal bleeding—for him to recall her fully. "Yes, that's right. I didn't notice her until the swelling in her face went down," he said. He leaned back in his tilting chair and looked at us with glassy eyes. "Although . . . you know, she wore her hair a certain way. A bob. Modern. It's always attractive when a woman takes care about her hair and wants it to be modern. Yes . . . You notice that even when her face is too swollen and out of shape to be good-looking . . ." He trailed off.

When Petrovich pressed him, he allowed that, before her stint in the hospital, she might have been one of the women assigned to digging peat over the summer. But he had no idea what had become of her now. How she'd gotten smashed up so badly—he couldn't say that either.

On the way down the stairs, Petrovich grumbled about morphine-addict medics, and wondered how the man kept himself in supply. Even so, he seemed pleased.

It was beginning to get dark. The snow had stopped while we were indoors, and a heavy new layer covered everything. Petrovich wanted to follow up our new lead before curfew.

"You don't think our pass will be good enough?" I said. Work groups went in and out all night, but after 6:00 Nikolski was closed to individuals, even those with passes, unless the pass authorized it specifically. Ours said we were to be let through under all circumstances, so I'd assumed we were in the privileged category.

"Ought to be," said Petrovich. "But after that business this morning, I don't want those thugs to have any reason for harassing us. When we see our friend tomorrow, we can have him add special instructions for the guards."

At that time of year, only one area of the peat workings was still active. To visit it meant first walking about a mile up the northern road, then turning east and passing over the broken grid of ditches and canals that drained the water from the bog. Plank bridges spanned the gaps in places, but Petrovich found these difficult going with his cane. We took the planks only where they looked sturdier or less slippery, or where we had no choice but to cross. We wended a much longer way than we had to, back and forth around the trenches' ends. The women were working in one of the eastern pits, near a tongue of forest still not cut down.

I'd never cut peat, but it looked like hard work. On the ground above the cutting trench were a hundred small mounds, spaced regularly, like miniature, snow-covered haystacks. Evidently these were bricks of peat arranged for drying; many mounds-in-progress were visible, being piled up clod by clod by the women. The pilers left careful patterns of space between each active layer, while others packed moss around layers that were finished.

A little distance away, bricks that had dried were stacked in a half-dozen wall-like ranks. These were much larger, forty feet long and ten high. Each must have comprised thousands of clods. Along one side of these larger mounds, a few rusted steel rails were scattered, as well as a single cart, overturned. A smooth stretch of ground headed east in a straight line, showing where there must once have been a track. The train line ran up the island's eastern shore, from a point just south of the kremlin to the Anzer ferry; I surmised some system for transporting the peat to that line for loading had been dismantled.

Jagged with snow, the nearby pines loomed in the darkening afternoon.

"How will we find out which one is Veronika Fitneva?" I asked. "She may not even be here."

"You tell a detective by how far the heels of his boots have worn down." Petrovich coughed thinly at my stare. "Start asking questions. There are thirty women here? It's not so many. Won't take long to question them all if we split up. Enjoy the company of the fairer sex. It must have been long enough since you've had it. All you have to do is ask them if they know the name."

Petrovich started among the mounds, leaving me to wander along the trench. Its wall stretched about two hundred feet, with cutters working with long spades over about half that length. Where there was no work, the peat had been covered with insulating moss, the same being used on the mounds. I thought I would start at the end and work my way back. That way Petrovich wouldn't have so far to come when he'd finished.

When I got there, two girls were readying a new section for cutting. They'd removed the moss and begun hacking through the frozen stuff with axes. Chips of ice and mud flew in the air.

Petrovich's advice just to ask about the name was fine, as far as it went. But my heart beat faster as I approached. Even in Saint Petersburg I'd never been very good at talking to girls. The fellows most liked were the worker-student types, who left the collars of their shirts open and wore high boots instead of shoes. My friend Arnold Palvo, despite being no great hand with ladies himself, had once tried to explain it to me. "It's a new age, Tolya. Girls now don't like you to hide anything. Don't treat them like they've never heard a vulgar word before. They're insulted: it shows you think they're sentimental. You and I were raised to think there are things called good manners, and that they matter. But listen, between the sexes, that's right out—those are just irrational bourgeois prohibitions on natural appetites." He'd shrugged. "At any rate, it seems they like you better if you're a little rude."

There was also the fact of this being my first interrogation as a detective. Apart from spilling news of the murder to Ivanov, which had been a mistake, I'd thus far only hovered behind while Petrovich asked the questions. It was an arrangement that had suited me. Now, however, I would have to work out the approach myself. How should one ask questions so as to get useful answers in return? How to broach the subject of the investigation?

My mind had been on Sherlock Holmes all day, ever since Petrovich had been so dismissive of my reading. When it was necessary to go among strange people to recover information, Holmes commonly disguised himself. His attention to fine details allowed him to pass for a stoker among train workers, a tribesman among Red Indians, a priest in the Vatican of Rome. I couldn't imagine how that might suit me here, however. Holmes sometimes impersonated an old woman, but I wouldn't be capable of it.

Nat Pinkerton offered a different sort of model—perhaps, given his nationality, a more American one. He disguised himself only occasionally, preferring to get what he needed simply by force of personality. It seemed his bluff, masculine character made people want to explain themselves to him.

The same couldn't have been said of me. But I had to say something. So it was in a kind of half-conscious imitation of the King of Detectives that I came out with: "This is where the peat for our stove comes from, then." One of the women, a girl with a blunt nose and red cheeks, looked up. I was standing above them, at the rim of the pit. My voice sounded louder than I'd meant. Maybe that was good. I went on in the same vein. "Next time I warm my hands, I'll think of you ladies."

"Do that if you like," she said. The one she was working with only glanced at me, and kept hacking.

"Some attitude," I said. "I guess you don't like the work. You'd rather be doing something easy than out here making sure I don't freeze."

That got a grudging laugh, but I could tell my act was failing to make a great success. "It's not that," the first one said. "Only that this work's stupid." She spat. "Half the bricks we lose to freezing. When the peat freezes, it crumbles up and falls apart. You can't cut a decent block." She made a chopping motion with the hand that wasn't holding the axe. "It should be even, you see? My old dad would have beaten us black and blue for a mess like this, back home."

"What about you?" I said to her partner. "You're intent on it, anyway." She didn't pause, only shrugged.

The blunt-nosed girl hadn't stopped looking up at me. "Why don't you tell us what you want, eh?" she said. She was young but stocky, with a face made for giving men looks that said they were ridiculous.

"I'm looking for a woman named Veronika Fitneva," I said.

"Oh? And what do you want her for?"

I explained as best I could about Infosec without mentioning the murder, with the result that I came off as both menacing and pompous. I couldn't seem to stop myself referring to "the investigation," as though I expected them to have been briefed on it already.

"Haven't heard of her," said the girl. She looked at the other, who shook her head. "You? No, she hasn't heard of her either."

"She would have been working on the peat in July. Possibly later as well, but we're not sure about that. There was an accident. She had to be sent to the hospital with broken bones."

"My friend Masha warned me about this," the girl explained to her still-unspeaking partner. "The Chekists get jumpy when the last boat is about to go. Think people are going to escape. They send informants around to get us in trouble—slugs.

It hit me like a slap. Everyone knew informants infested the camp like bedbugs; the term she'd used, "slugs," bespoke the disgust in which all other zeks held them. An exposed slug could expect ostracism and a beating from the men he'd told tales on. That was the best case. In the worst, it would be worth his life. We were not slugs, of course — I told myself I'd never have agreed to help Petrovich if that was what his investigation meant. But in the moment the best way to draw a quick distinction between what we were doing and what was done by Chekist informants eluded me.

"This one's ridiculous hat and scarf are just meant to put us off our guard." She turned back to me. "Well, even if she was about to fly away in a balloon, I couldn't tell you anything about it. I don't know her."

I heard myself stammering. "You—you're mistaken. We only need to ask a few questions. You don't need to worry."

"Well," the blunt-nosed girl said, "we don't know her. We can't help you."

Now staging my questioning in the conspicuous way I had, with the edge of the pit as proscenium, seemed highly imprudent. Perhaps it would have worked for Nat Pinkerton. I only felt myself growing nervous. I was sure I could feel surreptitious, suspicious gazes directed at me from all along the trench.

"My father," I said. "He taught me to cut peat as well." The lie had left my mouth before I realized it. My father, a native son of Petersburg, had no more cut a block of peat in his life than I had.

She had been about to start working again. Now she gave me a look I couldn't read. "Burned peat all winter, mine did, when I was growing up. Gone now, though."

I'd surprised myself by lying, but somehow her accepting it as truth made me feel a little better. Afterward I changed my approach. First I climbed down into the pit, so as not to be striding quite so stupidly across the horizon. The next peat cutter I approached as if she had been a friend of my mother's, rather than a girl student I wanted to impress. In this way I avoided being called a slug, but the woman admitted to no more knowledge of Veronika Fitneva than the first two. Neither did the one after that, nor the one after that. One group laughed when I asked if they'd answer a few questions, but most listened with hardened expressions.

If no one recognized the name, no one was prepared to say positively that Veronika Fitneva hadn't been there either. The peat operation had been much larger before the first frost. In October it drew only a fraction of the labor it had in July, but even so, women were transferred to and away from the pits every day.

By the time I'd finished, it was getting dark. Where the snow hadn't been trod into the mud, its surface had formed a crust that glittered in the light that was left.

Petrovich hadn't come down to help me, though his interrogation of the women working the piles seemed to be finished. I found him warming himself by a small fire. By now the women were preparing to return to their own dormitory. The noises they made carried to us through the still air: voices, and the scrape of tools being piled together.

"Learn anything?" he said.

"Nothing."

He grunted.

We were about to leave—I was worried about negotiating the crisscross of ditches between us and the road before the light got too dim—when a woman appeared out of the gloaming. At first I didn't recognize her. When she stepped into the firelight, I saw that it was the red-cheeked girl who'd thought my hat and scarf looked too foolish to be genuine.

"You're still here, then," she said. When I agreed, she sniffed. "I thought about what you were asking, after you went on. I still don't know that girl you were talking about by name. But I was working peat here in July." She paused. "I'm good at it, so they keep me on. Anyway, I heard about a girl who went to the hospital then. It was because she'd been beaten up. Some man hit her with a pipe."

"Did she ever come back to working peat?" said Petrovich.

The woman shook her head. "I don't know." She looked at Petrovich's face, then back at me. "You really want to find her, don't you?"

"It's all routine," he said. "We only need to ask her a few questions."

"Who was the man?" I asked.

"Her man." She looked at the ground, not meeting our eyes.

"A lover. That's what I heard, anyway."

"Thank you," I said.

The girl shrugged, then looked up at me. In the light from the fire her broad face looked especially flat. Her eyes were pale beads. "All right, then," she said.

Petrovich watched her leave. "I said there would be another man in it somewhere, didn't I? Not that that gets us much further, but it's something. Good work."

It was what I'd said about Father teaching me to cut peat that had made her come around, I thought—my lie. Impersonation, in the manner of Holmes, had been the right strategy after all.

Darkness did prove to make the planks bridging the ditches more treacherous. But Petrovich was still worried about reaching Nikolski before curfew; going around the way we had on our way out would have taken too much time. Twice his cane slipped on icy boards and I had to take hold of his coat to keep him from falling. The second time, only his weighing next to nothing kept us both from crashing into the mud below.

By the time we made it to Nikolski, the old man was panting, and my arm was bruised where he'd dug his fingers in supporting himself. The guards made a hostile show of checking our documents and the time—it seemed Petrovich had been right to be worried about what they'd do if we arrived late. But we'd beaten curfew by ten minutes. In the end they let us through without trouble. From the darkness outside, we passed once more into the whitewash and lamplight of the interior kremlin.

8

The barracks of Company Thirteen occupied the volume that had once been Nativity Cathedral. Space had been cleared for a large portrait of Lenin and a few painted slogans. "WORK STRENGTHENS A MAN'S BODY AND SOUL" and "WITHOUT EDUCATION AND CLEANLINESS THERE IS NO ROAD TO SOCIALISM," they told us. Everywhere else, the bunks crawled up the walls like crazing on porcelain, rickety and out of square. Just above them, you could see the plaster discolored in a band, a high-tide marker for the sea of prisoners that sloshed inside the building. Wherever men had been able to reach, the walls were dirtier.

On the floor you threaded a cockeyed, irregular grid. Narrow pathways separated the beds, with partitions of wood rearing abruptly up to block one work platoon's area off from another's. Boots upon boots, coats upon coats, man after surly man after hungry man. Haze filled the air. In the evenings, before the command for lights out, the din of voices became a weight dragging you down by the ears.

It sounds like squalor. Well, it was. Yet at the same time, you never stopped being aware of grandeur in Nativity.

How so claustrophobic and so grand at once? It must have been the space above. Nothing interfered with the arched vault's soaring. You traversed the stupid detail of the bunks, made your way from the back of the nave to a corner of the transept until, looking back over the beds around you, you found you had a clear view of the pillar you'd started under. Your tortuous route distilled itself into a straight line through the air. Sad-eyed saints, painted on the dome's ceiling in an earlier time, showed beneath its whitewash, stepping perpetually out from some mist. Entering through the main doors that evening, I felt the true cathedral had merely been translated fifteen feet above our heads, hovering there while men swarmed beneath it.

I'd come to show the Chekist's transfer order to Buteyko, leader of my now former platoon. That morning, I'd wondered whether I stood to gain or lose by being attached to the investigation. Now I was sure it would be a gain. After seeing how Petrovich and Antonov had lived, as well as taking stock of the dry ration I stood to inherit, I was anxious to make my membership in Company Ten official as soon as possible.

There was something else, as well. It was nearing seven o'clock. Surrounded by bunks, I couldn't see across the sanctuary to tell whether the nightly scrum around the side door had started, but if it had, Buteyko would be there, positioning himself for the distribution of rations that would take place in the alley between Nativity and Transfiguration. If I postponed talking to him until after food had been handed round, I might manage to enjoy a meal here in Quarantine, then another back at Company Ten. The man was no fool. He would be drawing a portion for me whether I reported the transfer or not. The question was simply who would eat it?

Ivan Kalishevich Buteyko. A decent, practical fellow. Well liked because he did well for us in the soup and bread queues. The technique was to be as close as possible to first in line for bread, then as close to last for soup: any bread that had gone missing in transit from the bakery to us—that is, any that had been eaten by those in charge of transporting it—meant less for the last few sections to receive. The opposite situation obtained with the soup: getting yours later meant you had a better chance at a scoop of sediment from the bottom of the pot. Either way, Buteyko had the knack. He had been a lawyer before his imprisonment. I remember that about him, as well as his shortsighted squint.

I didn't think he'd make trouble for me about the transfer. Whether I'd manage the extra meal was another question.

Our bunks were at the back. To reach them, you stepped onto a low, raised platform. Not far beyond the step, you could see marks where the iconostasis had been torn from the wall. We slept in the sanctuary, behind where the altar had stood. In the monks' time, the place would have been forbidden to congregants.

Foma, who'd pushed me forward when my name had been called that morning, was first to see me. "Had us worried, you did, when they dragged you off during roll. Then we worried worse when you didn't show up for grub at lunch." He grinned, showing bad teeth. "Got back here all right, eh?"

My friend had grown up in Ukraine, with Proskurov the closest city to his village. But, he reported, he'd never been there. Indeed, before his arrest he'd never traveled more than a dozen versts from the front door of his family's wattle-and-daub hut.

I could never quite follow Foma when he explained what he'd done to be sent to Solovki. Something about a disagreement with a local party activist, a night of drinking, and one of the new cooperatively owned farm machines found broken the next day. At any rate, he had been sent up as a wrecker, which earned him a three-year sentence, like mine.

Imprisonment, by shutting him up in cells with men from all walks of life and shuttling him from remand prison to remand prison about the country, gave Foma his first taste of the wider world. His principal reaction to this was a refusal to be impressed. In literature (before I met him, most of my exposure to the peasantry had been in the pages of books) you often see the figure of the country bumpkin who's convinced any new way of doing things is a trick, which will leave him poorer and sadder if he's fool enough to believe what the sharpers from town say about it. Foma was like that.

If his suspicion of new ideas could make him slow to understand politics—after several years of imprisonment, he remained convinced that a party called the Bolsheviks had started the glorious revolution in order to take land from the gentry and give it to the peasants, only to be displaced by another party, called the Communists, who stole the people's grain and took their land away again to give it to the collectives—on the whole, his attitude served him well. The knack, so important to survival, of working when you were being watched and resting when you weren't, came to him naturally. Whatever he was told to focus his attention on he quietly ignored, continuing to plan how to get a little more food, a little more sleep.

I'd learned to respect this single-mindedness. And perhaps even our sufferings as *zeks* were not sufficiently different from the ones he was used to for him to find them very noteworthy. He'd referred more than once to "the hard times," which I took to mean the famine everyone said had swept Ukraine in '21, despite official reports denying it. He wouldn't come out and say it, but I gleaned that he had watched several brothers and sisters die, as well as his grandmother. What the rest of the family had done to survive, I never knew. But it had prepared him for camp life.

"You think you were worried?" I said. "You weren't the one they marched off. What happened to my kasha when I wasn't at lunch?"

He was hunched on his pallet at the bottom of our set of bunks, arms draped over his knees. The freestanding bunks stood three high, but against the walls, where they could be secured with nails, they rose to four. Foma's and mine were the bottom two in one of these teetering stacks—his the lowest, mine the one above that. "Half to Panko. Buteyko said he needed it—he's got a cough. The other half I ate."

"And do I get anything, for providing you with a side of kasha to go with your kasha?"

He sniffed the way he did when something was funny. "Said I'd trade you a piece of my bread for it if you showed up tonight. So, I guess you showed up. What was that about this morning, anyway? Why'd they call your name?"

"Someone died," I said. "A man I knew. They wanted me to help identify the body."

Foma had a round face, and a sharp, thin nose. His coarse hair stood up in cowlicks no matter what he did. Now he frowned up at me. "Better to steer clear of that. You identify a man, and then he turns out to be someone else, and dead—that's trouble you're in. My advice is, keep your mouth shut."

I looked around. Our platoon leader was nowhere to be seen.

"It's more complicated than that," I said. "Is Buteyko getting the food?"

"He went with Kulkov and Goosev."

"I have an order to show him," I said.

A quizzical note entered his voice. "What do you mean, an order?"

"A transfer. I'm not staying. I've been moved to Company Ten." Like any good peasant, Foma could shut his face like a door when he wanted. It slammed on me now. I tried to explain. "It's only temporary. This friend of mine, they think he was killed. There's a detective here, a tsarist police officer. But he's an old man. He needs someone to help him. I doubt it will be more than a week or two."

No change in his face. "Investigation?" I nodded, and his lips tightened. "It was a friend of yours? The one who died?"

"A kind of friend," I said.

We were silent for a moment, Foma thinking, me waiting to see what he'd decide. At last he said: "I still say, why do it? Buteyko could say we need you because of all the logging there is now. All have to do our part in the socialist work effort. These investigations are a distraction."

"I don't think that would work," I said, picturing the Chekist. I didn't want to explain that I was glad of the transfer.

Before either of us could add anything, a reedy voice from above interrupted. "What's this? What's this? Our boy leaving us in the lurch?"

The face that squinted over the edge of the top bunk was frankly ugly, with a wide mouth full of teeth that were straight but too large. Before he was a *zek*, Vitaly Genkin had been a NEPman, one of the private traders countenanced, if barely, by Lenin's New Economic Plan. He'd been arrested for selling copper pipe purchased cheaply in Vladivostok at extortionate rates in Kiev. After Lenin's death, this was termed "economic wrecking," analogous to what Foma had done to his village's machine, only carried out with trade rather than a crowbar.

"Getting away from here, are you? I'll tell you what I think about that. I think it's a good idea." Genkin hopped down clumsily, taking my arm. He had the habit of gripping your biceps when he spoke, signifying either intense earnestness about what he was saying or unwillingness to let you go before you'd let him sell you something."Now, if you're wondering what my attitude towards this investigation is, I'm interested. Tell me, a detective probably needs to follow his clues everywhere, doesn't he? You're probably going to find yourself all sorts of places, inside the kremlin and out."

"I suppose," I said reluctantly.

"You'd have to, wouldn't you? Without knowing the details, it seems to me you'd have to. Now, listen, while you're out there, see if you can get me some rubber. Just a few scraps, you understand. I don't need much. I know a man who'll teach me to cut the stuff for galoshes. Rubber galoshes, just like that. Wouldn't that be nice? Keep your boots dry? Everyone would want them. Only he says I have to bring a supply before he'll teach me."

In 1926 there was not yet a revolutionary Penal Code in Russia: magistrates simply knew crimes when they saw them. But when the code did come into force the following year, we learned that, under Article 58-7 of it, men like Genkin were guilty of undermining, in the interests of former owners of capitalist organizations, state production, transport, trade, monetary relations, or the credit system. Genkin would have said that he undertook his schemes only in his own interests, but that was not a distinction the Code was written to acknowledge. There was always reason to be a little cautious around Genkin.

Foma hadn't moved from his crouch on the bunk. He looked up at us from between his knees. "Think it's easy to get something like that? They don't go around cutting up stacks of tires all day in the other companies."

"Easier for you to find some out there than for me to do it in here. Only keep your eyes open, and if you bring me some, once I've learned how, I'll make a pair of galoshes for you. How does that sound? To me it sounds fair."

"I'll see," I said. "I don't know how easy it will be to lay my hands on rubber."

"Still say you ought to stay," said Foma. "Never know what will happen."

Genkin had released my arm when I agreed to watch for the rubber. Now he gave me a sly look. "You said Company Ten, didn't you? What I'm told about that is, it's a good place to end up. A place a boy could begin making connections. They get a dry ration, don't they? Get to be in charge of your own meals. You could see if you can't make a few trades, if it's to your benefit."

"That right?" said Foma. "You get a better ration there?"

For a moment my friend had emerged a little from whatever unreadable place he went when he shut the door of his face. Now he'd retreated back to it. "Yes," I admitted. "A little better."

A long moment passed. "Told you," he said at last. "Buteyko's in line for food. No call to wait. You might as well find him now and go."

It put me in an awkward situation. As I saw it, my plan didn't amount to taking food from their bowls; they'd get exactly the same as they would have if I hadn't been transferred. But it was far from clear they'd share my view. "I thought I'd mention it to him after dinner."

Foma had clearly been thinking along these lines already. "Less for us if you stay," he said immediately. "Maybe you don't need it like we do, now you've got a good place."

"He'll be drawing a ration for me anyway. I don't see why you have a better right to split it up than I do to claim it for myself."

"Means two meals for you, doesn't it?"

As though he'd been appealed to for arbitration, Genkin raised his hands, palms out. "Now, I'll tell you what I think about all of this. What I think is, every man has a right to watch out for himself in this camp, when it comes to food. None of us can tell another he isn't hungry." He made a froglike face, pulling the corners of his mouth even wider. "But, you know, Anatoly, you're getting a whole dry ration. For us it's only an extra little mouthful of soup each."

The embarrassment I'd felt a moment before dissolved in a wash of anger. Foma was a miserable serf, Genkin a despicable swindler. I'd have smashed the teeth out of both their faces, if I could. The experience was new to my life in Quarantine, and strange: without circumstances under which it can be expressed, the *zek's* anger dies even more quickly than his sympathy. Hunger operates as a functional substitute for so many emotions.

But I did feel angry. Perhaps the privileges I'd begun to enjoy with Petrovich were changing my attitudes already. In hindsight, it's clear I should have tried to reach some accommodation with

Foma and Genkin. That would have been the rational course, the course of survival. For them, soup and bread split three ways would have been better than a mouthful each; for me, it would have been better than nothing.

I was not rational. Anger, and perhaps even that forgotten luxury, pride, made me say what I did instead.

"All right. All right, damn it. I'll go to him now."

Out in the alley, the only illumination came from the little kerosene lanterns brought along from the refectory by the cooks. The arc lamps attached to poles above our heads were dark. I wandered between the soup and bread lines for some time without finding Buteyko. The men waiting for their platoons' shares of the meal all looked the same: black silhouettes of coats breathing fog into the frigid air, one after another. Only the cooks in their pool of light, handing out the half-pound loaves and ladling slop into pails, did more than hint at human features.

Around the margins of the scene shambled even less definite figures. Like walking corpses, or shades haunting a certain stretch of ground, they moved aimlessly without ever seeming able to escape the orbit of the food. While I watched, one stumbled towards the soup pot, hands fluttering in front of his face.

"Have pity," he said. "Have pity. I can't see. A little soup. A little something. I can't see."

The two big men who'd carried the pot from the kitchen moved to intercept him. But the man actually ladling out the portions only laughed. Beckoning him over, he dipped out a tiny amount of watery soup from the surface of the pot, then threw it in the man's face.

The splattered man immediately fell to the ground in surprise. Rather than trying to right himself, however, he began running his hand over his face, wiping the residue of soup out of his beard, then licking it from his fingers. When he'd finished that, he began to run his hands over the snowy ground, feeling for any fragment that might have dripped from his face and escaped him.

The language of the camp called men like this *dokhodyagi*, goners. All of us were hungry: a *dokhodyaga* was someone from whom starvation had taken everything. In their need, they'd gone past care, past self-respect, past humanity. It was understood that a *zek* who'd reached the status of goner would soon be gone altogether. You identified one by his listlessness, his dull unconcern with anything other than putting another scrap in his mouth. They were a nuisance: one might sneak up to lick your bowl if you'd left it behind on the table with a film of grease. As a result of a group scrabbling for edible fragments among the rotted cabbage, a rubbish pile might be found scattered across the yard.

There were physical signs as well, of course. *Dokhodyagi* in Quarantine Company tended to be those who received a Class 2 ration because of some prior infirmity. Along with whatever individual trouble each had had when he arrived, malnutrition gave them all a similar set of problems. They came to look the same: cadaverous, filthy. Sores covered their papery skin, the teeth rattled in their mouths, their faces were skeletal. Many became night-blind, losing the ability even to make out shapes in the dark.

Having licked all he could from his beard and the ground, the one who'd had soup thrown at him scrambled up and resumed begging, his whine unchanged: "Just a little something. Have pity. I can't see."

This time one of the pot carriers aimed a cuff at the man's ear, knocking him down again. With a whimper, the *dokhodyaga* curled into a ball and covered his head with his arms. When, after a moment, no further blows came, he straightened a little, then crept off into the darkness on all fours without a word.

At length I came across Buteyko towards the middle of the line for soup. He didn't seem quite far enough back this time to thicken what would be scooped into his pail, but you could see he'd made an effort. The bread ration had already been collected, he said. Goosev had taken it back to our bunks in a basket. I must have passed him somewhere without noticing.

While I explained some of what had happened to me that day, Buteyko squinted at the paper I'd brought, holding it up in an attempt to make it out in the light from the lamps. "Just when they're pushing us the hardest with the timbering, too," he said. "Just my luck. And what do you think are the chances of their reducing the squad's quota to account for less manpower?"

"I'm far from the best worker on the squad. Maybe you won't miss me."

"A pair of hands is a pair of hands." With a stub of pencil, he made a note on one of the loose sheets he carried with him for tracking assignments. He could hardly have been able to read what he wrote in the dark. "Well, good luck to you. Maybe if you manage to make the transfer permanent, you'll be the first of us to get out of Quarantine." He folded up his paper, handing mine back to me. "Decent of you to come find me now instead of waiting. Eighteen rations split seventeen ways may not seem like much, but every bit helps."

"I know you work hard to feed everyone, Ivan Kalishevich." Having Buteyko think well of me was not as good as getting my share of soup, but it was something. Even in the best-case scenario, there was a good chance I'd be returning to his platoon for a time after this investigation. Maybe I'd be in a position to ask him a favor at some point.

Still, I was unwilling to go back to Company Ten and Petrovich with nothing. Buteyko's mention of Goosev and the basket of bread had reminded me: Foma still owed me for the afternoon's kasha.

Back among the platoon's bunks I passed Panko, the big blond Cossack who'd gotten the other half of it on Buteyko's say-so. He lay on his side, coughing. He was forty or fifty, a horse of a man without the vigor. His mustaches hung down morosely around his mouth. After a day with Petrovich's bristling whiskers, they looked deflated.

"That you, Tolya?" he said as I went by. "Genkin says you're leaving us."

"That's right," I said. He began to say something, but started coughing instead. I waited for him to finish before I added: "You got my kasha at lunch." I hadn't planned on mentioning it, but the *dokhodyaga*'s groveling had been bitter to see. Anything was better than the diminishments of hunger.

"Buteyko said I should have it," Panko said, blinking slowly.

"Yes, you're sick. But I got nothing. Foma is going to give me some bread for the share he got. Goosev just brought back your loaves, didn't he?"

"Ate it already." Panko gazed at me with his sad, equine look. It was no less than I'd expected. I managed to tell him to forget it, I'd eaten well enough today anyway. "Buteyko says you have to eat more when you're sick," he said behind me as I went.

Foma was where I'd left him. He lay on his back with his arms behind his head, staring at the berth above him—the one that had been mine. "You're back," he said when he saw me.

"I talked to Buteyko," I said.

"What are you doing waiting around here, then?"

"You said you'd give me bread in return for the kasha you had this afternoon."

He was slow to respond. "I did."

"So?"

"Didn't know you were getting a fine new ration when I said that. Maybe I need it more than you, now."

"My new ration starts tonight, now that the transfer is official. This afternoon I was still entitled to kasha. You ate it. You owe me bread."

He looked at me then. Maybe he expected me to look away. When I didn't, he reached into his jacket and pulled out the half-pound loaf he'd just received. He broke it in two and handed me the smaller piece.

"Thanks," I said. Foma shrugged. The bread was airy in my hand, barely more than a crust. I could feel the anger that had been driving me begin to ebb away. "I suppose I'll be back here soon enough."

His face, flat as a barrel head, stayed shut. "We'll see," he said.

Petrovich had good news when I returned to Company Ten. Cots were typically hard to come by; it had been suggested I might have to make do with a board and blanket laid out for me in the hallway. Fortunately, he had been able to remind the section leader about some space that had just opened up.

That night I slept in Gennady Antonov's bed, still wearing his sweater. The bed was short, so my feet stuck over the end when I stretched out. Despite the luxury of the straw mattress, I could only make myself comfortable by curling up.

Part Two

SOLOVETSKY LABYRINTHS

9

And so I come to the end of the first day. Strange how time dilates in writing. I have been at work on my *detektiv* now for weeks, scratching with my pen long into the night, and yet in the story have only lived long enough to sleep once.

Vasily-the-tank-commander has stopped asking about my progress. Now he only indicates his interest by alluding to literary subjects. He tells me a man must have a feeling for Chekhov. "I myself have recently reread 'A Story Without an End,'" he says. "All the problems of the old era are there, but presented artistically, beautifully. Have you read it?"

I tell him I haven't, but I am lying. It is the story of Chekhov attending at the bed of an attempted suicide, who mocks his offered commiseration. A portrait of a man at the nadir of his life: hostile, destroyed, trapped in an identity with no consolations left to offer. Vassilyev—that is the suicide's name, I remember it—postures and poses, refusing to tell why he's shot himself in the side. Gradually we reconstruct the story, without his ever quite confessing it: a young wife whose sickness and death resulted from their poverty.

Then, within a year, Vassilyev has recovered. Once more he socializes, presents himself as a guest, ventures charming opinions. They meet at a soiree; the writer shows him the account he's produced of his suicide attempt, the very account we are reading. "How does the story end?" he asks. Vassilyev goes pale, can't answer. Then: "What I have suffered, and what I am now, are absurd, like life. Give it a humorous end!" He straightens his tie and returns to the party. The writer regrets the sorrow he'd felt on the other man's behalf. Yes, I remember it well. That final line: "It was as though I had lost something . . ."

Vasily Feodorovich's critique is veiled, if thinly: I am the ungrateful Vassilyev in the first part of the story, who refuses to share the tale of his grief with the intercessor. Better to tell him I haven't read it.

I must say something about the situation with Vasily Feodorovich.

I know he is still curious about the manuscript. The visits continue. Our sessions of drinking and eating pickles occur now once or twice a week. Last week he brought herring he was able to get from the managers' store. The quality is good, but he insisted it was nothing. Prices there are cheap, he said. When I open the door to his knock, his eyes fly around the room.

I have learned to return these pages to a dresser drawer after I've done with them. Thus far his interest stops short of pulling on the handles of my furniture. He takes pains to demonstrate his literary sensitivity, and, when he is finished with that, he tells me about himself.

Vasily Feodorovich is an engineer at the plant where I work on the line. The workers respect him, the managers value him. Sometimes I see him, reviewing with intensity the welding on a machine's brackets, or arguing with other specialists out on the floor, pointing and gesturing. He struggles heroically to master the forces of production, a Soviet man in full. He is twelve years younger than I am, the son of workers from Moscow. A son of the Revolution.

Of course he is a Party member. Of course.

It was only his distinguished military service that made possible his studies at the university, he tells me. He is enthusiastic about building socialism, happy to be able to work for that goal so directly. "Only we must have reforms," he says. "For the State and Party to serve the people means concerning itself with their well-being, with their freedoms. There must be a sense of life . . ."

He rose to captain of his tank company from the ranks. With their commanding officer killed by bombardment during the second battle of Kharkov, only Vasily's quick thinking saved his fellows and their fifteen tanks from being cut off by the Germans.

He is dismissive of his own contributions, credits his successes to the men around him. Daring Vasily Feodorovich, quick-witted Vasily Feodorovich, humble Vasily Feodorovich. He is a hero.

During that time I was working with other ex-prisoners released with loss of rights, in a munitions plant to which they'd transported us by train.

He speaks sometimes of his wife. Vasily-the-tank-commander married a pretty redhead with neat eyebrows, one who manages to look the prim schoolgirl at the age of thirty. I have seen her sometimes in the hall. We have never spoken. He tells me she is the daughter of kolkhozniki, her mother the chairman of their farm. He wonders whether she fully understands him, he says. To me her mouth looks pinched.

His own face is flat, with an Asiatic slant to the eyes. The cheeks are pocked, but where this would be disfiguring in some men, in him it sets off his features. You can tell he is stubborn, strong-willed. It is the sort of face we reward, for which difficult roads are made smooth.

A stupid face.

This is the man I've lied to about Chekhov, to whom I will not show my writing.

In fact I've read Chekhov's tales often. There is much in their observing, inquisitive narrators that gratifies. Detective-like, they wander everywhere and look at everything. The Chekhovian narrator, like Nat Pinkerton and Sherlock Holmes, speaks with equal confidence to shopkeepers and invalids, privy councilors and nuns.

And yet Chekhov never wrote a mystery that could be solved. Perhaps it was a consequence of his honesty, his straightforwardness. Withholding nothing left him helpless to control the ways his stories would end.

By the time we left the kremlin the next morning, dawn was approaching. The steam whistle that marked the beginning and end of curfew had blown in freezing darkness. The air hurt: cold pressed its angles into any exposed skin.

I'd been expecting we would meet with the Chekist first thing, but Petrovich said there was something else we needed to do first. After a ten-minute walk along the northern road, he pointed towards a long, low stone building. It was the alabaster workshop.

"What are we doing here?" I said.

Petrovich was taciturn. "A lead. One I need to be able to tell our friend I am following."

For decades a small quarry on the main island had produced enough alabaster to be worked by a few monks. *Zeks* replaced them now, but otherwise things carried on much the way they always had, with a few loads of bowls and vases shipped to the mainland for sale every year. The workshop had been mentioned to me as a desirable assignment, if you couldn't get desk work. The pieces were simple enough not to require much expertise to produce, but the position was still designated as skilled. That came with benefits. Workers in other divisions had been transferred to lumbering for the last few weeks of the season, but I could see that wasn't the case here.

From outside, the door opened into a single room that ran the length of the place, with a broad pillar in the middle supporting the roof. The air tasted chalky and dry. White forms filled the shelves along the walls, cluttered the worktables. At different stations around the room, a dozen workers produced a din of rasping.

When Petrovich gave a name, we were pointed to a man using a handsaw on a large slab in a corner, his dark clothes covered with stone dust.

"You are Nail Terekhov?" said Petrovich. "Cavalry master in the Eighth Imperial Cavalry Division, and after that of the Volunteer Army?" The rank was a surprise. It made me think of Zhenov, whom we'd spoken to the day before. This made two White Army officers in the case. Whether Zhenov would prove to be truly in it was another matter, of course, as was what this Terekhov's involvement might be.

The man released a cloud of breath into the unheated room as he looked up. The face he showed was handsome, but puckered somehow, as though it had fallen in on one side.

"That's right." Parted lips revealed that the puckering came from six or seven teeth missing on the left side of his mouth; the words slurred a little. He looked at us suspiciously, a streak of white marking his left cheek.

"Can you account for your whereabouts between eight and midnight two nights ago, Prisoner Terekhov?" It interested me to observe the old man adapting his approach to his subject. What was it about Terekhov that made him decide the note to strike was that of a bored Infosec functionary? The appearance of fear, maybe. The man looked like someone who knew what functionaries could do.

He kept his face carefully neutral. "I was in the dormitory by curfew, same as any other night. I am always in my bunk by nine."

Petrovich consulted a sheet of paper he'd drawn from inside his jacket. "That would be Dormitory fifteen. Your cellmates will confirm this?"Terekhov nodded at the other side of the room. "Slavsky over there is in my cell. He can tell you." He seemed to relax a little, having been asked for an alibi. "What's this about?"

Petrovich made him wait, examining the paper again before he said: "Are you acquainted with one Gennady Mikhailovich Antonov, Prisoner Terekhov?"

The man thought. Several of his knuckles, I saw, had been bandaged, but the bandages were as covered with white dust as the rest of his hands. The large slab before him was marked out into squares. We'd interrupted him in the middle of cutting them out.

"No," he said. "I don't recognize the name."

"What is your familiarity with the collection at the Camp Museum of Anti-Religious Exhibits?"

"I don't have any familiarity with it."

"Be more specific, please."

"I only know the museum is in the kremlin somewhere. Never been inside. They assigned me here directly out of Quarantine. I couldn't even give you directions to the museum."

"What can you tell us about their collection?"

Terekhov spoke carefully. "Listen, I'll answer all the questions you like. The last thing I want is for Infosec to think I am not cooperative." Petrovich's act had effectively communicated the source of our remit without having to name it. "But maybe you have the wrong man. If I tried to tell you what they keep there, I'd be guessing. Is it the monks' old things? Gold candlesticks and so forth?"

"We are interested in icons," said Petrovich dryly.

Terekhov betrayed no more knowledge of the museum's icons than he had of anything else. Petrovich stroked his mustache and asked a few more questions along the same lines, without much apparent expectation of generating new information. Then he gave me a jolt.

"Explain our investigation to Prisoner Terekhov, Tolya," he said.

I stammered. I'd taken it to be my role to occupy the background, lending Petrovich the institutional credibility of plural pronouns. Now, suddenly, I was thrown back on last night's dilemma among the peat workings: how, conversationally speaking, did one put oneself into the role of detective?

Mindful of my mistake at the museum, I began by avoiding the subject of how we'd found Antonov's body, but Petrovich scoffed and told me not to dance around the issue. Terekhov took in my ensuing account of Antonov's being found in the bay, murdered, without giving any sign, either of bafflement or recognition. In fact, I found myself noticing the old man instead; during the whole time I spoke, he was watching my face intently, blue eyes searching for something. Even as Terekhov uttered his short responses, the gaze didn't waver. I ignored it for as long as I could—we were still cultivating institutional credibility, weren't we?—but eventually I couldn't help glancing back.

"Is there something I'm forgetting, Yakov Petrovich?"

"No," said the old man. "Go on."

When I'd finished, Terekhov said he was sorry to hear about my friend. "But I don't know anything that might help you."

Petrovich took over again after that. What about Terekhov's sentence? Ten years, because of his taking up arms against the state. And his arrest? He'd turned himself in at one of the Cheka's local offices in '22, naïvely believing that the published terms of an amnesty for White partisans would be adhered to. The man's suspicion and fear returned as he was asked questions about himself. His answers grew shorter and shorter.

It transpired that the position in the workshop had been

acquired for him by military colleagues; he had no experience working stone. He admitted to being acquainted with three or four men whose names Petrovich read from a list he took from somewhere, but resisted saying anything about them. Petrovich didn't push, only went on in the detached manner he'd adopted from the beginning. At last he said: "Fine. One more thing: there are rumors of an escape attempt being planned. Heard anything about that?"

Terekhov inhaled sharply. It surprised me, too. Admitting to knowledge of anything of the sort, even discussing it as a possibility, might be more than a *zek*'s life was worth. I could see the other man's tongue working nervously where his teeth had been, behind his left cheek.

"No," he said. "I've heard nothing of the sort. It would be a stupid idea. Nothing I'd want to be involved with or be told about."

Petrovich fixed Terekhov with his gaze for another long moment, but I thought I caught him glancing at me out of the corner of an eye. "All right," he said. "That will be all, Prisoner Terekhov. We'll be in touch, if there are more questions."

Outside, after the noise of alabaster being sawed and turned on the lathe, it was quiet. The air was no warmer than it had been when we went in.

The old man directed us south, towards the rendezvous with the Chekist. "I don't understand," I said. "Did you learn anything from that? What was that list?"

Petrovich didn't answer immediately. "Tell me," he said after a minute. The functionary-of-Infosec approach had apparently been left behind in the workshop, but he still didn't sound quite normal. "Did that seem to you like a man who was nervous to be talking to us?"

I thought about it. "He was nervous," I said. "But not more than I'd expect anyone to be, being interrogated about a murder."

We went on a few more steps without Petrovich saying anything. Then he stopped. When I turned, his look shut my mouth—the same fixed blue stare as in the workshop.

"That man," he said slowly, "was on a list of *zeks* Infosec is interested in in connection with this case. Our friend gave it to me yesterday."

"That's why you had to interview him before our meeting?"

Petrovich only said: "Can you think of any reason the Cheka should be so interested in him?"

"Can I?" I was surprised by the question. "No. No, I can't say I understand it. Do you?"

Petrovich watched me for another moment. Then he shook his head and wrinkled his mustache, as if there were something caught in its hairs he wanted to be free of. "They don't tell me everything. Only wondered whether you saw anything in it. But there's no reason you should. No reason at all. Come on, let's go see our boss."

The interior of the Chekist's cabin consisted of one bare room, with three shuttered windows and a chair in the middle of the floor. Not the sort of place a *zek* would usually be anxious to find himself. Two lamps gave yellow light, however, and the stove in the corner emitted welcome heat and the black smell of coal.

Petrovich had taken the chair. Standing behind him, I tried not to let the warmth make me drowsy.

"Gone well enough so far," he was saying. "Only, the guards at Nikolski didn't like us looking at their records. Their boss threatened to make trouble. Doesn't want anyone bigger than him involved in his business. Maybe you can send word to tell them we're not to be interfered with."

The Chekist sat at a table along one side of the room, his leather jacket and cap hung over the back of his chair, a collection of notebooks and folders in a neat stack at his elbow. Beside those, three pens had been lined up in careful parallel, along with a bottle of ink. He had the same air of quiet menace as before—a boyish menace that made you picture punishments that involved trampling with soccer cleats.

"Perhaps," he said. "First tell me how you're progressing."

Petrovich began with the examination of the body. The pattern of bruising and the lack of water in the lungs indicated the victim had been killed by a blow to the back of the head, then disposed of in the bay. This was old news, of course; the Chekist had been there. Still, both men seemed to regard it as the appropriate start to their review of evidence.

The old man continued. On the night of the killing, Antonov

had left the kremlin at a quarter past five, showing the guards there a pass from the museum director, Nikolai Vinogradov. We'd gone to ask Vinogradov about it, only to be told he'd departed on an expedition earlier the same day. No one left at the museum knew why Antonov might have been given the pass.

"What do you mean, an expedition?" said the Chekist.

"Hell if I know," said Petrovich. "They tried to explain. Some kind of stone circles out on Kostrihe. Apparently he's an archeologist."

"He's camped there?"

"Evidently. It's not so far as a straight shot, but with the roads as they are, I suppose he doesn't feel he can be making the trip back and forth all the time. Better part of his day would be eaten up traveling."

"Is Vinogradov one of your suspects?"

Petrovich made a face, considering it. "His leaving just before the murder is quite a coincidence. We need to talk to him."

"Nogtev thinks he's reliable. The museum gets special privileges."

Nogtev was SLON's administrative director, the Northern Camps of Special Significance's highest authority. Petrovich didn't flinch. "You think he's not a good suspect?"

"The opposite. If he keeps secrets he shouldn't, it would be interesting to know."

The old man gave a judicious nod, then went on. Everything about Antonov's work had seemed normal. The only irregularity involved a requisition order for icons—they were being broken up for planks. But we'd looked into it, and no one who'd been involved admitted to having seen Antonov since the collection. More pressingly, our search of Antonov's desk had turned up a note that suggested he was involved in an affair of some kind. The old man explained what we'd done to track down the "V" of the note, and about the two women we'd discovered at the hospital.

"We need authorization from you if we're going to look at their files."

The Chekist had listened impassively to everything Petrovich said, making notes in shorthand. Now he put down his pen. "You haven't mentioned the matter we discussed yesterday." I thought his eyes flicked to me.

"I interviewed Nail Terekhov," said Petrovich. As if correcting himself, he added, "We both went. He claimed not to know anything. There was no sign of the connections you wondered about. For now, I think the women are more promising."

"Only Terekhov? What about the others on the list?"

"Been busy. Start of a new investigation. Takes time to lay out basic facts."

"There's no indication these women are connected to the killing. You should be following the leads I gave you."

"Listen, I told you yesterday, my methods are different than yours. Otherwise what was the point of bringing me in? I have to learn what Antonov was involved in, what he was trying to hide. That's how I work."

"My organ works by taking vigilant action against threats, Yakov Petrovich. I am not the only member who adopts this attitude—my superiors do as well. I am taking a risk, bringing you on board like this."

"I understand that."

"And do you understand that your authorization is temporary? After a week, you go back to KrimKab, Bogomolov back to wherever he came from. If I see no progress in your reports, I may not bear with you so long as that."

"We're making progress. These women are progress. The talk with Terekhov didn't go anywhere, but I'll keep on with your list. I'll find out for you who the men on it may or may not be connected to. But if that's all you wanted out of our arrangement, you might as well have started on your own investigation."

The Chekist's face darkened. "Perhaps I'll do that still."

That gave Petrovich a pause. He spent a moment chewing his mustache. "I tell you, if I learned anything from Terekhov, it's that whatever you hoped I would find wasn't there."

"Even so."

"Fine. You'll do what you're going to do, even if it gets you nothing. But if you want me to continue with my investigation, I need to see those women's files."

The Chekist tapped his pen slowly against the table top. In the stove, burning coal hissed. Finally, the younger man gestured for Petrovich to go ahead.

As Petrovich gave Veronika Fitneva and Varvara Grishkina's

names, the Chekist turned over a new page in his notebook to write them down. Thinking it would spare us another hostile audience later on, in a low voice I reminded the old man that we'd intended to look at Antonov's file as well. "Remember?" I said. "We wondered whether the person who wrote that note might have been an acquaintance in Yaroslavl."

The Chekist laid down his pen and stared. Meeting his eyes, I stifled a cough; where he'd hit me yesterday, my sternum still ached. Sweat prickled under the collar of my coat. The heat of the room, so welcome at first, had become stifling.

Petrovich said: "It's true. We discussed seeing Antonov's file."

"You discussed it?"

"My eyes aren't so good," Petrovich explained. "Yesterday in the hospital went much faster with two to examine."

There was another long pause.

"No," said the Chekist finally. "The two women's files. No others. Absolutely not Antonov's. And I warn you not to try anything clever. If I hear you've even craned your neck to look at anything other than the two files listed here, it will go badly for you. Revoking your investigation authority will only be the first step."

Having written the authorization, he handed it over without saying anything else. When we reached the door, however, he called us back.

"One more thing. Once you've read these files, leave a note for me at the Infosec offices describing your plans for the rest of the day. I want to be able to find you if I need you."

Petrovich nodded stiffly, and we left.

It did not escape me that something about the conversation had been strange: the way their negotiations oscillated and changed trajectories suggested the existence of some hidden variable. But now that I come to it, I find it hard to recover exactly how much I guessed or feared. I did learn, in the end, what it was they were struggling over—learned it to my misfortune. Knowledge marks itself on my mind, writing over any memories of what I knew then.

Yet this is not the moment in my narrative to reveal what I know: it is a moment to withhold, to husband surprise and suspense. If I am to write the story I intend, I cannot emulate Chekhov's honesty. And so I collude with the other two, Petrovich and the Chekist, keeping the secret from myself.

The main administration building brooded over the quay, a pedimented and dingy white slab. A hostel for pilgrims under the monks, now it was offices, with several rooms devoted to housing Infosec's archives. Across from it was the *Gleb Boky*, which must have docked sometime during the night. The ship was for the most part white and dingy as well, but on its funnel had been painted a large red star.

Prisoners loading goods aboard the ship swarmed over the spot where the Chekist had shown me Antonov's body. No trace remained. I wondered where they'd moved him.

"Who are the men on that list?" I asked as we climbed the stairs to the door. "Why is the Chekist so intent on your investigating them?"

Petrovich shook his head. "I don't know myself. But he's the one we report to. It will have to be done at some point."

Inside, after showing our papers and being admitted to Infosec's offices, we were directed to a room on the first floor. What might once have been a dining hall was now packed with racks of dossiers. Our note from the Chekist got us two thick files from the attendant at the desk. We were required to read them there, at a table set up under a lamp for the purpose.

Thanks to the pulpy, acidic cheapness of Soviet paper and the tendency of our adhesives to disintegrate, the dust you breathed in that room was made up of material assembled by the State against its prisoners. Given the relatively short period of their existence, the decay in SLON's archives by 1926 was remarkable. The earliest files were nine years old at most, yet even the most damning accusations had commenced rubbing themselves to bits. Surveillance records had yellowed and faded, ideological mistakes were pulverized by the cardboard flaps of the dossiers containing them. The fug had a smell not unlike dry kasha, but unappetizing and headache-inspiring—largely mildew, I suppose. Powder filmed every surface, eddied visibly in the air.

At work in that brown, jaundiced light, we learned the following:

Varvara Grishkina had entered the Cheka's official consciousness only at the moment of her arrest, when she attempted to sell a pair of sapphire earrings to a Polish jeweler's factor (also arrested; he was the one who'd been under observation). Interrogation revealed her to be a minor member of the hereditary nobility, married to a count with an estate in Byelorussia. The two had lived separately for many years—in fact, he'd fled to Bulgaria in 1917, just before his lands were redistributed, and thence to Paris.

Grishkina had remained in Minsk. At first she continued to live in their townhouse. As her circumstances became more difficult, she'd moved with her lady's maid into a succession of less dignified arrangements. She had evidently been supporting them both with regular sales of pre-Revolutionary luxury goods—things like the earrings.

The agents who'd arrested her and the maid were congratulated for apprehending rampant female speculators and looters of Russian heritage objects. Little else was to be expected from the socialist state's class enemies.

That was in 1922. For several months after her arrest she'd been housed in a small remand prison outside of Moscow. At her trial she got five years. The first two of those she served in Lefortovo prison. Towards the end of 1924, she was transferred to Solovki, then a fairly new camp.

The note had referred to a package from V's mother. The file said nothing about Grishkina's parents, but Petrovich noted that she was forty-eight, just young enough to have a mother living who might send her something. There was little else in the file to suggest she could be connected with Antonov. Most of the material referred to her medical complaints; she'd fainted often during her initial round of interrogations, and her constitution did not seem to have improved since then. She'd had several hospitalizations before the most recent. Since 1925 she had been categorized as Class 2 Fit. Two months before her typhus infection, she'd been transferred to the camp laundry, and she worked there still.

By contrast with Grishkina, Veronika Fitneva, a Petersburg intellectual in her late twenties, had been under surveillance for some time before her arrest. Fitneva had been one of those irregular bohemians that our present regime, like the tsars' before it, is pleased to accuse of decadence and antisocialism. Until 1924 she worked occasionally as a translator of unpopular French novels, sharing an apartment at the bad end of Garden Street with her brother, a young man burdened with similar literary tendencies. In 1924 he was arrested for being a parasite on society. After that she lived alone and cleaned other people's houses.

What the file called her "counterrevolutionary cadre" was filled with poets and painters. It characterized the poetry as "puerile sexual drama," but its language concerning the paintings was surprisingly knowledgeable. Most were "post-Suprematist efforts, elaborating a modern and general fourth-dimensionism." I concluded that in this case the Cheka's bohemian spy was a painter.

Fitneva had been arrested in November 1925, six months before me, on a charge of hooliganism. For a woman, this meant prostitution.

Here is one of socialism's perversities: then, as now, our State could not be brought to admit that the exchange of sex for money might occur within its utopian borders. It refused to so much as acknowledge such a crime with an article in the criminal code. Thus its agents were denied one of the insults they might wish to use against state enemies. When they wished to dirty the characters of those they arrested, they had to resort to euphemisms.

This seemed clearly to be their motivation in Veronika's case. Her dossier contained evidence of her having taken lovers, but there was no evidence of her having accepted a kopek from any of them.

After her arrest, the file's cornucopia ceased to overflow. Formerly prodigal with implicating detail, the story her jailers told about her suddenly became thin and tenuous: from the various prisons where she'd lodged there came a series of pink intake slips and gray exit slips, followed by a pink with no matching gray. This memorialized her arrival on Solovetsky. At some point before she came to the island, a brief statement had been taken from an informer with whom she'd shared a cell: "Veronika Fitneva, a woman of loose morals, speaks callously of the Party and the project of her rehabilitation. She does not provide the names of associates." There was a record of her assignment to a peat-cutting squad during her first months on Solovki, then a note of her removal from it in July, when she was hospitalized. Where she had been assigned upon her release from the hospital, the file did not say.

Her past was weighty, but as Veronika Fitneva drew closer

and closer to the present moment, she converged to an insubstantial point, and vanished. We had to content ourselves with learning the floor and block number she'd been assigned in the women's dormitory.

I suppose our consulting the inmate files was inevitable. If not at this point in the investigation, it would have been another. As Petrovich had said, there were benefits to conducting your inquiry in a prison. What detective could resist the archives? They were a palace built by surveillance, whose paper-and-ink corridors were much easier to walk than Solovki's frozen trails. Personal history, a record of prior crimes, memos about work assignments and associations here on the island: individually, the details were almost too much to take in. If they didn't add up to an all-encompassing whole, the aesthetic effect for the reader was the same as if they had, a kind of overload of the sense of suspicion.

They inspired grandiose thinking. You could almost imagine that Antonov's murder had been witnessed and recorded by some diligent spy, who'd written it down in the illiterate style characteristic of confidential reports: *Oct. 21, 1926, 4 a.m.: Subject* X *was observed to kill Prisoner* GA, *following which action* GA's *body was dragged to the bay by Subject* X, *and thrown in. Subject* X's *antisocial tendencies confirmed.* Our work as detectives would only be a matter of finding the right document, then. Instead of looking for the killer out in the cold world, we would search instead for his file, among the indices and registers of the dusty one. Appealing thought—what else is a mystery novel, after all?

It can only have been Petrovich's high respect for his own powers as an interrogator that had kept him from starting our investigation within the archives—that, and the Chekist's odd unwillingness to grant us more access. In retrospect, it should have struck me as highly suspicious that we were not allowed to read Antonov's file as a matter of course. At the time I took Petrovich's meek acceptance of this as a sort of bow to the arbitrariness of Solovki Power.

What wasn't in those archives? I wonder. Along with a record of the murder, it would have been possible to imagine my own involvement with the investigation logged in their pages, my every movement and idea tracked by someone unknown:

Subject A. Bogomolov exited the administration building in the company of Prisoner YP. His gratification at receiving the dry ration in Company Ten is apparent. Appears distracted by own good fortune. Follows orders from YP without complaint. Full extent of undesirable associations still undetermined. Subject does not appear to suspect he is under observation.

10

A shoulder-high barbed-wire fence surrounded the women's barracks. The place was near the main administration building. We'd left the note the Chekist had requested, describing our anticipated whereabouts, at the Infosec office, and come here first, to see whether any trace of Veronika Fitneva could be discovered. Visiting the laundry for Varvara Grishkina would come later.

After showing our papers to the guard at the gate, we were allowed through the fence. Inside, the barracks were clean, but empty. Another converted building, their layout was much like the hospital's, with large rooms opening off a central hall. The tap of Petrovich's cane echoed in the uncluttered stairway.

The only lead we had was the floor Fitneva lived on, the third. There was no indication of which room or bed might be hers, but we found a woman nailing a loose board into place above one of the doors. "You'll want Alexandra Stepnova, then," she said when she explained we were looking for someone.

The room we were directed to was small and windowless, on the same floor. It was part office, part closet. Mops and brooms leaned against a few shelves of borax and soap along one wall. The middle-aged woman who sat at a table against the other stood as we came in. Alexandra Stepnova was tall and broad-shouldered, her brown hair piled in braids atop her head.

"We're looking for a woman named Veronika Fitneva," said Petrovich after we'd showed our letter from Infosec.

Her faint smile was less an expression than a way of holding herself. She gave the impression of being used to stepping out of the way as others tripped. "I see. And when you've found her?"

I looked to Petrovich, who raised his bushy eyebrows. "A few questions."

"Of course," said Stepnova. "Only, I'm interested in her, you see. Veruchka—Veronika—is by way of being one of my pets. I like to keep track of goings-on in her life."

"Your pets," said Petrovich slowly. "And just what is your role here, Madame Stepnova? The girl we talked to outside thought of you right away when we said we needed to find someone."

"Only Citizen Stepnova, please. There are a few fancy ladies here on Solovki, but I'd rather be a simple Soviet woman." She spoke slowly, confidently. This was not a woman who minded answering questions for Infosec. "I am only the floor mistress. My job's divvying up cleaning and maintenance duties among the girls, and it's me who decides when one of them needs to leave the dormitory. We're enclosed here, for our own protection, of course. It would be chaos if the girls all went tramping about the island."

"I see. A pet of yours would be in line to receive some favors."

Her shoulders hinted at a shrug. "We all have to look out for each other."

"Maybe you can tell us a little about Prisoner Fitneva. What kind of woman is she?"

Stepnova eyed him, her smile unchanging. "A charming one. Headstrong, perhaps."

"Headstrong?"

She shrugged again. "Well, who am I to say? Perhaps she isn't as receptive as some to the rehabilitation the Party hopes for all of us here on Solovki. But I am only the floor mistress."

"I'm sure you underestimate your judgment," said Petrovich dryly. "Would you say she knows many people on the island? Maybe one of your pets is able to go visiting more than others are."

Stepnova was all friendliness. "I could hardly say who she's acquainted with. Maybe I could be more help if I knew what you wanted her for."

"We are trying," said Petrovich, "to find out whether she knows a man named Gennady Antonov."

"Ah," she said. "Another man, then."

The old man was getting impatient. He was in danger of violating his own rule about getting more information than he gave out. Even I had noticed that she hadn't told us where to find Fitneva. "Another? Who's the first?"

Stepnova relented a little. "My role puts me in a position to play a bit of the matchmaker. Yes, love blooms, even on Solovki! I thought things had been going well between Veruchka and an important man in the machinist's shop, Boris Spagovsky. But something seems to have interfered."

"You think Antonov is what interfered?"

"Well, of course, this is the first I've ever heard of your Antonov. But you have to understand how it was. Boris Stepanovich came to me at first because he didn't know how to woo her, poor thing. He was bashful, as some men are. But Veronika had been coming around. He wanted to walk out with her, to spend time alone . . ."

Veronika's file was still fresh in my mind. "You call that bashful?" I said.

"Maybe your young man hasn't yet experienced the full flower of passion," said Stepnova to Petrovich.

"Maybe not," he said.

"Well, we had planned to have her transferred to work more closely with him. I was ready to give the transfer my full support. But then—well, then, all of a sudden, she was assigned somewhere else. Very unfortunate."

"Where was she assigned?"

"Not every bucket carries the same amount of water. Boris Stepanovich and I wanted her to go to him, of course, but a bigger bucket wanted something else. And the way she acted was very irritating. I tried to talk to her about keeping them together, but she just wouldn't listen. Now I wonder about your Antonov. Maybe there was someone else who wanted her near. It's too bad. Women need to be careful, or they'll get reputations. Then no respectable man will have them."

"Antonov wouldn't have had that kind of pull," I murmured to Petrovich.

"Of course it's possible I'm wrong," Stepnova said. "As I said, all of us here in the camp have to help each other. Perhaps you can tell me what's so interesting about the man?"

Petrovich said: "You still haven't told me where she is."

Stepnova nodded sympathetically. "Ah, I understand. In the past, I have done a few little favors myself for the apparatus your letter mentioned. I know how to stay out of what is not my business. I certainly don't wish to delay you. But I would like to know what is happening." She lowered her voice. "It would be better if I knew why an interest has been taken in her. Perhaps, after you and she have spoken . . ."

Petrovich frowned before giving one of his barks of laughter. "Fine. What if I came back this evening, after Tolya and I have interviewed her?"

Stepnova's smile broadened. "Perfect. It happens that Boris Stepanovich will be coming to see her this evening. I've arranged for them to spend time together away from the dormitory. If you came back then, you and I could talk without her feeling . . . uneasy about it. Maybe she will have said something I can help you understand."

"Maybe so," said Petrovich. "Where can we find her?"

"She will be at work. The transfer I mentioned moved her to the monks' fishery. You can't miss it if you take the southern road. It's on the way to Muksalma."

Petrovich lifted up his cane to stare at its head, then put it back down on the floor. "This Spagovsky you mentioned. He wouldn't have had anything to do with Fitneva's being sent to the hospital in July, would he?"

Stepnova's face didn't change—the same smile, the same faintness. She tilted her head to one side. "Do you know, that is an event she and I have never discussed?"

That was all we would get from her, it seemed. As we climbed slowly back down the stairs, I said to Petrovich: "That seems odd, doesn't it? Her unwillingness to talk? Perhaps Veronika Fitneva really is our V."

"Perhaps. Still want to talk to Grishkina, though."

The laundry was inside the kremlin. Before we passed

through Nikolski, Petrovich thought it would be wise to stop in again at Infosec and revise our report to the Chekist to reflect the trip we would need to take to Fitneva's fishery. That done, we headed to the gate.

They hadn't given us any trouble leaving in the morning, but this time the guard with the goiter, Vlacic, stood when we approached the sentry shelter.

"You two," he said, picking up his rifle. He sounded excited."Commander said bring you. Come with me."

Petrovich planted his cane. "What for?"

"Just bring you, he said."

"I don't have time to traipse around at your boss's beck and call. You saw our authorization yesterday. You know who we're working for."

The man sniffed. I could see his fingers tightening on the gun. "Going to have to make you come?"

I looked at Petrovich, alarmed all over again. Even with an authorization like ours, I doubted *zeks* could get away with defying an order from the guards outright. But the old man followed Vlacic through the gate, with me coming along behind. As before, the men in line behind looked anywhere but at us. You might focus the malignant gaze of authority on yourself by looking where it looked.

Just inside the gate, attached to the kremlin wall, the guards had a small building of their own, one that seemed as though it might have been a gatehouse under the monks. Vlacic led us down a hall before opening a door and motioning us in. We walked through into a dim space.

"Yakov Petrovich," I said.

The old man already understood: "Just a minute—"

But the door shut behind us, and a lock clicked. We were trapped.

There was a knob, but it wouldn't turn. While I rattled the door, Petrovich called out: "Damn it! What is this?" There was no response from Vlacic. It was impossible to tell whether he was even still out in the hall.

The place was freezing cold, bare. High in the wall, a shutter covered a tiny, glassless window. There would not have been space for both of us to sit down, even if we'd wanted to on the cold stone.

"They can't keep us, can they?"

Petrovich shook his head. "Our friend in the cabin draws more water than this piss-bucket in charge of the gate. They won't dare to do anything."

"He wasn't exactly reluctant to beat me up last time."

"I tell you, we'll be fine."

Still, anxiety trickled from my clenched jaw down into my chest. I wished there were room to pace.

We waited for two fearful hours, standing close to each other in the cramped cell. Petrovich leaned with more and more of his weight on the cane. By the end, his arm was shaking. Walking from place to place over the last twenty-four hours, he'd done well enough, but this enforced stillness, with nowhere to sit, seemed to wear hard on him.

We spoke very little. I had the impression neither of us wanted to discuss what might be happening.

At last we heard a key in the lock again. A guard we hadn't seen before appeared in the opened door. Like Vlacic, he carried a rifle. "You two go on, then. Commander says to tell you he can't see you now after all. Says remember what he told you before about not making trouble."

The old man said nothing, only pushed past out the door. No one stopped us as we left. Outside, he gestured for my arm.

"The man's an idiot," he muttered. Whether his hand shook with fury or exhaustion, I couldn't tell. Perhaps he felt the same relief and fear I did. "Doesn't want his authority challenged, but interferes just to remind us of his threats. Tell me, does he give me any option but bringing someone down on him? We can't be worrying about the damned guards every time we go in and out!"

"I don't understand what he wants from us," I said.

"Always this way. Those guards' boss is a man who gets things his own way—as long as no one pays too much attention to how he runs things. Out on the bureaucratic periphery, you see anyone who comes digging into your business from the center as a threat."

"Are we from the center?"

"To him it looks that way."

I considered that. It was hard to imagine the old man and myself as threatening, with him tottering along supported on one of my arms while I tried to pull my student's cap down more effectively over my ears with the other. Still, we were, officially speaking, the Chekist's agents. Just that morning, he'd been musing to Petrovich about the trustworthiness of Adminstrative Director Nogtev's inner circle. That did seem to place us close to the center of Solovki Power.

Gray skies threatened, though the air was still clear. Above our heads, snow shelved from the kremlin's eaves.

The laundry occupied the lower floor in one of the stone buildings along the southeast wall, not far from Nativity. When we arrived, two men were at work in front, unloading large bags of dirty clothing from a sledge.

"Just a minute, Yakov Petrovich," I said. "There's something I wanted to ask you. Would you mind if I helped with Grishkina's interrogation? Maybe I could ask her a few questions."

"Why would you want to do that?"

"Well—practice. I'm afraid I haven't done well when you've asked me to question people before now. I was awkward with Terekhov at the alabaster shop this morning, wasn't I? Perhaps I'd be less likely to hold back the investigation if I had some experience."

An uncomfortable look creased his face. "You did fine with Terekhov. You did what was needed."

"Even so. The Chekist said we'd need to finish within the week. Things might go faster if I were better able to help."

"All right," he said slowly. "All right, if you want. Just follow my lead. With Grishkina, we only want to start by learning whether she knew Antonov or not. If she won't admit to it, we'll probe to see whether she has any suspicious connections to the museum."

Inside, a few stairs led down into a low-ceilinged semibasement, white-washed, but green in patches with moisture. The damp air was cold and foul.

A dozen women scrubbed in front of a bank of windows along one wall, each at her separate sink. The rest of the narrow space was filled with soiled fabric, in places piled to the ceiling. While we watched, one of the men unloading the sledge outside shook another bagful out onto the floor. When a cascade of tiny bodies followed the shirts—lice and other insect vermin—he grimaced, tossed the bag onto the pile as well, then stepped back, brushing off his hands.

"Time to find our laundress," said Petrovich.

Asking after Grishkina, we were directed to a room further within. Here, another dozen or so women were washing—in tubs this time, not at sinks—while four others ran wet clothes through two mangles in a corner. This was a larger room than the other, with the remainder of the space filled up with clothing drying on racks. Even so, the amount set out to dry was much less than what sat in dirty piles in the other room. They could not have been getting through their backlog very quickly.

That didn't surprise me. I'd heard you might be offered a clean change of clothes every few months, turning your old stuff in, but it hadn't happened yet to me.

All of the women had noticed us come in. Grishkina, a short-haired person at work at one of the tubs, opened her eyes wide when we came over and Petrovich asked her name.

"Yes, yes? Me? Who are you?"

"My name is Yakov Petrovich. My young associate, Anatoly Bogomolov. We've come from Infosec, with some questions for you."

"Yes. Questions." Her face seemed to show more than the forty-eight years Infosec's file had charged it with. It was lined, fallen. Between it and her clothing—coat and trousers, both much too large—she looked like a feather bed missing half its stuffing. I knew she ought to stir my sympathy.

"You were arrested four years ago, correct?" said Petrovich. "In Moscow?"

"I've told all I know about the man who bought my jewels," she said quickly. Her voice was high, twittering. "I told it long since. They made me tell, in Lefortovo."

The old man shook his head. "That's not what interests us. We're here about your stay in the hospital last July."

Grishkina was still holding the garment she had been scrubbing. She moved it halfheartedly against her washboard. "I had typhus."

"Yes. Tell me, how long did they keep you there, with typhus?"

Petrovich had said to follow his lead. So far, his lead seemed to indicate that things should be allowed to proceed slowly, by stages. With Terekhov, he had launched in directly by asking for an alibi—I could only imagine that he was being more deliberate with Grishkina because she was a woman. At any rate, I hadn't yet seen an opportunity to join in.

"Ten days. Or perhaps—twelve? It took some time for me to recover. Then the quarantine. That was five days, before they let me go back to the dormitory. But I was still very weak when I came back. Very weak."

"Most people don't get typhus in the summer," said Petrovich. The old man was right. It hadn't occurred to me before, but you thought of the disease breaking out during winter, when people were crowded together indoors.

"It's this place," said Grishkina. "The clothes lice. Everyone gets typhus when she starts. If she hasn't had it before, I mean. Every louse in the camp—every louse in the camp ends up here."

I stepped back quickly, realizing how close I'd been standing to the pile of dirty shirts that waited by her tub. Lice were how typhus spread, their infected excrement rubbed into your skin when you scratched. The disease had been epidemic during the wars, both the World War and the civil conflicts that followed. On posters, Lenin's face had overseen citizens shaving each other's heads, treating their clothes with steam. "All attention to this problem, comrades," the newspapers had reported him saying. "Either lice will conquer socialism, or socialism will conquer lice!"

No one seemed to care much whom the lice conquered on Solovetsky. Outbreaks of typhus came with fever, chills, a characteristic rash, and a high likelihood of death. Petrovich flinched as well, reflexively brushing at his trousers. We had our own lice already, of course. But typhus was something else again. I didn't know whether he had had it before—in that case he would be safe—but I hadn't. It would be better to move the interrogation along.

"Whom did you meet while you were there?" I said.

"Whom did I meet? A few people. A few. I helped care for three they brought in while I was quarantined. They died. The others . . . there were several men. And Elena. She started working here at the same time I did." The woman she indicated, at work on the mangles, had hair cropped like her own.

"What about a man named Gennady Antonov?" I said.

"He had typhus?"

I looked at Petrovich, who shook his head. "No," I said. "Some other fever."

"With the other wards, contact was forbidden. The quarantine—we were quarantined."

It stood to reason, of course. The only way to be sure that a typhus patient didn't reintroduce infected lice into the population was to keep them isolated while they had the disease, and for some time afterward. If we'd thought of it, we might have ruled her out as the V. of the note from the first. Still, Petrovich was not ready to let her go.

"I think you have a husband," he said. "In Paris."

The question startled her, widening her eyes again. "Yes. I can tell you nothing about him. My husband does not communicate with me. He had nothing to do with the jewels. Nothing."

"I promise you, this has nothing to with your jewels. You say you don't communicate. Do you still consider yourself a married woman?"

Grishkina had given up on her washing altogether by now. She clutched the front of her coat with a wet hand. "What do you mean?"

"You've been separated from your husband for a long time."

"You think I had some—some connection with this Antonov?" What was it that made her begin to straighten up, put on that worn-out dignity? Sexual outrage, presumably. An angry bird had woken up inside the feather bed and begun to flutter.

Petrovich only shrugged. "Show her the note, Tolya."

It was all going on longer than I liked; I could feel my skin crawling with new lice, real or imagined. Still, I held out to her the note we'd found in Antonov's desk. When she gestured that her hands were wet, I unfolded it and held it up to her view.

'—has come from my mother with a few rubles,' she read under her breath. 'The thought of your goodness is all that enables me to continue.' She shook her head. "It isn't my handwriting. You thought this V. stood for Varvara? But my mother died at her estate. Fifteen years ago."

It wasn't her. Wasn't that clear now? In the other room, water could be heard running from a tap. The washboards made their dull ripping sounds. I was anxious to finish with the questions Petrovich had wanted us to ask. "Do you have any connection to the camp museum?" I said.

"What? The museum? No. No, I've never been."

Petrovich sighed. "Fine. Perhaps you'll tell us where you were two nights ago, between 5:15 and midnight."

Grishkina looked from him to me and back, bewildered. "Where was I? From here they take us back to the dormitory. That is usually around six. But why are you asking these questions? Who is this Antonov?"

"He was my cellmate," said Petrovich. "Someone killed him. Two nights ago."

"You don't know who?"

"We are trying to learn."

"You are from Infosec. And you thought that I —?" To my surprise, she giggled behind her hand. "Oh no. No, I'm afraid you have been wasting your time. And—tell me, gentlemen: have you had typhus? Too much light still hurts my eyes. And my hair! It's grown back so slowly where they shaved it off. But I was lucky to live. If you are assigned to work here in the laundry, the best thing is to have been infected before. Then, ossf course, you're immune. I wouldn't recommend spending time here for anyone who is not. Not without a good reason."

She picked up a shirt from the pile and held it out to show us. The fabric was alive with insects.

Apparently the old man was no more immune than I was; we left hurriedly. For the rest of the day, I would be trying to ignore the feeling of tiny movements between my shirt and my body. There was nothing to be done about it now.

11

Apportioned an impressive-enough area under the old monastic plan, the cemetery had recently expanded. Just south of the kremlin, new graves spilled out past its edges, a dropped box of index cards: haphazard, crazy, everywhere.

We had left the kremlin again, without any trouble from the Nikolski guards this time. The road that led to Veronika Fitneva's fishery took us along one edge of the cemetery, near where a chapel called Onufrievskii humped dully out of the ground. Years had grayed its whitewash, eroded its steeple to ghostliness. Returning from work in the evenings, I'd sometimes seen candles glowing in the church's windows. Today they were mostly shuttered. The ones left open were dark.

The candles appeared, when they did, because it was in Onufrievskii that the monks were allowed to hold their services. This was the contingent we'd discussed with Ivanov-the-Anti-Religious-Bug: a remnant of the group that populated the islands before the Bolsheviks took possession, kept on in the site of their former devotions. They were essentially prisoners like us now, but they knew from long experience how to catch the herring and *navaga* cod that swam in the area. As it happened, these were delicacies the appetite for which the Revolution had done nothing to reduce. Party officials in Moscow appreciated the Solovki herring's characteristic tenderness and delicate flavor no less than aristos in Saint Petersburg had under the tsar. Thus, on the condition that they continue to ply for the Cheka the fisherly expertise they'd developed on behalf of the Lord, the monks were exempted from the standard companies, allowed to govern themselves to a certain degree, and granted a few religious privileges. They even passed in and out of the kremlin through their own small gate, called the Herring Gate, on the western wall.

A long avenue approached Onufrievskii's doors from the west, with the cracking crosses belonging to the dead monks of earlier eras drawn up in unsteady ranks to either side. Then, beyond the old monks' decayed graves: disorder, the disorder of a project without an ending. Heaps of naked earth, shovels left to stand upright in the snow. Frozen tarps covering tools, or supplies, or perhaps bodies.

Men died constantly under SLON's care, and though sometimes there were bottlenecks, and in fact it was more or less normal for things to proceed by fits and starts, their bodies were interred, on average, at the same rate. To dispose of the corpses was the job of Company Sixteen, whose work was eased (so the joke ran) by the fact that they were their own most frequent clients. A prisoner was likely to get a transfer there when he was no longer good for anything else.

Their rations were known to be meager, their work shoddy. But, to be fair, the poor *zeks* in Sixteen weren't entirely to blame if things were in a bad state. The same problems of management and supply that afflicted other companies were twice as bad for them. What could their supervisors do, when some company commanders simply would continue refusing to transport the dead from their work sites as they succumbed, in a measured, orderly manner? In winter, a month's worth of dead from remote work sites would sometimes be delivered all at once, in one sledge-load after another.

For such arrivals, coffins might be available, or might not. Along with its casket (even in these hypothetical best of circumstances not very waterproof), a body that appeared at the right moment might get an individual grave of reasonable depth, a board with a name scratched on it, and even some record of the burial date. Coming at the wrong moment meant being tipped into a pit with a dozen others. Most found accommodation somewhere between these two extremes.

In short, a man's treatment after death was liable to be as arbitrary and insufficient as in life. Why, then, had the Chekist considered Antonov's corpse worth the effort of investigating, when others were simply filed away or discarded like so many unread memoranda? Petrovich had suggested that the Cheka wanted to be the only ones to employ killing as a tool in the camp, but I wondered. Dying was such a wholesale business that one or two irregular entries in the account book could hardly matter.

But, then, there were other questions as well. What was it that had made the Chekist seek me out the previous morning? What had made him agree to Petrovich's suggestion that we be authorized to make inquiries?

I reached no conclusions as we approached the graves. Did I even frame the questions to myself clearly enough to answer them? Their elements swam somewhere in my consciousness, true. But perhaps I only pose them now because I know how they were to structure the story to come.

While I watched, a ray of sun broke through the gray overhead, blazing white over the half-acre of snow it fell on. The dark headboards swam over the ground like spots in front of my eyes.

Then the wind blew the gap in the clouds shut again.

With Petrovich and his cane, what should have been a thirty-minute walk took more than an hour. At last a path off from the main road brought us to a little bay. At a place where the rocks came steeply down to the water, buildings had been built out on a platform. Two sheds flanked a larger house in the middle, all gray with steep roofs.

That was the fishery. From the middle of the platform a pier jutted out into the deeper water, where a small boat floated at anchor. Our steps and Petrovich's cane made hollow noises on the boards. I remember looking out and noticing that the boat was chained to the dock in two places, both fastened with padlocks.

A bearded monk met us at the door to the central building. When we asked for Veronika Fitneva, he glowered sternly, then directed us to the shed on the left. She was at work when we came in, something involving a tangle of ropes spread out on a table.

Noticing us, she put it down and looked up, but said nothing.

The woman before us stood several inches over five feet, neither tall nor short, loose-limbed and pale. Her large features complicated the face they were in, made it full. Just as the file had described, her eyes and hair were black.

"Veronika Fitneva?" said Petrovich.

"That's right," she said. She had a low alto voice. Bundled under men's clothes—brown trousers, a sweater with a stretched-out neck—her body showed only when she shifted. I couldn't stop noticing her breasts and hips hinting at themselves beneath the heavy wool, then disappearing again, like shapes moving under water.

"My name is Yakov Petrovich." He indicated me. "My assistant, Anatoly. Long walk from the kremlin, for an old man like me. Maybe I could sit?" Her eyes followed his to a stool over by the wall, but she didn't move. Petrovich shrugged and limped over to pull it out himself. "Fine, then. There are a few questions we'll need you to answer."

The room was dim. Above, a gust of wind rattled a window, then stopped. The squawking of the gulls came into the building from every direction, now louder, now softer, as they wheeled themselves into and out of knots.

Veronika Fitneva sniffed and flipped her wrist. "I doubt I can tell you anything very interesting. Is it something about tying nets? Because I speak with great authority when I say it is not an interesting subject." While she spoke, she went over to a row of pegs that hung along the wall and pulled down a coat that hung there, put it on. There was a stove, but it hadn't been lit. We each breathed out our own wreath of fog. Cold as it was, the place still reeked of fish. Nets lay limp and kelp-like about the room, draped over its rough tables and benches and uneven shelves, piled on the floor. "It is moderately engaging for about a day and a half, while you're learning and it's still difficult. After that it is incredibly boring. But maybe you're here for something else?"

"We're looking into a certain matter," said Petrovich, "for the Information and Investigation Section."

She shrugged, but looked away. "In that case, I imagine you'll ask your questions whether I have anything interesting to say or not. What's this all about?"

"Are you acquainted with Gennady Mikhailovich Antonov?" said Petrovich.

"No," she said. The way she said it was too quick.

Petrovich sat forward on his stool and leaned with both hands on the cane between his knees. His expression was amused, like a man preparing to enjoy himself. "Very well."

Have I made it clear I found her very beautiful? I did. At the time, I thought she was the most striking woman I'd ever seen.

But it's strange, remembering her looks. Sometimes her image in my mind's eye is unlovely. As the years pass, it comes more and more to resemble everyone else I met on Solovetsky. Hungry, dirty, too thin. Suspicious. Hardened around the eyes and mouth. And it is not only a matter of the coarsening effects of the camp. Her big features were unusual. From certain angles, I think, perhaps you would have called them ugly.

What renews her for me, in those moments, is the memory of that graceful flip of her wrist when she replied to Petrovich. A woman's wrist is the part of her most capable of preserving beauty in the camps. Her face, her figure, her hair: all quickly spoiled by ill-fitting clothes or heavy work or simple filthiness. But when her sleeve pulls back as she moves her arm to place a cup on the shelf, or to lace her boot—something shows, something naked and lovely. Most of all, the wrist moves, a verb. Veronika Fitneva's wrists rippled in response to her thoughts. They spilled out a cascade of unconscious, minute gestures, so that you felt that to know the range of movement of the wrist would be to know all its owner's moods.

Even a wrist, of course, can be ruined by hunger. The starved wrist becomes an apparatus of grating bone, curtained behind loose skin. Starvation ruins everything. The wrist sustains beauty longest—not forever.

Still, when I met her, Veronika had beautiful wrists. No trick of time can alter that.

Petrovich nodded at her. "Very well," he said again. "But tell me. You had a stay in the hospital this past June, didn't you? You were pulled off the peat workings."

"Yes," she said curtly.

"Yes. A broken rib or two, wasn't it? Antonov would have

been in the men's ward with a fever at the same time. An older gentleman—younger than me, of course, but old to you. Longish pointed beard. You know the camp museum? He worked there, on the icons."

"I've told you. I don't know him."

Petrovich pulled on his mustache and said: "You've told me. Only, we're wondering who might have written a certain note that was found in his desk. Show it to her, would you, Tolya?"

The note was in my coat pocket. I pulled it out and handed it to her. She read calmly, then folded it and handed it back. Our fingers did not touch.

"Look familiar?" said Petrovich.

She set her chin. "I've never seen it before. Why are you asking all these questions? What is it you think this Antonov has done?"

Petrovich's amusement grew savage. "What's he done? He's died."

Her face went blank. "What?"

"Gennady Antonov, the man you don't know, is dead. He was murdered. That is the matter we are investigating for Infosec."

For a moment, she turned her face away, down and to the side. Then she raised it again and spoke quickly.

"You're investigating a murder? Do you think that's quite smart? When it comes to killing, the most prolific workers I can think of on this island are your bosses in the Cheka. Wouldn't it be a shame to find out they'd done the murder, then simply forgotten to tell you about it? They might not appreciate your apprehending them, in that case. Yes, statistically speaking, I'd have to say that's a fairly likely outcome. If you could line up all the men who were killed on Solovki in a year and throw a rock at them, you'd bet on hitting one who'd been done in by the Cheka, wouldn't you?"

She mastered her voice, and the words came on in a rapid stream. "But then, they wouldn't have sent you out to ask your questions if they had any doubts about what you'd turn up, would they? No one seems to find anything except what they were expecting here, least of all the Cheka. But it is true for the rest of us as well. It's certainly been true for me—things are bad here in just the ways I anticipated. Maybe I should have exercised more control over my expectations. If only I'd been picturing myself being reformed into a model of Soviet womanhood! I would be married to a local Party boss on a new collective farm by now. What about you, gentlemen? Were you expecting me to be uncooperative? You were, weren't you? I've observed that policemen like us to be uncooperative exactly as much as we like being uncooperative. Otherwise what reason would you have to exist? So there is another proof of my rule. We only ever find what we are looking for."

It was a performance. Veronika Fitneva, threatened, was always headlong and maddening and desirable and grand. I knew that about her, even then. I'd seen it already, in her file.

That file. V. Fitneva's I had read much more intently, more avidly, than V. Grishkina's. Where Grishkina's was dull and matter of fact, Fitneva's gave the effect of a kind of spy-comedy. The entries for March and April 1925 had reported her being regularly tailed by a team of four men. One of these she'd learned to recognize, and whenever she spotted him in a crowd she'd accost him and ask for a cigarette. Again and again he was forced to record the time, date, and location of her request, never saying whether he gave her one. The list went on, page after page, until it became a kind of dry joke, one she'd orchestrated for whatever anonymous Chekist might ultimately compile her case. Or for anyone else who might read the official account of her life—for me.

Once, noticing a stranger shadowing her on her way to a rendezvous with a friend, she turned on her heel in the middle of Zagorodny Prospect to excoriate him: "Subject VF used language more common among street hooligans and loose women than among the debased intelligentsia," the man wrote in his report. "Subject refused to proceed until this agent had walked two blocks from where subject stood on Zagorodny, then darted into an alley and eluded pursuit."

She was courageous, she was dignified. As her circumstances became more and more straitened after the arrest of her brother, she began to spend time with needle and thread, couturiere of her own penury. She would return home from her day's work garbed as a domestic, spend two hours behind a drawn shade, and emerge into the splendid evening wearing the same dress, now rendered à la mode with dropped waist and raised hem. Her feat of transubstantiation duly entered the record: "Subject regularly alters appearance and costume. Attempts at disguise possible. Officers take care not to be deceived by any change in subject's appearance." She frequented tearooms and dingy salons. Occasionally she was observed quite drunk.

One informant, evidently a member of her circle but identified only by his initials, wrote of her: "V. M. Fitneva dresses extravagantly, wearing 'elegant' foreign fashions in the bourgeois 'flapper' style. The most counterrevolutionary among the girls in the group are attracted to her rooms, where they discuss getting a good fiancé and foreign dances ('Foxtrot,' 'Charleston'). Often heard to mention her brother Emil, and known to send him packages in prison." Elsewhere he wrote: "Sexual depravity likely in Fitneva's case." The file did not mention the author's sex, but I was sure he was a man. I recognized the desire and jealous reproach a man would have to feel, forced to watch her life from a distance. I desired, I reproached, along with him.

Yes. It is a special kind of love, the love a young man conceives for a young woman while reading the evidence compiled against her by the secret police. Her file, hefted back onto the desk of memory, presents itself as a plume of dust, as an effluvium rising up from its heaped mess of paper, string, and paste flakes. Somewhere in my mind, I shut my eyes and sneeze.

Petrovich allowed her a moment to collect herself after she'd finished. He examined the head of his cane before he said: "Let's talk about something else for a minute. What can you tell me about Boris Spagovsky?"

She made an expression as though she held a small oval stone tightly in her mouth. "You've been talking to Alexandra Stepnova," she said.

Petrovich nodded. "She wonders why you spend your time here, when you could be keeping house for a boyfriend."

"Why? Because I've been assigned to put a million knots into a million nets with Brother Cyril. It's the nature of a prison camp. You don't get to choose how you spend your time. Or is one of the perks of working for Infosec picking an assignment you like? For the rest of us, it isn't like that."

"I'd say Stepnova knows something about how favors in this camp work. You might have called one in. Maybe you don't like

Spagovsky so much."

Her eyes flickered to the side. "I like him. I like him perfectly well."

"All right," said Petrovich. "Then you're in love with him?"

She made a "huh" sound that was half a laugh, half an angry sigh, and glanced at me. When our eyes met, I looked away despite myself. "What does that have to do with anything?" she said. "I'm a modern woman. Who says I even believe in love?"

Petrovich sat still on his stool, intent. "Those broken ribs in June. That was Spagovsky. He put you in the hospital."

"I'm surprised Stepnova would tell you so much. In her eyes, Boris is an angel."

"Not her. We heard it from a woman you worked peat with."

Veronika Fitneva lifted her shoulders, refusing to be impressed.

"But now you like him," Petrovich went on. "This man who beat you that badly. You see him of your own free will. Getting out from under him has nothing to do with why you're working here."

"Every man has his own idea about how to court you," she said dryly. "First he wrote me a note: 'Let's live together, and I'll help you.' Then, when I said no, a few blows with an ax handle. It wasn't as endearing as he thought, but he used the pull he had in the machinist's company to make sure I got good care in the hospital. He was sorry, after his fashion—a visit every day! Sometimes he brought wildflowers. There are worse men. I don't mind spending a night with him sometimes." She looked back and forth between us. "Is that scandalous to you? As I said, I'm modern."

The old man's blue eyes narrowed. "'Sometimes'—but if you let Stepnova make you his housekeeper, it would be all the time."

"Maybe."

"And it wasn't Gennady Antonov who kept that from happening? You haven't been relying on him to protect you, to ensure you remain assigned here?"

"I've told you. I don't know anyone by that name."

Petrovich moved his jaw back and forth, sucked his teeth. Finally he sat back in the chair and said: "All right. But I expect we'll have more questions. We'll be back soon."

"Fine," she said. "Next time, tell your silent assistant not to leer at me."

"I—you're quite mistaken," I said. I could feel my face turning red; my embarrassed heart squirmed. I hadn't realized my staring was quite so obvious.

Petrovich was raising himself with his cane. "Let's go, Tolya," he said.

That was Veronika, then. She of the charming surveillance file, whose existence had been nearly erased from the Cheka's archives once they had her in prison. How much more effectively has she been erased by now, each passing year moving her further along the axis of oblivion?

Veronika, are you still alive? Tonight, as I remembered and put down the words you said, it was as though you were here, speaking to me and telling me to stop looking at you that way. You made me feel all over again what we would and would not be to each other, as if you were still the unanswered question of my life.

But no. The question was answered long ago, and you are gone. It is most likely you died in the camps, as so many did. If not on Solovetsky, then perhaps you were transferred to the Belomor Canal Project, like me, and unlike me died there. And if not there, then somewhere else, and if not in that place, then in another. If you lasted beyond the White Sea Canal, the possible settings for your death multiply beyond what I can track.

But then, of course, one is never capable of tracking as long a path as one can calculate. I thought of myself as a mathematician once, didn't I? Then assume, for the sake of demonstration, that you lived through five camps after Belomor. And say there have been a thousand camps established since then. Then it is a matter of elementary enumerative combinatorics: for every camp you lived through, the possibilities multiply. In choosing your first place of confinement, State and Party possess one thousand options. But, since it is beyond even the power of the Central Committee to change your camp assignment without assigning you to a new camp, in every subsequent choice they have only nine hundred and ninety-nine. So, given my assumptions, there exist one-thousand-by-nine-hundred-and-ninety-nine-to-the-fourth-power paths that you may have followed to your grave.

One thousand by nine hundred ninety-nine to the fourth

power! A huge number. But the figure is for demonstration purposes only: no one knows how many camps there really are. My neighbor Vasily-the-tank-commander is outraged by this. "Perhaps a thousand camps, of ten thousand souls each," he cries in my room late at night. "Fifteen hundred camps, perhaps, scattered across Siberia like drops of blood. How can the cult of a single personality have caused ten million to disappear, to be forgotten?" Soviet history, he says, must hear my tale, and the tales of those, like you, that may be lost from every mind but the survivors'.

Vasily still seems to me like a stupid young man, Veronika. I will not allow him to read this. No one else will read it either. I will not—laughable thought!—attempt to publish it. I will cease writing. What has been put down so far, I will burn.

Why send my story out on its own path from point to point, possibility to possibility? You know, don't you, Veronika, that the whole edifice of possibility is a trap, another camp. What chance is there that this story's path might meet yours, or that of any reader who could understand?

Veronika, I must say it: I hope that you are dead. I have decided to destroy this writing. No one living will ever read it. And so these words can't be addressed to you, not really, if you are still alive.

But who knows what the dead read?

Enough. I have been drinking while I write this. I am drunk. Enough.

12

At the road Petrovich stopped and looked back in the direction of the fishery and ocean. "So much for our leads from the museum," he said. "For now, at any rate. At least we know where our V is."

"You feel sure she was the one who wrote the note?"

He snorted. "You were less eager to interrogate Fitneva than poor Varvara Grishkina. What, not interested anymore in improving your contributions to the investigation?"

"No, that's not it. I—"

"Never mind. Bashfulness may be your best response. Dealing with a woman like Miss Fitneva takes some experience of the world. You're how old, twenty? You've been in prison during the years you would have been becoming worldly, maybe."

Seeing my discomfort—after my awkwardness with the girl digging peat, this made the second day running I'd put my inexperience with women on display—Petrovich grinned. His mood had been improving all day. Every uncooperative answer, every new door we knocked on, increased his appetite for what we were doing. His physical frailness was undeniable. He'd done nothing when the crate fell, and wasn't faking his need for help on the snowy paths. But the fragility generated a kind of headlong energy, a confidence that only grew as he poked around the island on his cane. Even being locked up by the guards at Nikolski had only subdued him briefly.

It seemed to have been a relief for him to be removed from his normal assignment at KrimKab, the Office of Criminology. There his colleagues were—he said the word with disdain—sociologists, more apt to chatter about the symptomatology of antisocial affect than pay attention to real crimes. We'd discussed it over our meal the night before. "Forty years with the police force in Odessa," he said, "and now this."

Resuming the role of detective suited him—especially when, as now, it allowed him the didactic pleasure of correcting my views on women, crime, and the world.

"In fact, any man ought to be careful around this Fitneva," he said. " A woman, with a man to do the killing. That's what I said we should look for, didn't I? You can see she'd be the type to take sinister suggestions from, eh? The woman who exercises the greatest power of attraction isn't always the one with the prettiest face." When I didn't reply to that, he lit up. "Oh ho! Or maybe you already find her a beauty? Advanced that far, has it? Well, be double careful, then. You're too young to remember that woman in Venice, Tarnovskaia, who was in the headlines for years. Kept getting her lovers to kill each other over her, never laid a hand on them herself. A fatal woman—*rokovaia zhenshchina*. Papers talked about her as though she were a new phenomenon of the new century. Nonsense, of course. This type has been around forever. But when it appears in your case, your ears perk up."

I don't know whether he noticed my bristling at his calling Veronika a type, but it was enough for me to momentarily forget my embarrassment. She'd been so personal, so distinct to me, that Petrovich had to be wrong. "I didn't see anything sinister about her," I said. "Mostly she seemed worried that she would become the target of an Infosec inquiry."

"Ah, but she lied to our faces, didn't she? Never mind. Time will tell."

It was getting on into the afternoon as we approached the kremlin. We were on our way to Company Ten, not having eaten since the morning, when Razdolski met us. Among the southern outbuildings, there was enough foot traffic that I didn't recognize him approaching.

"You two're to come with me," he said.

"What is it?" said Petrovich. "What happened?"

Scratching the back of his neck, the guard only shrugged. "Come on."

It was dark under the evergreens' canopy. Razdolski led us along the northern road, then turned off onto an uncleared logging path that made Petrovich wheeze. I helped him as best I could, but my own concentration was slipping. The case had held my attention so far today, but with every step taking us farther from our meal, food had begun to master my thinking again, pushing even my shame about leering—had it truly been leering?—at Veronika to the back of my mind.

At length we came to a small clearing near the forest's edge. You could hear gulls, see the glimmer of water through the trees. On one side, a carved crucifix, the wood cracked and gray—one of the monks' old shrines. The Chekist waited underneath with another guard, standing over a pile of dark clothes.

"Ah, good. When we saw your note, I was afraid Razdolski would be longer finding you. Your forensic skills are required once again, Yakov Petrovich."

Not clothing at his feet: someone's body, dead.

Petrovich panted, looking at it. "This is related to our case? To Antonov?"

The Chekist gestured. "As you see." It was Nail Terekhov, the White cavalryman. "And the manner of death is the same as before. A blow to the back of the head."

Alive, Terekhov's face with its jaw of missing teeth had looked deflated. Now it looked like a rag with features. He wore the same dark shirt and pants he had when we'd seen him before, though brushed free of much of their white dust. "We were talking to him just this morning," said Petrovich. "How would he have ended up here?"

"Who knows?"

"How was he found?"

The Chekist hesitated. "A logging team, working in the area. They noticed the body. Infosec was informed."

"When?"

"Not long ago. Around one o'clock."

"It's a narrow window. He'll have left the alabaster workshop sometime after we left him. That was six, a little after dawn. We can begin tracing his movements there."

"I only need you to examine the body, Yakov Petrovich."

He didn't like that, I could tell, but he bent down, lifted the head to look at the back of the neck. The hair was sodden with blood, and a bloody whitish substance bulged from the wound. The stuff was Terekhov's brain matter.

"If you know the cause of death already, why do you want me to examine him?" said Petrovich peevishly.

"I want to know what you can tell from looking. Weren't you just telling me to respect your methods?"

"All right. Yes, fine. Then, looking at this, I observe that the blow was sloppier than last time. Likely done with a heavier weapon. With Antonov the skin was unbroken." He surveyed the body. "Have you moved him?"

"No."

"Someone else did, then. He's been brought from elsewhere. A man hit from behind doesn't fall face up. Plus, there are no signs of struggle, and if he'd been hit here there'd be blood spatter. Don't see that either."

The Chekist listened, but he was staring at me. "And what about you, Bogomolov? What do you make of it?"

"What—me?"

"Yes, you. You must have some reaction. Yakov Petrovich says you are capable of assisting intelligently with his investigations."

I could have told him that seeing Terekhov's slack face and seeping brains had brought my stomach into my throat. No, the reaction is not exactly nausea, I could have explained, since, there in my throat, my belly is still twisting with hunger.

But that was not a reaction anyone had any interest in.

"No," I said. "No, I can't think what it's about. It—it must mean he was connected to Antonov somehow. I wouldn't have said so. I believed him when he said he wasn't, this morning."

This time, I noticed, the Chekist had prepared for his time out of doors by donning a thick wool coat. Had the leather jacket been left back in his cabin? His expression was remote, heavy, one hand moving slowly over his smooth chin. Meanwhile Razdolski had moved up to stand behind me, the way he had before I'd been punched the day before. I kept myself from looking over my shoulder to see how close he was.

"This is not living up to the reference Petrovich furnished you with, Prisoner Bogomolov. He said you were clever. You must have more thoughts than this. Nothing seems significant about his having been found so close to the shore? Antonov was found in the water as well."

Yes, I was right: this theatrical approach was a threat. But what did he want from me? "I don't know. I couldn't say. If the body was moved—"

"You sound upset. You were more self-possessed looking at your friend yesterday."

"I'm only hungry. I can't seem to think . . ."

Petrovich interrupted, sparing me further questioning. He was still kneeling by the body. "His buttons are crooked."

The Chekist turned. "What?" Petrovich didn't answer, instead indicating Terekhov's shirtfront. I felt relief. Something about Petrovich's observation had disrupted the other man, unbalanced him. "Well, and?"

"Let's see," said Petrovich. He opened Terekhov's shirt. Beneath a surprisingly thick mat of fur, a mess of welts showed on the dead man's chest. "Someone gave him a beating before he died. Meant it, too. This wasn't any tickling with a feather. Help me undress him, Tolya."

I had the impression the Chekist was about to object, but he didn't. Terekhov was less stiff than Antonov had been, and his clayey skin still felt lukewarm. We were able to remove his coat, shirt, and trousers without much difficulty. Despite what the Chekist had said about my agitation, it was easier to bring myself to touch Terekhov's body than Antonov's. Once we'd examined him, however, I felt my hands shaking. Bruises like the ones on his chest covered much of the body. Cigarettes had burned angry red eyes, some still blistered, into his skin.

"Whoever did this was in no hurry," said Petrovich. "They worked him over. Somewhere they had the leisure to take off his shirt, burn him with their cigarettes. Killed him with that blow to the back of the head, put his clothes back on—always hard to do with a corpse, no wonder they fouled the buttons. Then they dump him here. Leaves us with three questions. What were they trying to find out from him that they needed to torture him? That's one. Where did they do it? That's two. And three: what, if any, is the connection to Antonov's death?"

"They were both killed the same way," said the Chekist shortly.

"Apparently. But there are differences as well," said Petrovich. We all regarded Terekhov. Where it wasn't bruised, his naked body looked blue. The bandage I'd noticed on his knuckles that morning had been lost, and you could see old scabs on his hand. Petrovich sniffed and resumed. "They didn't mark his face, did they? If they were going to kill him, I don't see the point in covering up the damage."

"Who can say?" said the Chekist.

"Anyway," said Petrovich, rising. "It's as I said before. The first thing we need to do is find out when he was last seen at the alabaster workshop. Tolya and I can go there now."

"No," said the Chekist.

"What do you mean, no?"

"Your contributions to this side of the investigation need only be forensic. I will handle Terekhov. The two of you will continue looking into Antonov's circumstances."

"You can't be serious! This is a major lead. The man was killed not eight hours after he talked to us. He may have been killed *because* he talked to us. Someone may have seen us go to him. Or there was something he told us worth killing over, something we didn't recognize. It's clearly a part of the case!"

"Yes. A part of the case for which I bear responsibility, first and last. Don't forget who you are working for, Yakov Petrovich. Anything you discover serves the goals of Infosec. Your instructions are to forget about Terekhov, regardless of whatever sort of lead you think this is, and report whatever you learn about Antonov to me."

Petrovich fumed, moving his wrinkled lips in anger. He seemed to be on the point of saying something back to the Chekist, before he stopped himself. After a moment of sour-looking reflection, he turned to me instead: "At least we will finish investigating the scene. Tolya, I'll handle things here. You look to see whether you can discover signs of the body being dragged in through the snow. You'll need to walk a circle around the body—

say a hundred paces out."

That was a surprise. "You want me to find footprints?"

The old man rolled his eyes. "Yes, yes, I know what I said before. But the snow isn't so disturbed here in the forest. Maybe you'll find out what direction they brought him from. Look for blood, signs of dragging. Anything like that. A wide circle, understand? The further out you go, the more likely you'll find something we haven't covered up by walking around already. Go on, get moving." I spared a glance for the Chekist, but he was watching Petrovich and didn't say anything. In fact I was glad to be released—glad not to stay there and try to justify my inclusion in the investigation, or to get involved in whatever struggle was going on between the two of them.

I began by going Petrovich's recommended hundred paces back up the path we'd come down. The ground beneath the trees here was smooth and flat, interrupted only in places by stones and old stumps. The trees were dense. I could sometimes make out the others grouped around the body, but mostly I lost them among the trunks. Taking my time with the search did not help me uncover anything. The snow on the stones lay undisturbed; the stumps were gray, cut long before. Soon enough my circuit brought me out of the trees and down to the shore. The Chekist was right—Terekhov's body truly was close to the sea, close enough that the water's edge laid a chord across the circle I'd been tracing. Petrovich had said Infosec was concerned about Antonov being found in the bay, and the questions he'd asked Terekhov at the Chekist's behest had been about an escape plot. Was that what the Chekist had expected me to have ideas about, back in the clearing? It was bewildering.

Regardless, there was no sign of a body being moved here either. When I'd come full circle and reached the path again without finding anything, I could only conclude that Terekhov had been brought in along the path, the same way we'd come.

Back in the clearing with Terekhov's corpse, Petrovich and the Chekist seemed to have finished whatever remained of their examination of the scene. Having seen me coming, they stood waiting by the still-naked body. Razdolski and the other guard had taken seats on a log.

"Nothing," I said.

"All right," said Petrovich.

The Chekist nodded as well. "Then the two of you are to continue your investigation into Antonov's death. You'll continue working your way down the list of persons of interest. Meanwhile I will investigate Terekhov's killing."

"And if any more of the men we interview come up dead?"

"Then I will issue instructions for handling the matter in due course. Just do your job, Yakov Petrovich."

The old man made a gesture of begrudging acceptance. "You haven't heard yet what we found out about the women we talked about earlier."

"You haven't found anything conclusive?"

"Not yet."

"Then you can brief me on the matter tomorrow."

Petrovich spent another few minutes complaining about what had happened to us at Nikolski that morning. That seemed to engage the Chekist's interest a little, though in the end he only agreed to speak to the gate commander when he next passed through. Razdolski and the other guard sat in silence. The sound of Razdolski scratching himself—his chest, his neck, his thigh—was audible in the quiet forest.

The big guard had never paid me any attention before, not even when his explicit job was to watch me. But this time, I thought his and his partner's eyes were on me. I was glad when we left.

13

Back at the cell, we finally ate. A cold meal: it was too late to cook, the afternoon's supply of peat having been used up. Each of us had been provided a pound loaf of black bread that morning. The old man fretted his, tearing one end to bits with gnarled fingers. I stopped before I'd eaten half of mine, having decided to allow myself a bite out of the beet in Antonov's chest as well. What remained I broke in two, putting the pieces in the usual spot in the lining of my coat. The pound loaf was better than the half we'd gotten in Quarantine. I told myself I wasn't hungry enough to care about errant crumbs, but not one of the fragments that fell around Petrovich's boots escaped my notice.

"What do you think about Terekhov?" I asked. "It's surprising, isn't it? After we talked to him this morning, I'd have sworn he had nothing to do with Antonov."

Petrovich grunted, not looking up. "Nothing surprises me."

The maddening black snowfall of bread continued. After a moment of watching it accumulate, I tried again. "I don't see why the Chekist doesn't want us to ask questions about him. It's all part of one case. How can we ask people about Antonov without asking about Terekhov?"

That got a reaction. "Our friend wants to wrap the case up quickly, whether we find the killer or not. Yesterday he actually seemed to care about coming up with the truth. Today, not as much. We've got less time than I thought." He sounded more petulant than usual, sour rather than gruff. "Need to start casting a wider net. Time for a visit to the sauna."

The word disagreed with everything I knew about Solovetsky. When I was a boy, my father had sometimes taken me with him on his regular visits to the steam room at the neighborhood's public bath. I had memories of peering through white clouds at the men around us—sweat covering my body, a towel wrapped around my waist, tile slick and unaccustomed against my skin. Sometimes the heat had made me nauseous. But on Solovetsky, maybe a sauna would be more like the one I'd once used on a hiking expedition with the Academy of Uncertain Arts and Ephemeral Sciences. That had been a rural affair, wooden walls and benches blackened by the smoke that was allowed to fill the room while it heated.

Even that seemed wrong. A sauna combined concepts of leisure and extremity in a way that did not belong on the island. Here we schemed and plotted to experience moderation.

"What does it mean?" I asked "'The sauna?'"

"It means we're going somewhere I didn't want to have to go."

"Is it for division commanders?"

He barked a laugh. "What, do you picture them whipping themselves with birch sticks to relax? That's not the way things work. Here, to relax, they whip us. No, it's not a proper sauna. Only a place where one of my old friends can be found. I don't know whether he'll have anything useful, but sometimes when you're under pressure, taking a shot in the dark is worth it."

"All right," I said. "But who are you talking about?"

"One of the most useful things a detective can do is know the local criminals. My friend is an old *urka*."

The *urki* were "legitimate thieves," career criminals who lived by their own code of conduct. There was already a distinction between "politicals," and *zeks* who'd committed more ordinary crimes. The difference between run-of-the-mill criminals and the *urki* was something else again. To be an *urka* meant not only to commit crimes, but to be committed to crime as a mode of existence. Imprisonment, for them, was only one of the stages of life, the way childhood or marriage were for others. They had their own culture, their own rules. The first of these was to take every opportunity to rob and terrorize those who were not members of their criminal community. Finding yourself in a cell or barracks dominated by them was bad. They would play cards with their neighbors' belongings as stakes. Any objection you might make to finding you'd lost your coat in a bet made by someone else was likely to be answered in a way that left you pissing blood.

"But why is it called 'the sauna'?" I asked.

"Long story. The men there—they don't work. It's a kind of protest. Or you'd call it a strike, maybe."

"A strike?" I had never heard of such a thing on Solovetsky. It sounded as farfetched as a sauna itself. "But they'd never allow it! Any *zeks* who announced a strike would be dragged to Sekirnaya immediately. That's if they weren't shot on the spot."

"They didn't announce it. Not exactly. There are parties in Moscow who wouldn't like to hear they'd been rounded up. The way I understand it, the ideological line is that urki are 'socially close.' Stealing, murdering – just misdirected class warfare, if you aren't part of the bourgeoisie. Our gangsters are only an eyelash away from being heroes of the working class. They can get away with a lot, if they only come up with a story that doesn't make it look like they're going against the state. You'll see."

As he stood, Petrovich dusted the crumbs he'd allowed to fall into his lap up into one palm and rolled them up, popping the resulting marble into his mouth "Come on," he said around the bread.

The building was just inside the kremlin gate, one of two against the northern wall. Around one side, a sunken stairway led down to a door. Snow lay on the steps in undisturbed piles, where it gave Petrovich some trouble.

"These aren't nice men," he remarked as I helped him. "One of the reasons they get away with what they're doing is that they're a hard bunch. While we're here, I do the talking, understand?" He sounded nervous.

The opened door breathed an assault at us, the stale air warm and suffocating. It was like stepping into the bottom of a laundry sack. Undershirts and pants crammed the low-ceilinged place.

Only as your eyes became accustomed to the gloom did you perceive the bodies behind the dirty clothes.

We'd interrupted a palpable boredom. Men lay on cots, propped arms on tables, leaned against walls, or stuck their legs out across the floor. These were the *urki*, thirty-five or forty of them, a whole platoon or more. This was the sauna, then: with every one of them undressed and lounging, they looked ready for an afternoon in the steam room. How could they get away with it during working hours? The room was too crowded for me to take in every corner, but there was no sign of the heaps of clothing the men would have produced if they'd simply disrobed. Somehow they'd gotten rid of them entirely.

I wondered whether their "losing" their things had something to do with the urki's undeclared strike, but the inquiring glance I directed at Petrovich was ignored. Glances slid over us from every direction, none quite willing to offer acknowledgment by resolving itself into a stare. From somewhere a voice said "Oy, Boris," and a bare-chested man rose from his card game by the door.

"I'm looking for Golubov," said Petrovich.

Boris was a lean, hard-looking man. On his chest were tattooed two large, intricately drawn stars, one at the top of each pectoral muscle. "What do you want?" he said in a high, reedy voice.

"Tell him it is Yakov Petrovich, from Odessa."

After a moment of consideration, Boris moved his head minutely, flicking his eyes towards the back of the room. One of his cardplayers headed off in that direction.

Light only entered the basement through a few small windows up at ground level. As my eyes adjusted to the dimness, I began to notice Boris's other tattoos. A devil grinned on his ribs, and I glimpsed spades on the knuckles of both hands. And so, too, for the other men lolling around us: every one of them half dressed, but three-eighths clothed in ink. I'd known already, from my time in Kresty, how the elaborate code of tattoos could indicate an *urka*'s rank, criminal specialty, or even the details of his biography. An inverted cross might signify a housebreaker, a series of interlocked circles could mean their wearer had been betrayed to the police by a woman. I'd never seen the system on such full display, however. In the sauna, no one's markings had to peek out from beneath sleeves and collars. Here, when a man crossed his bare feet in front of him, the bells on them rang.

Oddly enough, the effect of all this was only to intensify the boredom we'd disturbed by entering. The dancing girl whose breasts stared out from a man's thigh: boredom pointed her nipples. The half-human wolf-beast on someone else's neck: its snarl expressed boredom, too. Almost every tattoo was done in the same blue-black ink. Yes: with their white pants and shirts and the scribbling on their skins, the *urki* wore a kind of uniform. They'd dyed themselves with insignia and talismans: stars and crosses, arrows, daggers, dots and dragons, skulls. How was this any different than the medals worn under the tsar by my father's staid and respectable superiors in the civil service? Too profuse and detailed to be taken individually, as a mass these inked symbols, like those molded ones, were monotonous and senseless—the boring marks of boredom.

What was it that bored the men so? And, of course, again: why were none of them dressed?

There was little time to consider. The cardplayer had returned, catching Boris's eye.

"Where's Golubov?" said Petrovich.

Ignoring him, the man gave Boris a gesture with his chin. Without another word, Boris stepped over and struck Petrovich in the jaw. The old man fell like a dropped sack, and Boris fell on him, continuing to punch. I stepped forward—cried out, I think. There was time to see blood in Petrovich's face. Then I was slammed down. A dirty cement floor slapped the air from my lungs. My arms were gripped. A knee ground itself into my back.

"That'll do. He didn't say kill him," said a voice. "Bring that one, too."

The knee was removed and I was pulled roughly to my feet. Petrovich, insensible, had to be carried. I was frog-marched.

They pushed us to the floor at the feet of a man sitting on a stool. His bare legs were covered in ink like all the others, a pair of crucifixes wrinkled by the skin on his knees. One elbow rested on a small table that also supported a bottle of vodka and a glass. And then, his face—

"So, it is him," he said.

Instead of seeing his face, you read it: INDIAN. The blue

letters of the tattoo blocked their way over the cheeks, three to a side. They were like a cloud, a haze. Somewhere behind them were wizened features, hooded eyes.

"Yakov Petrovich, fuck. You know I'm always glad to see you, but do you really think coming here was a good idea? The boys don't like it when you let in the cold air. Shrinks their pricks. I can tell them we are old friends, but . . ."

That got a round of nasty laughter. The man in the chair—he had to be the Golubov that Petrovich had asked for—not smiling at his own joke, waited for the chuckling to stop. For all the world he looked like a monarch attended by courtiers in the privacy of the royal chambers. A glance at Petrovich showed me he still wasn't supporting himself. His eyelids fluttered, and his head hung limp on his neck. Blood ran from his nose and a cut on his cheek.

"If you really don't mean for him to—to be killed, you should be careful." The laughter stopped abruptly. My voice had come out louder than I'd meant, more shrill. But somehow it felt less dangerous to speak up than to wait and see where this went. "He's an old man. He can't take anymore than what you've given him already."

The seated man turned the letters on his face towards me. "Who says I don't want to kill him?" From behind, someone cuffed me. Golubov addressed the room. "This fuck wants to come into our place and tell me what I want and don't want. What do you think of that?"

"Yakov Petrovich," I said desperately, "he has friends. People you wouldn't want to have as your enemies. Just let me take him to the hospital and we won't bother you any more. We made a mistake coming here."

"Fuck your mother, I'll say you made a fucking mistake."

"We weren't trying to cause you any trouble. Our case doesn't involve you. Petrovich only—"

He cut me off. "Your case involves your mother's cunt-hairs. But this is fucking interesting. 'Your case.' You're telling me this old prick has gotten himself set up as a detective here, too?"

"Yes," I said. "Yes, he told me you knew each other in Odessa. We only wanted to ask a few questions. A man was killed—"

"The cunting fuck. Should have known he'd find a way to

keep sticking his prick where it didn't belong. The great inspector!"

"He never thought you had anything to do with it. It was a man named Gennady Antonov. Listen, let me take him—"

"Shut your fucking mouth." He swore at me with a voice grown small, almost prim, with authority. I stopped talking.

Above the tattoo, the man's brown hair was thin and graying. He sat back in his chair, taking a sip of vodka. When he spoke again he was once more addressing his men, not me. "Inspector Yakov Petrovich, from Odessa. Yids, you know, they're thick on the ground in Odessa. Not the Inspector, he's all right that way. But in Odessa, the yids are organized, ganged-up like you would not believe. These are none of your egg-sucking peasant Jews who pull the plow themselves because the horse has the shits. No, these ones are smart like you and me. At least like me. They have guns, women. They wear fur coats, they like diamonds, they like vodka. And they deal with their own kind, like they always do. This is my home town. Disgusting. Sometimes it gets so that a real Russian cannot make a living with honest thieving.

"One yid is Red Shloem. This is fifteen years ago, during one of those not-so-good times, understand? Back then I had a little gang that worked the port warehouses. This is mostly good work. Easy. You find the right guard, who will consent to being knocked out in return for a share of the profits, and your only other worry is hiring boys who can carry heavy boxes without dropping them.

"Well, this changes when Red shows up. First he kills two guards who won't work with him. Both Russians, by the way, so who can blame them for not wanting to help the kike? Okay, after that everyone is more on edge. It's much harder to find a guard willing to lie down for you, because he's not sure he'll be getting back up again. This would be aggravating on its own, but it gets worse. Somehow, after doing this stupid thing, this Red Shloem is the only one able to do business in all of Odessa. Somehow he has an inside line. You have heard about a promising shipment that you might lift? Oh, too bad, Shloem's gang got it two days ago. Naturally he is drinking champagne in all the places Jews drink and driving around in a new Kraut car all day with two whores who don't mind a circumcised prick, maybe they are Jewesses as well, I don't know. You can tell this is a fucking mess.

"So then, what? Shloem has an inside line? That's okay, I have my own lines that are not so bad. I hear about a shipment of fancy women's things due to sit on the dock for a few days. Underthings, you know? To cover up their cunts. You laugh, but these things are easy to sell if you know the right places in the city, and light to carry. Plus, wherever you go, whores like them, so the boys will take payment in kind because they know they can exchange two dozen pairs for about three good fucks. Depends on the going rate. Anyway, the important thing is, the way I get this information, I am sure Shloem will have gotten it, too. We know some of the same people. I am a bit disgusted by this, because he's as greasy and offensive as any Jew, and I like to think better of my circle of acquaintance, but it's true."

Sweat crawled down the collar of my shirt, but I dared not move. The room's boredom had converted to hostile interest with Boris's first blow to Petrovich. By now I felt that the men's tattoos had become a hundred violent eyes on their skin. Still Petrovich hadn't stirred. Even if he had, there would have been no chance of making a break for it.

"I have not been doing much business, and a job would be nice. But what would be nicer would be to see Shloem crawl back up his mother's cunt and disappear. So I think I will send a note to someone on the police force. Inspector Petrovich here, he's known. Competent man, people say. They say he knows how to take a hint. Also they say he's a bit of a dick-head, likes being a policeman very much and thinks that it makes his balls enormous, but in the end I decide, okay. I get a message to him, to let him know about this shipment I know about.

"Easy, right? I thought so, too. When Red Shloem finally gets around to lifting these underpants, the cops, led by the heroic inspector, let him and his gang break into the warehouse. Then they surround it and tell him to come out with his hands up."

He stopped, took a drink. "It goes even better than I hoped, because Shloem decides not to put up his hands and instead to shoot his way out with his little revolver. Lo and behold, he gets shot in the prick by a policeman who actually knows how to handle a rifle, and then they put one in his head for good measure.

"Okay, then. Everybody should be happy, wouldn't you say? I am certainly happy. So what do I do? I go to see the inspector. I figure we're friends now. I want to explain how I helped him, talk with him about what he might do for me in return, as a friend. The inspector has an office that you have to walk down a dozen halls to get to, then you give your name to a cop sitting on his cunny behind a desk. Okay, I give my name. They know me at the station, know who I am. I wait."

Golubov steepled his much-inked hands in front of him and sighed. It was an asymmetrical gesture: the left ring-finger had been cut off at the second knuckle. "Who do you think comes out to greet me? Is it your fucking inspector? No, not likely. Two overgrown cocksuckers in uniforms made for elephants appear and throw me in a cell. The fucker has me put in a cell for questioning about four other jobs, two of which I had nothing to do with. And he doesn't even appear himself to do the questioning, he has some other son of a bitch do it. Can you believe he would squeeze my balls that way? After I did him such a favor?"

There'd been more laughter while Golubov told his story, but Boris had held his face still as a mask. He'd taken up a place near Golubov, and now watched me with a look of deadpan aggression. I was trying to think of what to do next when a voice interrupted.

"Doing you—a favor now." It was Petrovich, breaking off in the middle of his sentence to shake his head and catch his breath. His gaze seemed a few degrees off from where it ought to be, and an effort to wipe the blood from his cheek had only smeared it. But at least he'd pulled himself most of the way upright.

Golubov concluded without acknowledging him. "Of course I'm telling this fucking story to show you can never count on a cop. And maybe to show you've got to squeeze his balls back, and fucking harder, till they pop, when you have the chance." At last he turned to the old man. "So why should I trust any fucking favor you offer to do me now? Why not have Boris give you another kicking?"

"We should talk in private," said Petrovich.

"You want me to give you the kicking my fucking self?"

"Golubov," Petrovich muttered, as though to himself. "Always with you gangsters, it's take out our schmeckels and compare before we're allowed to get down to business."

"What? What? This yid talk is supposed to remind me of the

good old days, maybe? What fucking business do you think I have with you?"

"—'S your schmeckel," said Petrovich, still in his own world. "Who am I to tell you not to take it out? Only, no need to rattle my teeth. Loose enough already."

"What do you want, you old fuck?"

Somewhere behind my anxiety, I was amazed that the old man could keep his brashness up, even after being knocked out. In a way I admired it. But Boris only seemed to be waiting for a hair to vibrate the wrong way. "Yakov Petrovich," I hissed.

The old man shook himself. "All right. Yes. What I want is only a few answers to a few questions. If you know anything that helps, it would be good for you. Earn you a good opinion in certain quarters." He gestured vaguely around the room. "Good opinion for the lot of you."

"I need your good opinion like I need a cunt with ears."

"Not mine. Infosec's. That you need a lot. Who do you think I'm working for? Information and Investigation. You know something that helps them, that would look good. Proves how 'socially close' you are."

"You sound like you are recommending fucking graft to me." He looked at me. "Do you know what fucking graft is?"

"No," I said.

"This is funny," Golubov said without smiling, still talking to me. "Because there are obviously no bigger fucking grafters in this camp than you and this fucking old man. Graft is when someone like you or the inspector here, in between sessions of licking his jailers' balls, helps to run his own prison. You see? The toadying fuckwit works to keep himself in jail. Going out there to work in the forests, that's graft. Nosing around and ferreting out information on behalf of the camp bosses, that is major fucking graft. You want me to answer questions for the Cheka, you want me to graft. Are you telling me I should go out and find some secret policeman's balls to lick?"

Petrovich was dabbing at his bloody face with the sleeve of his coat. "What I'm saying is you need friends. All of you here in your sauna do," he said. He seemed to be growing more lucid rapidly, but the continued dabbing robbed the words of some of the conviction they might have had. "Tell him about the case, Tolya."

"The man who was killed first was named Gennady Antonov," I began tentatively. To my surprise, Golubov didn't cut me off. "And now another, too, Nail Terekhov. Antonov worked at the camp museum, Terekhov in the alabaster workshop."

"That means fuck-all to me."

I tried to keep the tremor out of my voice. "Antonov died yesterday morning, down by the bay. Terekhov they found today, out in the forest."

"Like I said, you can go fuck yourselves. I know fuck-all about any of this."

"Fine," said Petrovich. He'd gotten some of the blood off, though it left his mustache pink. "You've never heard of either of them. Let's come at it another way. What do you know about the quay? What's happening down there that I should know about?"

Golubov sighed. "Go fuck yourself, Petrovich. Really, it's fucking lucky for you the Reds sent you to the camps, isn't it, old man?" For the first time, he sounded a note of something more than urbane brutality. His voice had grown tired. "Couldn't believe it when I heard you'd retired from the force. You'd have never given it up yourself, it would have been like yanking your own balls out. Someone must have had enough and kicked you out, was that it? I heard from someone you were living with a daughter, playing cunting nursemaid to a pack of fucking grandchildren. But now you're here, doing whatever it is this is a part of, and you get one last chance to act like Chief Fuck again. Is it doing it for you? Does it put a little blood back into your dried-up old prick? That's even worse than graft, really. You want me to call you 'Inspector'? Now? You're an informant. Even the grafters out there, your fucking 'politicals,' call an informant a slug. And I know you. You don't even do it for whatever you get from it. You do it because you like it."

There was silence for what felt like a long time. Petrovich didn't move, but what Golubov said had affected him. I could see his mustache flutter each time he inhaled—he was breathing heavily. With every second that went by, I felt the danger rising like mercury. Around us, the diamonds and lines and circles, the devils and naked ladies waited. Shoulders and fists knotted in the human wall. I tried to read Golubov's expression to see what he would do, but with the tattoo I couldn't.

At last the *urka* boss opened his mouth. "Get them the fuck out of here. I don't want to look at this son of a whore for another minute."

Outside, cold air rinsed the odor of unwashed bodies from my nostrils. The place had reeked like a zoo. My relief at having escaped with our lives mingled with gratitude at returning to the world of more-or-less human smells.

"Are you all right?" I said to Petrovich.

"Give me my cane."

He'd dropped it during the attack, of course. Spotting it on the floor as we walked out, I'd calculated rapidly that picking it up was worth the risk of drawing the anger of the *urki* hustling us out. We'd need it: Petrovich had been able to stand up on his own, but his arm had to be slung over my shoulder just to reach the door.

"We should go to the hospital," I said.

"Not necessary. Just need to sit down. Take me back to the cell." We went a little way, Petrovich laboring and leaning hard on my shoulder, me taking short steps to keep pace with him.

After a minute he stopped. "Thought Golubov would be willing to talk," he said breathlessly. He was aiming at the tone of instruction I'd grown used to, but I could hear the strain in his voice. "Didn't think he'd do that. Should have tried to get him alone. Might have gotten more out of him. He had to act hard in front of his men, but you see he knows he needs Infosec."

"Are you sure? That wasn't what it looked like to me."

He waved for me to take him over to the wall of a nearby building. When I did, he propped himself against it with one arm. "You saw how they've managed the strike? Got rid of their clothes. What they did was throw them into the stove, one pair of trousers after another. Fed Camp Administration a line about how it was all lost in the laundry, and they can't go out and work naked in the snow, can they? Well, fine—but try a stunt like that without friends in Administration and see how long it is before you're out in the wind with your fingers and toes turning black."

I took the point, but it still didn't make much sense. "You said before they were socially close. You mean to tell me they can get away with something like this, as long as they don't let it look like they're defying Administration?"

Petrovich nodded. "But they've got to keep it plausible,

and they've got to hope no one's patience runs out. And by now they've been at it four or five weeks, ever since it got cold. They're pushing their luck. When the bosses send new clothes, they just get rid of those, too. Someone's sure to resent that sooner or later. Means Golubov's going to need some help if he's going to make it last much longer. I thought being owed a favor by Infosec might tempt him."

Four or five weeks without a visit to the bathhouse would explain the smell. Even in Quarantine we'd been taken to bathe every ten days or so. Better to stink than work, maybe, but the *urki*'s plan still seemed crazed.

Petrovich could see my incredulity. "Give me some snow," he said. He rubbed what I handed him against his cheek and lips to get some of the blood off, then held what remained up to his eye. "It sounds odd to you, but I promise, this is what they've been babbling about every day back in KrimKab. I've had to hear about it all month. They're fretting over the 'effect on prisoner morale,' the 'very real possibility of violence.' They worry about the situation 'getting out of hand.' Whose hands do they think it's in now, I wonder?"

He was still slurring some words, but I couldn't tell whether that was from concussion or only damage to his mouth. I hoped it was the latter. It wouldn't do our investigation any good if he had to be put to bed for a day.

He continued, "Of course there really could be violence. Golubov's men wouldn't be the only casualties, either. Holed up in that cellar, their position is good, and none of them are scared to fight. Guards could flush them out, of course, but it would be bloody, and not just for the *urki*. They'll be armed, that's certain. Knives, axe handles: they've got that much down there, at least. Then you'd have to explain to Moscow why you got your men killed massacring a group you ought to have been practicing social closeness with."

He dropped the snow from his eye. That left ice crystals and blood in his mustache, but he didn't deign to notice: what I was watching was the laborious reconstruction of his dignity, brick by brick. "S'not an outcome anyone in Administration wants. And Golubov doesn't either. But he's a cagey one. Wish I knew his endgame."

The sweat that had trickled down my neck and soaked my shirt was beginning to chill. "Has he always had the tattoo?" I asked.

"The one on his face? No, no, only after they locked him up. They use a needle or a piece of razor. Make the ink from soot and soap. Some things, even an *urka* only does when he's facing a long stint. 'Indian,' ha. People say he scalps his enemies, but that's all made up. Prison's been good for his reputation."

Maybe Golubov's not the only one, I thought. Petrovich had dignity to rebuild, here on Solovetsky. It had never occurred to me to wonder whether that would have been the case back in Odessa as well. So far he had conducted our investigation with such energy and authority that he'd struck me as inexorable — he was a rule of arithmetic or logic, not to be denied. But had it ever been more than a part he needed to enact? Did it have any connection to the person he'd be outside? Golubov had said he'd been living with his daughter. An old man huddled by a fire, wiping the noses of grandchildren.

Petrovich heaved himself away from the wall and we got going again, this time with him holding on to my shoulder with both hands. He muttered, half to me and half to himself as we went.

"Said he didn't know the name, didn't I? Got that much out of him, at least. And maybe we find out later he lied..." I turned and looked at him as we negotiated a raised spot in the path. "Only for now, it doesn't get us any further than we were before. Shot in the dark. Came up with nothing."

The blood had begun to run from his nostrils again. I could see his mustache was turning pink, but I said nothing.

14

Since his shot in the dark had turned up nothing, Petrovich said we needed to make progress on the Chekist's list.

After giving his face a more thorough wash back at the cell, he'd sent me downstairs to make him a cup of tea, then sat on his pallet drinking it and looking out the window for a long time. While he ruminated, an impressive shade of purple-red spread over his wounded cheek, the bruise swelling until it nearly forced his eye shut. When he finally put his cup down on the sill and stood, however, he seemed steadier. Evidently he'd been right about not needing a doctor. I still felt concerned about him, but the old man was tough.

The next name on the list belonged to one Zuyev, a former military engineer who worked in the tiny office of canal management, north of Nikolski. We found him in a room whose walls were covered with maps drawn on flimsy paper. Apart from that difference of setting, the interview proved nearly identical to Nail Terekhov's. Like Terekhov, Zuyev had been an officer in the White Army. Like Terekhov, he swore he could tell us nothing. He didn't seem to have heard about Terekhov's fate, and true to the Chekist's instructions, we didn't ask him about it. I hoped he wouldn't be the next to turn up dead.

By the time we left him, the five o'clock whistle had already shrieked. *Zeks* had begun to trail back from work sites, and the setting sun was dragging northern twilight across the island, early and heavy. Atop their poles, electric lamps flickered on.

I'd thought he might want to return to the cell for more rest, but Petrovich was intent on keeping the appointment he'd made that morning with Stepnova, Veronika Fitneva's floor mistress.

I hadn't liked Stepnova, and the feeling had grown to full-blown resentment now that I'd laid eyes on Veronika and heard her voice. For all the queasy, voyeuristic excitement elicited by her becoming a focus of our investigation, I also felt she needed a protector. "Do you really think Fitneva was involved?" I asked. "Even after that business with Terekhov?"

"She knows something she thought was worth lying about," he said. "Maybe finding it out will convince the Chekist there's more to this than he thinks. And there's the suitor, too, the one who beat her up. To me, that still seems promising. At least it will show we're doing something."

Stepnova had asked Petrovich to brief her privately, while Veronika was engaged with Spagovsky, the man Petrovich had called her "suitor." The timing was tricky. The guards at the gate to the women's enclosure let us wait in their sentry box while one of them went up to the dormitory to let Stepnova know we'd arrived. Word came back that we should wait: Fitneva hadn't returned from the fishery yet, but she would soon, and it wouldn't do if she found us inside. Once Spagovsky had whisked her away, Stepnova would send word. Then we could come up.

With four in the box, our shoulders were pushed up around each other's ears. The stamps on our permit had been so imposing, however, that neither guard dared make Petrovich or even me stand out in the wind. That may have had something to do with his face as well; they seemed impressed by the damage. Soon the stream of women returning from work grew steady enough that they had to stay down at the gate to deal with them all, and the old man and I had the place to ourselves, with room to unfold.

"All right, I understand the interest in Fitneva," I said. "But what more are you hoping this Stepnova can tell you? She's no more than a madam."

"You don't think madams have useful information? You do have a lot to learn. At the very least she'll be able to tell us something about the girl's circumstances. Probably has a better idea of her movements than anyone, too. Would be good to figure out how she and Antonov arranged their meetings. Anything that puts pressure on Fitneva is progress."

We were calling her Fitneva, but already I thought of her as nothing but Veronika. Every time a group of women came up the path past the sentry box, I hunched down in my coat and turned my face to the wall, worried she might be among them. If someone had asked, I'd have explained it was because Stepnova had warned us not to be spotted. But it wasn't that, not really.

She'd told me not to leer. What is a leer, after all? A sidewise glance, a desire that expresses itself by trying to hide its interest. Inevitable, perhaps, to leer at a person first glimpsed through the window of the Cheka's file on her. Yes, surveillance is the leer of the state: a prurient interest that simultaneously declares and hides itself.

Perhaps it was only more leering, and not, as I thought, desire to prove my usefulness, that made me suggest what I did.

"What if I followed her?"

"What?" said Petrovich.

"When Spagovsky comes. While you talk to Stepnova, I could tail them, find out where he takes her. Maybe I'd be able to overhear something. If they really are mixed up with Antonov's death, she would at least tell him about our visit, wouldn't she?"

Petrovich rubbed his mustache with the knuckle. "Putting a tail on someone isn't so easy," he said. "Especially not alone. It's better with a team, in a crowd."

"We'd learn at least as much as you will taking tea with Stepnova."

"You're getting bolder, eh? You stared down a roomful of criminals this afternoon and now you think a paper from Infosec will protect you from anything. No great risk to have a man find you trailing along after him like a bad smell. But what about my face? That paper of ours didn't protect me then."

I hadn't considered that Spagovsky might resort to violence if he noticed me. But it was true: I did feel bold. Tailing him could hardly be more dangerous than marching into the sauna had been that afternoon.

"I'm not proposing to confront them," I said.

"No, and you shouldn't. I want to know more when we question this Spagovsky," he said. He eyed me, however, eyes glinting in the dark. "In there with Stepnova, there's nothing for you to do, of course, only get in the way. I won't need you . . . All right. Yes, it might work. We'll do it."

Only now that he'd agreed did I begin to feel concerned. He seemed well enough, but tailing the others would mean leaving the old man to negotiate stairs and snowy paths on his own. "You'll be all right?"

"Don't be patronizing. It's not the first beating I've taken. Now be quiet and listen. There's more to shadowing a subject than you've read in your silly Pinkertons. It's not just walking along with a quiet step. I couldn't teach you all you ought to know in a year, much less ten minutes."

The old man's advice amounted to behaving always as though you were on the way to some destination of your own, and giving the subject of your pursuit plenty of space. In fact, this was precisely what I had gleaned from reading about Pinkerton's tracking of the devious Hairy-Man William through a German cathedral cloister and market-fair stalls in "Tiger of the Hamburg Dom," but I thought it better not to mention it. "I'll be back at Company Ten before you are," he concluded. "And I'll leave your name with them at Nikolski so they know to expect you. We can only hope you won't have trouble getting in."

With his one good eye, he scowled down at the white cap in my hand. "You look like a lit candle in that thing. But it'll be conspicuous if you don't have a hat. Give it here." He pulled off his own and handed it to me. It was a sailor's knit cap, unraveling in places but still better than mine in every respect. "We'll trade. Thank God I won't have to wear yours long."

He jammed it onto his head, rendering himself ridiculous enough that the guards exchanged a glance when they brought their lamp back to the sentry box. The old man only stared straight ahead, frowning and extravagantly bruised beneath the brim.

At last the figure of a tall, thin man appeared at the gate. The guard spent longer than usual examining his credentials, then waved him through. Back at the box, he confirmed that it was Spagovsky.

The old man nodded to me. "Once he's collected Fitneva, Stepnova will send for me. You go back and wait back up the road. You'll see when they come out."

"All right," I whispered.

Some way up the path, the lamplight cast a shadow from the corner of the main administration building. I took cover there and waited. Five minutes, then ten. The pounding of my heart went on and on. I'd just started to think something had gone wrong, when finally they came out.

Night was closing down Solovetsky's horizons as they passed my hiding spot. Back above the kremlin's wall with its squat towers, the cathedrals' burnt spires dwindled and disappeared into the blackening sky. From the trees to the north and east, the buildings to the south, and the wide sea to the west, the limits of vision shrank down to a series of bright hemispheres centered on lampposts. I trailed them along the path that circled the kremlin, fifty paces behind, following their silhouettes from light to dark, light to dark.

Following proved surprisingly easy. The pair was too far away for me to make out their features, but I could identify them as a couple walking together. They curved around to the north side of the kremlin, then took the road that led north among the larger outbuildings. As we emerged from among the buildings and the lampposts began to come at longer intervals, I'd occasionally lose track of them in the dark, but they would always reappear again a little further down the road. Veronika strode in front, with the shape that was Spagovsky never quite catching up. Neither looked back.

After half a mile they turned off the road onto a path that led to the machinists' shop, a low building that had been a smithy under the monks. Many of the more specialized and privileged work groups lived outside the kremlin, nearer the sites where they worked. Evidently that was Spagovsky's arrangement. Snow-covered lumps of machinery were strewn around the yard. A long building with a few windows looked like a barracks to me, but Spagovsky and Veronika headed towards a little cabin at some remove from it.

Stepnova had only said Spagovsky was a machinist. I knew next to nothing about the actual techniques of machining, but you could not help noticing that the parts of Solovki's many mechanisms broke down continually, whether from hard use on the one hand or neglect on the other. With the closest industrial centers days of travel away, it was obvious how crucial the work of manufacturing replacements was to the camp's operation. Men with even minimal experience in the trade could expect to be snapped out of Quarantine the moment their term was up. If this Spagovsky had a cabin of his own, it meant he was a particular expert, someone Solovetsky couldn't do without and therefore had to take special care of—perhaps a die maker or even an engineer. That would be consistent with his having been able to come to an arrangement with Stepnova about Veronika, I reflected.

From a distance, I watched them enter. Soon light appeared under the door. I waited what I thought was five minutes; Petrovich had recommended letting them settle in. Then, skirting the edge of the yard, I crept around to the side of the house and crouched down uncomfortably beneath a windowsill. There I waited, hearing nothing—only my own breathing, the blood pounding in my ears, the noises my boots made every time they shifted. Would I be able to hear them through the wall and the windowpane? Maybe the cabin had more than one room. Had I picked the wrong window?

No—a light spilled out onto the snow, to prove they were inside. And as I had the thought, I heard a man's voice, only a little muffled on the other side of the glass.

"Have some pickled apple."

That was Spagovsky, then. It was hard to tell much about him, just listening to him offer pickled apple. He clipped his words off at their ends, his voice neither low nor high.

"That's what you have to say?" It was Veronika, of course. Every thrilling note I'd heard in her voice that afternoon was still there, but she sounded disturbed, unmoored, almost wild, in a way she would never have allowed herself to be with us. "Have some apple?"

"What should I say? You are babbling at me."

"Nothing." Having seen her so passionately before—it was a passion of seeing, I felt hungry to look at her again—it was thwarting now to be only able to listen. I thought I could picture what exasperation would do to her expression.

Another period of silence. Flurries of snow were falling past the window; I was aware of them coming to rest on my shoulders. I inhaled through my mouth, trying to control the sound of my breath. Something was passing between them inside, but without being able to see it—their bodies, their faces, their attitudes to each other—there was no way to tell what it was.

"You liked that apple before," said Spagovsky.

"Did I? I don't remember."

"You liked it. I got a jar on purpose from the specialist's commissary. Not cheap, I'll tell you."

The cabin's shingles smelled of pine tar, even in the cold. I realized I was staring at a particular point on one shingle, as though my looking hard enough would make the scene inside show through.

"You worry too much," said Spagovsky. "Stop thinking about so many things at once."

Veronika laughed, a little breathlessly, as though it squeezed her in a way she liked. "I realize you only want me to sit down and be quiet, but I think you're right. Do you know, I have always thought that of myself? I can never look at only what's in front of me—I'm always seeing something else as well. When I was a little girl I was always seeing soldiers or foxes in the sums I was assigned. That's why I am a better translator than I am a poet. I'm always thinking about something else, not the page before me. I can't finish the poem I'm working on. Another one emerges out of it before I get done. Sometimes I think it's a problem of concentration, but at other times I think it's because I concentrate too hard. Because I can't relax. You see what I mean, don't you?"

"I don't know what nonsense you're on about," said Spagovsky. "You're lucky your voice is pretty."

This time she didn't laugh. "That's both flattering and not," she said evenly.

My left thigh had begun to cramp, but I didn't dare move into a more comfortable position.

"Tell me about your day," said Veronika.

"Same as every other day here."

"How can you say that? Every day has something about it different than others. Even in our frozen island prison."

"Nothing worth talking about," said Spagovsky.

I heard footsteps cross the room. When Veronika spoke again, she was close to the window. "What did you have to give Alexandra Stepnova so she'd allow you to drag me off this evening?"

Her voice had changed, hardened. She must have been standing just on the other side of the wall, looking out into the dark.

For the first time, Spagovsky raised his voice. "All you do is mock. Don't you see how things are hard for me?" It was the first sentence of his that had had any emotion in it. One of our good Russian lamenters, Spagovsky. The best of us all have that confidence behind our groans.

There was more silence I couldn't interpret. Once again, my gaze bored fruitlessly into the shingle I'd chosen. "Oh, don't look like that," Veronika finally said. There was the faint sound of glass clinking on the other side of the wall. "Here. Drink some vodka and I'll sit on your knee. That's what you want, isn't it?"

There was the scrape of a chair moving, and more footsteps. Spagovsky said something I didn't catch about the vodka, and they exchanged a few more remarks about pickled apple. Was she sitting on his knee? I preferred not to picture it.

Instead, I wondered: had she told him about our visit earlier in the day? Did he know about Antonov? They were not talking about it now, but what had they discussed while I waited to take my place under the window?

"Did you know a causeway connects the main island and Muksalma?" Veronika was saying. "Brother Kiril was telling me about it today. A pile of stones that snakes over the shallowest part of the channel. There was a dairy on Muksalma; any cows to be added to the herd had to be driven across. And they built it in the 1600s! Imagine the monks dropping one stone after another into the water. I picture them all lined up in a procession, each with his own stone. That's probably not actually how it was. I'm sure the seventeenth century had its own techniques of engineering. But it was like they were building a wall in the sea. That's what it is. The water itself was already a kind of wall against the rest of the world. Then the wall around the kremlin, and then, when they wanted to cross the water to another island, the causeway. Even when they were trying to get somewhere, they built a wall."

She'd wandered back over to the window as she talked. Again

the bottle made noise against the rim of a glass.

I could see her procession of monks: the ropes hanging from their waists a-sway, the heavy stones they carried straightening their elbows. Icons carried before them, incense rising into the gray sky. That was the woman whose file I'd fallen in love with—I'd known she would be capable of that kind of visionary non sequitur.

It hurt to have her lavishing it on someone else. He'd beaten her with an ax handle, sent her to the hospital, and this was her voice when she talked with him. How had she talked with Antonov? How would she talk to me?

Her footsteps moved away.

"Earlier today someone asked me whether I loved you," she said. "I told him I might."

Spagovsky smacked his lips and exhaled. The glass clacked down on a surface that sounded like wood. "Quiet with all that, now. Bring another, Veruchka."

"That's all you say, when I tell you something like that?"

"Bring another."

Footsteps, clinking, more footsteps. "There," said Veronika's voice.

"No," said Spagovsky, "you drink it. I've had two now to your none. Have to keep up."

Silence for a moment. "There," said Veronika.

"Just a sip? Take it all quickly, like I do."

"You want me drunk? Even a little kvass makes my head spin."

"Ahhh, give it here. Open your mouth."

There were sounds of movement. Veronika laughed another of her stifled laughs. "Borya." Then a thump, and the scuffling of feet moving on the floor. Something coppery and afraid came through in her raised voice. "Borya, no, I don't—" She made a choking sound, and began to cough.

Spagovsky chuckled, perhaps a little nervously. "There, you see? It's good for you. You women don't know how to drink."

She coughed once or twice more, but didn't say anything. I heard only his heavy tread and the clink of the bottle, hard and careless, against the rim of the glass.

"You see?" he said. "You like it, don't you?"

Here was another moment I could not picture. He was near the bottle—was it sitting on a table? Where was she? Her silence was charged.

"I am ready to go back," she said in a low voice.

He didn't say anything for a long time. At last he came out with: "It's not time yet."

"I am tired of being here. I'm ready to go back to the women's dormitory."

"You'll see what happens," he said sullenly.

"I know what will happen," she said. Suddenly her voice was loud. It sounded again like the voice that had spoken to Petrovich and me that afternoon. "Get on with it."

More snow joined what was already on my shoulders. Then there was a sharp sound, and the wall I was leaning against shuddered as something fell to the floor. Veronika cried out, first in pain, then yelling, "Boris—"

Before she could say anything else, I heard him hit her twice more. The blows were somewhere between a slap and a thud.

In memory, we only experience the past layer by layer, never swallowed in one dense bolus as we felt it at the time. I remember that I counted the times he hit her. Yes, counted them, all nine. And then I remember that, while I counted, the sound of struck flesh was reminding me of my mother pulling fish from a pail and slapping them on the kitchen table to kill them. That is another layer.

And then, of course, I did not know what to do. I thought I loved her. At least I loved her file. I wanted to help her. But also—also she had embarrassed me that afternoon, and I was lurking beneath her window. I wanted to see her, I wanted to hide, I wanted to hide my seeing her.

How many more times did he hit her while I crouched there counting, simply because I was ashamed?

I stood up, framing myself in the window, and rapped on the glass.

15

Staring into the room dazzled my eyes. A shape on the floor, supporting itself with one arm, was Veronika. From where I stood at the window, a metal bed frame and mattress blocked my view of her shoulders and face. The man was another shape, a hostile one. He lowered his fist and looked around. "What's that?" he said in a loud voice, taking a step towards the window. "Who is it?"

It was my first view of Spagovsky as more than a figure moving over the dark road. Out of his coat he was splinter-thin. He looked thirty, though with a grizzled and angular face. The light cast by a lamp hanging overhead on a rafter made his eyes into pits.

"God damn it," he said, muffled by the glass. He'd come the rest of the way to the window and began fumbling with the latch. I hadn't thought beyond getting him to stop.

"Wait," I said, leaving the square of light.

By the time I'd come around the corner of the house, he was waiting for me in front of the open door, a large wrench in hand. "What is this? What are you doing fucking sneaking around my cabin in the dead of night?"

This was the voice I'd been listening to silently only half a minute ago. Now I heard my own voice answering it. "Listen," I said. "Leave the lady alone." I sounded thin and distant.

"Fuck you. Who are you?"

Who indeed? *Leave the lady alone* was quite clearly a phrase from a detective story. Properly delivered, it might have had the characteristic Pinkertonian flavor of bravado, in which physical bravery guarantees a cause's rightness. But the plaintive noises I'd produced did not match the voice that sounded in my head when the King of Detectives spoke on the page. What should a nonfictional detective sound like, then? Petrovich's cantankerous, impatient authority depended on his age. That, I'd never manage. What model did that leave me?

Perhaps at the time I was only half aware of the answer, but in retrospect it is obvious. Wasn't I acting as Infosec's agent? Hadn't Petrovich said our authorization from him would protect me from any threats of violence? Notwithstanding the persistent ache in my chest from where he'd hit me two days ago, only a version of the Chekist's curt sarcasm gave me anything to say.

"I work for Infosec. Veronika Fitneva is needed. I'd rather she be able to talk when I bring her in."

"Infosec? What —?"

"That's right." My voice still shook. I hoped he didn't notice. "Is this going to be a problem, Prisoner Spagovsky?"

Hearing his own name brought him up short. "I—listen, what's all this about? Why were you outside my window?"

"I've told you already. I need Fitneva. What we want her for is our business, not yours." I jammed my fists into the pockets of my coat and took two steps towards him, feeling grateful to Petrovich for relieving me of my hat, which no one out on Infosec business after dark could ever have worn. "If you're considering cracking my head with that wrench, I'd advise against it. They will wonder what happened to me, and then who knows what will happen to you?"

"What? No, no, I—" He trailed off as I pushed past him and stepped to the doorsill. That was good. I had the investigation authorization in my pocket, but I didn't want to have to show it.

"Prisoner Fitneva," I said.

She'd risen, now leaning on the table in the middle of the room. On it were the glass and bottle of vodka I'd been hearing, along with the jar of pickled apple, a half loaf of black bread, a knife, and a small piece of hard sausage. Her face was already starting to swell—an impastoed canvas, as though he'd added something to her with every blow of his fist.

"Prisoner Fitneva. Come with me."

It took her a moment to look up, then another to recognize me. She shook her head. "You? Why would I want to go with you?"

"Your presence is needed," I said.

She stared for what felt like a long time. It was what I had come all this way for, to gaze into her face again. Even so, hunger intervened, the way it did at the worst moments on Solovki. I felt the sausage end on the table pulling at my eyes.

Finally, she shrugged and picked her coat up from where it hung on a chair. Spagovsky stood by the door as we went out, but didn't block our way. "Veruchka," he said as she passed him without looking. "What is this? What do they want with you?"

"How do I know, Boris?" she said. "Go back inside."

We left the buildings around the old smithy and followed the narrow path that led back to the road, her walking ahead with quick, stiff steps. We'd gone a short way when, without any warning, she fell forward into the snow on her hands and knees. She shook her head when I tried to help her up.

"Are you all right?" I said.

Her voice sounded thick, as though she held something under her tongue. "No."

I looked back at the lights of the buildings. When I turned back to her, Veronika had gotten to her feet, but she was bent, holding her side.

"Let me help you."

She looked at the arm I held out to her, then took it slowly. We went a few steps. "I'm only dizzy. It will pass soon."

After a moment I said: "You did know Gennady Antonov, didn't you?"

"That was obvious, was it?"

"I knew him as well. So did Yakov Petrovich. They were cellmates. We aren't quite as bad as you think."

We went a little further, with her holding onto my elbow with both hands. "How did he die?" she asked.

Feeling her fingers gathered in the fabric of my sleeve, I had to remind myself she was a suspect. Petrovich had warned me in the museum the other day not to share information about the body too freely. "We are still trying to find that out."

"I want to know if he suffered," she said quickly.

I shook my head. "No. Petrovich doesn't think so." I looked at her face. Even in the dark her contusions were obvious. I went on, despite my better judgment. "His neck was broken. It would have been quick."

"Oh." After another minute of limping she stopped, taking her hands away from my arm. She straightened her coat, then looked at me. She was still hurting, I could tell. But suspicion has dignity, and makes certain demands. "So," she said. "You told Boris Stepanovich you were bringing me in."

"I only said that to stop him hitting you."

"I see. A kind of figure of speech." She reached down slowly to brush snow from the front of her pants. The thick quality was still in her voice. She worked at pronouncing the words. "In that case the question is, what are you doing here?"

She couldn't have seen me flush in the dark, but I felt embarrassment bloom in my cheeks, caught once again in the leer of surveillance. My arm still seemed to tingle where she'd touched it. "We thought there might have been something you hadn't told us this afternoon."

Even the low laugh she let out made her wince. "So your boss sent you to listen under Boris's window. I see. Well, whether or not I believe you, I suppose I have to be grateful for what you did, but you'll understand if I beg off another battery of questions. Being spied on doesn't make me feel forthcoming."

"But why did you lie to us this afternoon?"

"Why should I tell you the truth? My relationships are my own business. As you see, there are reasons for me not to want my acquaintance with Gennady Mikhailovich to be too widely discussed. And I don't much like the idea of helping the Cheka either."

The going grew easier when we reached the main road and left the path. A wilderness of stumps attested to logging in the area around us. At a distance the road curved around the wall of pines that still stood between us and the kremlin. I could see its towers above them, vague outlines through the snow and the dark.

"I'm from Saint Petersburg, too," I said.

"What?"

"I saw your file. My family lives a few blocks from Liteyny Bridge." She didn't say anything, and I heard myself stumble on. "I—I learned to swim there, in the Neva, by the bridge. I grew up there."

Who knows why I said such a thing? I had been a good swimmer as a boy. Perhaps I was trying to brag.

She shook her head. It was restrained, as though the movement made her sick. "What was it your friend said your name was?"

"Anatoly. Anatoly Bogomolov."

"Anatoly Bogomolov, something's clicking in my jaw." She reached up and massaged beneath her ear. "I can feel it when I talk. It hurts."

"I can take you to the infirmary."

"No. If I am not at the fishery tomorrow they'll begin looking for someone else. I only need to sleep."

"All right."

She had mapped the afternoon's struggle into a new space, transformed it while preserving its properties. In the game of information we were playing, she won, or thought she won, by withholding, whatever the means. What did it matter whether it was a flat refusal or a plea not to hurt her jaw anymore? My move had been to try being her friend, and she'd read me, read my desire to protect her and be thought well of, then played her injury and powerlessness like a card.

Well, and so? Maybe it should have been a winning card. In another version of his life, Tolya is a nice boy, one who pities and accommodates an injured woman, even when she uses her injury to thwart him. He's not angry at her, he doesn't wish to prove to her how wrong she is about his earlier leering. He is not driven by his need to find a killer and secure himself a place in Company Ten, nor by his desire for her, nor by jealousy of a relationship he thinks she may have had with his dead friend Gennady Antonov. Nothing drives him to make her speak to him with a possibly dislocated jaw.

This version of Tolya, however—he dies much earlier than

the protagonist of our story. Starves, perhaps, or coughs his life out in the following year's typhus epidemic, or becomes someone's victim among the bunks or the trees.

Even in this version, I was silent for the time it took to bring us around the pines. I had been listening to Petrovich's interrogations now for two days, long enough to be able to come up with a list of plausible questions. As the kremlin wall came into view, I put out a hand to stop her.

"What?" She didn't pull away. There was something in her voice I couldn't read.

"You're the second person today to tell me they don't want to go to the hospital."

"Who was the first?"

"Yakov Petrovich. Beatings are going around."

"The old man? I'd've thought the two of you would be protected. Who'd have beaten him up?"

"Things aren't as easy for us as you think."

She frowned. "Well, I'm sorry for him."

"Where were you two nights ago?"

"You think I killed Gennady Mikhailovich?"

"I don't think anything. Others might. It looks suspicious if you won't answer any of our questions."

Sighing, she looked at the kremlin's lights, then past the collection of buildings on the quay and out at the darkness of the freezing sea. "All right. I was in my dormitory. Any of the women there will tell you. That's where I always am in the evenings, unless Stepnova sends me out with Boris." She shrugged and I let her go. "That's what you wanted to know?"

"What about Spagovsky? Where was he?"

"What does that have to do with anything?"

"Petrovich will want to know."

"Boris didn't know anything about me and Gennady Mikhailovich. There's no reason for you to suspect him."

"Did you tell him we came to ask you questions earlier today?"

She pursed her lips. "No."

I'd steeled myself to interrogate her as roughly as necessary, but a certain warm reluctance still rose as I approached the question. Snow-shagged branches encroached on the other side of the road. When I looked back, she was holding her hand to her bruised face, absently.

"Spagovsky wouldn't have liked your relationship with Antonov."

"He's jealous."

"Did he—was there something for him to be jealous about?"

She looked at me incredulously. "'Something to be jealous about'? Tell me, Anatoly Bogomolov: how old are you?"

"I—I'm twenty."

"Twenty! Well, all right. But even at twenty I don't think I'd have needed to mince words like that."

I'd held the upper hand in questioning for a moment, but any advantage I had crumbled under her derision. "You know what I mean," I said weakly.

"Do you mean were we lovers?"

"Yes."

"I don't know," she said. "What is a lover, here on Solovki? He never brought me flowers."

"But you . . . spent time together."

"Yes."

If I could have analyzed it, I suppose my inner tumult would have proved to be nothing complex: it was jealousy again, a minor, predictable convulsion of the heart and lungs, exacerbated by her identifying the difference in our ages. It only felt incomprehensible. The sole mystery is why it should have bothered me in particular to have her relationship with Antonov confirmed. It was already clear what kind of arrangement she had with Spagovsky.

My throat felt dry. "Do you know where Spagovsky was when Antonov was killed?" I said.

"No. But I've told you, he didn't know anything about it. He couldn't have."

"Why not?"

She waved a hand in the air. "You see what he's like. If he'd found out, my face would have been first to hear." Then she shivered and pulled her coat more tightly around her shoulders. "Are you going to ask him—tell him—about it?"

Petrovich had, in fact, mentioned wanting to confront Spagovsky. It was easy to see what would happen to her if he did. "What about Nail Terekhov," I said instead of answering. "Do you recognize that name?"

It was a question I'd wanted to be sure to ask before this period of forthcomingness ended. Petrovich's warnings notwithstanding, it couldn't hurt to mention the second murder to her. The Chekist had said he didn't want us to interfere, but he wouldn't be interrogating Veronika unless she proved to know something significant. If she did, it would be good to have asked. If she didn't, no harm done.

She shook her head. "No."

"Another dead prisoner," I said, watching her. "He was once an officer in the White Army. Someone killed him this morning—while we talked to you, perhaps. It was done the same way as Antonov."

"Awful, but the name means nothing to me," she said. "It still strikes me as most likely that your bosses murdered Gennady Mikhailovich. Maybe they murdered this Terekhov as well. Are you going to tell Boris about me?"

She was not willing to be brushed aside. That was all right; I had what I wanted. She'd hardly been able to control her face when we mentioned Antonov that afternoon, but discussing Terekhov seemed to have no effect on her. Either she'd become a better liar, or she was telling the truth.

"Yakov Petrovich may want to talk to him," I said. "To see what he says."

She laughed again, bitter and low, still musical. "Well, you spared me the worst of one beating. Maybe I can't complain if you cause me another." She exhaled hugely. "Are we done? I've answered enough of your questions, haven't I?"

"We can walk," I said.

We walked. She was favoring her side again, but I hadn't quite finished. "When did you last see him?"

"Antonov?"

"Yes."

She shot me a glance, but answered. "It had been some time. Since that note you found—that would have been about two weeks ago, when the package from my mother came. That was unusual. Usually it's easier for him to leave the kremlin than for me to get in."

"Did he seem strange, or worried?"

I heard her sad smile as much as saw it. "He was always a little strange. I don't know whether he seemed worried. I wouldn't say so. He seemed the same." She shook her head. "I don't know anything that will help you."

As it ran along the lake's north shore and approached Nikolski Gate, the road became a bright corridor, hemmed in on either side by the height and length of the wooden buildings. We were the only ones out walking, and the ground showed white under the lamps' electric glare.

Were there further questions I should have been asking? I'd learned things, but they seemed to lead nowhere. Veronika and Spagovsky's having anything to do with Antonov's death did not seem more or less likely than before. Knowing more only traded old ignorance for new.

Looking up at Nikolski Tower, I said: "I . . . overheard what you said about the causeway to Muksalma."

"You were eavesdropping for quite a while."

I ignored her tone. "I see what you mean about it. Building a wall to cross the water."

"That is what interests you?" She sounded surprised.

I couldn't have said why I'd lit on that, of all the things I'd heard her say to Spagovsky. "Antonov told me once that, properly perceived, the faithful were the living stones of the church. He thought the church itself, the building, is only an image of something spiritual." It was embarrassing to be so incapable of explaining. If I'd been imitating the Chekist's restraint, I wasn't any longer. "A living stone in the wall of a church. It's beautiful, but horrible, too. I don't think Antonov understood that. Imagine being alive, stuck like a stone in a wall of bodies."

She didn't say anything until we'd come to the barbed-wire fence surrounding the women's dormitories. Then she said: "Yes. That's part of what I meant." She gestured with her chin, a pale angle on which spread a shadow of bruise. "Here's the gate. Goodbye, Anatoly Bogomolov."

16

Vasily Feodorovich asks, am I still writing?

It is the first he's spoken of it openly in some time. It was four months ago that I first told him I was writing a *detektiv* and refused to let him read it. Lately his eyes have not darted about when I first open the door the way they did. I thought he'd ceased to look. But last night he asked again.

I hedged, said I wasn't sure it was worth finishing. Let him decide whether that means the story is abandoned or I am still at work.

But the truth is I am still writing. Why? After first describing Veronika, I put it down that I would stop, throw the pages I'd produced in the stove. For a week I did stop. But since then I've filed four more chapters with the others in their box, and on the page Veronika and I limp back from Spagovsky's cabin to the Women's Quarters.

Every night, I write. My shift ends at ten. I wash in the factory showers, walk home. In the kitchen I am allowed to use on the first floor, I cook myself something to eat. By then it is eleven-thirty. I descend. I write until three, three-thirty, four. Sometimes later. When I wake up the sun is shining brightly in through my ground-level window, and sweat soaks the bed.

The workers' store at the factory has cheap pads for sale, and these are what I write on. The paper is lined, gray, bound with a coil of wire at the top. Each pad has a thin, pale blue cover. When I complete a chapter, I tear the pages out and put them in the box. When I am done with a pad, only a fur of paper is left within the spiral, and the cover flaps on the empty coil. There are five pads empty now, all saved in the drawer along with the manuscript and my shirts. Soon there will be six.

Even in the din of the factory, my pen's scratching seems always to be in the back of my mind. Filling these pages, tearing them out . . . This story is inside me. I have never felt the desire, the need, to write it before. But it comes over me now, a compulsion.

What does it mean? I once saw a film set during the construction of the Belomor Canal. In it, two Komsomol members, a boy and a girl, left Moscow and traveled to the canal so they could inspire the *zeks* to work hard. They were in love with each other. A strong man with a beard, a criminal who'd killed his own son, was so moved by their example that he stormed through his labor assignment. In the end, he worked so hard he died. Everyone sang a song about him, and finally the Mosfilm logo appeared onscreen.

I was an accountant at Belomor. From a window of the office where I had my desk, I watched the Canal's real workers march down the road to their labor sites. They went to dig, to pour concrete, to dynamite. I saw them, their coats and beards, their prisoners' boots. I could see their faces from the window, almost as clear as the ones I'd see projected before me years later.

I knew how the film would end—with a song, with triumphant death. I know how the real story ends as well. I was there. I saw the food expenses remain constant as the number of prisoners assigned to the work companies increased, increased, increased. They say 12,000 died before the canal was finished.

And the end of this story, the one I cannot stop writing: I know that too. My pen drags me towards it by the hand.

Back at the cell, I told Petrovich what had happened. He listened closely, only interrupting to ask the occasional question. By now his face was lurid, a pool of ugly color behind his mustache. It occurred to me to wonder who would look worse in the end, him or Veronika.

"I know you didn't want me to confront Spagovsky, but I didn't ask questions. All I did was stop him. I didn't give anything away."

"That's fine."

While we talked, I spooned up tepid soup. Arriving after the stoves had been put out, I'd had no chance to cook, but the old man had saved me a portion from the pot he'd made earlier. It tasted watery, the same as the day before.

"They give you any trouble at the gate?" he asked.

"No, no. They said they'd been waiting for me and let me right through."

"That's good. Maybe our friend gave them a talking to after all." He watched me eat. His blue eyes seemed less sharp than usual, filmed over by something. "You did well. You've been doing well. Better than I expected."

"Thank you."

"I was lucky to have you there at the sauna today."

"I'm not sure I did much."

"Better to have someone with you when you're knocked out than no one," he said. Then, after a pause: "I've been teasing you about your Pinkertons."

"I know I have a lot to learn."

"It's not that." He resituated himself on his cot, favoring his back. "Back in Odessa, in the department, we were out on the street all the time. You go everywhere, talk to people. In my day you were expected to cultivate a network of useful types, the sort you could send out to learn something for you. Usually for pay, yes, but you had to know them. Well, the point is I spent time in all sorts of places. The boy who sold me my newspaper—sometimes I'd see him in one of the grog houses I frequented, with a beer before him, following the lines of a magazine with his finger and moving his lips. No more than ten, eleven. After a year I lost track of him. Heard later he'd been picked up with a gang of kids. They'd hit a man they were robbing over the head. Killed the fellow."

His voice was thick. I hadn't heard him so sentimental before. "That is how I know about your Pinkertons. He read them, always. So did all the others on the street with him. And there are more than ever of these street children, *besprizorniki*, these days. They belong to no one, and in the end there's no choice for them but crime."

The remark was out of place—the sort of thing people said all the time outside, but rarely on Solovki. It hung in the air. "You'd think the stories would have been a positive influence," I came out with at last, for lack of anything better to say. "Usually the wrongdoer is punished. The whole point is to see Pinkerton chase down the criminal."

He shook his head vehemently. "No. It's the opposite. They see a detective catch a murderer in the pages of your pulps and they think, 'It isn't me!' The one who reads it gets a chance to enjoy the body, all the gore. Then he gets off scot-free. A made-up person punished, and your own crimes ignored. That is what your street hoodlum sees in a Pinkerton."

"But hoodlums aren't the only ones who read them. I liked them when I was eleven, too, but I hadn't committed any crimes."

"Not even the most innocent cherub is without a crime or two to his name. A policeman knows. Everyone hides something guilty somewhere."

I'd finished my soup, and I put the bowl aside. When I suggested we turn in, the old man leaned over and blew out the candle that burned on the sill.

"You'll learn," said his voice in the darkness before I fell asleep. "You're a fast learner. You're doing well."

That night Petrovich snored like an engine. I suppose something about his injuries brought it on. A swelling of the nasal passages? He would growl and rattle endlessly, then stop and, after a moment, emit an alarming gasp. During the periods of silence that followed, I found myself contemplating Veronika and the difference in our ages. According to her file she was twenty-eight—not a huge difference from twenty, surely? But she seemed so much more experienced, more confident than I. And so on, until the rattling and growling resumed. By the time the steam whistle blew to rouse us, I'd barely managed to snatch an hour of sleep altogether.

At his cabin the next morning, the Chekist was in a sour mood. "What was it you were telling me the other day, Yakov

Petrovich? My method works when I know in advance the result I'm looking for? To me yours seems woefully diffuse and undirected. Without a sense of the political and class forces at work in a situation, you barely know where to begin. A classic liberal fallacy. You believe staring at facts will simply yield up the truth. Not so. You require a proper theory to orient you towards productive avenues of inquiry and labor. It's precisely this that's the proper dialectical relationship between theory and factual knowledge, and precisely for this reason that the masses must be educated in the tenets of dialectical materialism."

Here, reproduced extemporaneously in response to the old man's report of yesterday's activities, was the language of a hundred speeches and newspaper articles: the empty (or inspiring, depending on your perspective) discourse of revolutionary authority. It was hard to know what he meant by it. He couldn't really have been saying our investigation had the wrong political outlook, could he? Petrovich had given no hint so far that our authorization rested on the conviction that we would reach some predetermined end. If that was what the Chekist wanted, why choose Petrovich for the job? But it would never be wise to treat official discourse ironically in front of a member of the secret police—even if the secret policeman himself seemed to be deploying it for ironic effect.

"All right," said Petrovich. "You wish we'd made more progress on the list you gave me."

"What I was not expecting," said the other man, "was for you to spend the time since I last saw you having your face pounded by those antisocial prisoners who burned their clothes. You look horrible."

"Could be worse."

"Fine. But you received clear instructions yesterday, none of which included these *urki*."

Outside, it was still dark. To arrive at the time the Chekist had appointed, we'd had to get up earlier than the rest of Company Ten. Quarantine Company had still been calling its roll off between the churches as we made our way to Nikolski.

"Golubov is an old contact of mine," said Petrovich. "I thought he might provide background. You never know where a clue will turn up."

"And now you've sparked the attack on an agent of official business that the Administration Section has been worrying about for a month. You'll have made things very awkward for me if word gets out."

"I got my drubbing before he knew I was working for you. Involved our bad blood outside, nothing to do with Infosec. In fact, he got helpful, a bit, once I mentioned your agency. You don't need to do anything to Golubov."

"I don't intend to. Not before the time is right, anyway. And you, Bogomolov. You've been off chasing girls. You find that stimulating, do you?"

A bell of warm alarm rang below my throat. In this room, it did not feel safe to become the person of whom questions were asked. "Fitneva did have a relationship with Antonov. And she denied it at first. That's worth looking into."

"Impressive. You have discovered that Antonov was not in fact a holy fool, but was motivated by the same instincts and appetites that drive the rest of the species. For me," the Chekist continued, turning back to Petrovich, "it is an axiom that the religious are hypocrites. Do you really believe this is a good use of the time granted you?"

"I'm not ignoring the men you're interested in. We talked to one of them last night. Zuyev. I only want to keep all avenues open."

"And what do you believe Fitneva's avenue to be?"

Petrovich didn't flinch. "The only thing more common than a dispute over a woman in the murders I've investigated has been vodka. And vodka is like air when it comes to murders. Not everything is a conspiracy or a plot. Sometimes a man gets hit over the head because someone found him under the wrong blanket."

"That is your theory? That this—" The Chekist broke off. "What is his name?"

"Boris Spagovsky."

"This Spagovsky broke Antonov's skull out of jealousy?"

"I don't have a theory yet. I'd like to know more about him. According to Fitneva's floor mistress he's a lamb, too innocent for the world. Once I explained we were investigating a murder she was at pains to make it clear that no one in her little circle could possibly be involved. She even about-faced and doubted that her Veruchka would ever have taken up with anyone like our Antonov." He chuckled and ran his hand over his mustache, showing the spots and veins on the back of his hand. "Listen, I told you yesterday. Your list of these officers isn't promising. The signs we thought might have appeared haven't turned up. It's possible you had bad information."

"Yakov Petrovich," I said. "Are you forgetting Nail Terekhov? He was on the list as well. His murder counts as a sign, surely."

The two men stared at me for a long moment. Coal hissed in the Chekist's stove.

"Of course it does," Petrovich said roughly at last. "But that side of things is being investigated via Infosec's methods, not mine. I can't say what anyone might turn up about Terekhov. But I think there's good reason to believe we can break this thing open just by figuring out what happened to Antonov. To do that, Fitneva needs to have the screws put to her. Spagovsky needs to be questioned. There's also the matter of Vinogradov, the museum director. His being away on Kostrihe has delayed us. We ought to know why he wrote Antonov that pass the other night. That would help us start tracking his movements the night of the murder."

The Chekist frowned. "I believe I recall you saying he would return to the kremlin in a week."

"Five nights from now, according to the man he left in charge at the museum. It's too long to wait. I know you want us to hurry." He leaned forward, both hands bearing down on the head of his cane. "That's why we need you to order him to come back here and talk to us. You can do it, can't you? Send someone. Tell him Infosec requires him to come back to answer some questions.

"I can," the Chekist said. "But I won't. Vinogradov's friends are powerful. And I don't care to use up my store of goodwill in the service of an investigation being prosecuted in as leisurely and haphazard a manner as yours is."

Petrovich cleared his throat but didn't say anything. The Chekist continued: "Interrogate the men on the list I gave you. All of them. Make them talk to you. Only after that are you to proceed with your investigation of anyone at the museum, of this Spagovky or this Fitneva. You will report back here in two days." He pulled a date book from an inner pocket of his jacket and consulted it. "At 10:30 sharp. I expect to hear of concrete advances in the case. Otherwise you'll return to me the documents I gave you and resume your normal work at that time. Your investigation will be over. Understand?"

I rose, anxious to be gone, but Petrovich stayed stubbornly in his chair. "That's your final word?"

"Yes. Get to work."

We left.

The old man held on to my arm as we went down the path from the shack. "All right," he said. "All right, I'm surprised. I'd thought he would give us more time. Apparently he's not so respectful of my approach as he made out."

I waited for him to say more, but he looked lost in thought. The electric lamps along the road had been turned off, but it was still dark. Only the faintest hint of dawn showed me his face.

"I'm sorry I brought up Terekhov," I said. "The two of you seemed surprised I mentioned it."

"No, that was fine," he said distractedly. "That was good."

We reached the road.

"What will we do now?" I asked.

Petrovich shook himself, cleared his throat again. Then he said: "Things are getting more and more urgent. He wants two things that are impossible together: for us to go down his list, and for us to produce results. I wasn't lying to him when I said I thought the list was a waste of time. But whether it helps the case or not, it has to be done. It would be more than our skins are worth to refuse."

He heaved a wheezing breath, settling down on his cane. He'd been making a good pace so far this morning, but I could tell he ached. "So that's what I'm going to do. If there's any time, I'll follow up with Fitneva. We still have to follow our best leads, or we'll be sunk all the same." He looked up at me, his face hard to read in the dark. "That's why you're going to go to Kostrihe. If we can't bring Vinogradov to us, someone has to take our questions to him. I'd never make it there and back in a day. But you can handle the walk, and you performed well with Fitneva last night. You'll do well enough on your own."

17

By the time the sun cleared the horizon, I was trudging south. Last night's clouds had dropped their snow and disappeared; the world was a glass box filled to the brim by the sounds of my steps and breath. Only when I stopped for a moment could I hear axes and the drone of saws, somewhere off in the forest.

Sometime earlier I'd crossed the dark, frozen ray of a canal. Now, following the road to the top of a low bluff, I caught a glimpse of the sea. Here the water was still water. Only a sluggish flickering near the shore suggested crystals forming.

The air was bitter, painful and inert in my lungs. On days like that, you labor in the morning's grip for each breath. As the last pools of darkness evaporated, sky and ground turned fragile lilac, a spreading facsimile of warmth. Pines cast their pale shadows over the snow, interrupted at intervals by stands of ash and birch. Where the road ran near the water, these were gracefully doubled over, like ballet dancers. They all bowed in one direction, trained as they grew by the force of the wind off the sea.

What was it, that morning, that brought Solovetsky's beauty to life for me? I hadn't slept, and after the meeting in the Chekist's shack, I ought to have been worrying about being sent back to Quarantine. I ought to have made plans for smuggling what remained of Antonov's ration back into the cathedral, or schemed about how to turn my interlude in Company Ten into something more permanent. And then, of course, the landscape should have bored me, the subarctic vistas worn me down. They had been spread before me every day since my arrival on the island, without a break.

But no. Today—today's scenes were new. And the visit to Kostrihe would not have to be repeated tomorrow. These trees, this snow, these canals: none of it was freighted with the fear of seeing the same image every day for the rest of my life. I could let my mind wander—had Veronika known what I meant when I mentioned swimming in the Neva the night before? Would Antonov have seen the line of her wrist in the arched birches, the way I did?—and I could experience as a kind of frisson, rather than a handicap, the ambivalent sensations my reflections raised?

I've written that it was a labor to breathe in the cold, and that is true. But I was walking a straight line to an unseen location, one outside my normal round. At least I didn't have to feel I was taking the same breath over and over again. I was an arrow fired from one point to another, and the snow painted white symmetries for me on either side of my path.

It was something like five miles to the cape. No one had made any effort to clear or manage the snow, but as much as possible I walked where sledges and footsteps had packed it down. As the road took me farther from the kremlin, these marks of prior passage made less and less difference. By midmorning I was tired and had to stop to readjust the wrappings in my left boot.

It was not until '27 that the flimsy bast shoes, which caused so much frostbite, became standard issue on Solovki. At the time of Petrovich's and my investigation, most of us had *valenki*. The beaten felt boots were warm enough. With a pair of galoshes, they would be waterproof—that was what Genkin, back in Company Thirteen, had been so eager to capitalize on when he asked me to get him rubber. Otherwise, all that kept your feet dry was the snow's being too cold to melt much.

We'd received ours earlier in the season. Naturally, a nobody like myself had not had his choice of the supply. By the time my work platoon entered the washhouse to claim them, the giant pile had been picked over. I'd found a right boot close to my size and without too many worn-thin places, but there was a small hole in the sole of my left, near the ball of my foot. I'd padded it with rags. For some time I'd felt them loosening with each step.

I brushed off a fallen log and sat. The wind on my socked foot made me shiver. After that I walked along with less of a sense of possibility.

Sometime before midday, I plodded among the sparse trunks of a few final trees, then stepped out onto the cape, a white expanse stippled with stone and brush and framed by saltwater. The trees had petered out, but off to the west a line of them kept me from seeing the whole of the promontory. Stands broke up the view to the south as well.

The wind had died while I walked, the day growing overcast. A fine icy haze drifted inland from the sea. When a seabird's loud cry pierced the gloom, it was a surprise.

Vinogradov's camp was nowhere to be seen. Petrovich and I had visited Ivanov briefly at the museum before I set off. The Anti-Religious Bug was not thrilled to see us, but he'd showed me a few places on a map where I might look for Vinogradov. The cape was about a mile wide, and that long again. "These stone arrangements he's studying are found at several sites," he said. "Can't say which one he'll have decided to camp by. The director's going to make the arrangements that seem best to him."

I started by following the western shoreline. Beneath the snow the ground was rocky, with boulders strewn here and there as if carelessly dropped. The clusters of low scrub I stepped among cast no shadows in that wide gray noon.

I'd circled around the butt of the cape and begun coming up the other side of the trees before I noticed smoke trickling into the sky from a campfire. At some distance, three tents stood at the woods' edge, sheltered by some birches. They were low affairs, sides heaped with snow. I could see a few figures among them, one standing and moving, the others seated.

Setting off in their direction, I came around a stand of scrub and found a man crouching over the earth. He squatted strangely, tense and ready, like a marionette or an ugly bird. The hem of his belted peasant coat brushed the ground. When I said, "Oh," he stood and turned.

The face he showed was strange as well. Beneath a furred *ushanka*, the features might have been pinched or molded into the ball-like head. Half-lidded eyes moved behind the round lenses of a pair of wire glasses. The thin lips turned down at the edges of the mouth, never quite forming a frown.

"Yes," he said. An acknowledgment, not a question. I might have been the next person in a queue. "What can I do for you?"

"I am—excuse me, I'm looking for Nikolai Vinogradov."

"Yes."

"You are—he?"

"Yes." A tidy rectangle of mustache centered itself beneath his nose, the bubble in a spirit level. He gave the impression of having been distilled, drop by drop.

"Excuse me," I said again. "I expected to find you at your camp. My name is Bogomolov. Your assistant Ivanov said you could be found here."

"You've come a long way from the museum."

It seemed abrupt to launch into the interrogation here, out in the wind. But Vinogradov gave no sign of being about to invite me back to the camp. He looked like nothing so much as a man who wanted to conclude this distraction and get back to his work.

"Yes. I—we—have a few questions for you. About an—an important matter." His features were utterly still. "I am sorry to tell you that Gennady Antonov is dead."

He looked at me for a long moment. "You've come to talk to me because of his work at the museum."

"That's right."

"It is sudden. I spoke to him before I left the kremlin. He was quite well."

"Yes. He died two days ago."

"And here you bring news of his passage into the underworld to the mouth of the labyrinth. The ritual of stone age man recapitulated in our modern era."

I blinked. "I don't—"

He gestured at the ground. Where he'd been crouching, a rough circle of some twenty feet had been cleared in the snow. Within it, a pattern of stones, also brushed clean. They were uniform, none more than a foot high, packed close together in arcs and curls. They made a spiral.

Or not quite a spiral. The form teased you. At any given point it was simple, but the principle of the whole's construction never made itself obvious. The path your eye traced seemed always to be turning away from its expected destination. Now inward towards the center, now out to the edge, now nearly back to the point where it had started. On one side the pattern divided into two lobes or leaves, while on the other it looked like a simple series of concentric circles.

At a height of about two feet, thin ropes were strung between four stakes. The ropes met at right angles, dividing the whole into quadrants. They were an addition of Vinogradov's, obviously, something to do with his work.

"This is a figuration of the city of the dead," said Vinogradov. "Not merely a depiction, you understand. An image with the power of the thing it represents. Man has always wished to dictate the lower world's structure. Here on Solovetsky they tried to do it with the arrangement of their labyrinths. They are designed to confuse and trap the souls of the departed, to keep them from returning to torment the living.

"What is puzzling to modern archeology, however, is that all of the apparent tortuousness is false. In these structures there is only ever one path, looped back on itself—no chance of a wrong turning, you see? One cannot become lost. But perhaps the dead are easy to fool. Some believe structures like this are modeled on primitive fish traps. The fish swims in, and is only prevented from swimming out again because it lacks the intelligence to realize it must go back the way it came. If the dead are like that . . ."

He trailed off, and was silent for a moment before he continued. "It seems the island itself was a kind of marginal space for these ancient men. An outpost on the border between our middle world and the lower world of the dead. An image for our own state as prisoners of SLON, perhaps. Gennady Antonov has crossed the boundary on which we all exist."

His hooded eyes flicked once, from my cap (I'd returned Petrovich's watch cap to him) to my boots. In his right hand were a little book and a pencil, which he now transferred to the pocket of his coat. "And there is something unusual about his death. Otherwise bringing news of it to me here on the cape would not have been worth the trip. Forgive me. I am dismayed, of course. It is unfortunate. He was a man of rare skills, and he had been with us for some time. My plans for the collection will have to be entirely changed. How did it happen?"

Lulled by his discourse on the labyrinths, I almost said. But that would have been giving too much away. Petrovich had been quite explicit: I wasn't to tell the museum director anything about the circumstances the body was found in, or about the cause of death.

"That is what we are hoping you can help us discover."

"An inquiry, then. The matter is very serious. Tell me, on whose behalf is it being made?"

I explained about Petrovich and Infosec. I'd had to leave the investigation authorization back at the kremlin, but Vinogradov didn't ask for it. The old man hadn't thought he would.

"And your name is Bogomolov," he said when I'd finished. The glasses perched on the bridge of his nose as though balanced there. "Perhaps I've seen you somewhere before."

"I knew Antonov. Sometimes I came to the museum to watch him work." He considered this for a moment, then nodded once.

The night before, I'd had to improvise my list of questions for Veronika, doing my best to ask what Petrovich would have if he'd been there. This time the old man had had me commit an ordered list to memory. I started down it. "Can you think of a reason anyone might have had to hurt him?"

"No. I would have described him as an inoffensive man. He was killed, then? Someone did this?"

I didn't see any point in equivocating about it, Petrovich's advice notwithstanding. "So it appears."

Vinogradov frowned. "I see."

"You can't think of anyone who might have wanted to hurt him? Maybe someone at the museum? There might be jealousy or competition about the work."

"No," he said. "Nothing of the sort."

"He never mentioned any danger to you?"

"No."

"Was there anything out of the ordinary about how he acted recently, or about his work? Did he seem worried?"

"He did not. I would not have said he had been acting any

differently than usual."

"Can you think of anything we should know about him, then? About his life here on Solovki, or before? Anything out of the ordinary might be a clue."

"Gennady Mikhailovich was a man worth talking to, but not the type to discuss himself when he could be discussing his subject. I know very little about his life apart from his work."

The next question gave me pause. It would have been a mistake to bring her up, but Veronika was in his background. Anything related to her made me doubt myself. "He would never have mentioned a relationship with a woman to you, then?"

Vinogradov pressed his lips together. He took, then released, a large breath through his nose. "No."

All of this was as expected. We'd asked the same questions of Ivanov and Sewick, with the same responses. The crucial moments, which Petrovich hoped would advance the investigation, were still to come. But there was some context to be provided first. "How did Antonov come to work at the museum?"

"Ah. In that he was unusual. Most of those I employ are referred to me—I am known as someone who will find places for members of the intelligentsia—but he presented himself. Once he'd described his training and experience, it was immediately clear he would have to work with the collection. There are few enough men with his expertise in Russia. At SLON he is—was—quite unique."

"Most of his work was restoring icons, then. Did he do anything else?"

"Basic maintenance work. Ensuring the pieces were stored safely, things like that. Some identification and cataloging. The records of the monks are not always clear about dates of acquisition. The artist responsible for the production of a given piece is not always known. At my direction he undertook a few archival research projects of that sort. But for the most part he simply worked on the damaged or faded pieces." He looked away. Annoyance flicked across his face, the first emotion I'd seen on it. "The work plan for all of the religious paintings will have to be altered."

He hadn't mentioned the requisition order, but that would have been an irregularity, not a normal part of Antonov's work. I was meant to ask about it at a later stage anyway. The bird I'd heard when I stepped out onto the cape called again. It made a sound like a gull's kee-kee-kee, but lower, harsher. It sounded predatory. It was time for the first of my difficult questions.

"Can you think of any reason he might have had to be outside the walls three nights ago?"

"He was found outside?"

"Yes." Leaving out what we'd discovered at Nikolski was purposeful, but it didn't depend on Vinogradov not knowing about the body. Either way, if he didn't mention the pass he'd written, we'd have something on him. Petrovich had instructed me to watch him closely, even if he came back with the right answer.

"There is a reason. Certain supplies had gone missing from his desk. I'd written him an exit pass so that he could look for them. If you check the logbook at the gate, perhaps you will find a record of his using it."

"Supplies?"

"Tools and materials used in his restoration work. Solvents, sable brushes. I was most concerned to recover a quantity of gold leaf. There was a—requisition." You could hear his distaste for the word. "It is a farce the Camp Administration sometimes requires of us. A way to demonstrate to those parties in Moscow who care about such things that SLON is seized by the appropriate revolutionary fervor."

"Ivanov mentioned it to us," I said.

His eyebrows arched slightly above the rim of his glasses. "You will be acquainted with the details, then. The supplies disappeared after the workmen from Anzer Division had come to collect the icons. Antonov was to begin by inquiring with their superior."

Petrovich had told me not to act excited, even if I learned something. "A man named Zhenov?"

"You know him."

It wasn't what I'd been sent to look for, but it seemed important. Zhenov and his foreman had claimed not to have seen Antonov, but this would make Petrovich want to take another look at them. Maybe it would convince the Chekist as well. I tried to think back over what Vinogradov had just said. "You keep a stock of gold leaf here, on the island?"

"What was lost amounted to only a fraction of an ounce of

gold," said Vinogradov. "The sheets are extremely thin. But they were all we had, and Antonov needed them to complete work I had scheduled for the winter." He glanced down at the labyrinth's stones idly, as if they were a supply manifest for the museum. "Leaf is not quite as dear as it sounds. But it would have been troublesome to replace."

I pictured Antonov's desk as it had been when Petrovich and I searched it two days before. Nothing had been locked, not even the drawer behind which I found Veronika's note. Antonov carelessly allowing himself to be robbed did not seem unlikely. "Why did you send him to Zhenov? Couldn't it have been taken by one of the other workers in the museum?"

"It is possible. But I would not call it likely. It is well known at the museum that Antonov uses leaf, as well as where he stores it. I can't think why one of my colleagues would have decided to steal it directly after the men had come from Anzer Division to take our icons."

"To cast the suspicion on them, maybe."

"Perhaps."

"And how would Zhenov's men have known where to find it? And what would they have wanted with the other supplies?"

Vinogradov shrugged. "I assumed they somehow saw the leaf in his desk. The rest—who knows? One of the solvents was alcohol. *Zeks* always have a use for that."

"How would we recognize the supplies if we needed to search for them?"

"The book of leaf is three and a half inches square. There should be between twenty and forty leaves in it, each between tissue. As for the other things, there is not much distinctive about them. Solvents in glass bottles, brushes, and two scrapers."

His bringing up the requisition himself made the next of Petrovich's questions easier to ask. "We found a list of icons in Antonov's desk that Ivanov thought were the pieces meant to go to Anzer. Some were crossed out. Places where someone hadn't wanted him to send what he proposed."

"Yes."

"That was you, wasn't it? What did you disagree about?"

Vinogradov was silent for a long time. It was like reaching a wall: I waited, but his expression didn't change. I could still make out the shapes of the tents off across the cape, against the trees. Men moved about in front of them. There was time to wonder whether I should have insisted on having our conversation over among them, by the fire.

At last he said sharply: "Is your investigation focused on matters related to the collection?"

I shook my head. It was a relief to talk again. "We're only trying to understand. It was an unusual-seeming thing to find in Antonov's desk. My partner says you have to understand every detail of a man's life. He's the one with experience in these investigations, not me."

Vinogradov nodded slowly. He thought for another minute, then said: "The collection is an aberration, of course. The same as the museum itself. I imagine nothing like it has ever before been administered by prison labor, within a prison system. The situation poses special threats that most administrators of antiquities do not have to address. Deputy Camp Director Eikhmans is usually an ally—but there is reason to be especially vigilant when he fails to protect us from things like this 'requisition.'" He shrugged, another even raising and lowering of the shoulders. "I wished to be sure that Antonov's choices about what to sacrifice were correct. In the event, he seemed to me to have made a few errors. He proposed to give up pieces that were more important or valuable than others in the collection."

"Wasn't he an expert? Shouldn't he have known what was worth keeping?"

"Yes. I was surprised we disagreed. But there are different ways to evaluate. I supposed there was some religious scruple that counted for more with him than with me. To him, certain pieces may have seemed more or less spiritually important. We didn't discuss it."

I looked down again at the labyrinth. Whoever had cleared the snow had done a thorough job. It stuck to the stones only where it had frozen, and you could see blades of grass poking through it on the ground. Some still showed a little green. I almost thought I could smell the earth beneath them, the way you do in springtime. But it must have been frozen solid.

"Tell me about your work here," I said.

"What would you like to know?"

"What are you doing with these ropes?"

"They are a drafting aid. My diagrams can be more precise when I draw them in relation to a set of axes."

"Diagrams of the city of the dead? You know what they represent already, don't you? What more are you hoping to learn?"

He sniffed. He'd been reluctant to talk about the collection and the icons, but now, on the topic of labyrinths, his suspicion abated a little. I made a mental note of that, to see what Petrovich would make of it. "The symbolic and religious content is easy enough to see. In other parts of the island there are cairns and burial markers that make the funerary role of the labyrinths obvious. The more interesting questions relate to classification and techniques of conception and construction. Simply put, I want to know how they were made, why some were made differently than others. This one, you see, approaches the form of a horseshoe—this side is flattened. Others are closer to perfect circles or spirals. It is not a random distinction. If I could discover the separate schemae behind their construction, I might be able to date them, see how one has led to another. I hope to make some contribution to the study of the dissemination of the figure of the labyrinth across the ancient world." He was gazing down at the ground again. This must have been the same intensity I'd seen in his back when I arrived. His face had somehow become even more expressionless, more doll-like, as though, looking at the stones, he turned into one himself. "In archeology it is generally the material structure of a thing, not the meaning attributed to it, from which we learn most."

"And what is it about your work that requires you to undertake your expedition just now, in the snow, the day after one of your workers has been killed?"

He looked sharply up at me, frowning. I'd sprung the question on him the way Petrovich had instructed me to, down to drawing him out on another subject first. It was almost annoying to see the technique be so successful at getting a response. It was only a frown, with perhaps an indrawn breath, but from Vinogradov that was something, his first sudden movement since I'd arrived.

"I see. That appears suspicious to you. But I had planned this trip for some time, with the goal of presenting its findings at the next meeting of the Solovetsky Society for Local Lore. That will be January. Diagramming these sites in the spring would be too late. October is a challenging time to make camp, but I could not arrange it earlier, and next month it will be even worse."

"Aren't you the chairman of the Society for Local Lore? Couldn't you move the date of the meeting?"

"I wouldn't wish to. The membership should not be made to wait because of one researcher. They expect a meeting in January."

"You'd describe your being here now as a coincidence, then."

"Yes. A coincidence."

That matched what Ivanov had said, but if it was a coincidence, it remained a large one. This was the sort of thing Petrovich had told me to take note of. We might be able to convince the Chekist we needed more time to check the story.

Something Petrovich hadn't asked me to look into was whether Vinogradov had any connection to the other murder. But I had been planning to ask about it anyway. The same calculations that had applied to asking Veronika applied here as well.

"Just one more question, then. Are you acquainted with a man named Nail Terekhov?"

"Terekhov? I am not familiar with the name."

"A cavalry officer with Denikin. He worked in the alabaster workshop."

"I have nothing to do with the alabaster workshop."

"Thank you, Director Vinogradov," I said. "I believe that is all. You're scheduled to be here for four more days, aren't you? If we have any questions during that time, maybe they'll be able to answer them at the museum."

He watched me. Having come to the end of the list, I felt whatever wave of authority Petrovich's inquiries had been allowing me to ride dissipate abruptly. It would have seemed appropriate to be preparing myself to go, but there was nothing to prepare. I hadn't taken off my hat, unbuttoned my coat, or spread papers anywhere. I'd neither sat down, nor opened or closed any door. I'd walked up to him in the middle of a field and asked several questions. Now I was about to turn around and walk away again.

"Yes," he said, "four days. Before you go—Bogomolov, wasn't it? You said you were acquainted with Gennady Mikhailovich?

You came to watch him work."

"That's right."

"You are educated. Perhaps you were recently a student?"

"I was at the university in Saint Petersburg."

"Of course. And your interest in Antonov's work is part of your general program of mental cultivation. What did you study?"

The seabird shrieked again, closer than it had been. At first I waited, but this time it didn't stop after a few cries. It went on and on, filling the air with the raucous sound.

"Mathematics," I said.

"I see." Vinogradov's lips turned up slightly at the corner: a tiny, cold smile to match the frown of a moment before. "I mentioned finding positions for intellectuals. Do you know what the greatest obstacle most of those I help must overcome, before they can do valuable work here? It is the idea of prison. They are particularly susceptible to believing in our imprisonment. Now, in one sense, of course, our imprisonment is an incontrovertible fact. If we should attempt to leave before the end of our sentences, we would be stopped. But in another sense—in another sense there is a fiction at its core. That fiction is that we have been removed from the world. Do you see my meaning? The central symbolic fact of prison is that prisoners exist separately from nonprisoners, that time flows differently for them, that their place is somehow alongside, not with, the other places people inhabit. But, of course, this is manifestly false. This is the real, material world, the same as anywhere else. Have we been removed? No. We remain within our boundaries, without being gone from existence. At most, we've been removed from a world of symbols, the social world. A world that history, recent history especially, has already shown to be ephemeral and unreal enough in any case."

"I can think of a few things there that I would call unreal and symbolic back in Petersburg," I said. "But I seem to recall it as a world of sufficient food and beds with sheets."

"This is precisely my point. It is those circumstances that differentiate Saint Petersburg from Solovki, not concepts like freedom or imprisonment. The world is full enough of things that demand our interest without insisting on the preservation of some meaning for the word 'freedom.' As I observed concerning archeology, so for the rest of life: it is more important to attend to the physical realities of a thing than to the symbols men make of it."

"You are a materialist."

"I am a collector. Here I have been given charge of a marvelous collection. A real thing, you understand? It is full of objects made by men's hands, which I can touch and see. If the cost of proximity to these things is that I am called a prisoner, what do I care? I care for the things themselves, the artifacts. It matters no more to me that I am believed to be a *zek* than that Antonov believed his restoration work to be inspired by Christ. In both cases, someone has merely draped his idea over what is real without affecting it. I care for the real. I can ignore the drapery."

He spoke evenly, carefully, as though he were reading from a book. "You, too, might find it worthwhile to focus your attention on your material circumstances. You should avoid being distracted by any roles you are asked to believe you are playing. As you suggest, the simple physical demands of survival here are severe. And there are other sorts of dangers as well. Real dangers, which don't depend on any story about guilt or responsibility. I would hate to see a promising young intellectual such as yourself stumble into them because he could not stop telling himself a certain story. And, conversely, you may find that opportunities present themselves if you only keep your attention fixed on what is tangible and real."

That seemed to be all. He pulled the notebook and pencil from his pocket and crouched down over the stones again. For a moment I watched the smoke that rose from the camp's fire, but in the end I turned and followed my tracks back over the bouldered and uneven snow. The cape's muffling gray sky began, it seemed, six feet above your head, as though it emanated from the ground and was not, after all, the sky.

Back on the road, I trod over the same canals and bluffs I had coming. I passed the same snow-bowed branches. Seen again, views that had promised something new expressed only the same monotonous truths as ever. The morning's journey was an arrow, aimed at a new destination. The trip back converted it, step by step, from arrow to dull loop.

On Solovki, I always seemed to be returning to the kremlin.

18

Intelligence of the missing gold leaf changed things.

I arrived back at our cell late in the afternoon, as the sun was going down. Not finding Petrovich there, I ate a cold meal of bread, onion, and a little salt fish soaked in a mug of water, all taken from Antonov's dry ration. The cell was warm after my long walk through the snow. Soon I dozed on my cot.

It was well after curfew by the time the old man appeared, creaky and exhausted. Even so, he immediately wanted to know about my conversation with Vinogradov, taking particular interest when I described what the museum director had said about the gold. One of his eyes had swollen almost entirely shut by now, but excitement flattened the other.

For his own part, he was able to report crossing off eight more names from the Chekist's list. With Terekhov and Zuyev, that made ten who'd been talked to, out of seventeen total. It had been a full day's work, but none had had anything suspicious or illuminating to say. Each knew most of the others on the list, but none would admit to an acquaintance with Gennady Antonov. He had not asked them about Terekhov, since our instructions to leave that alone had been explicit and we were already pushing our boundaries. It was impossible to say what the Chekist thought connected them to the case.

Whether the news of the leaf would alone be enough to convince him that our investigation ought to be extended was hard to say. "The trick," said Petrovich, "is to do enough of what your superior says to make him feel he's being taken seriously, but not so much it keeps you from presenting him real results. Misappropriations at the museum will intrigue him, at least. And these Whites Army types are getting us nowhere. But I'm worried he'll take it as insubordination if we don't make a show of looking into all his suspects."

At length it was resolved: having nothing to show for ourselves when we next went to meet the Chekist at his cabin would spell the end of our deputization just as certainly as having ignored his orders altogether. The leaf gave us a new lead to follow, one that might finally produce some results. We would prioritize tracking it down, with any time left over devoted to interrogating the rest of the list.

That was settled, then. What was not settled was what to do about Veronika.

True to his suggestion, Petrovich had visited her at the women's dormitories before coming back to our cell. This, too, had taken priority over questioning the last seven men. It was important, he said, to begin putting our leverage to use. What this had meant, practically speaking, was that he had threatened to tell Spagovsky about her affair with Antonov unless she cooperated. Of course, he explained, he hadn't discarded the possibility Spagovsky already knew—that was required by the hypothesis of his killing Antonov, which it would be premature to give up—but, regardless, he thought the proposition would put strain on the suspects, which was desirable. The best way for us to get something on Spagovsky would be for Veronika to crack and give it to us.

Predictably, the conversation had gone poorly. She'd denied knowing anything about Vinogradov, Zhenov, the strange business of the icon requisition, or anything else that Antonov might have been involved in. Petrovich had been ordered in the strongest terms to leave. He had, but not before issuing an ultimatum: bring us something we could use by the end of the day tomorrow, or he would go to Spagovsky.

The idea of what such a step might make her say when next I saw her made me uneasy. From Veronika's perspective, it would look as though the old man was offering her a choice between a stay in the hospital and giving up her dignity. She'd indicated how she felt about such choices the night before, and would have no reason to exempt me from her disdain.

"She didn't respond well to threats from Spagovsky," I said. "I don't think it will be any different coming from us. She's stubborn." It was true: she was more than stubborn. A beating wouldn't scare her. Hearing myself say it made me realize that if I didn't like the prospect of her withering looks, I liked even less the possibility of her allowing herself to be destroyed before submitting.

"Rather you were allowed to work your charms, would you? I'm afraid we don't have that long to wait. I told you before, it could take you years to catch her up." The old man chuckled. "Let me worry about the methods, Tolya. You only have to listen and keep your eyes open."

The next morning was clear again. Freezing winds spun the day past quickly; gray clouds scudded across a pale blue sky overhead. Zhenov and the men at his warehouse would need to be questioned again, obviously, but Petrovich thought we should start our search for the missing gold leaf at the museum.

Ivanov's eyes widened only slightly at what the bruise was doing to the old man's face, though it had certainly acquired new shades of purple and yellow since he'd seen it yesterday morning. By this time he seemed to have grown used to helping us, and when we asked for any material he might have related to Vinogradov's expedition, he produced a file from his desk marked "Kostrihe." Inside, memos from Vinogradov detailed the plans. There were copies of receipts for supplies, as well as carbons of two letters arranging permission for Vinogradov and five assistants to be away from the kremlin, addressed to Camp Director Nogtev's office and copied to Deputy Director Eikhmans. The earliest memo was dated September 8. "As you see," he said, "the director's expedition had been planned for more than a month."

"What about this gold leaf?" said Petrovich.

Ivanov knew Antonov had had some, but hadn't heard about it going missing. It would have been in his desk somewhere, he assumed. If we hadn't seen it when we searched the other day, then, as the director said, it wasn't there. He couldn't say exactly who had known about it; that Antonov had used leaf in his work was common knowledge. When Petrovich asked whether there wasn't some kind of inventory where the things being issued to Antonov would be recorded, Ivanov looked unhappy but nodded.

He disappeared into the director's office, then returned from a hallway towards the back of the sanctuary with a slim black ledger, which he laid open before us on his desk. "There." A stubby finger pointed to a line that read *Sept. 3: 1 book (25 sheets) leaf issued Antonov.* He flipped back a few pages. "And here." *June 28: 1 pint spirits and 1/3 pint turpentine issued Antonov.* Both had been marked *Missing Oct. 14* in the rightmost column. "That's the director's writing."

Petrovich turned back and forth between the pages and reread the entries slowly. Without looking up from them at Ivanov, he said: "You think it's plausible one of the men who came for the icons took these things?"

"They might have," said Ivanov slowly. "We didn't think to take precautions. And they had to pass Antonov's desk to reach the staircase to storage."

Another search of Antonov's desk turned up nothing new, and we weren't able to tell where the leaf or the solvents had been stored. The rest of the morning we spent questioning the other men. As Ivanov had said, most were aware Antonov had worked with gold, but none admitted to knowing it had gone missing.

Petrovich asked a number of them about the day of the icon requisition as well, without producing much of interest. The men from the warehouse had been up and down from the courtyard a good deal, carrying the pieces a few at a time out to the sledges they'd brought, but it hadn't taken long. No one had noticed any of them take anything from Antonov's desk. None of them were men that anyone had recognized or seen before. Johan Sewick attempted to reconstruct the morning for us at some length, but in the end he said the same thing as everyone else.

Before we left, Ivanov escorted us down into the museum's storage area, explaining that the requisitioned icons had been stored here before the men from Anzer Division came to collect them. A set of stairs at the back of the chapel led down to windowless rooms that must have occupied a space in the wall just to the side of the Holy Gates. Here Vinogradov's collection resided: a wealth of crates stamped with numbers. A few pieces of furniture had been draped with white sheets, and a row of cases with sliding drawers had been lined up against one wall.

The icons were stored vertically in racks constructed for the purpose, each wrapped in a white cloth bag. Covered that way, there was something funereal about them, like shrouded bodies stacked in a crypt. When we took one out and undraped it, the lamp showed a haloed saint busy before the wooden gates of a city, appealing to the Virgin Mary and an infant Christ for a blessing.

As so often with the icons of Antonov's I'd seen, I felt there was something peculiar about the piece's composition, something that eluded me. Mother and Son peered down at the scene from an ornate red patch in the panel's top left corner, as though the ivory sky had peeled away to reveal a crimson heaven behind. Past the city's walls ran a ribbon of blue hatched with white—a river—and the saint had planted his slippered feet on a brown disc that appeared to float in the middle of the stream. What the disc represented was hard to tell—perhaps a clod of earth or a round stone—but with it and him done in much larger proportions than the river or the city, the bearded figure resembled nothing so much as a gigantic circus bear on its ball. Why the ball? Why the filigree in Christ and Mary's red ground? Why the strangely regular undulation of the river's banks?

Even answered, such questions would mean nothing for our investigation, of course, and I couldn't think of any others more productive. After Petrovich had turned the icon over and rapped a knuckle against its wooden back—indeed, it was smooth board—we wrapped it up again. Back in the chapel proper, the old man stopped at Antonov's desk to run a hand over the surface. "I don't know. It isn't in the middle of the room, but it's out in the open. You'd expect someone to notice a stranger rooting around."

But the icon had pushed the details of the case from my mind. With the field cleared, there was nothing to keep worries about Petrovich's intentions for Veronika at bay. She was never far from my thoughts in any case, and shame over what he planned to do to her had been stabbing at me from around corners all morning.

It should not have surprised me to be shown his character in a new light, but it did. I'd known there was a core of something canny in him underlying the bluster and the hectoring, something wry and knowing. Now I saw that it was not only canny, but ruthless.

The fact of the matter is that I never did get to really know the old man. There wasn't time. Our acquaintance ran its course over just eight days. That was how long it took to conclude Antonov's case.

Eight days will allow you to begin your mental portrait of someone—I began several of Petrovich, with each of my later efforts painted over an earlier one that had come to seem entirely incorrect—but it isn't enough to make the face resemble your subject more than superficially. Our glimpses of others' characters are fleeting. It takes many to build a comprehensive picture. As if you were rendering a face whose features—the curve of a cheek, the bridge of a nose, the left eyelid—appeared only intermittently, out of the dark. Assembling fragments like that into something remotely human is painstaking work. Often enough, even after much careful collection and collation, the image that emerges is monstrous anyway. Why should it have surprised me to learn Petrovich was willing to see Veronika's ribs broken again, if it meant we got our man?

This conceit is drawn from portraiture, of course. That wasn't Antonov's sort of painting. He would have thought of these things differently. The details of the face, he would say—he would have called it "the physiognomy"—are unimportant, merely a gate through which passes a higher, diviner truth. I will never, he says, come to true understanding of Man or God while I persist in this false conception of the Image.

But he is confusing my metaphor. Very well, there is purported to shine through a man's face a kind of truth, which some call his soul and others his personality, and which makes sense of how the face looks. But it isn't the face I need sense made of. I am asking the more concrete thing to stand for the more abstract one—the face for the personality.

Petrovich's actual face is tediously clear to my memory: mustached, floridly bruised, the one open eye flat, sharp, and above all, blue. I don't require anything shone through these features to be satisfied. It's the inner man who's remained fragmentary and vague. So, all right then, Gennady Mikhailovich, if the soul unfractures the physiognomy, what unfractures the soul? If some higher truth is expected to redeem and complete the passing accidents of Petrovich's character, which are so hard to assemble into one man—well, fuck your mother: what is it?

No, the only images of others available to us are the ones we produce ourselves, from the materials we are given. And I was never able to create anything satisfactory from the gleanings the inspector from Odessa afforded me.

What about Antonov's voice, the one I carry on the argument with? Why should I retain a confident version of that, when I knew him barely longer than I did Petrovich?

I can't say.

At the Anzer Division warehouse, the only sign of the accident we'd witnessed three days before was the block and tackle having been removed from the crane in the front. Zhenov looked askance at Petrovich's face, then blanched and patted his hairline with his fingertips when we told him his men might have taken something from the museum.

He wrote out a list of the warehouse's fifteen workers readily enough, but couldn't say which had been assigned to go for the icons that day. "Ivan was in charge," he said to Petrovich. "He might remember."

"Fine. Get your men together. We'll talk to the ones who were with him. The others can help search the warehouse."

"You don't suspect these stolen goods are being stored here?"

"Plenty of spots to hide something in a place like this."

"Well, I doubt—that is—" Zhenov was taken aback. "Forgive me, Inspector, but the disruption of our work a search would entail—"

"I showed you our documents before, didn't I? I think your operations can be interrupted for an hour on Infosec's authority."

We waited downstairs while someone rounded up the workers. Zhenov fidgeted. I'd been sure to take off my cap when we came inside this time, but the subcommandant still managed to vent his anxiety by lecturing me on follicular analysis: "Even if your working schedule won't permit daily region-by-region sweeps with a comb, there are other methods. For instance, along with my more careful daily examinations, I place a sheet of newsprint over my pillow every evening before I go to bed. I record the hairs I lose during the night, you see? Of course, your data concerning location are less precise with this method, but it requires a minimum of effort."

Kologriev, the foreman, arrived with the last group, a stub of pencil behind his ear. He'd removed his coat, but the blue shirt was once again buttoned tightly at the neck and wrists. It made him look like an oddly grimy priest. "You two," he said, noticing us. "Fuck your mother, that was something with the winch the other day, wasn't it? What's going on?"

Zhenov cleared his throat. "These gentlemen have a few more questions about the requisition, Ivan. I will need you to come up to my office." He raised his voice. "Those of you who went along to the museum last week to collect the icons—that is, the lumber order—will come and wait upstairs as well. The rest of you are to stay here. The warehouse must be searched. There may be an object hidden somewhere, a booklet of gold leaf. It is either to be located, or confirmed to be absent. You will work in pairs. Any suspicious behavior or attempt to keep this object hidden is to be reported directly to me."

The men grumbled, and a dubious look passed over Kologriev's face. He glanced at me, conveying skepticism eloquently, even with his beady eyes. But he followed Zhenov without complaint, identifying five others who had helped him with the collection.

"You stay here and help look," Petrovich said to me in a low voice. "Keep an eye out—see whether any of them try to leave. No need to stop them, just note who it is. I'll handle the interrogations."

"What are you going to ask them?"

"What they noticed on the day of the pickup, and whether they know of anyone coming into vodka or money. Don't worry, if there's anything to get out of them, I'll get it. You just keep your eyes open."

Searching was slow. Snow covered the warehouse's small, high windows, turning the morning light into blue shadows as we searched. And the place was too large to comb systematically: too many barrels might have been knocked open and resealed, too many crevices might have had a small book of gold leaf slipped into them.

It would have helped if the other men had been less wary. Zhenov's order was carried out with little enthusiasm and many sidelong looks in my direction. Things improved a little when Kologriev came down and set the others moving, making a show of friendliness by partnering with me. We'd covered most of the obvious places by the time Petrovich and Zhenov came down from the office, but I couldn't have sworn the booklet wasn't squirreled away in some spot we'd missed.

The subcommandant was clearly getting impatient after sitting through six rounds of Petrovich's questioning. "I can assure you, Inspector, my men and I will be on the lookout for any sign of your missing objects. But I fear there is little else we can do. I see no evidence that anyone here was responsible for their going missing."

"We're almost finished. Explain to me again what happened to the icons after your men retrieved them."

Hurriedly, Zhenov ran through it the way he had the other day: the train, the ferry, the coordination by wireless. The icons had been transported directly to Anzer, not stored in the warehouse.

"And you visit Anzer regularly," said Petrovich. "You've seen that the icons arrived at the cabinetry workshop as expected, then?"

The other man made a pained face. "Well, no. It was the wrong time in the cycle; I have not made an inspection since they shipped. In fact, my next trip to Anzer is scheduled for tomorrow."

"So you'll check on them then."

"Just so. And the calendar says the workshop is to ship the finished product back here in four days' time. I will have returned by then, to ensure personally that nothing has gone wrong on this end either. You can be sure, Inspector, that I have taken a special interest in this matter. There will be no more irregularities."

"That's fine," said Petrovich. "Next place we need to look is your men's quarters."

Zhenov coughed. "Now, really, Inspector. I have many demands on my attention today. I regard this matter with utmost seriousness, of course, but . . ."

"Want me to take them, boss?" said Kologriev. "You could get back to work."

Petrovich didn't object. With Zhenov anxious to get rid of us, it was quickly arranged. The big *zek* led us out of the warehouse and into the cold. It was past noon, the sun high in the sky.

"Anyone try to leave?" Petrovich asked me.

"No, no one."

Petrovich had emerged from his interrogations with a better picture of how the collection of the icons had gone, but little else. Each of the men told a similar story: two sledges, difficulty negotiating the stairs with the paintings, and no way to be sure whether anyone had been rummaging in one of the desks.

I listened with half an ear. I was still worrying about Veronika.

"We're still going to the women's dormitory this evening, then?" I said when he'd finished.

"No, not the dormitory," he said. Kologriev glanced back over his shoulder, his interest apparently piqued by the mention of women. The old man waved a hand "She said she'd be working late at the fishery with the monks. Something about a rush to finish the nets so they can be tanned. So, another hike. I don't expect to find anything out to change that."

Zhenov's men had their quarters north of the kremlin, above what had been the monastery's kvass brewery. The first floor, still full of tuns and barrels, went unoccupied; the men stayed on the second, in two large rooms intended for storage. The windows were few and small, the ceilings slanted. It had been a long time since kvass was brewed there, but a yeasty, sour smell lingered.

Their beds were worse than ours, but better than the ones in Quarantine. I spent a quarter of an hour down on my hands and knees, checking underneath them. Kologriev indicated which beds belonged to the men who'd helped him collect the icons, but I found nothing to distinguish any of them from the others.

While I crawled, Petrovich went through the men's belongings. The old man unfolded the few articles of clothing stored on them, looked into a pair of shoes someone had managed to hold on to, and generally made a mess.

Kologriev leaned easily against the doorframe, watching the search. "The old man really knows what he's doing, eh?" he said to me as I rose after examining a loose floorboard Petrovich had pointed out. "The two of you Infosec?"

"Not exactly," said Petrovich, shaking out a shirt. "We've been deputized."

"I'm only the assistant," I said. "Yakov Petrovich used to be a detective."

The two rooms were very similar, but one had two improvements the other lacked. In one corner was a chipped ceramic stove, unlit, clearly not original to the space. A widening scorch mark spread like a stain across the wooden floor beneath it. The chimney had been arranged so as to vent, not through the roof, but out a window, with a plank cut to shape to hold the pipe in place.

Petrovich opened its door, but there was only coal ash inside. "You brought this in yourself?"

Kologriev grinned. "Well . . . could have been here when we got here. Who's to say?"

"And this is your bunk?" said Petrovich, indicating the one closest to the stove.

"Sure. I get cold."

The other improvement was a set of curtains that had been hung over a window—again, the one nearest Kologriev's bed. These Petrovich only pushed out of the way with his cane.

It was clear we were not going to find anything. The first floor was no better. We combed through it in a cursory way before leaving the building, but even if the gold leaf had been there, I doubt we could have found it. The space was smaller than the warehouse, but more disorganized, and with as many places to hide something. I poked around the dusty equipment without much hope. Kologriev brought down a lantern, and even helped me move a few barrels, but soon Petrovich called a halt.

"At some point the chances of turning anything up aren't worth the time it takes anymore," he said. "This was a good start. We still have those men on the list for this afternoon."

Outside, Kologriev took his leave. It appeared we had reached the end of our investigation into the leaf, for the moment. The rest of the afternoon would be spent on the list. First we headed back to the cell to eat.

"Listen," I said as we went by the bay. "Why don't you let me go to Veronika tonight? Alone, I mean. Even if we're still working on the Whites, you won't need my help. And with her I'll—I'll see if I can talk something more out of her. You can always give her until tomorrow morning before you go to Spagovsky, can't you?"

Petrovich sighed. "What are you going to say to her that you haven't said already, walking her back from Spagovsky's place?"

"I don't know," I began. "But one of us should be on her side, at least. She needs someone to trust, if we're going to learn anything from her."

He stopped. "Tolya, I've teased you before. But, fine, I see you like her. You're taken with her. Sometimes this happens in an investigation, particularly when you're young. You begin to uncover a woman's secrets, it's like being invited into her boudoir. It's exciting. But you must not let an infatuation interfere with your case. You can like her, but be suspicious."

"I'm telling you, you can't expect to convince her with threats."

"Threats. All right, then. Tell me, why do you think I'm not annoyed at having spent all this time searching that warehouse without turning up the leaf? It looks like we wasted the morning, doesn't it?"

"Well, we had to look, didn't we?"

"We did. But there's a reason it's not a disaster that we didn't find anything. It's because Zhenov's men saw us looking. Now we'll wait and see what kind of trouble is stirred up by that. None yet. But something may still come from our banging around."

That made a certain amount of sense. We had certainly demanded their attention. "I don't see what that has to do with Veronika," I said.

"In my professional life, Tolya," said Petrovich slowly, "I had two tools. The first was men, the police force. That's good for when you need to find a pistol thrown into the long grass, or when every train leaving the city needs to be checked for your suspect. Men are a broom, they sweep up. Throw enough of them at a search, usually they find something, whether that's a book of gold leaf or a witness. Here, unfortunately, I have only you. Zhenov's men helped well enough, but since any one of them might have been in on the theft, you couldn't say that using them was what you could call a failproof method. And even if I had a hundred trustworthy officers, it wouldn't make the job of talking to Fitneva any easier. Piling uniforms into a room wouldn't make that one talk."

The temperature had dropped as the sun began to go down. Petrovich coughed and rubbed at his shoulder. "That is a job for the second tool, one I still have at my disposal. It is knowing secrets. A secret is a hammer. It knocks away wedges that hold your suspects in place and prevent them colliding. Once they've smashed pieces off each other, you sift the gravel to see what they've left behind. Then you use that to plan your next blow. This is detective work, do you understand? I don't care about threatening her. I need to put her in motion. Maybe she turns against him. Maybe she sets him on us. Maybe she calls in a favor from a friend we haven't heard of yet. You see? And it sets him in motion as well. I'm not hoping he hurts her. The most interesting outcome would be that I tell him about Antonov and he does nothing. That would mean he knew already, you see?"

It put what we had been doing in a new light. Yet another reconfiguration of my image of the old man—only the mustache and blue eyes seemed to be constant. "All right," I said. "All right, I see what you mean. But I still think we should give her one more chance to talk to us. Then if you still need to tell Spagovsky, we can do it in a way that's safe, make sure she's protected . . ."

Petrovich mused. "Whatever she knows, you're probably right she won't give it up just because of the threat. If Spagovsky does beat her up, she'd be the kind to hold it back from us, just out of spite."

"I don't want her smashed," I admitted.

Both of us raised our eyes to the kremlin's wall, first him, then me. Its stones were massive. "This is what I have been telling you, Tolya," he said. "You need to think: what are you going to do if she proves not to be so innocent?"

19

A secret is a hammer. That was Petrovich's approach to mystery. A different one than Sherlock Holmes's or Nat Pinkerton's, but as effective, I suppose, for driving a story forward as deduction or adventure.

With Vasily there has been more literary discussion, though its focus is belles lettres rather than the mechanics of detective pulp. His subject remains Chekhov. I must have let something slip—the lie about "A Story Without an End" did not put him off.

Last night he asked whether I knew *A Journey to Sakhalin*, our great writer's survey of the tsarist penal colony. "A masterpiece," Vasily says. "An example of the way genius may be put into the service of true social transformation. The man's humanity, his attention to material forces!" And more in this vein.

By "attention to material forces," I believe Vasily Feodorovich means that the illustrious Anton Pavlovich spent months conducting a census of Sakhalin, a godforsaken island in the Sea of Okhotsk that the Imperial Army once seized from the Japanese. He presents the results to the reader hamlet by miserable hamlet. "In Upper Muckstead live twenty-three men, twelve women, and three children. All of the men are under sentence, and eight of the women, with the rest being the wives of those transported under sentence. Sixty-eight percent of the population is between twenty-five and forty-five years old, prime working age. For each household or single man there is a third of a hectare of arable land and half a hectare of hay meadow. People here give the impression of being morose and complain of the climate. In Lower Muckstead . . ." I informed Vasily of the truth, that this is exactly as boring to read as it must have been to carry out.

He refuses to believe I am serious at such moments. When had I read it, he wanted to know? Was it after my own imprisonment? Then hadn't I recognized my own sufferings in what he described? Hadn't I felt myself to be known and empathized with by a capacious intelligence?

Since Chekhov describes the horrors of the tsars' prisons, not ours, the book is approved of by the censors, available in all libraries. I did read it after my release, in the time before the war. I wanted—well, who knows what I wanted from the thing? All I found to recognize in it was the story of a doctor who, when a shoemaker arrives with the latest shipment of convicts, commits the man, perfectly healthy, to the hospital, to be released only once a pair of shoes has been made for the doctor's son. That sounds like the camps I know. Whatever else it was I was looking for, I did not find it.

Not even the usual pleasures of reading Chekhov are there. His prose is that of a punctilious functionary throughout—or, at best, that of a man who has put off genius and taken on responsibility. Two occasions only do I remember when his writing rises up to its usual intensity. One, a description of a prisoner wedding in a remote church. The other, a recaptured escapee receiving ninety strokes with the lash. What inspires the writer in Chekhov, then? Religious ceremony, and torture.

There is perversity in everyone who puts words to paper, if you only look.

Vasily does have some taste, evidenced by the thoughtfulness with which he took my remarks about style. I went on to venture with him the observation I put down before, that Chekhov writes as though he is telling a detective story, only without the crime or the revelation of guilt. I maintain that my basic insight is correct. However, my neighbor points out that one of Chekhov's early works, and his only true novel, *The Shooting Party*, concerns a murder at a provincial estate. By his account it is a more or less normal mystery, with an unfaithful wife murdered in a forest, several suspects, and a magistrate who tells the story of his investigation. I gather there is some ambiguity about the narrator's reliability, which is perhaps an artistic touch; Vasily suggests the magistrate himself may bear some of the guilt. But otherwise it sounds as lurid as Nat Pinkerton.

I am forced, therefore, to acknowledge that Chekhov did, at least once, write a mystery that could be solved. Still, a minor work, one I could not be expected to have read. Chekhov is, of course, not known as a novelist.

In the end Petrovich and I agreed that I would go to Veronika, and I set off along the southern road just after the sun had gone down. Even in the dark, it was familiar; I'd walked this stretch twice in the past two days. The last redness died from the sky, like the reflection of candlelight licking out over a glass dome. The trees were silhouettes against the night air, with the fishery's lamps visible through them before its outline appeared.

When I knocked, Veronika's voice called out for me to come in. It was the same room we'd found her in the other day; she was sitting again on the box beneath the lamp. The nets spread from her lap across the floor, yards and yards of them in the shadows, filling the room like an impossible skirt.

"Anatoly Bogomolov," she said. "Where's your partner?"

"It's just me."

"The two of you are duplicating your efforts. You do know he came to see me again the other day? We were quite the pair. I couldn't decide which of us was more beautiful." Now that I was closer, I could see where the bruises bloomed around both eyes and on her left cheek. Even the bridge of her nose was swollen, but in fact she didn't look quite as bad as the old man. "He told you about his ultimatum?"

"I didn't know he had that in mind. It wasn't something I wanted."

"I see. So, you intend for us to continue being friends, is that it?" The anger thrilled in her voice. She hadn't stopped moving her hands in the net. "Why are you here, then, my friend?"

"I want to help," I said. "If you tell me what you know now, he won't feel he has to say anything to Spagovsky. We could protect you."

"You want the same as your partner! Only you want me to think you're doing me a favor, as well."

The truth of what she said bit at me, but I couldn't see any other way to spare her. "We don't have to be enemies. There's nothing sinister or secret about what we're doing. Antonov was murdered. We're only finding out who killed him."

"Maybe you even believe that!"

I didn't stop to ask what she meant. "It doesn't look good, your refusing to help. Petrovich is convinced you know something you're not telling. If there is, you should tell me. If not—you could just tell me more about what your friendship with him was like. Whatever you don't mind saying. Maybe there will be something useful in it."

"What makes you think telling you about our friendship wouldn't be betraying a confidence?"

Her black eyes were huge under the lamp, even with the swelling. It was quiet. Outside, waves slapped against the pier.

She'd identified my youth and inexperience immediately the other day. There was no point in trying to conceal it or act as though I could browbeat her into cooperation.

"The note we found," I said. "You wrote about his goodness—that it was all that let you continue. I knew what you meant right away, before we had any idea who'd written it. He was a kind man."

"Yes."

"We only met because he took pity on me. I was dawdling at the museum after the end of a lecture. He introduced himself when I knew no one. Do you know about the Quarantine Company? I don't know if they have anything like it for women." She nodded, and I went on. "He knew how meager my rations were. He was willing to help a—a young person in need. He gave me onions—more than once, in fact. That was kindness. But there was more to him, wasn't there? He'd have something to say about man living not by bread alone, don't you think? Or by onions."

I looked, but couldn't tell whether she had softened. Anger and sadness were always close together in her face.

"Once he learned I'd studied mathematics at university, he would always ask me to explain the geometry of perspective to him. I think he understood it quite well, really, but I only had to start to explain linear transformation for him to stop me and ask how distorting a distant object's real shape could be thought to produce a so-called realistic image. We'd end with him shaking his head over anyone ever thinking anything other than its spiritual importance should determine a figure's size in a painting. The kindness was in giving me a chance to talk, you see? He knew I missed being a student, an intellectual."

Veronika finally laughed, in spite of herself. "That sounds like him."

"How did the two of you meet?"

"As you surmised. It was when we were in the hospital."

"Yes," I said, "but how did you meet once you were there?"

Her sigh was barely audible. "Ah. That." Her hands had fallen still, buried in the ropes. "Well, it might as well have been a novel, really. He came in when I'd been there for a week already. They'd put me to work while my ribs healed, helping nurse the sicker ones. He was my patient."

She was talking, at least. I didn't want to push her too soon. "What made you like him?"

"He didn't ask about my beating. Maybe he'd heard about it already from someone else in the hospital. But I appreciated that. How dull, having to explain the hows and why of being beaten up over and over. No, instead we talked about . . . well, about his work. About Petersburg. How can I say it? The conversations were mundane. But they were like nothing I'd heard since they arrested me. He talked—he talked as though he were a friend of my father's, one interested in my schooling. You're right, he was compassionate to youth. But then, of course I am not a little girl. When they were about to discharge me, I begged him tearfully to come and find me when he was well. I said I couldn't live without him. That wasn't true, it now appears, but it felt right to say so at the time."

I swallowed. Whether the sound she'd made was a laugh or a sob, I can't say. "And he came, when he'd recovered?"

"I wasn't sure he would. In the hospital he closed his eyes while I expressed my feelings. All he would say was, 'God bless you, dear girl.' But then, after another week, he came. He said—he said he'd missed me. He said the ward had been dark after

I left. And he said, 'Veronika Filipovna, I am ready to sin with you.'" Her chin took a new angle. She must have noticed my flushing. "It was while I was at work, out from under Stepnova's eyes. I'd told him to do that. You didn't think it was all chaste between us, did you? I'm not ashamed. When we managed to be alone, we slept together."

"No," I said, willing myself not to show any awkwardness or emotion. "I didn't think you were chaste."

"Good. I liked him already, but his frankness was attractive. It wasn't the customary hypocrisy. Plenty of men will act like they can't help themselves, their lust is overwhelming them. Not Gennady. He was gentle, but—deliberate. It was like he'd seen us together in bed, and had decided to make it real. He was ready. His thinking it was sinful wouldn't stop him. It didn't even trouble him, once he'd made his decision, not really. It was all a scene he'd laid out. He was . . . unlike anyone else."

My ears and chest felt hot. She looked away, at the floor, as if she'd said more than she meant to. I cleared my throat, but she was the one who continued: "So, you—you liked him, too, then. That's why you keep harassing me with these questions?"

"Partly. He didn't deserve what happened."

"Partly?"

Our eyes met. I wasn't expecting it. Always her gaze pushed when I looked for her to pull, pulled when I thought she'd push. Now, just when I thought she'd relented, there was something hard in it. Something that hardened me to the point of honesty in turn.

"The other part is that I'm transferred to Company Ten for the duration of the investigation. The ration is better than in Quarantine. Much better. I'd like a place there, instead of in hard labor, when my term in Quarantine is over. Chances are better if we find the killer."

She nodded, slowly. "Yes. Even I agree that's a better reason."

The nets on the floor kept me from coming any closer. I did not want to lose the progress I thought I'd made. "Did you ever watch him at work on the icons?"

"Yes. Twice. Once recently. That was after I wrote him that letter, when I was able to come inside to go to the commissary." She pressed her lips together. "It was his way of socializing, wasn't it? He showed people icons. That was how he spent time with them."

"Did you notice the sorts of things he used, restoring them?"

"The things he used?"

"Supplies. Anything of that sort."

"There was something he cleaned the surface with. I thought it was alcohol. Otherwise—the pigments, his brushes. There was a little knife I saw him cut canvas away with. Is that what you mean?"

"Did you ever see him apply gold leaf?"

"No." She narrowed her eyes.

"It's gone missing. We'd like to know what happened to it."

"I'm sure."

"You don't know anything?"

"You think perhaps I took it? You think I would have had anything to do with killing him for that?"

"No," I said. "I don't think that."

"Then why do you keep pushing me?"

"Petrovich thinks you're hiding something. Maybe you are. But I don't believe that is your reason. You're scared—but we can protect you, Veronika!"

"Ha! You don't find it brazen to make that offer twenty-four hours after your partner offered to have me slapped around if I didn't help? Why, you're exactly like Spagovsky! 'Let me protect you, and if you don't you get a smack.' You think the offer is different for being a hair more subtle? It is not." Again her fingers began to ravel up the net. She shook her head. "You may as well go. I don't think you are going to be satisfied with anything I can tell you. If you would really like to help me, convince your partner not to have Spagovsky beat me. I would appreciate that. Otherwise—well, who cares if you've wasted my time?"

I couldn't think of anything else to say. I had not managed to bring her around. Petrovich would tell Spagovsky, and there was nothing I could do about it.

Before I reached the door, I turned to look back. "Veronika Filipovna," I said.

In her pool of light and nets she was a sculpture with living eyes.

"I can see why he was ready to sin."

With that I stepped out quickly, cheeks burning.

That was Tolya: foolish enough to say it, not bold enough to stay and hear her reply. Out on the road, I stepped quickly over the snow, as if I could leave my embarrassment behind if I only walked fast enough. Her voice was in my ears as I made my way back to the kremlin. *I begged him to come and find me when he was well*, she'd said. *I couldn't live without him.* Somewhere in my mind was a picture of myself with Antonov's beard, raising a hand—was it fatherly? was it desiring?—to Veronika's cheek.

It can only have been its stillness that made the figure pierce the fog I was in. No one stood still outdoors on Solovetsky. It was a waste of heat, a waste of calories.

I'd come about halfway back from the fishery by then. The man stood off to the side of the road beneath a stand of trees, some hundred yards away. I'd just come around a bend, in a spot where the road ran close to the sea. Now, seeing him, I stopped.

There was a moon, but with the trees crowding the road it was dark, and I couldn't make out anything about him. Was he facing this way? Was he looking at something? Was he waiting?

Was he waiting for me?

A gust of wind blew, and there was time to shiver. By now I thought he'd noticed my presence and was looking in my direction.

The situation said danger. I hadn't expected to see anyone out so late. I remembered Petrovich advising me not to confront Spagovsky two nights before.

Something about the situation said danger.

In a moment I'd decided: I would simply turn around, go back the way I'd come. The thought of explaining to Veronika that I'd returned because someone scared me on the road was excruciating, but the *zek*'s sense of self-preservation already outweighed my tenderer feelings. Perhaps I wanted to see what she would have said to my parting remark as well.

When I turned, a second man had appeared behind me. This one was closer than the other. I could make out an anonymous watch cap, a scarf wrapped around his face.

I was sure no one had been following me. He must have been hidden in the trees alongside the road, only to step out after

I'd passed.

I thought the first figure had taken a few steps in my direction, though it wasn't moving now. The new one was looking back over his shoulder in the direction of the fishery, as though he expected something. When I tried to think of what to do, my mind stalled, produced a blank page. For a long moment the three of us stood there. I could hear the blood pounding in my ears.

Then the man standing between me and the kremlin shouted something that sounded like "This one!" and everything was in motion.

I could hear the one who'd appeared behind me coming as I broke for the cover of the pines. A branch pushed me back as I got among them. Something gave with a crack and I stumbled, then righted myself without slowing down. Fingers of snow shook down my coat.

Beneath the canopy it was far darker. Snow squeaked and crunched under my boots, and my breath roared in my ears, whipping away in flags.

The ground sloped up as I ran away from the water, and the trees were thick enough to slow me. To avoid crashing into a trunk or another errant branch took care, but at least they'd put me out of view of the two men. I thought the second one had followed me into the woods, but when I chanced a glance back I couldn't see him.

Who were they? Why had they been lying in ambush for me? It had to have something to do with the case, but panic drove any further conclusions from my mind.

After a short time the slope evened out again, with the snowy ground interrupted here and there by depressions that the boughs filled with shadow. By this time I was panting, and beneath my coat I could feel fearful sweat running down my chest. When I looked back again, there was still nothing. I needed to think. When I passed a spot where an overhang of roots and stones created an especially deep patch of darkness, I checked behind me one more time, then crouched down and hid.

My thighs felt made of gruel. Again I wondered who they were. But there was no use wasting time on that question now. For the moment their identities didn't matter, only what they might do if they caught me. I tried to control my breathing, the trembling of my muscles. I needed to listen.

The kremlin was to the north, which I thought was on my left. That would be the only safe place. My earlier idea had obviously been wrong. Why would men willing to chase me through the forest balk at following me into the fishery?

But what was the fastest way to reach the kremlin? And how far had I run already? Even if I was right about which way was north, simply blundering off through the trees might bring me up on the wrong side of the Holy Lake. That would mean more time in the woods to be found and caught.

I'd been listening, or thought I had. Now I heard the crack of a branch, shockingly close. When I peered around a stone, the man was there. He was coming slowly, following the tracks I'd left in the snow.

My tracks! Hadn't Petrovich and I been discussing footprints all this time? Hadn't I been pondering Sherlock Holmes's forensic expertise? I should have known all along that I left behind my own trail of signs, leading to me as surely as my *detektivy*'s clues led to their villains.

I held my breath, but again thought failed me. I could hear his boots crunching in the snow now. He would be on me in a moment.

Finally consciousness snapped back into place. Before he could come around the mound and see me, I broke from cover.

"Here!" I heard him shout behind me. "Here!"

I thought I heard an answer from somewhere past him, towards the kremlin, but by then I could do nothing but run. I couldn't look back, but from the sound of it he was right behind me. As we wove through the trees the ground began to rise again, until it became clear we were climbing a significant hill. Breath came raggedly, and the terrain was treacherous beneath its layer of white. He was gaining on me. Every time I felt myself stumble I expected to feel his hands around my neck.

As I came over the crest of the hill, the ground fell away in a much steeper grade on the other side. For a moment I slowed to look for another way, wary of tumbling down the slope.

That was all he needed. I heard him grunt as his hard body slammed into me from behind, felt myself trip and pitch forward. Then the world turned end over end and I fell, the skin of my face raw against the snow. Stones slammed past, whirling about me as I rolled.

It can only have been luck that kept me from dashing my brains out on a rock. I came to a stop when I struck a tree at the bottom of the hill. Aching all over, I had bruised ribs and a sharp pain in my shoulder, but did not seem to have suffered any worse hurt than that. Miraculously, even my hat had stayed on my head. I can hardly have noticed it at the time, but I still had it later, so I know that it must have.

I shook my head to clear it.. Back at the top of the hill, some forty feet above, I thought I saw movement. My pursuer hadn't registered the drop that yawned in front of us when he tackled me; instead of catching me and finishing me off, he'd given me a lead. Before he could figure out a way down, I scrambled to my feet and set off running again.

My understanding of the game of flight and pursuit was growing by palpable leaps. Though I'd gained some ground, I was still far from safe. Now that it had entered my consciousness, I felt my track erupting out of the ground beneath me with every step. The man who'd been closer to me on the road had followed my path directly, while, judging from what I had heard when they called to each other, the other must have moved off into the woods to keep between me and the kremlin. I was disoriented, but thought they would both be behind me now. If I were somehow to double back and make it past the one, the other would still be waiting to sweep me up.

All I could think to do was keep running.

When a break in the trees appeared, I thought at first I might have reached the road again. Plunging through the last layer of branches, I instead found myself teetering at the top of a stone-lined embankment.

Twenty feet below lay a frozen canal. A system of waterways connected the island's lakes and ponds, I knew. Once dug by monks for travel to outlying hermitages, now it was one more way to move lumber from place to place. A rough channel had been hacked in the ice, just wide enough for a floating log to be dragged by a hook.

I slid down the embankment in a frantic crouch, nearly sitting. Here the moon was bright again, among sparse clouds.

Looking up and down the length of the canal, I saw that muddled boot-prints had packed the snow into ice and the earth into frozen mud at its edges. To the right, the canal gave into a small lake, while to the left it continued straight for some distance before disappearing around a curve. Prisoners' boots had churned the ice and frozen mud along its edges into a landscape of craters and ridges. If I hurried, my tracks might be lost in the muddle.

I leapt the channel easily. On the other side of the water, between the curve and where I stood, sat a few piles of boards, heaped around a series of rickety, trestle-like constructions whose function I didn't know.

I looked back over my shoulder, expecting the man to appear at the top of the embankment at any moment. The boards weren't a much better hiding place than the overhang back among the trees had been, but I'd never make it back around the bend before he saw me. If I lay down, I could at least put them between me and anyone who ran down the middle of the canal. This time I hoped he wouldn't be able to follow my footprints.

I lowered myself to the snow just in time. Through a crack between two stacks I saw him emerge from the trees. He followed the furrow I'd made sliding down the embankment easily, but drew up short when he came to the canal. For a moment he looked at the bank on the opposite side, searching for signs that I'd climbed back up and continued on into the woods. Seeing nothing, he turned and began jogging in the direction I had taken.

There was time now to look at him. The man coming towards my hiding place over the ice was thin, his height more or less the same as mine. He wore his scarf up over his nose, hiding his face. What I could see of his eyes I didn't recognize. He wore a standard *zek*'s coat, felt *valenki* like mine. In his right hand he held a wicked-looking curved knife with a naked blade.

The gap I'd been peering through didn't cover his whole approach. After he'd passed out of view, I could only hear the sound of his footsteps coming closer and closer. Now they were a few feet away.

Now they were here.

I began to breathe again once I'd heard them pass and begin to fade. And yet it is there, waiting to emerge and cross the water again to lose myself in the forest, that the memory of terror returns to squirm in my throat. I had to wait long enough, but not too long. If I thought he would continue on around the bend, I should wait until he had. But if I thought he would reconsider before that and come back to check my hiding place . . . There was no way to choose. How could I know what he would do? Yet the alternative was to stare helplessly at the boards around me until the knife arrived.

Shaking, I raised my head. He was not around the bend yet, but he was close to it, and still looking the other way. Immediately I darted out from my hiding spot, leapt the canal a second time, and scrambled up the north bank. In a moment I was in the trees again.

Had he seen me? I hadn't been able to tell, and it would have been foolish to stop to check. Again I ran.

Noise would be important now. If I'd lost him, he would be searching for me soon, and the other man was presumably still somewhere in the woods. The worst thing to do would be to broadcast my position. I tried to slip between the trees quietly.

That was a longer run than the others. At one point, I thought I heard the sound of a voice somewhere off to my right, but I couldn't be sure. If I did, it was one of them talking at a normal volume to the other, not shouting like before. Afterward I passed over a fresh trail of footprints in the snow. That was a good sign—it meant I'd gotten behind the other man, didn't it?—but if it occurred to him to double back, he'd find where I'd crossed him. The thought made me willing to risk more noise for speed. Shadows barred the snow in blue and black.

At long last I came to a break in the trees again: the edge of the Holy Lake. The moon shone in the sky on the other side of the water, lighting up the monastery's towers and walls, the power lines that ran along the road.

I breathed a sigh of relief; disoriented as I'd become, I'd managed to head mostly north, towards the kremlin and safety. I did, however, seem to have veered to the east significantly. I could make out Nikolski Tower, but the gate was well out of sight. To reach it, I'd need to circle around the lake in one direction or the other. The way around the north shore looked longer, but I thought it would be safer as well, since my pursuers would be coming up from the south.

After another period of running, the trees around me gradually gave way to stumps, until I found myself about to emerge onto the road east of Nikolski. Through what remained of the treeline I could see the outbuildings and a few lamps.

The prospect of exposure made me stop to think again. If my pursuers were smart, they'd have made directly for Nikolski as soon as they realized they'd lost me. I'd been telling myself that I'd been eluding them. Had I really only been giving them time to set up another ambush?

The nearest outbuilding was more than a hundred yards away. If one of them was lying in wait and watching for me, there would be no way for him to miss me dashing for it.

The chase had wound its pattern through the trees and around the lake, until now all the turnings looped on each other fell away. From here there were only straight lines.

I took a breath. I dashed.

The snow was treacherous as ever, but I barely had time to notice myself stumbling before I'd picked myself up again. I did not look back when I reached the road, but I felt sure that I heard the sound of pursuit behind me. The dark windows of the first outbuilding passed me, then the second. I came to the turning for Nikolski and took it without slowing.

There was no one in the guards' hut. When I reached the gate, it was shut.

The sounds of my shouting and pounding shattered the night's stillness. I expected at any moment to feel hands grabbing me.

There were sounds within, and a crack opened. I pushed through. The light of a stove flickered on the arched walls of the tunnel that passed through the wall.

"What's this all about?" asked the guard I'd shouldered aside. "Don't shout like that."

"Behind me—" I gasped. "Shut the door. They're coming."

His gray, exhausted face looked at me, baffled. He wore the normal guard's uniform—belted gray tunic under his coat, high boots, cap with a gleaming black brim—but wrapped around his neck as a scarf was a filthy scrap that had once been a red-and-white-checked dish towel. He glanced outside, then reached up to rub one gaunt and hungry cheek reflectively. Here was a guard, but with the embarrassment of the camp prisoner, who grasps so humiliatingly little about the world that entraps him. Who knows not to seek out any more understanding than he has. He avoided meeting my eyes.

"I don't know about any of that," he said. "Need to put an entry in the book about you coming in after curfew, though."

I was lucky, perhaps, that he was so meek. It hadn't occurred to me to worry that I might be met with hostility by the Nikolski guards. They hadn't given us trouble for the past few days. But it could easily have gone differently.

After I had showed Petrovich's and my pass, I went back to the gate to look out. The snow-covered roofs, the lake, the trees in the distance: the moon shone on all of them, motionless and white.

20

The first thing Petrovich said was that it was a good sign. If it had been worth someone's trouble to chase me through the nighttime forest, he reasoned, it meant we were closing in on something, making people nervous. Veronika had known we were coming, hadn't she? It would certainly be a development in our investigation if she'd tried to set someone on us. Perhaps Spagovsky. There were many possibilities. It was a pity I hadn't gotten a closer look at the two men.

The old man paused when he saw my expression. "But, after all," he muttered, "under certain circumstances, too close a look can be unhealthy. I'm glad you're all right."

My muscles still shivered. It was after curfew, and we were in our cell. We were not supposed to have a light, but Petrovich had turned the lamp on the windowsill down low. Bent over it, his face glowed. Each wrinkle, each unshaven hair, cast its own distinct shadow. From behind the mask of his bruise, one eye looked out, pink-rimmed and flat.

After I'd described the chase, he wanted to know the details of my conversation with Veronika.

"She admitted to being Antonov's lover," I said. "They slept together."

"We as good as knew that already."

"Yes, but she confirmed it. That's new. And she was more open about how they had met."

He nodded. There was no need for either of us to say it wasn't what I'd hoped for. It was not a new revelation that would keep Petrovich from going to Spagovsky. I could hardly even say if I wanted that anymore. What if the old man was right? What if she'd told the men in the forest where to wait for me?

After we put out the light, it took me a long time to fall asleep.

Each morning the inmates of Company Ten awoke, waited in line, then performed the necessary morning ritual standing shoulder to shoulder at an open stone gutter in the basement of their barracks. The flow of piss through a drain at one end trickled and splashed a mazurka into the cistern below.

That morning, as I stepped up to take my turn, I felt myself panic. The men standing to either side of me were too close, a danger. That there should be lavatories inside the kremlin was a result of the same sophisticated monastic drainage system I'd encountered at the canal the night before. My hands shook, spattering, as I felt myself there again. I hurried back upstairs to the cell as soon as I was done.

Petrovich was calmly reading a piece of paper when I came in. "Change of plans," he said. "Before we question Spagovsky, we're going back to the sauna."

While I had been trudging to the fishery last night, the old man had gone to see his colleagues at KrimKab about Golubov. The gold leaf was the kind of thing the *urka* might have heard of, if it had come up for sale. At any rate, it would be worth asking him. Our first meeting had gone poorly, of course, but there were other ways. The mistake, he said, had been to think that their connection in Odessa would allow him special access to the *urka*—approaching Golubov along with all his men had forced his hand, obliging him to make a show of force. Doing that again was out, but given their desire to resolve the situation without violence, the Administration Section had to have a private channel of communication with the sauna's leader. Asking among the criminologists had duly yielded someone who thought he could get Golubov a note via contacts in their office. The response had come while I was downstairs.

"I wrote that I had more questions, and notwithstanding my treatment last time, my offer was good. Told him we should meet privately. He writes here for us to come this morning."

In fact the note simply read, *Saturday, 7 a.m. Side door. Three knocks.* "It could be a trick, couldn't it?" I said. "Are you so sure he's willing to let bygones be bygones? He didn't seem like the type last time."

"I tell you, that was theater, to impress his rabble. Golubov may not care for me, but he knows how to advance his interests."

"What if those two were his men, waiting for me on the road last night?"

"It wasn't. What reason would they have? We need to hurry. Come on."

I wasn't reassured—my hands still shook, and Petrovich's face looked worse than ever—but could think of no way to delay. Bread had already been issued, and it was getting light. Seven would be here soon.

We found the side door Golubov had mentioned on the opposite side of the building from the stairs we'd gone down last time. Petrovich delivered the requested three knocks with his cane.

After a minute of waiting there was the sound of a bar being raised, and Golubov himself opened to us. Still wearing only an undershirt and drawers, he shivered in the cold air.

"Come on, then. I don't have all day," he said.

We followed him down a stairwell. The density of the blue-black ink that stormed over the *urka* boss's skin surprised me; somehow my memory had erased a large number of his tattoos. The word INDIAN was still there, blazoned across his cheeks. There was no forgetting that.

The room he brought us to was at one end of a hall. I thought the other end might lead to the barracks we'd been in before, where the other men stayed. It was all connected, at least; you could tell that by the stink. Smelling the place again was like having an animal squirm through your nostrils and nest in your throat.

Inside, Golubov sat down at a table, where a young blond woman waited for him. In contrast to his dingy underthings, she wore a blouse and a skirt with stockings, along with a heavy jacket.

As he began to peel an egg, she leaned against him, her cheek on his shoulder, her body half-covering the image of a ship under full sail on his arm.

"So, Inspector," he said. "Here we are, together again. What the fuck do you want? Wasn't I clear last time about not telling you anything?" He gestured with the egg at Petrovich's bruises. "Your face says I fucking was."

Petrovich took the remark in stride, along with the girl's presence, and I tried to as well. Frightened as I'd been last night, the chase hadn't put the boldness of my talk with Veronika from my mind altogether. Still, a moll waiting attendance on her half-naked gangster had no precedent in my experience.

"Oh, come, Golubov," the old man said. "There's no one here but us. Why let us in if you weren't interested?"

"You want something from me? You want to do business? Make me an offer, something we can actually trade. Don't be a silly cunt. Don't try to put my cock in with the pickles. Fuck your mother, how do I even know you can deliver anything from Infosec?"

"All you have to do is listen. Perhaps take a look at something. If, after that, you feel like talking to us, you can, and I'll report that you were helpful. Otherwise, we'll go away." Petrovich gestured at me with his chin. "Tolya heard about some stolen goods the other day. We thought that might be in your line."

Both men looked at me. The blond girl, paying no attention, sat forward and helped herself to a piece of bread from the table."Our friend Gennady Antonov," I said. "The one who was killed. He worked restoring icons in the museum collection. I heard from his boss that some supplies were taken from his desk shortly before he died. Alcohol, turpentine, some brushes. What seems like it would come up for sale is a book of gold leaf."

Golubov looked interested despite himself. "The fuck you say. Restoring icons? Here? I figured they would have thrown that stuff on the fire years ago. Or sold it off, at least. What do you mean by icons?"

"Just like your poor grandmother used to pray for your soul in front of," said Petrovich. "There's a whole chapel-full above the Holy Gates."

"I don't fucking believe it. They can't have saved that stuff.

The Communists would get their dicks tied in a knot all trying to piss on it at once."

"It's true," said Petrovich. "Have you heard anything?"

If a man with writing tattooed on his face can look mild, Golubov looked mild. "If I were saying anything to you, I'd say I haven't heard a fucking thing about it."

"What about a man named Zhenov?" said Petrovich. "Military—a former White. He manages a warehouse that supplies Anzer Division. He ever sell surplus to your boys?"

"Think I keep track of all the tsar's son-of-a-whore lieutenants who ended up in this camp and got bent? Who'd have the time?"

Petrovich sighed. "You're determined to be difficult. All right. Just one more thing." He handed him the list we'd gotten from Kologriev with the names of the men who'd collected the icons on it. "Recognize any of the names on that list?"

Golubov glanced over it languidly, then started and held it up. The N on his cheek twitched. "Ivan Kologriev? That prick? Him I know. I know he's lucky to fucking be alive." Hardening, his face receded behind the letters on it. Anger made him less of a man and more of a word.

"What do you know about Kologriev?" said Petrovich excitedly.

"Didn't notice the tattoos, Inspector? Should have been a fucking giveaway."

"You're saying Kologriev's an *urka*?"

"Something like that."

Petrovich stroked his mustache. "He buttons his shirts at the wrists and neck."

"Waste of his old man's spunk, is what he is. How's he mixed up in this?"

Petrovich smiled. He said: "You'll help us, then?"

"All I know about is Kologriev. How did you two come across him?"

"He's Zhenov's foreman," I said. "It's like you said, some of the higher-ups in the OGPU don't like the icon collection. Others protect it, but evidently they can't always. Zhenov seems to have gotten permission to use some of the icons we were talking about for boards at the Anzer cabinetry workshop." Golubov frowned, so I explained. "They're painted on wooden panels. Kologriev was in charge of going to the museum to go and pick them up. The gold leaf we're looking for went missing around then. He might have taken it."

Golubov looked down at his undershirt and brushed an invisible speck of dirt from its shoulder. When he looked up at me, he looked human again. "This business with the museum is all news to me." He took his glass from the table and waved it at the girl, who poured vodka into it. "But Kologriev—I never worked with him, but I know him. He was a stick-up artist in Moscow. One of us. No fucking longer, though."

"When did he start grafting?" I asked.

"Picking up the lingo, are you, schoolboy?" He tossed off the vodka. "It was spring before last. The camp bosses started offering deals to any *urka* who'd whore for them. Sweet positions, extra rations. Trash like that."

"They've got to be able to say they've reformed you," said Petrovich.

"That's what gives them a hard-on. Kologriev teased them just right. One day he's one of us, next he's transferred to a new unit and works for them with a grin like he's figured out how to get his prick into his own mouth."

"In Odessa," said Petrovich, "anyone who tried leaving the life like that wouldn't have lasted long."

Golubov spat. "Goddamn right." He lowered his voice. "But we aren't in fucking Odessa, are we? Word came around that if anything happened to the sorry cunts who took their offer, these Cheka fucks would put certain of us in the ground, regardless of who'd done it. They aren't so stupid."

"Don't you have a tattoo somewhere that means you care less about life than the honor of thievery?" muttered the old man.

"Fuck yourself. That stuff's for children. You think anyone who gets to be as old as I am believes that? Why do you think I'm talking to you?" He looked down at his uninked palm, then turned it over to the symbol-speckled back of his hand. "Point is, Kologriev's protected. I had someone go talk to him at his new place. Just talk. Next day a prick from Infosec showed up in a leather jacket, gave me to understand that if anything happened to young Ivan, I'd be screwed with a splintered table leg. No debate about it. They don't want us fucking with the grafters, but even for a grafting fucker, Kologriev has special connections."

The girl looked supremely bored. She had a few tattoos herself, I noticed, one of a heart with wings above her wrist, another that I couldn't identify peeking from beneath the neck of her blouse. "You think he might have taken the gold leaf?" I asked, looking purposefully at Golubov and not her. "He's the kind of man who could kill our friend Antonov?"

"Sure. Cock-gobbling graft artist, but he used to rob for a living. He's a killer. He'd fucking do it without looking, just by feel."

"Anything else we should know about him?"

He looked thoughtful. "Before all this, he was trusted. Did time in work camps under the tsar. Even broke out of two of them, made his way back to his people in Moscow. Smart guy. Tough. Only he turned out not to be worth more than a dead dog's prick."

Petrovich and I exchanged a look. "All right, Golubov," said Petrovich. "This has been useful. I'll put in a good word for you, and I'll let you know what happens."

From the expression he looked at us with, the *urka* might never have smiled in his life. "I wish you luck. Nail his balls to the roof of Sekirnaya, and his cock somewhere else."

Outside, we hurried towards Nikolski. Petrovich thought we should try to get as much as we could before meeting the Chekist at ten. There was still Spagovsky to talk to. Then Zhenov, to see whether he had anything to say. Finally we would go to Kologriev, try to press him with Golubov's new information.

In the courtyard, where waiting *zeks* snaked out from the gate in a line, a monk who had been sitting on the stoop of one of the buildings stood up and hurried over to us. "Bless you," he said abruptly. "I am Brother Kiril. I am looking for a Yakov Petrovich, along with an Anatoly Bogomolov. You are they, yes?"

The man's beard was a breastplate that covered his chest. It tapered into matted points as it met the flapping belly of his robe. Except for the odor of fish, he might have stepped out of an anchorite's crypt-adjacent cell, with the eleventh century's dirt smudging his wide face.

"That's right," said Petrovich.

"You are known to me. You've come to speak with Veronika Filipovna at our fish house several times."

"You were looking for us?"

"A letter for you." The man moved his mouth like he was tasting something he didn't much like, eyeing me suspiciously. "Usually she keeps a decent silence, but this morning I found her outspoken and insistent. She demanded I bring you this. An errand of mercy, she said. But women are easily led into sin."

Petrovich was suspicious. "Why hasn't she come herself?"

"She knew that my brothers and I can use the Fish Gate." He gestured towards Nikolski. "She would not have been allowed through here. It was important that I find you at your cell as soon as I could, she said. Not finding you there, I decided I would wait to see whether I would recognize you here."

"Fine," said Petrovich. "I'm glad you found us."

Brother Kiril nodded but held back the letter. "I regard Veronika Filipovna as a soul in my care." The way he peered back and forth between me and Petrovich suggested he was trying to decide who would be more likely to drag his charge down the road to licentiousness.

"That's not what this is," I said hotly.

He stayed in case we would let him see what the letter said, but left when I shot him a look.

It began, *To the Hon. Detectives Petrovich and Bogomolov:*

I am ready to tell you what I know, though I expect it will be less than you hope. It has nothing to do with Boris and little enough to do with me. Nevertheless, perhaps you will find it helpful.

I have sent the monk to give you this so that you will not say anything to Boris before talking to me. I will return to the Women's Dormitory at the regular time. If you care to wait, I will speak to you there. Otherwise, you do not seem to have had any difficulty finding me at the fishery in the past.—V.F.F.

"You see," I said to Petrovich, who was reading over my shoulder. "I told you she'd be on our side."

"That's what you think, eh?" He kept squinting at the note, as though something new might swim up out of its seven sentences. "To me this looks like what a woman would do if she knew her man's attempt on you last night had gone wrong. You may be wrapped around her finger, but someone needs to ask hard questions about this secret of hers. About your chase, too. We'll need to go through it again before we see her. From the beginning, in as much detail as you can remember."

"We don't know Spagovsky was one of them," I said.

"No. But we don't know this new forthcomingness means she's on our side either." He shrugged. "She's bought herself some time, at least. Spagovsky will have to be postponed until we see what she has to say."

The line for Nikolski was not excessive, and we soon drew to the front. The two guards on duty were the same ones we'd interrogated on the first day—Vlacic, with the goiter, and his friend, who'd smacked his lips. They worked slowly, uttering queries and commands as they checked papers and made entries in their book.

"You're them," said Vlacic as we stepped forward. I'd retrieved the gate pass from my coat and given it to Petrovich, and the guard snatched it as the old man presented it. He looked at it and nodded, but didn't hand it back. "Basil, go and get him."

"What is this about?" asked Petrovich tiredly.

Ugly anticipation clenched in the other man's face like a muscle. "You just wait." *Zeks* shuffled about us, creating a little zone of emptiness to separate them from the scene they sensed developing. "You made trouble for us the other day. Word came down we were to leave you be."

"Did it?"

"We'll see how smart you are now."

Petrovich began to say something, then didn't. He and I didn't look at each other while we waited.

When they had come to arrest me, back in Petersburg, during that family dinner, the officers had graciously allowed me a final few bites of my meal before carting me off. Dinka held my hand, the secret policemen looking on with strange courtesy while my fork clinked against my plate. Objects in the dining room somehow folded in on themselves that evening, as though the surfaces I could have touched were being turned away and replaced by identical surfaces inaccessible to me: the lamp hanging from the ceiling, the tablecloth, the bow in my sister's hair. A tureen, a pitcher on the sideboard.

This was like that. A false sky covered the sky, the kremlin's walls turned into incredibly detailed paintings of themselves. Nikolski Gate was a trompe-l'oeil effect, giving only the impression of depth; the zeks murmuring around us, actors. I've often noticed this phenomenon of cognition in moments of catastrophe—a feeling of the world becoming less real without any change to the visual field.

Trailed by Razdolski, Basil-the-guard, and the commander who'd swung his baton at me when we first examined the entrance logs, the Chekist came around the corner. He was pulling on his gloves; coming out of whatever warm spot he'd been waiting in had flushed his cheeks, and he looked more boyish than ever.

"Petrovich," he said without a nod of greeting. "You're carrying your papers with you? Give them to me."

"Just a minute," said Petrovich. I could hear him try to be gruff. My heart had started pounding. "Tell me what's happened."

"Don't be stupid, Inspector." The glove on the hand he held out was well made, I remember thinking. It fit him well. "Give them to me."

The guard with the goiter handed over our gate pass, while Petrovich's tongue moved behind his lips without his saying anything. Finally the old man gave in. "Get them out, Tolya." I fumbled in my coat for the transfer order, the investigation authorization, and the pass for the Infosec archives. Petrovich took them and handed them on to the Chekist. I almost handed over Veronika's note, but at the last minute I summoned the presence of mind to keep it back.

When I recall my state of mind, I see I did not fully comprehend what was going on, much as I felt that something terrible was about to happen. It should have been clear enough, I suppose. But the moment seemed to promise anything. Had the investigation into Terekhov's death paid off? Had Infosec caught the killer by its own efforts? Were we to be issued new authorizations?

The Chekist was looking through the sheaf of documents. As he did, Petrovich found his voice. "This is ridiculous. You haven't heard our latest progress. We are closing in. Someone thinks we are a threat—there was an attempt on Bogomolov's life last night!"

The Chekist barely acknowledged me. "Was there? How interesting. I will debrief him on that subject at some later point."

Petrovich took hold of the younger man's sleeve. "Listen.

There's more. This business at the Anzer Division warehouse is developing. One of their—"

"Yes," said the Chekist. "Anzer. You haven't been outspoken about that connection, have you? All your business about icons and cabinetry and missing supplies—but you left out your traipsing around the warehouse."

"One of their workers was an *urka*. Our investigation—"

"Enough!" said the Chekist, cutting him off. "Be silent, Yakov Petrovich. Your investigation, as you call it, is over." The flames leapt up when he opened the door to the guards' stove. In one swift motion he tossed in our bundle of papers. "Razdolski will escort you to Company Ten. See that they remain in their cells," he said to the guard.

Fear somersaulted in my heart. There was a tone in the old man's voice I had never heard before, not even when he'd been attacked by Golubov's men. "Do I take it this is—what? A punishment?" he said.

"Just stay in your cell."

"What is going to happen to us? You'll send Tolya back to Quarantine and me back to Krimkab? Or you have something else in mind? I've done nothing but help you, you devil!"

"Razdolski, take them." The Chekist began to walk away, but turned back as the guard took the old man's arm. "You will know, Yakov Petrovich, when I've decided to punish you."

Petrovich didn't resist as he was led away. I remember walking behind them stunned, as though the false, hard surface the world had turned to face me had suddenly jerked forward and struck me between the eyes. Goitered Vlacic grinned, Razdolski scratched his neck with the hand that wasn't gripping Petrovich, and the zeks in the line continued to look at anything but us.

In the eyes of Solovetsky, we were no longer investigators.

21

Waiting is the essential activity of prison life. Whatever else you do, in prison you wait.

Sometimes the waiting kills you. But since that can only happen once, and since there is so much more waiting to be done than can be measured by only one of anything, most of the time it doesn't.

Waiting comes in different textures, different flavors. It is dull, sharp, bitter, glassy, friable. It gags with sweetness. Men choke on terror. They do it while they wait.

You wait to be fed. You wait in lines. You wait for your work assignment, or for the necessary tools to be delivered so that it can begin. You wait for winter to end. You wait to board trains. You wait to move, and you wait to be allowed to stop moving. When winter is over you wait through the summer, anticipating the frost that will kill the mosquitoes. You wait for something, anything, to break the monotony. You wait alone and with others. You wait for the present crisis to blow over; for God's sake, keep your head down in the meantime. You wait for the end of your sentence, or to see whether there will be tacked on to it, via telegram from some functionary in a distant city, another three years. You wait for punishment, for revenge, for a clue that will tell you how much longer you will be waiting.

I waited on the bed that had been Antonov's. The straw in its mattress poked at me, the board underneath bruised my hip. Petrovich sat on his own bed, reading Antonov's old Bible. If I'd swung my legs to the floor, our knees would have collided.

Razdolski had brought us here and seen that we were installed. He'd made a face like he didn't like us sharing the room—the Chekist had said "cells," not "cell"—but in the end he left us. Taking a stool from the hallway, he'd gone out to sit on the landing in the staircase. He was still there now.

Your guards wait, too, in prison. Their hats wait, their belts wait. Their fists and weapons wait.

After what had happened, I couldn't say what waited for us. Though I tried to put it from my mind, what the Chekist had said—"You will know when I punish you"—skittered fearfully along my spine, over my ribs. I raised my head and watched Petrovich turn a page. Antonov's Bible was dense and black.

"What should we do now?"I said.

"There's nothing to do."

"There must be something. He said we had three more days."

Petrovich did not look up. "No good asking," he said in a low voice.

"But the two of you had an understanding, didn't you? What did he say to you when you first arranged this?"

"Nothing that makes it a good idea to harass him."

The old man didn't want to talk. And maybe he was right: for all my jangling anxiety, the food problem made more urgent claims on my attention. I climbed off the bed and opened Antonov's chest.

Even in the best case, of my merely being sent back to Quarantine Company, what had happened was not good. To return in the Chekist's bad graces, and without Petrovich being in a position to do much for me, was essentially worse than never having left at all. I'd need to take as large a share of Antonov's rations with me as possible, simply to break even. I could improve my nutrition for the next three weeks that way, if I was sparing. But it would mean making arrangements to keep my bounty from being taken from me, whether by stealth or by violence. Violence seemed more likely. Hoarding calories invited danger.

I'd moved a few things in the chest around, mainly the food, but the arrangement inside was mostly the way Antonov had packed it. Spoons, bowl, safety razor, and soap atop a little pile of clothing. The dried greens wrapped in a towel. I rubbed the wool of his green sweater between my finger and thumb.

He'd been kind to me, Antonov. He'd taken pity on me, that night in the museum, offering me the patronage I'd come looking for—that's what I'd told Veronika. He'd treated me to several of his eccentric conversations, provided some fish and part of an onion. Then he'd died, a murder victim. The investigation that followed seemed to have been about everything in his life but him. Passing back and forth from side to side of the kremlin wall, following figures down one snowy road after another, asking question after question—so far it had told us exactly nothing about the man.

But then, my chief concern had always been the investigation's effect on my prospects for survival. Justice for Antonov—it was secondary, at best. Why should I have expected to learn about him?

I tried a few ways of distributing rations around my coat, moving them between the two pockets and the hole torn in its lining. It appeared I could take either the potatoes or the groats without making it obvious that I carried something. Not both.

Petrovich had put aside the Bible, laying it on the windowsill next to his chess set.

"Did you ever play chess with Gennady Antonov?" I said.

"No."

"Why not?"

He huffed in amusement. "Said he had a distaste for moving 'the little idols' around in their different directions. That was precisely the phrase he used. I remember it. It was a competition to see who could tie the tightest knot on the board, he said. 'There ought to be something in another man's strategy to make it worth so much effort to perceive. But men's strategies always disappoint.'" He shrugged. "Always talked as though his preferences were religious scruples. Who knows, maybe they were."

"What's going to happen to us, Yakov Petrovich?"

"I don't know."

"What do you think?"

He shook his head. "They didn't send us to a penal cell right away. Maybe that's a good sign."

Despite the chill this remark gave me, I was able to kill an hour dozing. When I woke up, I tried again.

"Shouldn't we try to explain what we've found out to the Chekist? This afternoon, in front of all those people, he wasn't about to listen to you. Like Golubov. Maybe he'd be more reasonable if you went to his place and explained."

Petrovich was sitting back against the wall with his eyes closed. His wrinkled face looked dead. Only the mustache was lively, with its crazed hairs vibrating as he breathed in and exhaled. "It wouldn't do any good."

"But the note from Veronika, what Golubov just told us about Kologriev—we're making progress for the first time. I was chased! You said it yourself this morning, that's a sure sign we're on the right path. If we stop now—"

"It's not us stopping. We've been stopped." He opened his good eye and squinted at me with it. "You don't want to go back to Company Thirteen. I don't blame you. But you should see that that's the best thing that could happen now."

"What you said before, about the penal cell—is the Chekist going to punish us? Why would he?"

"I don't know. And anyway, there's nothing I can do."

"I don't believe that. We should make him understand how we've advanced the case."

He looked up at the ceiling. "Do you know what I was doing before they sent me here, Tolya?"

"You'd retired, hadn't you?"

"I retired fourteen years ago. I was last a policeman in 1912. Do you know what I was doing when they came to take me away? I was shouting at my daughter's children, because their noise kept me from reading stories from the morning's paper for a second time. My daughter had twice already made her usual suggestion. Maybe I'd enjoy getting out of the apartment and taking a long walk? I'd refused because of the pain in my joints, and because I had no one to visit. Now she sends me money and hopes no one in her building remembers I was sent off to prison. She leaves it out of her letters, but I can tell things are not going well for her with the building manager. Or at work either. You expect too much of me."

This was said with his usual matter-of-factness. Except for a certain clipped manner, he might have been talking about a witness in a case he was working, one he did not have much respect for. It was like watching someone smash his hand against the edge of a table to demonstrate that it was numb.

"You still know police work," I said. "Look at how much I've learned, just working with you for five days. And about Golubov—you were right, we only had to get him alone. We're closer than we've ever been!"

He closed his eye. "Don't say I've taught you."

"Well, you have. Of course you have. And the Chekist isn't stupid. He knows your value, whatever else may be. He wants to find the killer, doesn't he?"

"He wants an investigation. He'll carry it out however seems best to him. You've been arrested once. You ought to understand that it's dangerous to tell them you don't want to go along with how they do things."

"Veronika Fitneva will never talk to him," I said.

"She's barely talked to us."

"She wants to tell us something." He shrugged but didn't say anything.

"Well, fine. But tell me the truth, Yakov Petrovich. Do you think he'll be able to solve the case?"

A moment passed before he said:"I don't know."

"You can't tell me you're satisfied with that—with the possibility Antonov's murderer might go free. That's not to mention poor Nail Terekhov."

"No one here is free."

But his gruff voice was quiet. I thought he might be coming around. "I'm worried about being on the Chekist's bad side. And I do want to stay in Company Ten. You're right about that. It's been good for me to be here, to have my own bed and dry ration. But it's more than that. Antonov was my friend. If we even understood what made the Chekist give up on us, I might be as discouraged as you are. But as it is, don't we owe it to him—owe it to the dead—to try to go on? The Chekist would listen to you, if you'd just explain it all to him."

Did I believe what I was saying? Only an hour before I'd been reflecting that such considerations were peripheral, secondary. But as the words left my mouth, I think I did believe we owed something to the dead. Hunger and fear will make you believe anything.

Petrovich pushed his body painfully to the edge of the bed and stood. He gestured impatiently for me to hand him his cane. I did.

"I need the lavatory," he said.

He still hadn't come back when the bell began to toll. A church sound, a steeple-and-spire sound. I associated it with the city, with distance. If someone had asked me, I'd have guessed the monastery's bells had melted when the cathedral towers burned in '23. But something rang through the island's early arctic twilight.

"What is it?" I asked Petrovich as he limped back into the room.

"Early curfew. They are calling the men in from work."

I went to the window. Outside the sun was setting rapidly, but this was different from the usual steam whistle that signaled curfew. "What does it mean?"

His voice was quiet, still grating. "Last time, they rounded up a dozen prisoners and took them out to the graveyard to be shot."

The bell continued to peal. Five times, then six. I told myself the icy tendril that curled in my gut was only a product of the general circumstances. Executions were always alarming, and any *zek* would be jumpy after an encounter like the one we'd had with the Chekist. I had already been afraid. If my body's reflex reaction to new stimulus was more fear, it only meant my nervous system was working properly, not that things had grown more dangerous.

(But how to be sure? a voice in my head answered back. Where was the guarantee the two things weren't connected?)

Petrovich didn't say any more. The bell went on, reverberating through the empty dormitory, a dome of sound that covered the kremlin. The pealing, repeated and repeated, grew monotonous.

Gradually the sound of men arriving reached us in our high cell. Their shuffling echoed up the stairs like water rising around the bell's pilings of sound, until drips of conversation, of throat clearing, of boot removal, along with the minor adjustments of furniture as it was sat on, flipped from background to foreground and submerged the ringing.

Petrovich and I sat and waited.

At last it stopped. Still we waited.

There were five at first. We became aware of them when someone down the hall cried out that everyone should look outside. In the twilight below us they were only shapes, and we couldn't tell exactly what they were doing. But our view of the courtyard was good. Our two neighbors from across the hall, men I'd seen before but hadn't been introduced to, joined us at the window.

The number swelled as men were pulled from the dormitories. Each door they went to spilled forth a new figure, stumbling between the men who'd gone in to fetch him. Once they came out with three at once, one member of the group holding the door for the others, allowing light from inside to paint shadows of their legs across the snow.

I couldn't look away from the window. The breath rasped in my throat as I watched to see whether they would come to the door of Company Ten.

There was a period of milling about in a crowd—I thought there were fifteen or so down there, the guards indistinguishable from their victims in the oncoming blue darkness. Then someone marshaled them into a group and marched them off.

They had not come for us. They had not come for me.

Instead of towards Nikolski, they headed to the Holy Gate. We could see them waiting while the bars were unchained and raised, the doors pushed open. Then the group disappeared behind an angle of the wall, leaving the emptiness and the darkening blue snow of the courtyard behind.

As I was to learn later, this was standard procedure. I've mentioned that the rule was for the Holy Gate to be kept barred, haven't I? An exception was made for the larger sorts of execution. It had been the main gate for the monks, and it was closer to the graveyard than Nikolski. The effect of funneling regular daily traffic through the smaller gate was to constrict it, to choke and slow the flow of prisoners so it could be monitored and controlled. During roundups like the one that had unfolded below us, however, with everyone consigned to his cell or barracks, no one else would be going in and out. Why not relax?

There's a certain gross symbolism to throwing wide the kremlin's largest doors only for those *zeks* who were leaving it to be killed. I don't believe it was intended. Organizers of these events have many factors to bear in mind. They take advantage of every opportunity that presents itself to make their plans more efficient. This is something I have come to understand.

The whole kremlin waited, listening. During executions the bullets were rationed like bread. One per victim. Everyone knew it. You could tell how many they killed by counting the shots.

Bang. One.

It startled me, though I'd been waiting for it. It hadn't taken them as long to reach the graveyard as I'd thought it would. The second followed immediately. *Bang*. Two.

We pulled open the window to hear. The guns sounded tinny and small coming from the field, but they echoed in the kremlin's empty courtyards. *Bang. Bang. Bang*. Three, four, and five.

The old man stepped back and looked at me. Even now, after thirty years during which the thing he was on the point of revealing has abraded my consciousness, I cannot visualize the expression he wore at that moment, cannot picture his abrupt-as-ever mustache, without seeing them as unreadable ciphers. As the shots rang out I looked nervously back and forth between Petrovich's face and the blackening sky outside the window—from one emptiness to another. Cold air poured into the room.

Bang. Six. *Bang*. Seven.

"Jesus Christ have mercy," said Petrovich finally.

The words came out too loud for the small space, with a sound that made you realize things—teeth, tongue, glottis—were grinding together behind his face. One of the men from across the hall twitched.

Bang. Eight.

"Are you well, Yakov Petrovich?" one of them murmured—not the one who had twitched.

"Never mind, Mikhail Sergeyevich," said Petrovich. "Doesn't matter."

There was another moment before the next shots. No one said anything else, as though no one wanted to be interrupted.

Bang. Nine. *Bang*. Ten.

A gust of wind rattled the window. The twitcher—he was

standing over my right shoulder—shook his head and turned away. You could hear him crossing the hall back to his own cell.

Bang. Eleven.

"Fuck your mother," said Petrovich quietly. "Here it is. Already. And what's next? Christ forgive me."

Something about that brought me up short. He sounded the same as always, but wrong. I said: "What do you mean, what's next? Why would there be anything next?" When Petrovich didn't say anything, I said it again. "Why would anything come next?"

"It's stopped," said Mikhail Sergeyevich. "Hasn't it?"

It had.

Petrovich shut the window. Mikhail Seregyevich took one look at him and hurried out of the room to join his cellmate, muttering something about it being a terrible shame. Outside our door, conversations hummed, muted and energized. Prison is waiting: a violent public event, which punctuates the wait and gives the *zeks* something to talk about, is like water poured out for thirsty men.

It afforded us a kind of privacy.

"They didn't come for us," I said into the still room. It should have been relieving, but wasn't. I steeped in a brew of doubt. "They didn't take us. So how could this have had anything to do with us? With the investigation?"

"I don't know anything," he said. "Only that it's a bad idea to try again with the Chekist."

"What do you mean? What could we have found out that would lead to that? No one's been implicated yet. We've barely started to—"

He cut me off without turning to face me. "Listen. Go back to Thirteen. Keep your head down. Don't act like you know anything. Don't involve yourself. The best thing you can do now is pretend none of this ever happened, that you never had anything to do with it."

The room had grown dim. The lamp would only have made it harder to see while we looked down into the courtyard, and we'd left it alone. Now the only light came from out in the hall. Petrovich lowered himself slowly onto the bed. For the first time since his beating, he sat like a man with a wound.

"What does the Chekist have to do with it?" I said.

He shifted, then coughed twice. His lungs made a noise like tiny twigs breaking. "I haven't told you everything about—about what the Chekist wanted me to look into."

"He wanted you to look into Antonov's death."

"That. But they don't set up an investigation for every *zek* who dies under mysterious circumstances, do they? Don't deceive yourself. Men die up on Anzer as badly as Antonov did out in the bay, and no one ever thinks about it again." He looked tired, deflated. "No, it was because the Chekist had heard about some kind of escape being planned. He thought Antonov was involved."

"Antonov? What do you mean?"

"He wouldn't tell me details. Something to do with those Whites he had me interviewing. Whatever it was, Antonov's death surprised him, surprised all of them at Infosec. I think he hoped if we solved the killing, we'd learn something about how they were intending to get away. Maybe he'd done something to get on the wrong side of his fellow conspirators, and they'd done for him."

"But that makes no sense. No one from the Chekist's list even knew Antonov. We haven't heard the first thing about any escape. You don't believe it, do you?"

His voice scraped in his throat. "No." He jerked a thumb at the window. "But that's what they would do if they believed, isn't it?"

"I don't understand. It must have been obvious to them that there was nothing in it. What about Nail Terekhov? Why would his former comrades kill him? He didn't even seem to recognize Antonov's name. Was he supposed to have crossed this conspiracy somehow as well? No, the story doesn't make sense. That can't be the Chekist's theory."

"It isn't. He already knows perfectly well who's guilty of that murder."

"What do you mean?"

"No *zek* killed Nail Terekhov. Our friend did that himself."

I struggled to grasp what he was saying. "What?"

"Didn't you see the cigarette burns? The bruises? Terekhov endured an interrogation before he died. There's only one group able to arrange something like that on this island, and it isn't any squadron of White officers. It's Infosec. I expect they tried to get him to talk about this escape. Maybe he'd even have lived through it if he knew anything."

"But that's madness. If the Chekist killed him, why have us come and examine the body? What could he have hoped to learn?"

Petrovich shook his head. "It doesn't matter. We've been pulled from the case. You were there. You saw how that went this morning. It's what I've been telling you. What we've found doesn't matter now. Not in the slightest. At best, we're beside the point. At worst we have something that conflicts with their story." He'd set his jaw but still wouldn't look at me. "Go back to Quarantine, Tolya. Don't show an interest in any of it. Not in the executions, not in Antonov. None of it. Your best chance is to let them forget you were ever connected to him."

The cold I'd felt wrapping my gut while they rounded them up curled again. This time it reached into my chest, and I felt my heart twitch with it. "My best chance?"

"Do I have to explain? You ought to understand this. It's never been good to find yourself on the wrong side of something they've already decided to go forward with."

"You're in danger, too, then?"

"It's not as bad for me."

Still he wouldn't meet my eyes. The room was darker and darker. I opened the tin door on the lamp and lit a match.

"You're warning me?" I said around a tongue thick with fear.

"I'm warning you."

"It doesn't seem fair, it being worse for me than for you. It's only an accident that I ended up helping you."

The match was burning down in my fingers. "Light the lamp," said Petrovich.

I did. The flame guttered, then burned clean.

The understanding coming over me was nothing at all like light. It was smoke, gradually spreading in my chest.

"How did I come to be involved in this case, Yakov Petrovich?"

Now that I was beginning to understand, he sounded miserable. "I am only telling you to keep your head down. That's sound advice, whatever else may be. I don't want to see anything happen to you."

"The Chekist knew about the time I came here. With Antonov." He'd interrogated me about it, with those slippery changes of subject and demeanor, that needless punch in my gut. I thought of Petrovich's meetings with him in the little wooden cabin beneath the kremlin wall.

The old man's breathing was heavy. He didn't say anything, and I went on: "I came to get some food from him. I met you."

"How do you think I made it through Quarantine, Tolya? Do you think I would have without help? What work platoon would want to carry crippled Petrovich on its back? Hard to claim your share of the bread when you can't handle your share of the work. I had an . . . arrangement already. When I arrived. From the warden in Odessa, where they first kept me. Not stupid, him. He ran the place . . . call it respectably. An old Bolshevik. No police background, but he said he'd spent enough time in the tsars' prisons to want to understand how they ran." He chuckled, then grimaced. Finally he stared up at me, his eyes blue and pained. "You've seen the skills I have left. Do you think being a detective is simply solving crimes? No. Being a detective is learning secrets, then telling them. Someone's always needed to peer behind the picture one person presents to the world and tell another what's really there. That I am still good at. That is always going to be worth a share of bread."

"You told him about me. You're the one who told him I knew Antonov."

It was a long moment before he answered. "Yes."

The icy feeling made another turn in my intestines. For all its twists, it led to one conclusion, like one of Vinogradov's labyrinths. "And now you're telling me he thinks I am part of this escape. You thought they might come for me just now. Not because we made him angry. Because they thought I was one of them. You thought they might take me out with those others to be shot."

"Yes."

A disgusting thought welled up. "Terekhov's body. That's why he showed it to us. He didn't want you to examine it at all. He only wanted to see my reaction. He wanted to see—what? Whether I'd give some kind of sign that I'd been colluding with the man?"

"Must have hoped it would rattle you. He wanted me to watch to see whether you made contact with anyone afterward."

"And you—you knew. You knew what had happened to Terekhov. You knew about all of it. And you wouldn't tell about it because it would have given away your blasted secret." My voice shook. "Damn you. You—you bastard. You old slug! Golubov was right. You're an informant! I've carried you around this island. On my back, almost. And all the time you were selling me out."

"Keep your voice down!" Petrovich hissed. "Tolya, please. I am sorry. I never meant you any harm. I didn't know what he had in mind about Antonov. I thought it was ordinary surveillance. They want to keep track of everyone. Most of it comes to nothing. Harmless, you see?"

I could hear the fear shaking in my throat, but fury kept driving the words through it. "Harmless? You were the one who brought me on as an assistant. You—you've been meeting with him. While I've been gone. Reporting on me. You have to have been. What have you been saying?"

"That you have nothing to do with it. That there's nothing for you to have to do with—I haven't seen any more evidence of this escape plot than you have. I only asked for you to be assigned to help me because I was sorry for having gotten you involved. I thought I could get you a better ration, be in a position to protect you. He said he wanted you close to the case, that I should watch you, but all we turned up—I thought we would find the real killer, you see? But he kept pushing me to find more about this damned escape, harder than I thought he would. And now—"

While he spoke the bell began to ring again. There were three long peals, then it stopped. Petrovich and I both looked around.

"What is it?" I said. I could feel the pulse in my neck, my heart pounding somewhere in the body below it.

"The end of curfew."

I went to the window. It was dark out in the yard. I couldn't tell whether anyone was moving. My breath fogged on the glass.

"You're probably all right," said Petrovich quietly. "If they were going to take you tonight, they'd have rounded you up with the others."

To that I said nothing. The anger that had washed over me continued to build, a rising wave in the current of my fear. If I'd tried to answer, the eddying might have choked me dead.

We were interrupted by the floor section leader, who appeared in the door, apologetic. An order had arrived from Administration: I was to be transferred back to Company Thirteen. I would have to leave tonight. In fact, now.

The two of them watched silently as I gathered my things. It embarrassed me now, to pull on Antonov's sweater and wrap his scarf around my neck: what had been a fortunate windfall, sign of my ability to grab opportunities as they came, now marked me as a dupe and idiot. Whatever good a sweater would do me, it had cost me more. In the end I fit two pieces of fish, three potatoes, and what was left of the bag of groats into the lining of my coat. I stowed both of Antonov's spoons in my sleeve. I no longer cared about the things being obvious.

As I stepped through the door, Petrovich said, "Tolya."

"What?"

"Whatever you think about me now, my advice before was good. The best you can do is act like you never had anything to do with it. Stay away from me. Stay away from the museum—from anything related to Antonov. Don't go to the Chekist." He looked at me grimly, his mouth pulled tight. "And . . . be careful, won't you?"

I met Razdolski on the stairs. When he saw me, he turned around without a word and went down ahead of me. Out in the courtyard he held up a dirty finger in my face. "You're to go back to Quarantine. Don't you go anywhere else." With that he turned and went off. Having waited so long, why didn't he escort me there? Razdolski: inscrutable and lazy to the last.

The lamps that usually lit the yard hadn't been turned on, and clouds covered the moon, so bright during my run through the woods the night before. The walls and arches around me were only thickenings and smoothings in the black, perforated in places by dimly lit windows.

I could hardly make out where I was going, but I knew the way well enough that I didn't have to. In the quiet I could hear my heart beating. It had slowed down from its hammering when the bell had rung again, but was still fast.

The paths of the kremlin carried me my short and undiverging way through the cold dark.

Part Three

GONERS

22

It never ends for the *zek*, even after his release. Putting down my memory of that night and those bells, I have felt the same sickening fear return, as though those men are still being killed. As though I still do not know whether I will be rounded up and shot along with them—even thirty years later, even having heard the report of the gun with my own ears and been spared. I know what happened, and yet still it seems I must relive it in ignorance, in the dark.

And of course it would be perfectly irrational for the *zek* to relinquish his fears after his release. He will never again be free of such threats.

Eleven months in Kresty and the other remand prisons, three years on Solovki. Three in the Belomor accountancy, including a two-year extension of my sentence. (Labor was needed for the completion of the Belomor Canal; why shouldn't prisoners be asked to make sacrifices, along with everybody else, for the building of socialism?) Since the end of 1933, I have lived a free citizen of the Soviet Union.

But no. Free, but released "with loss of rights." I must have been among the first to have the famous "minus" on my passport, which has grown so much more common as the survivors of sentences handed down in '37 and '38 have finally been amnestied and begun to trickle back from Siberia. When your local representative of the MVD (*Ministerstvo Vnutrennikh Del*, the Ministry of Internal Affairs, is one of the Cheka's latest titles) sees your minus, he knows how you are to be handled. You are to check in at his office once every ten days. You are not to travel within fifty miles of certain cities. You are to be addressed with hostility, mocked and abused when the opportunity presents itself. He is to squeeze silence from you like oil.

The minus presents itself differently to a prospective employer, or to the member of your local housing committee. For either of these, you are a liability. What if you should be given a job, assigned a room, only to make it necessary for the police to arrest you again? How would that reflect on the man who hired you, who took you into his district? Better to send you away. If you try to talk him out of it, that is worse. Who knows the kinds of things you might say, with a minus on your passport? Things it is the duty of the listener to avoid hearing. The best course then is to slam the door in your face, to hurry away down the street without acknowledging you. You can find work somewhere else. You can move on to another town.

That was how it was for me, from '33 until the start of our Great Patriotic War. Work hard to get, and once gotten, inevitably temporary. At intervals I would appeal to the local NKVD (by then the acronym had changed from OGPU). With their intervention a *zek* might find a place for six or eight months. The formula was: "You must do something with me. If I cannot work, you must send me back to prison, where at least I will be fed."

It was a ritual, a piece of flattery. Everyone knew the camps were not places to go for food.

In '38 I was rearrested as a matter of course. Nor was I the only one: that year was a time for former *zeks'* nightmares to rise out of our beds and walk about in daylight. To my surprise, I was neither returned to the camps nor killed but, after two weeks of imprisonment and interrogation, released. I moved on to a new city, different work.

In January of '42, those whose backgrounds made us unsuitable for the front (I almost wrote, "unsuitable for war," but no, everything was suitable for war, everything was war, war was total.) were rounded up and transported to factories still further east.

There we worked under guard, manufacturing first munitions, then the T-34 tanks Vasily Feodorovich speaks of so reverently.

That plant kept me for a year after the Germans surrendered. Then another period of moving from place to place, chasing work, leading to a third arrest with no cause in '49. That time I was imprisoned for fifty-one days, with only two interrogations. My hair turned gray. On release, transfer here.

Vasily-the-tank-commander says that if I were pursuing rehabilitation, it would be easier for him to explain the time he spends in the basement to his wife. He laughs, but I can tell what is and is not a joke. The subject has come up before.

Rehabilitation means they give you a certificate saying certain inferior agents of the State erred when they handed down your sentence on its behalf; really, in the eyes of the State, you are not so bad. Your minus is removed. To receive such a certificate you must appeal to the Procuracy, which ensures (ensures!) all types of Soviet legality are maintained. There follow applications, endless forms, letters from all quarters attesting to your character and behavior. Or, perhaps, smearing you anew. I have watched others attempt the process. It means disappointment, insult, striving. It means the bored, deadly attention of our police focused on you once more.

Few are rehabilitated. Some are sent back to the camps.

For me, perhaps, my successful rehabilitation would mean a better room, the chance of promotion at work. The question is: what might it mean for friend Vasily Feodorovich? Perhaps only that justice had been done. He seems to struggle with the idea that the best of all possible lives might not be one that includes Party membership. He considers himself a good Communist. "Only Russia could have defeated fascism," he told me last week. "A free socialist people can endure anything, accomplish anything, in the cause of justice and humanity."

A comforting belief for those who can hold it. I remember a time, before I was arrested, when I, too, thought the Bolsheviks' revolution was for the best, all things considered. My parents were appalled at what they called lawlessness, at the seizure of property. For myself, I was never a true believer in the cause, but I was young. Things were changing, they were exciting. After the bad times of the Civil War, it seemed to people my age that things might be good.

Then came Solovetsky. And now a soft voice whispers to me: perhaps my neighbor worries about my rehabilitation because he anticipates our connection will need to be justified to someone in a dark room. Perhaps he has not been as upstanding a comrade as he believes. Perhaps, absent my rehabilitation certificate, I should be watchful that he does not feed me to the beast in his place. Vasily-the-tank-commander has voiced opinions before me that our local Party leadership might be interested to hear. As Petrovich said, a secret is a hammer.

No. I do not think that Vasily would betray me, idiot that he is. What whispers is only the part of me still waiting to be taken from Company Ten out through the Holy Gates.

At Nativity, it was some time before Buteyko could be found. The guards at the main door held me while someone went for him, and when he came he hadn't heard anything about it and had to go off again to look into the matter.

Here was another period of waiting.

Even Nativity's din had been settled a little by the executions. Things were hushed enough that you could hear the hum of separate conversations instead of one endless roar. The acoustics of the space meant that the noise, reduced, floated up to circulate somewhere far above your ears, just beneath the high ceilings. The screech of a shifted bunk would suddenly descend on you. Laughter caromed in from overhead angles.

At last Buteyko came back. He'd talked to his superiors. A note reinstating me had come to them that afternoon. He showed it to the guards, who waved me on, bored.

It was late, almost time for lights out. Buteyko had told me to take my old bunk, but when I came to it Foma was lying on it. "You're back," he said, not moving.

Panko climbed down to shake my hand, and Genkin stuck his head over the edge of his pallet to see whether I'd been able to bring back any rubber for his galosh scheme, tsk-ing when I said I hadn't.

"The one underneath you can have, but this one's mine now," Foma said when I asked about the bunks. "There's no one to hold your place for you if you leave."

Previously the order had been Genkin on top, then Panko, me, and Foma. Now I would be bottom man. There was not much to distinguish one level from another. Being at the bottom meant everyone's lice and bedbugs fell down onto you, but we were all infested enough that that made little difference. Beyond that, the only reasons to prefer a higher spot were symbolic.

"It doesn't matter to me," I said.

"Good then."

I slept fitfully. The plank was narrow and hard after Antonov's straw mattress. At Company Ten, it had most commonly been Veronika who came into my head as I was drifting off, but now discomfort and fear kept her image at bay. It was hard to believe I would ever see her again. Every time I woke up, I seemed to have just been asked a question I didn't know the answer to, or to have heard the crack of a gun.

"You were tossing and turning last night," Foma said as we were pulling on our boots the next morning.

"I didn't sleep well."

"You'll be wanting to get back to your feather mattress in Company Ten. Back's too soft now for an honest pallet."

Though no one seemed to have been listening to us, his talking about Company Ten didn't help my anxiety. It had been Petrovich who recommended letting the world forget as soon as possible where I'd been for the past few days. With what I'd learned, I didn't like taking the old man's advice. But about this he was right: it would be safer for Foma not to mention it.

Roll call in Quarantine Company had not changed. The count-off snaked through the ranks of *zeks* the way it always had, translating the mass of men into one straight line. The readdition, in me, of a single item to the series made no perceptible difference.

It was dark, light still an hour away. While men called out their hoarse numbers between the two great churches, cold powder blew up the leg of my trousers at unpredictable intervals. I tried not to shiver, or to think about what I'd learned the day before. My eyes felt gritty and hot, even in the wind.

Behind me, Panko groaned quietly. After him were several more men, and only then Foma. He'd always stood with me before.

With the eastern horizon lightening, we were marched out

through Nikolski to the trees, where they split us up into several work groups. The sea still hadn't frozen, and so the mad push to maximize the year's last shipments of wood continued. My platoon was assigned to a site a mile or so east of the kremlin, where logs had been cut and left the day before. Our first task was rolling these to the road, where they could be loaded onto sleds. To do this you used a cant hook, a kind of blunt pike with a swinging, curved arm attached to it a foot or so from the end. Driving the spike at the end of the arm into the log, you could grasp it between the arm and the shaft, and drag or roll it that way. The long handle provided leverage. You were expected to move at a good clip, usually two to a log. Someone strong and experienced could manipulate a moderate-sized log fairly nimbly, but I was neither of those.

Hooks had been left under a tarp for us, but their metal parts were stuck together with frost. Buteyko had to break them apart, and even the wooden handle of the one he gave me was so cold it was clumsy to hold, larger than its own dimensions.

"All right," he said. "One for each of you. Bogomolov, you work with Panko." I was used to working with Foma, but while I was gone he seemed to have been partnered up with someone else, a man named Milyutin, whom I didn't know well.

In this part of the forest, the trees were tall, straight pines. Piles of amputated boughs from the ones that had been felled lay in green mounds. Their long needles were everywhere underfoot, spread over the snow and mud like cut hair on a barber's floor. The scent of resin rose all around us.

To roll the log, you bent over and pushed with your hook while walking along behind. The posture this required was torture. The hook's length being what it was, you teetered constantly between stumbling forward to bash your face on the log and losing control of the thing altogether if you straightened up. Either of those positions would at least have put a body into equilibrium. The special suffering of rolling logs is that you must be continually adjusting back into instability.

The ground was clear-cut, but it had been done carelessly. Stumps that should have been trimmed close to the ground stuck out of the snow, each at its own height. My arms and thighs shuddered already after an hour of work. That was before I hit the stump. The blow drove the handle of my hook into my breast, and I gasped. Panko got a shock, too. He groaned a little and slowly picked up his hook from where he'd dropped it.

"Ought to watch Panko to see how he does it, Bogomolov." It was Foma's voice. He was with Milyutin, hooks over their shoulders, the two of them returning to the piles from the sledges to fetch a new log. "Maybe you won't have to push logs when you get back to Company Ten, but as long as you're here, it's hard on the rest of us if you can't use the hook."

"I know how to use it," I said.

Panko rubbed his chest and blew out a shallow breath. "You line up a position for yourself, while you were gone?"

My arm was still deadened from the blow. The joints felt like loose glass. "No."

"No reason not to say, if you did," said Panko.

"I would, if I did. But it didn't come to anything."

Foma kicked at the snow. "It's connections," he said to Panko. "What you have to do is make connections. Once you have connections, they'll take care of you. Tolya knows how it works. But he still has something to learn from us about cutting trees."

"All I did was play attendant to an old man who couldn't walk well. An old bastard who bossed me around. Nothing more to it than that."

"Not what you said before," said Foma. "You said there was a killing."

"There was," I said. "But all I was doing was trailing after the old man."

Milyutin, silent, wore a small and neatly trimmed mustache. He was my father's age, his bearing dignified but athletic. He looked like someone it would be good to know. As he and Foma left us to wrangling our log, I thought I caught him looking at me askance.

That was the morning. By midday we'd finished. Buteyko accepted back our hooks and placed them with the logs on the sledges, to be pulled back to whatever depot they'd come from. We made our way over to the mess area, where midday kasha simmered in huge iron pots over fires of newly cut branches. Cooking steam wafted through the stink of mud and pine, the smell of a few more hours reprieve from starvation. I found myself in a group Foma was part of as well. We ate standing, out of bowls handed to us. Most lifted the bowls directly to their mouths, or scooped kasha with two fingers. I held my own bowl in both hands while the others dug in, wondering whether it was a good idea to show off my newly acquired spoon so soon.

"Probably you got used to better meals," Foma said, noticing my hesitation. "If yours doesn't taste good, I'll have it."

I should have treated it as good-natured abuse, laughed and made some joking answer. I'm sure turning away made it worse.

The arrangement we'd reached on the train from Moscow—"We'll stick together, and keep an eye out for each other," Foma said—had abided until now. We *had* stuck together. We'd bunked next to each other during our stay at the transit camp in Kem and, after standing packed together in the hold of the *Gleb Boky* as they brought us to the island, had managed to be sorted into the same platoon.

The opportunities to benefit from our partnership were few, but we took them. Once, Foma had smuggled a pine branch into the kremlin in the sleeve of his coat, and we used it to sweep up the worst of the filth from the area around and under our bunks. Unfortunately, once we'd pushed it into piles, we discovered there was nothing to do with the dirt and rotting detritus. Nothing could be dumped in the yard, Buteyko informed us, since we paraded there for roll and the bosses demanded public order. As for waiting for regular garbage pickup—well, there was no such thing. It was why Nativity was such a mess to start with; the nearest dump was outside the kremlin, a mile away. Instead, we waited until *zeks* began to leave for roll call next morning. Then I kept watch while Foma pushed the pile we'd accumulated under the beds of some unfortunates two rows over from us.

Now, from his perspective, I'd split us. Never mind the fact I'd come back—I might do it again.

I never understood why he'd chosen me. Because I was crushed in against him on that train, because I'd once had hard-boiled eggs to share and might get more in the future? (If the latter, he was disappointed; after those I spent during the train ride, I never received another ruble from my family during my sentence.) I suppose our friendship was an accident, like most are, no more purposeful or distinct than stubbing your toe. If we'd met in any setting other than the one we did, packed together with a dying old man on a train car trundling slowly north, he might have been—what? Too wary, too resentful, too suspicious to enjoy my company. I'd have expected him to feel whatever restrictive emotions a serf's grandson does for the urban bourgeoisie. I would have had the feelings of my own social class.

But he hadn't, and I hadn't, and now the prospect of my being assigned away from work he was able to do felt like betrayal to both of us. He'd grown up during a famine, after all, and worked in the fields since he was a boy. The hunger and hard labor we suffered—were they special punishments for him, or just intensifications of the Foma-ian condition, translated into a new location? Did he see that I was trying to save myself? Did he think of himself as needing saving, too? Or did he only see me taking advantage of a resource he would never be able to use?

That resource was my connection to the murdered Antonov, of course. It had come to me to seem less like a resource than a catastrophe. Whatever Foma thought, I don't believe he meant to endanger me. After Petrovich's revelation, however, I didn't need him reminding people I'd been involved in strange affairs.

I told him no, the kasha was fine. There was a little chuckling. I decided to use the spoon after all. At least a few of them noticed, I could tell.

In the afternoon we moved from hauling to felling and bucking. I was assigned to fell. To my relief, Foma was bucking.

But still the work was hard. The difficulty was to hack out two notches in the tree, a deep one in the front and a shallower in back, leaving a thin hinge of wood that controlled the direction in which the tree toppled. Do it wrong and you might smash yourself or someone else. Or the trunk might kick back as it came down, breaking your leg with its newly cut end. Maintaining the necessary attention was not easy after I'd swung the axe two or three hundred times and my shoulders had begun to quiver.

Luckily we did not face the same pressure to work quickly that we had in the morning. It was easy for Buteyko's superiors to track the progress of our hauling: if we did not move all the logs within a given radius, we did not get our six ounces of kasha at midday. Actually chopping down the trees was a different story. No one would be counting too carefully, and taking credit for a stack of logs cut by someone else earlier in the week was merely a matter of brushing the snow off of them. Buteyko let us take our time, as long as we looked busy when the guards came by.

There was conversation while we worked, most of it about the executions. I tried to listen without making my interest obvious or participating

"Finland is not so far from here,"ventured one *zek*.

"It was not an escape," said another. "They were caught stealing something, or failed to pay off the right man to turn a blind eye. Mark my words."

"Is there a boss on the island who really cares whether we steal? As long as it's not from him?"

"What I think is, you should try it, and see what happens. Mark my words, it was an escape."

That was Genkin, with a few others, talking in low voices as they sat on a log. Later, a group of us sheltered from a sudden squall under a pine.

"I heard it wasn't the guards. Just a few old Chekists with pistols. Men serving sentences like you and me."

"Did it right there in the graveyard, did they?"

"That's how it works."

"Had a pit dug. Shot them and dropped them right in. Bang and bang."

"Tell me, is that justice? Out in the world they brag about rehabilitation, but you wouldn't shoot a dog that way."

And this I overheard among the trees as I returned to Panko after relieving myself in the woods:

"You mean to say they were readied for them specially? That would be unheard of! Absurd!"

"Nah. That's normal. Nothing gets more preparations than the shootings."

"Fellow I heard it from said they were painted, the coffins. He saw them carried off the train down from Anzer. How do you like that for preparations?"

"I call it perverse, prettying up the box you're going to drop a man into when you shoot him."

"I'll tell you what's perverse: they painted them inside, not out."

I couldn't see the speakers, only the snowy trunks around me. It was getting dark by then. The snow of earlier had stopped, and blue shadows filled up the space between the trees.

As the afternoon wore on, the temperature fell sharply. By the time we began the march back to the kremlin, I could feel my eyelashes freeze together and pull at each other whenever I blinked.

Back at the cathedral, the soup Buteyko returned with was thin and gray. Grinding routine had resumed. Nothing had changed in the time I'd been away. Already the shared meals I'd cooked with Petrovich seemed far away, behind a curtain of anger and fear.

Of course the spoons from Antonov still hung in the interior pocket of my coat. I felt the weight of the food I'd brought back in its several places, too. That, at least, was different. I went looking for Foma, found him sitting on my old bunk, tipping his bowl up with both hands to drink from it.

"Listen," I said. "I wish you'd give me a break. My time away, it didn't go well for me. I won't be going back there."

He didn't look up from his meal. "May as well go where you want, if you can get them to give you a transfer."

"That's what I mean. There's no transfer waiting for me. But look." I took out the spoons. "I got these out of the deal. Little enough. But I'm giving one to you."

He snorted. "I can still drink from the bowl, can't I? Don't need it."

"No, you take it," I said. "What would I do with two?"

The answer, of course, was that I would trade the second for something. But that was what I was doing now.

Foma said: "Fine." He took the metal spoon from me, looked at it. He dipped it carefully into his soup and raised it to his mouth.

"So," I said. "You and I are friends again? When something doesn't go well the way this didn't go well, you need all the friends you can get. The investigation—I'd say it was a disaster."

He spooned more soup into his mouth, still dubious. "Where'd they have you bunking, then?"

"Company Ten, over across the courtyard above the dispensary."

"Food all right?"

"Not bad. They get a dry ration," I said. I'd already given him the spoon. I wasn't about to share the fish and groats. Not yet, anyway. Let him show some goodwill before I fed him. "It's good to be able to cook for yourself. While I was there they let me use what was left from what the man who was killed had."

"Did you some good, if you got two spoons out of it. Can't have been that bad."

"Company Ten is better than here. You're not wrong. But in the end, the business my friend was mixed up in . . . It would be better for me if everyone forgot I was involved. Do you understand? I don't need to be hearing about it all the time, in front of everyone."

He scraped the bowl with his spoon. "Told you you should have stayed."

"You were right."

The soup was gritty and tepid, with a tongue-coating, tripe-like flavor. I didn't like it, but it meant meat somewhere in the stuff's history. At the other end of the sanctuary, a man's rough voice sang a song was called "Hot Buns," about the misfortunes of a private peddler girl. We could hear the laughing and clapping as it finished.

When he was done, Foma licked his spoon clean and put it away in his own coat. "Why'd they need your help, then?" he said. "You have so much experience solving murders?"

"That's . . . something I'm wondering about myself." My thoughts had been returning to the question throughout the day, with my anger against Petrovich rising at intervals. But the prospect of explaining was exhausting, and there was nothing for Foma to do about it, even if I could make myself understood. "The old man I worked with, the detective. I was meant to be doing things for him, things he couldn't do himself. But—well, there was more to it than that."

"Like what?"

"It seems they wanted to keep me close to the investigation."

"What's 'close to the investigation'?"

"I don't know. I suppose they thought I might have something to do with it. I knew the man who died. The old bastard was spying on me."

When Foma devoted his attention to a thought, he was as intent as someone working a bellows. I watched while he assimilated the idea. "Did you ever figure it out? Who killed your friend?"

"No."

"What'd he do to get mixed up in bad business?"

"I have no idea. He was only a painter, at the camp museum. It's where they keep the old icons, the ones that used to belong to the monks. He restored them."

"What does that mean, 'restored them'?"

"Cleaned them. Repainted where the paint had come off. Fixed their gesso—the plaster they're painted on—when it needed it. I seem to have learned as much about it in the past few days as I ever did when he was alive."

He nodded. "Probably had plenty of them, the monks. Guess there would be a lot of work for you, if you knew how to do it. There you go, Buteyko."

The section leader had appeared before us carrying two towering stacks of bowls, and we handed ours over to be returned to the kitchen.

"My little granny had a good icon," Foma continued. "Virgin Mary with the Christ Child. Big, too. Always there in its corner, with a candle in front of it when she could."

"We were never very devout in my family."

"Not like my granny, then. Always talking to the priest, she was. She liked to have things done the right way." He put his hands behind him on the pallet and propped himself up. "When Granddad died she wouldn't rest until we had a swan brought in."

"Did you say a swan?"

"Right." His coarse and dirty hair stood up elaborately. "Our chapel got burned by Reds from the city. No one left to give him a confession. She made me go out to the pond and catch one and bring it into the room with him while he died. Tough to catch. All that hissing, running around on those black feet. Big. The one I finally grabbed got me in the nose with a wing. Bruised across my face for a week, like I'd got hit with a plank."

"But why bring a swan at all?"

"Gran always said a swan is very like the Holy Spirit. Same as when you get an icon and it heals someone sick. Better than a week of prayers. Christ has mercy on you when you bring it in the room." My expression must have been doubtful. For a moment,

Foma looked embarrassed. "Never heard that about a swan?"

I hesitated. I didn't want to interfere with the reconciliation we were managing. "Well, I told you, we weren't devout. But Antonov believed in the power of icons. According to him, the Church Fathers said the icon is the symbolic image of Christ, so it doesn't matter whether it looks the way he really did in life. 'Not a likeness, but a window on glory,' he'd say. Why not a swan, in that case? Maybe a bird is as good a window as anything else."

"Don't know about that. My little granny always said, 'A swan's good as St. Basil for a fever.'"

"There you are. The same thing."

We sat and watched the activity in the cathedral. Genkin was talking rapidly to two blond Finns over by the next bunk. "Did she want the swan to heal him, then?" I said. "Or to absolve his sins?"

"Eh, well." Foma stroked his chin and looked off wistfully at the walls rising above the bunks on the other side of the chancel. "Granddad was an old man. Had the cough and the fever. Couldn't recognize us. Not much chance he'd get better. Mostly she was sorry he couldn't be confessed. Must have figured, swans being holy as they are, it would be good to have one."

He heaved a breath and lay back on the plank, propping himself on his elbows as though on a wedge. "Dirty thing, that swan, all green round its feathers with scum. We'd pulled the bed over by the stove for Granddad. Swan finally settled on Granny's linen chest under the window, one leg stuck up funny. Got to have a good look at it, while we waited for him to go. Granny kissing the icon, swan on the chest, and I just sat. Lots of little black scales on their legs, like a snake . . ." He raised himself and moved his fingers in that way he had, making little pinching gestures to illustrate the smallness of the scales.

Soon it was curfew. As the whistle screamed, I lay down in the bottom bunk, and Foma climbed up to the one that had been mine. Before long the lights had been put out, and the sound of men turning in their beds subsided to scattered snoring and the occasional scratch.

It was fully dark when I heard Foma drop to the floor with a bump.

"Oy, Tolya," he whispered. "Take your bunk back. I like my bottom one better."

"That's all right, Foma. I don't mind."

"You take yours back. I want mine."

Already he was shoving his coat and other little belongings onto the cot. I sat up, and without being able to see each other we maneuvered awkwardly, nearly embracing, until he had lain down. Now I was the one standing and facing him. "Thank you," I said.

"I like mine better, I tell you."

Taking my own coat, I climbed up and settled myself again. With the haul of Antonov's rations secreted about the coat, I couldn't wear it comfortably when I stretched out. Instead I pulled it over me like a blanket. The sweater I'd acquired, interposed between my jutting bone and the wood beneath me, made a decent hip pillow. I fell asleep quickly once it was all arranged.

Later that night, the sound of killing woke me up.

I had been dreaming. I never remember my dreams, but in this one I rode a horse through the classrooms and halls of my gymnasium in Petersburg. I had never ridden a horse, and never have since. In the dream I gripped its mane and held its giant back between my legs. It galloped easily through doors and around the desks of my teachers.

Then came the point when the dream changed. The horse no longer huffed its regular breaths. Instead, it began to grunt and moan. I felt the sounds vibrate through its ribcage in my groin. The sound of its hooves became a ringing of metal on metal, and it bucked. I woke.

In the dark, I could still hear the dream sounds. Close by, the horse was moaning—no, a shout, but muffled, like a hand being held over someone's mouth. There was a ding of metal being given a glancing hit. Then a curse, and my cot moved, struck from below.

I groped blindly over the edge, touching flesh moving under cloth before someone struck my hand aside. By this time the others had started waking up as well. I heard Panko above me, high-pitched, alarmed.

"What's this? Genkin, what's happening?"

"Shut up, fucking cocksuckers," said a voice I didn't recognize.

The muffled shouting came from directly below me.

"Foma!" I yelled.

A fist caught me in the shoulder, then solidly in the chest.

There was the distinct, ringing sound of a hammer striking metal. A solid blow this time. In the darkness the sound was unreal, like someone had brought his work to bed with him and continued it in his sleep.

The person hitting me managed to get an arm across my chest, holding me down easily. The fist of his other arm connected with my ear, my mouth. I tasted blood. The hammer rang out below, four times in rapid succession, and the moaning turned into a rattling gurgle. We heard the sounds of footsteps, many of them, running away.

"Foma," I cried again.

"What is it? What's happened? What is going on here?" That was Buteyko's voice. I could hear him stumbling towards us. I'd climbed out of bed and was down on the floor, kneeling by Foma. He was still making sounds. My hands located his face. His lips were moving, and his shoulders jerked.

"Foma, say something," I said.

"It's Pavlyuk," said Genkin's voice. "What I think is that something's happened to young Foma Pavlyuk."

Flecks of something warm hit my face. I could smell that it was blood. When I moved my hands down to it, his chest was wet and hot.

Foma had stopped trying to say anything.

There was more talking. I wondered whether I should do something, slap his cheeks or try to revive him some other way. I touched his face again, but the gesture meant nothing. He twitched a little, but I didn't think he could tell I was there. Soon he didn't twitch anymore.

After a long time, Buteyko came back, holding a lamp.

"Dear God," he said.

I looked at the blood and the expression on Foma's face a little, but the light made no difference. I'd felt it all for myself already. I didn't need the image.

23

The sun was beginning to rise as we marched out to the work sites. I recall staring stupidly at a hare that twitched its nose a safe distance from our path, struggling to bring the animal's name to my mind. Every impression came to me smudged, as if much handled. I had never been more aware of being one of many.

Foma was also one of many, having passed without a ripple from the monotonous throng of the living to the monotonous throng of the dead. Timbering continued without him.

I could not seem to order my thoughts. When the first signal had blown for roll that morning, I still hadn't slept. Genkin had climbed down from his bunk before anyone else. "I will tell you," he said when he saw me. "I think you'd better go wash."

Buteyko had told me to do the same during the night, but I hadn't. Why had Foma been chosen as a victim? They'd taken nothing from him—he'd had nothing worth stealing. Revenge and competition were other motives, but who would want to revenge himself on Foma? Who was there for him to compete with, and over what? He barely knew anyone outside our platoon. How had he ended on the wrong side of a gang of killers?

No, no one had any reason to do what had been done to Foma. But, after my flight through the woods two nights before, I knew someone was out there who had reason to do it to me. And hadn't Foma and I switched bunks? Had it really been him they were after?

The question hammered in my head with every pump of my heart. It had not made me anxious to follow Buteyko's advice. How could I go out alone into the dark to wash? The men who'd opened Foma's chest were still about somewhere, inside the cathedral with us.

And so I'd spent the night smelling blood as it dried on my hands and shirt.

After the tumult of the murder, it had grown quiet again quickly. Buteyko and a few others had wanted to take Foma's body outside, but agreed that it couldn't be done before curfew was lifted in the morning. Instead they carried him to an out-of-the-way vestibule. I didn't ask whether they'd found the spoon I'd just given him.

Those nearest us must have realized what happened, but it would have been bad policy to show it. Before the light was put out again, I caught a man two rows down staring at me, terrified. He turned over as soon as he saw I'd noticed him. All night I listened for footsteps coming back, hearing only the sounds of a thousand men breathing in their sleep, their bunks creaking as they shifted. Outside, the wind shrieked through the kremlin's gaps.

Before roll, I had taken Genkin's advice, scrubbed the dried blood from my hands and face with snow outside. There was not much to do about my clothes. The sweater I'd taken from Antonov's chest, once gray, had turned brown and sticky. I wondered where they would have dumped Foma's body, but didn't linger to look for new humps in the snow.

Back inside, Buteyko was talking to one of his superiors, a man I'd seen before but whose name I didn't know. A woodcarving chisel and a bloody hammer had been found kicked beneath the bunks next to ours. It had taken less than a minute, start to finish, Buteyko explained. They'd held him down, cracked his ribs, and neatly gashed his heart.

"Are they going to do anything about it?" Genkin had asked after the man left.

"He says it's regrettable."

Antonov's murder had only been investigated the way it had because it was unusual—and because, evidently, he was an object of Infosec's suspicion. But Foma's death was routine. I wondered dully who'd ordered it, but no one would care. The hands that had staked him could have been any of hundreds. It made no difference.

And so timbering continued. The work assignment that morning had me and Panko stripping some of the logs our team had felled the previous day. We were to use hatchets to remove their branches, preparing them for the bucking team. The old Cossack communicated his sorrow about Foma by nodding whenever he caught my eye, then shaking his head or shrugging.

The sighs, his dull chopping, the occasional crack as he pulled off a small branch—all of it was remote. My mind wasn't on the work. Panko had to have noticed me idling, but he let me be.

I was in danger. That was certain. Only three nights before—it seemed like a long time now—I'd hesitated to acknowledge the threat posed by the figure that waited for me on the road. The inexact thinking that followed had let my pursuers catch back up to me after I'd put some space between us.

Numb as I was, I would have to be alive to events. I would have to think.

How would Petrovich have advised me? But no. I was still angry. A mistake to model my thinking on the old man's, when he had been the very one to put me in this situation.

Instead: what would the heroes of my boyhood *detektivy* have done? How would Sherlock Holmes have reasoned the mystery out? How would Nat Pinkerton, King of Detectives, have chased the culprit down?

That was clear enough. Establishing his premises through careful observation, Holmes would have proceeded logically, systematically. So did I. Pinkerton would have no time or patience for equivocating about the evidence before him; he'd face the facts manfully, letting them dictate his strategy. Having reached a conclusion, he'd stop thinking, and act.

So did I, so did I.

Start from the fact most basic and salient: the night before, three feet below me, men had wedged apart my friend Foma's ribs and hammered a chisel through his heart. From this a number of conclusions could be drawn: there must have been several of them, since hammering a chisel through a man's heart is difficult and he must be held down tightly. Four or five, in fact, since one had been busy hitting me, and even so Foma had barely been able to struggle. And—my mind stuttered over the next step, despite my having known it was coming—these men could not have known it was Foma's heart they were hammering, since he and I had switched bunks after the lights had been put out.

It had been me they meant to kill.

There. Confronting it squarely sped my heart's pounding. I'd intuited it the night before, but it was easier to acknowledge here, subordinated to a chain of inference. Imagination loops, spirals, returns you to the same horrible ideas again and again. Reasoning proceeds. And to proceed was what I needed.

Who might have reason to kill me? I could conceive of three possibilities, which I listed in order of increasing likelihood. (But why was it so important to proceed? To escape a corollary, perhaps: Foma had died because of me. If fear gaped on one side of my trail of logic, guilt loomed on the other.)

First, thieves. It wouldn't be unheard of to be targeted, even attacked, for a share of food like the portion of Antonov's ration I'd smuggled into Quarantine. However, no one knew about it. I didn't think the bulges in my coat were very noticeable, and Foma, the only one I'd shared any of my new wealth with, hadn't been out of my sight in the interval between my giving him the spoon and his death.

On to the next hypothesis, then. I'd learned from Petrovich that the Chekist, and perhaps others in Infosec, suspected me of involvement in an escape plot. Suspicions in those quarters could certainly be deadly—see the executions of two nights before. However, Infosec and the Camp Administration would not dispatch their victims via a squad of killers wielding a hammer and chisel in the night. They had better methods. See, again, the executions.

No, not the Chekist then. That left as most likely the possibility that was also most frightening: someone believed we'd learned something about Antonov's death that made me worth killing, too, even with a stop having been put to our investigation. What the deadly information was, I couldn't say, but it did look disturbingly like I had it. I'd been stalked through the forest already, of course: Petrovich had taken it as a sign our investigation was on the right path. If the persons behind that were still after me, wouldn't they arrange something like what had happened to Foma?

Ratiocination had produced a result, then: because of what I knew, I was a target. Someone wanted to kill me. Swapping beds with Foma last night had saved my life, but by now the killers would have realized their mistake. I could see no reason for them not to correct it after lights-out this evening. There was little chance I'd prevail against four or five experienced men, even being more prepared for them than Foma, and escaping them would be difficult, not to say impossible, while I remained confined within the cathedral.

And even if I somehow managed to survive the night, it wouldn't be warranted to assume my enemy would stop there. If the same party was behind the attack in the forest and the men last night—and it stood to reason they were—it meant their reach was long. There were many ways to be killed on Solovetsky. Not knowing who my unknown enemy was, I couldn't say which they might be capable of bringing to bear against me. How could I protect myself? How could I act against them?

The questions brought me to a blank halt, surrounded by the sounds of axes in the forest. Reasoning had proceeded, but nothing had changed. Panko was at the other end of the tree we were working on; my own cut branches lay around me. The air was already frigid, but now I began to feel the cold in my chest, in my throat. Soon I would be shivering.

It was fear coming on. I struggled for mental purchase on the dilemma—how to protect myself? how to act against my enemy?—but could find none. I couldn't answer. The fear seethed, threatening to overturn my careful train of logic and leave it lying in the snow like so many pine needles.

Then, on the brink of panic, I had it.

If what I knew about Antonov's case marked me for death, then what I knew was dangerous to my enemy. What was dangerous to my enemy was useful to me. If I continued with the investigation Petrovich and I had been working on—if I solved the case of Antonov's murder—I might learn enough that I could to save myself.

And there *were* ways of learning more. Petrovich and I had had leads. Before the Chekist revoked our investigation authorization, there had been the note from Veronika, and we'd heard from Golubov about Kologriev's past life as an *urka*.

To pursue either lead, of course, would mean defying the Chekist's explicit order. It would be doing precisely the opposite of what Petrovich had advised: keep my head down, forget about Antonov, submerge myself. It would expose me to a new set of dangers. A bullet to the head in a basement interrogation room would prove just as deadly as a chisel through the heart in the cathedral.

But what else was there to do? The more I considered it, the more impossible remaining in Company Thirteen for even another night appeared. To submerge myself meant to drown. I had to get out from under the point of the chisel that had killed Foma. I had to discover who'd killed Antonov, and whom that knowledge threatened. Any trouble I caused for myself with the Chekist by such ostentatious behavior was secondary.

There: a conclusion. So much for ratiocination. If my story had been a Holmes tale, it would have been nearly over; they tended to end expeditiously once the puzzle was solved.

But, of course, there are variations to the genre. Pinkerton was known less for merciless ratiocination than for feats of bloody derring-do. A true Pinkerton story never concludes without a few pages of cathartic violence. And simply knowing what I had to do was not quite the same thing as knowing how to go about it. (In the back of my mind, Petrovich's voice whispered: solving a case isn't ever about reasoning out the truth. What you do is smash together people and facts.)

The King of Detectives solved mysteries, then shot his way out of them; had he needed to escape Quarantine, he'd have done it by punching a hundred jaws and kicking the bellies of a thousand gangsters. If these weren't entirely realistic options in my case, still I believe the plan I conceived did exhibit a certain Pinkertonian resolve and disdain for physical perils. The fact that it only required me to hurt one person does not, to my mind, diminish these qualities.

On the first attempt at cutting off my smallest finger, I managed only to make myself hyperventilate.

If you are going to mutilate yourself this way, you must not blink. I wanted to preserve as many knuckles as I could. If I was to convince the necessary parties my wound was serious, two would have to go, but I thought I could keep the one at the base of the finger. And I certainly didn't want to damage my ring finger before it proved necessary.

But let your eye flick from the spot before it's done, and maybe you'll hack off more than you intended.

It felt prudent, therefore, to remove my glove. As well as being able to see what I was doing, there would be no dirty wool to contaminate the cut. I raised the hatchet to my shoulder.

The urge to turn my head was so strong I saw spots. I gulped.

Panko gave me a curious look. Once I'd steadied my breath, I cut a few branches to prevent his realizing what I was up to.

His interference could spoil everything. A sort of fiction had to be maintained. It wasn't necessary for your "accident" to be truly plausible, but it had to be plausible enough that your superiors could claim to believe it. Then your bloody stump bought you a pass to the hospital, which guaranteed at least a few days of rest and quiet.

When I was convinced Panko was no longer paying attention, I began again. I stiffened the little finger of my left hand and laid it out before me, using the felled tree as a block. The other fingers I curled beneath my palm. I positioned my hand behind a thick branch that stood out vertically from the trunk, so that I could use it as a guide for the axe. Wrapping my fist around the haft at about its middle, I brought the blade level with my shoulder.

This time I carried out my idea.

It must have been pain I reeled with, but it felt as though my finger had gone suddenly, appallingly weightless. The experience is hard to describe. Perhaps it most resembled losing my balance. An equilibrium I hadn't known my hand maintained was disrupted. For a long moment, a nauseous blackness swirled before my eyes. I shut them tight and waited.

When I could look again, blood was everywhere. Or no, not everywhere. Red dyed the snow by my boots, and the tree was spattered, but I hadn't imbrued my coat too badly. My sweater was already a mess from Foma, I thought distantly. It would have been inconvenient not to be able to cover up the gore.

Somewhere Panko was shouting: "Oh! Oh! Look what he's done. Genkin! Look what Anatoly Bogomolov has done!"

I was looking. Where my little finger had been was a stump, shooting one jet of blood after another into the air with surprising force. I shut my eyes again and aimed it away from my clothes. I did not think I would bleed to death.

Pain throbbed now through my entire arm, a root growing out from the wound into the rest of my body. I'd dropped the hatchet, and had to use my now-empty right hand to steady myself on the bloody log.

Oh, said a voice in my head to match Panko's *Look what Tolya Bogomolov's done!* There on the log was my finger, right where I'd left it. It lay on its side, slightly curled by the force of the blow. A kink of flesh and bone. It did not look like it had ever had much to do with me.

"Oh, I'll tell you what you've done now, Bogomolov. You've gone and put your cock in the soup. Christ, Christ, Christ." This was Genkin, arriving panting, ever anxious for excitement. He was followed closely by Buteyko.

"Anatoly Pavelovich! What's happened?"

"An accident," I managed to murmur. My throat felt dry. Buteyko was the first person I'd have to involve in the process of receiving a pass to the hospital. He didn't have the power to issue it himself, but I'd need his support if the man who could was to be convinced. "My hand slipped on the branch."

Buteyko removed his hat and pulled at his hair with thin, frustrated fingers. It was his job to be sure all could work, so that all could eat. I know he saw me as a kind of shirker. But even so, through the haze of pain, I felt sure of him. Buteyko was one of those men who, if you identified yourself to them as the liberal product of bourgeois parents, would help you out of a sense of social decency. It was a kind of clannish obligation—an atavism, a response evolved to suit them for a vanished environment. Their social glands continued to control their behavior long after there was any use in it. They were, in a word, decent. Their limbs, hacked off, only needed a current run through them to spasm decency.

"Let's hurry," he said grimly. "You need to see the site boss before they'll accept you at the infirmary."

By now the rest of the section had gathered around. "Put the finger in the snow," I heard someone say. "Sometimes they can put them back on." Panko returned from the bog nearby, having fetched a clump of icy moss. I pressed it to the stump to stanch the flow of blood and held my left hand above my head with my right.

I don't know whether the finger was ever packed into the snow. If it was, I never got it back.

Soon Buteyko and I were out on the road, the others having filtered back to their jobs at his urging. Sounds of axes and saws came from where other platoons worked in the trees around us, syncopated with the pounding in my ears. The pain grew deeper with each throb.

At a certain point it all rose and washed over me in a wave, and I stumbled. Buteyko reached out an arm to steady me, then said, without meeting my eyes: "This is all I can do. First Foma, now you. Whatever's going on, I am sorry for it. But this is all the help I can provide. Understand?"

The site boss was working beneath a lean-to, a piece of corrugated iron atop four posts. He sat on a stump by a small fire, with two others, guards, standing to either side.

"An accident in my platoon, Igor Sergeyevich. I'm sorry to say that I need a pass for the hospital."

The man had been staring into the fire. He looked up. "What happened?"

"Anatoly here has lost a finger. You remember that we are limbing and bucking today."

"Pretty stupid thing to do, boy," the man said to me, eyeing the bloody moss around my hand.

"My hand slipped," I said. The pain, and perhaps the loss of blood, were making me nauseous and light-headed. My voice sounded insincere in my ears. "The axe—the axe hit a knot."

"Bogomolov is a good worker," said Buteyko. "It was just an accident."

Igor Sergeyevich waited to see if either of us would say anything else. Then he shrugged. "If you say so. He can spend the night in the surgery. Not the hospital—I can't see this being bad enough for that. The infirmary, just long enough to get bandaged."

"You know where it is, Anatoly Pavelovich?" said Buteyko.

Going to the surgery inside the kremlin would mean passing through Nikolski. There was no chance of my receiving a pass that would let me go back out again once I'd done that. And, of course, I'd have felt safer with the walls of the kremlin between myself and Foma's killers.

Nevertheless, I nodded. I'd simply have to do what I intended before having my hand seen to. The plan was working so far.

Buteyko's softheartedness almost sabotaged me. He said: "I can send someone with him, to be sure he gets there safely."

I flinched. I wouldn't be able to investigate either of my leads if they gave me an escort. It would be direct to the surgery, a night or two there, then back to Nativity to be killed.

"You want to disrupt your whole platoon? The camp's mobilized for lumber. You give me lumber. He can get himself there."

"Go directly there," Buteyko said to me quietly. "Don't stop to rest, even if you're tired. Do you understand? It's dangerous to stop, with a wound like that."

Igor Sergeyevich licked the nib of his pen. "What's the name?"

Buteyko told him. Anatoly Pavelovich Bogomolov. That was me.

Once again I was free from Company Thirteen.

24

Released from work, I could go where I needed. *Zeks'* papers were typically checked only when they passed a guard station, entering or exiting one of the camp's secured areas. I wouldn't have to do that. The only other way an agent of authority might find out I belonged in the infirmary was a spot check by a patrol. I did, at one point, see a pair of uniformed guards on the road ahead, but they turned off onto a different path before I met them.

The moss did its job for a while, but by the time I arrived at the fishery, it was sodden with blood. I'd tried to walk with my hand upright, above my heart, but after a few curious looks I'd begun to put it in my pocket whenever someone drew near on the road. My head bobbed, a balloon strung to my body by pain.

It was Veronika I'd come for, again. Luckily I found her in the same back room as before. At first, with her back to the door, considering some piece of work on the table before her, she didn't notice I'd come in. The way she stood, she might have been posed. It was the relation of her arms to the rest of her: a jutting elbow, a cocked hip, and then the line of her neck curving smoothly out through her arm to dangle in her wrist on the other side. Her boots were the same dirty gray felt the rest of us wore, with the cuffs of her brown trousers pushed carelessly into their tops. The extra fabric rucked around her calves.

"Veronika Filipovna."

Is it ever accurate to say a face is beautiful? Or is it that all of its expressions are? I can hardly picture what her face was, only what it did. Her wide mouth perched, billowed through the air, and perched again, a flock of birds rearranged on the same branches.

Seeing it was me, the flock of birds frowned, intent but off-kilter. The bruises on her face had begun to fade.

"Bogomolov," she said. "I didn't think I'd see you again."

"Your letter. You wrote you had something for us."

"Two days ago I did! I thought you'd be here making a boil over it. Then nothing." Her eyes moved to the door. "Where's the old man?"

I couldn't think of a way to answer that. "Please. I don't have much time. Whatever you were going to tell us—I need to know. And—" I gulped a breath. "I need you to talk to the monk you work with. Brother Kiril. I need them to let me through the Fish Gate."

She barked a laugh worthy of Petrovich. "What?"

"You can do it. He is . . . he's taken with you."

"Taken with me!"

"He brought your letter to us. He used the gate for you then, so it would reach us."

She shook her head. "You scared me, you know. When I didn't hear from you, I was sure you'd gone to Boris, even with Brother Kiril swearing up and down that the Lord had helped him find you before you did. But here I am, no new broken bones or bruises." She swept a hand down from her head, showing the extent of her intactness. "Your partner should know that if you don't follow through on your threats I'm not going to be as intimidated next time. Why should I tell you anything? Why should I help you with the monks, even if I could?"

"It was—" I shook my head and began again. "Things have developed. The situation—"

"Christ, are you bleeding?"

The wounded hand had come out of my pocket. Drops of my blood were bright on the floor. Somehow the sight focused me. "I need you to tell me what your letter mentioned. What you thought we would find helpful."

"What happened to the old man?"

"He's no longer on the case."

"And you are, in this state?" She was cagey, waiting for me to answer. The swelling in her cheek brightened the eye peering over it. "You're telling me you're in charge of finding out who killed Antonov now?"

I'd planned, back when I had ten fingers. The plan specified that I was to go to Veronika Fitneva and get from her the promised information along with a pass through the Herring Gate. What it did not specify was how. Somehow I hadn't considered that Infosec's backing might have been the only thing that made her willing to help us. Faced now with a choice between the truth and a lie, I settled on the lie. "That's right."

"I see," she said. "Infosec has delegated its authority to a twenty-year-old student with no Party connections. And in the course of your investigation, you had an accident, and then you thought, 'Say, I haven't been to see Veronika Fitneva since she wrote that letter. I'll just stop by before I get this stitched up, see if she'll provide me free passage in and out of the kremlin while I'm at it. Won't take a minute.'"

There was nothing to say to that. We looked at each other, and she pursed her lips. "Let me see your hand."

Her fingertips were dry and light. The throbbing in my arm made them hard to feel, like being touched through a rubber glove. Even so, I winced.

Her face changed when she saw the finger wasn't there. She examined the wound, not touching it or the moss Panko had dressed it with. It was like disgust, I thought, the pity that flickered over her features.

"It's still bleeding," she said. "Take off your coat and pull up your sleeve."

I sat down on the barrel she pulled over. Navigating the wounded hand through my coat sleeve proved difficult. Every catch of moss on the wool was agony.

She was staring at my bloody sweater when I looked up, but when our eyes met she shook her head and turned away. "Close your eyes," she said.

When she told me I could open them again, she was tucking

her sweater back into her trousers and holding the blouse she'd been wearing underneath. From a cabinet, she retrieved a small knife. Scoring the fabric first, she ripped a band of cloth three or four inches wide from the garment's bottom. Without the blouse, her neck emerged naked from the sweater's collar.

"You did this to yourself?" she said as she wrapped the band around my forearm.

"Yes."

"The blood on the sweater is yours?"

I shook my head. "No."

"The old man's?"

"No. A friend."

She surveyed her work. She'd tied the cloth in a light knot, just above my wrist. "It will be better than nothing. Just a minute."

She rummaged in a nearby barrel, coming up with a slat that might have been split from a shingle or an old board. She tied another knot over it, then gave it a dozen hard twists. The cloth tightened, and my hand began to tingle immediately, though the pain didn't go away. It wasn't like numbness. The balance I'd skewed by cutting off my finger had been adjusted again.

"Hold this." While I held the slat with my other hand to keep it from spinning loose, she tied three more knots to fix the whole assembly in place. Then she examined the moss again. "There. That's the best I can do for you. I can't tell if it's stopped the bleeding, but it should be slower, at least."

"Thank you."

"You should see a doctor. They say it's not good to wear one of these too long."

"Thank you."

The scent of her body, not quite too faint to notice, rose from inside her sweater. Her breath tickled the hair on my arm. "You're in some trouble," she said.

"Yes."

"What happened?"

I reminded myself that I'd trusted Petrovich too quickly. Her helping me like this didn't mean she had my best interests at heart. Don't let my infatuation interfere with the case, the old man had said. But then, I had needed the help, and I would need still more. What option did I have, other than to trust her?

"We lost our permit," I said slowly. "The investigation—they called it off. There was much more to it than—than I'd imagined. The Chekist who gave us the permit thought Antonov was involved with something with a set of White officers. Petrovich thinks it was connected to those executions the other day somehow. They think—Infosec thinks—I may have had something to do with it, too. That's why they brought me on the case. To see whether I'd give anything away when Petrovich looked at the clues."

She was unmoved. "What are you doing here, then?"

"I was sent back to Quarantine Company. My friend—" I indicated my sweater, using the right hand. "The men who did this to him were coming for me."

"Why?"

"I don't know. It must be related to Antonov. His name was Foma. They stabbed him with a—with a chisel. We'd switched. He was in the bunk below mine. I—" There was a bubble in my chest that might have broken if I'd gone on.

"So this was your way of getting away from them," Veronika said. "A few days in the hospital are worth a finger?" When I nodded, she sighed. "And what does any of this have to do with my convincing Kiril to let you use the monks' gate to get into the kremlin?"

"In and out. It has to be both. The guards at Nikolski, they were . . . hostile to us already. Then our contact in Infosec had them stop us. He waited for us at the gate, with them. I can't go in and out through there. They'll know me, report to him. But the Herring Gate—"

"I see. But they'll never let you through without a pass, you know. The monks won't lie. Uttering a falsehood is still a sin, even if it's lying to our jailers. That and the fish are the only reason main Administration trusts them even to the degree it does."

That I hadn't known. It gave me pause. "Maybe I will be able to get a pass. And if I do—you can convince your Brother Kiril to tell them to let me through?"

"I doubt it." She leaned back against the worktable as she watched this sink in, her palms against its edge. With her chin she indicated my hand. "I've never done that for a real wound before. Mitya and I—my brother—we'd practice tourniquets on each other when we were children. We liked stories about explorers being carried back to camp through the jungle or the tundra after accidents."

I waited. Cradled in my lap, the stick of its tourniquet protruding awkwardly, my hand was less like itself than ever. I tried to think how to get what I wanted from her.

She said, "We were very close, Mitya and I. We shared a flat as adults. Had all the same friends. When I had translation work, I would always have him read it over when I was done, even though his French was much worse. After they arrested him, I knew it was only a matter of time for me. It was a kind of relief, maybe, when they finally came."

That flock of birds that were her face had flown up while she spoke, an unreadable cloud. Now, as we watched each other, they settled again into a guarded expression. Above us, a window through the gabled end of the wall let in weak light.

"You cared for Antonov," I said. "I don't think you had anything to do with killing him."

"I've been saying that, haven't I?"

"All I want now is to find out why he died, who killed him. If you know something, you can help me. Infosec had some other motive. You were right to think so. But I don't."

She pushed herself away from the table, turned away from me. "I cared for him. Why should I care about finding anyone? Revenge is for little boys."

"They came for me once already," I said. "Please. Whoever's after me, whoever killed my friend Foma—they can only be trying to hide who killed Antonov. Finding it out is all I can do against them. The hospital will buy me a night. Two at most. It's my only chance."

"You're telling me that if I don't do what you're asking, my fine first-aid work will go to waste?" She let out a large breath, then turned to face me again. "All right. All right. Other than not wanting to be involved, I suppose there's no reason for me not to help. I don't know whether what I know will do any good for you."

Looking into her eyes, I could barely distinguish the pupils from her black irises. "Your letter," I said, my voice catching. "You wrote you had something."

"Something, yes. It's less a clue, maybe, than a piece of leverage. Or maybe it is a clue, I don't know." She was talking more quickly now, as if, having determined to tell what she knew, she was in a hurry to get it out. "You understand my work assignment? How I got here?"

"We were never sure. That woman Stepnova thought someone, maybe Antonov, had arranged your transfer."

"'Arranged my transfer.' That's decorous. You're right, better to bracket the question of how these things are arranged. Looking too close is not very flattering for anyone. What really happened was that a bribe went to someone in Administration, so that even though Boris had bought me from Alexandra Stepnova, I would get a job that made me less available to him and a little more available to Gennady Mikhailovich. Of course, Stepnova was irate when I didn't go to clean Boris's house and warm his bed full-time. No one is so irate about corruption as a madam who has made all the proper arrangements." She smirked. "At any rate, the bribe was a piece from the museum's collection. I can give you the accession number."

"Antonov was stealing from the collection?"

"Not him. His boss. A man named Vinogradov."

"Vinogradov? The museum director? What did he have to do with it?"

Her eyebrows arched, another expression distorted by her bruises. "You know him?"

"I've met him. He is—was—part of our investigation."

"Well, maybe you were onto something, then. He and Gennady Mikhailovich had an arrangement."

"Which was?"

"My reassignment, for I-don't-know-exactly-what. A favor to be named later. I got the impression Vinogradov liked having his men owe him. Anyway, he took care of the whole thing, from making the arrangements to providing the bribe."

"Whom did he bribe?"

"That I can't say. I don't think Gennady Mikhailovich knew either. Maybe someone in the Fisheries section."

"How did you find out about it—the arrangement?"

"Antonov told me. He never said exactly why the deal with the director worried him, but it did. He wanted me to know what Vinogradov had done—a kind of insurance, I suppose. I don't know how he figured it out, but he was able to tell me the accession number. I was to threaten to take it to someone high up in Administration, in case I ever had to negotiate with Vinogradov on my own behalf."

"Why would you have had to do that?"

"I don't know." She shook her head. "Sometimes Gennady Mikhailovich seemed worried that things would sour between them."

"But you haven't renegotiated with Vinogradov. Not even when we came to tell you Antonov had been killed."

"Why would I? There hasn't been anything to suggest my position was at risk—not yet. Reporting his little misappropriation would make him unhappy with me, for certain. I'd rather not provoke him unless it's necessary. Should I have risked my position here, just on the chance he was the one who'd hurt Gennady Mikhailovich? Which makes me think: I expect my name to be kept out of it, if you take this to anyone, understand? If anyone asks whether you heard this from me, I'm going to deny it."

"Don't worry," I said. My throat felt parched. "I'm grateful."

"All right, then." She shoved herself up onto the edge of the table again, sighing. "The accession number is 7-dot-38. That's all I know. I can't tell you what it actually is. Who can say what the price for removing a woman from servitude and getting her put into a fish house with a pile of monks' nets is? I like to think it was a jewel-encrusted crown, but that's probably not right."

There was nothing to write the number on, or with. I repeated it to myself: 7.38, 7.38. Once I thought I'd memorized it, I asked: "Do you think Vinogradov could have killed him?"

"I don't know. I don't know why he would have. But Gennady Mikhailovich was worried about something. Maybe it was Vinogradov! Maybe you'll find out that Antonov incurred a debt on my behalf that he couldn't pay, and the nefarious museum kingpin had him killed." She threw up her hands. "Then it would turn out it was my fault he died all along, just like your Petrovich wanted. But I can't say. I've told you everything I know about it now."

I watched her face. "Why didn't you want to move into Spagovsky's place? Why take up with Antonov at all?"

The laugh was the brilliant, warlike one she'd favored us

with so freely when we first questioned her. It ended with her tapping her bruised cheek. "Weren't you there the other night? You know that wasn't the first beating. Do I have to explain it to you?"

"I was there. I heard."

I'd made her angry. "Why are you asking, then?"

"When Petrovich and I first talked to you, you said you liked Spagovsky."

"You think I like being beaten up?"

"I don't know."

Those expressions of hers—that flock of birds. They'd have pecked my eyes, if they could. Sometimes when I remember that conversation, it seems like only a series of silent looks, separated by empty sounds. Even missing my finger, even under threat from the chisel that had opened up Foma, there was still a corner of my mind in which how she looked at me was all that mattered.

"All right," she said at last. "I like him, sometimes. It doesn't mean I like the beatings. It doesn't mean I have to like liking him. The fact I like him doesn't mean I can't like anyone else. It doesn't mean I want to be his slave. Antonov . . . he offered something else. I told you, he was gentle. He was an artist. Why wouldn't that be appealing? Why shouldn't I come here and see what happened if I was away from Boris?"

"All right," I said.

Nothing about her had relented, no part gave in. She spoke more quietly, her voice folded in on itself, but intense. "Gennady Mikhailovich would be the one who this would happen to. It's what I was telling you about him when I saw you last. He was going to put it before himself, no matter what—the image he wanted to see. Whether it was wrong, or rash, didn't matter. He was an artist. It was what I liked him for, but you can't do that here and expect to survive. That's something to remember." She'd looked away. When she turned back, she gestured at my hand. "You need to go and have that dealt with. I told you, you'll lose another finger if you leave the tourniquet on too long. Go see a real medic."

"The monks at the gate. You'll talk to Kiril?"

"I can make you no promises. Where should I send word, if he agrees?"

"The infirmary. Not the hospital. The infirmary inside the kremlin."

"Fine. You should go there right away."

It was hard making myself stand up from the barrel, but I did. We did not shake hands, did not touch each other again. She stood apart as I left, leaning back against her table, hugging herself.

My hand didn't feel better. I told myself I was getting used to it.

25

What they say is true: you do feel pain in the missing part. Even now, as I write this thirty years later, the ghost of my finger throbs. It stabs dully with each heartbeat. My hand with its shortened digit, the stump still pink and raw-looking, lies alongside my pad of paper. A reminder of what survival costs.

I was sufficiently discerning to identify the price, then, and canny enough to pay. Now, I wonder. Has old age dulled my instincts? Life makes demands of those who would avoid being ground to bits in its machinery. Have I deluded myself into believing those demands could be less cruel, less rigorous than they truly are? This writing, the late-night conversations, the pickles shared, all that has transpired since my assignment to this building: have I been the idiot all along? The men at the plant have begun to talk about Vasily-the-tank-commander. *Vasily Feodorovich is overstepping the mark*, they say. *Vasily Feodorovich risks damaging Party unity.*

The man himself remains stupid as ever. "Every Party member has an obligation to criticize," he says. "He criticizes the mistakes of the Party manfully, just as he criticizes his own. You don't understand, Anatoly Pavelovich, for the very reason that you've been kept forcibly out of the vanguard of socialism. Comrade Khrushchev's speech marks a new era. The time when all that was accepted was toadyism and eyewash is over. What's needed now is the truth."

In the spring, shortly after that speech, four young physicists elaborated somewhat on Comrade Khrushchev's ideas at their local Party meeting in Moscow. They dared describe the scale of imprisonment, of killing. Workers should be armed, they said. Only then could they be sure of protecting themselves from a berserk Party.

These scientists were crucified in the press, fired from their jobs. When I point this out to Vasily, he only says, "Yes, but they didn't send them to the camps, did they? And in the past what they said would never have been reported. This means there is approval of their ideas at the highest level, even if support can't be shown openly."

Vasily Feodorovich is placing his own concerns above the Party's. Isn't that the true definition of the Cult of Personality? These remarks are not addressed to me. They are the sort of thing I overhear, one Party member speaking to another. The few of my fellow workers, marginal as I am, who might care to address me, say, *Stay away from that one. He's a danger. The head of wheat that pokes up above the rest of the field gets lopped off.*

Vasily-the-tank-commander says, "No man must be destroyed for uttering the voice of conscience. There are retrograde elements in the Party, yes, but they will be reformed. It takes courage to build a socialism that truly acknowledges and supports the life of the people." *No man must be destroyed.* But men have been destroyed by the millions for far less than uttering the voice of conscience. Their families, colleagues, and even their basement-dwelling, peripheral acquaintances have been destroyed. Even if I believed Vasily Feodorovich about the Party's desire for reform, I would ask: What about socialism for the dead? What sort of a State will we build for them, who proved unable to buy survival at any price?

He asked once about my finger. I told him I lost it on Solovetsky. He has not asked again.

He is putting me in danger. He is in danger as well. I do not know what to do.

Things were proceeding, but not everything was going according to plan. As I made my way to Warehouse Three, I was thinking about what Veronika had said: that, even if she convinced them to make an exception to the usual rule that only monks were permitted at the Herring Gate, the brothers wouldn't let me through without authorization. The Chekist was out, of course. Where else could I find a patron?

Outside the warehouse, there was someone at work hammering a runner back onto a sledge. "Is Zhenov in his office?" I asked.

From the way the man looked at me, I could tell he recognized me from our search of the warehouse the day before. I didn't remember him. He was middle-aged but weathered, with a heavy black stubble.

"No." His jaw barely moved when he spoke, but his Adam's apple bobbed wildly.

"When will he be back?"

"Don't know."

I'd mastered myself a little on the walk back from the fishery, and was feeling more capable than I had with Veronika. The man was not disposed to be friendly, clearly, but I couldn't let that stop me.

"He was to take the train to Anzer, check on your supply chain. Surely he's back from that trip by now?"

"He's back. Haven't seen much of him since then, though."

"Why? What happened when he came back?"

"He heard about that shooting."

"Why should that matter to him?"

"The ones they killed, all Whites. All friends of his, I hear."

"He thought he'd be linked to the men they killed?"

The man shrugged.

I tried to connect it up. Zhenov had issued a requisition order, one whose consequences Antonov was meant to be dealing with when he was killed. That had set our investigation in motion. Now, it emerged, the same investigation had been halted just as Infosec was preparing to round up and shoot a group of officers associated with Zhenov. Petrovich hadn't even entertained the possibility of its being a coincidence that our papers were burned on the day of the executions.

But what did those things have to do with each other? I couldn't see it—not quite. During my first year at the university, there came a time when I realized I was not an exceptional mathematician, only a competent one at best. It had been when I tried to work problems in multivariant calculus. I could understand enough to feel the equations clicking in my mind, wanting to complete themselves. I could not understand enough to do it. This was like that.

"A group of your men took some paintings from the museum, then sent them up to the cabinetry workshop on Anzer," I said. "Has what they made with them been shipped back down to the kremlin yet?"

"I don't track everything that's shipped."

I call it perverse, I'd heard someone say, *prettying up the box you're going to drop a man you shot into*. That was a click. "They were the coffins, weren't they? The coffins they used for the executions."

"How do I know who they stuck in them?"

But I was right: they were coffins, and they had returned from Anzer. "Were you expecting them? Were they due to arrive that day?"

"Came early," he said reluctantly.

Another click. I couldn't say what this meant any more than the last, but the circle drew tighter.

"The things we were looking for the other day, here in the warehouse. Have they been found? Has Zhenov looked?"

He shook his head, jaw rigid. "Don't know anything about that. You want to ask any more, I'll fetch Ivan Kologriev. He's in charge while the boss's out. He's about here somewhere—been seeing to a shipment of salt. You ask him."

Kologriev. The *urka* past we'd learned about from Golubov made him more suspect, but more dangerous, too. I thought of the way he'd lifted the crate from Luka, of his laughter and violence. I didn't care to meet him. I'd probably stood exposed in front of the warehouse for too long already.

"No," I said. "No, that's all right. It's not important."

The wind began to build as I turned back towards the kremlin, raising chop in the water's icy slush. What, so far, had I gotten back in trade for my finger? Freedom, yes. Information, yes. But I still needed something I could parlay into an investigation that would continue after I'd committed myself to the infirmary. Simply returning to Quarantine with more knowledge than I'd had when I left would do nothing: knowledgeable and dead was still dead.

Beneath the snow that clung to the big stones in the kremlin wall, I could make out patterns of brown lichen. The pain in my hand was keeping me from thinking purposefully. I hunched against the wind and tried to concentrate. Instead of turning off the road to follow the path around the south end of the kremlin, the most direct way to Nikolski, I continued along the water. On the north side of the bay, the administration building loomed, a constant white presence.

The problem was leverage. I did have something on Vinogradov. The accession numbers might buy his help, or blackmail him. Antonov had given them to Veronika for just that purpose, to bargain with. And the museum director had been able to write Antonov a pass out of the kremlin. He could write me one as well, maybe even keep me out of Quarantine.

The trouble, of course, was that the man might very well himself have been behind Antonov's killing. Could I risk putting myself in the very hands I was trying to escape?

I looked again at the dead windows of the administration building. If nothing like what had happened to Foma had happened to him, Petrovich would be there, in the Criminology Department offices.

I admitted it to myself: I wanted his advice. He would know how to go forward, how to turn the information I'd gathered into something more. I needed, at this moment, not the deductive genius of a Holmes nor the violence of a Nat Pinkerton—my imitation of those had taken me as far as it would—but someone who knew how to use knowledge as a hammer. Someone who knew how to break off new pieces of this case.

Yes, and with a partner, I'd have someone to secure my safety if I went to Vinogradov. But would Petrovich be willing to help?

My hand hurt. Every so often it surprised me how much. Out at sea, gray clouds moved in endlessly, appearing over the horizon and disappearing past the kremlin walls.

The old man had brought me along when he collected his temporary discharge, on the first day of our investigation, so I knew where KrimKab's offices were. They occupied two good-sized rooms on the third floor—not, luckily for me, in one of the secure wings. I was able to make my way up a stairwell and down the hall to the door without being challenged.

His cough reached me before I saw him. The old man's hacking snaked around a corner, through a door, and past a large, out-of-place wardrobe filled with cartons of files. I mentioned his name and was duly waved through, my hand hidden in my pocket.

There were two windows in the back room, along with five desks. The old man sat at one. Of the others, only two were occupied, over against the other wall. Out the window, the wind continued moving the bay and gray clouds around.

"Tolya." His swollen eye had opened again. Blue as ever, it flicked to the door, looking for anyone who might come through behind me. When no one did, he continued. "Wasn't expecting you."

The bruise from where the *urki* had hit him seemed to have slipped down his face, as sometimes happens when the blood moves under the skin. Now it was the lip beneath his white mustache that showed lurid brown and purple. Under his breath, he said: "What are you doing here? If the Chekist hears we've been seen together—"

"Who'd tell him? Does someone else in this office share your special relationship?"

He glanced to the other side of the room. The other men hadn't looked up from their desks. "We'll talk out in the hall. Come."

He took his cane, and we proceeded back out the way I'd come in. A few heads turned, but he only uttered a quick excuse to his department head as he closed the door, then turned to me. The hall was empty. "All right. What do you want?" His eye caught on the tourniquet's slat as he looked me over. "What have you done?"

"I need your help."

He narrowed his eyes. "You're making a mistake, Tolya. I don't know what you think you're doing, but you're being stupid. You put us both in danger. I told you the other day, didn't I? You have to keep your head down, act like you don't know anything. Coming here, leaving your own work—it's the worst thing you could have decided on."

Now that he was in front of me, I was angrier than I'd expected. "You asked what I'd done?"

He hesitated. "Yes."

He waited silently while I extricated my wounded hand from its pocket. He must have known already—he was nothing if not observant. Still, his expression was gratifying. I gave him time to examine the damage.

"They came for me last night, after lights out," I said finally. "Four or five. A hammer and a chisel. I'm only standing here now because they had the wrong bunk."

"The wrong—?"

"I'd switched. A coincidence. The man below me—his name was Foma."

"He was killed?"

"He was my friend."

He grimaced, looking away. "I see. And today you arranged to be removed from your platoon before they came again."

"That's right."

"You have more grit than I gave you credit for."

The hall was narrow and dim, the only light a square window at one end. The faint sound of voices drifted out from one of the other offices. "How long do you think I'll be safe in the infirmary?" I leaned forward, close to his face. Where I grabbed it above the elbow, his arm was driftwood wrapped in fabric, brittle and light. "How long do you think you'll be safe? In Company Ten you may be harder to reach than I am in the cathedral, but any *zek* on this island is fragile as an egg. And anything I know, you know as well."

He pulled away, but I didn't let go. "Maybe," he said. "Maybe. But there's nothing I can do for you that won't make it worse."

"You don't know all I've learned. Those executions: Antonov is connected to them in too many ways. There's something off about it. At the cabinetry workshop they made his icons into coffins that were shipped down the day of the execution."

"Then you think you're going to solve our case."

"We are, you and I. The men they executed, the ones who went into the painted coffins—they were the Whites on the Chekist's list, weren't they? That was your hypothesis. I'm sure you've confirmed it by now."

He nodded grudgingly. "Yes. I wasn't positive the other day, but I am now. Just listening in on the gossip in this building, I've heard the names of three men I spoke to." He hemmed loudly, rasping at his throat, then smoothed the mustache.

"There's something to that," I said. "You must see it. And it's the only move. Who would have sent men to hammer a chisel into me except Antonov's killer? Someone connected to him, maybe, but in any case they're afraid of something we found out. What defense do we have, other than to figure out what it is?"

At the other end of the hall, a door opened and someone walked to the stairs. Petrovich's eyes darted after him. I released his arm, waited.

"Damn it, Tolya," he said after the man's footsteps had died away. "What do you want from me? What do you think I can do? My pull with the Chekist burned up with the investigation papers. He hasn't contacted me since. I can only scramble to keep the boot off my neck, the same as every other worthless *zek*." He looked down at his hands. The way he hunched over them reduced him, turned him inward. His shoulders enfolded his thin chest. "I appreciate the warning. Maybe it's more than I deserve, for you to come. If there's anything I can do for you here, I will. But keep chasing the killer, after being told not to in as many words? It'd be as much as my life and yours are worth if the Chekist knew we'd even talked about it. And what do you even think we could accomplish, without a pass?"

Perhaps the betrayal was not necessary for the way I felt. Perhaps every good student feels such anger for his teacher, submerged somewhere, latent. Why learn anything, if not to prove that your subordination in knowledge and skill was temporary, accidental? If not to annihilate the authority that sets the instructor above you? Petrovich had taught me something about interrogations, something about moving within the world of the camp. He'd certainly taught me something about betrayal. I understood better, now, the uses to which one human being could put another.

"If you won't help me protect myself," I said, "maybe your colleagues here at KrimKab will. They might be interested to learn that they have a slug sharing their office." He looked at me.

I had expected the blue eyes to flash with their old sharpness, but they didn't. Back inside my coat, my mutilated hand felt gigantic with pain, as if the opening of the pocket led to a much larger space. A barn, or a gymnasium. A hot, sour worm of nausea wriggled in my esophagus.

"It's your fault," I said. "You gave him my name."

He sighed. "I did. But Tolya, I didn't know what it would mean. That's the truth. The first time I head anything about an escape was after he brought me to look at Antonov's body. Before that, he only wanted updates on my cellmate—who he met with, where he went. Often enough, nothing comes out of these things. When I saw you standing there over the body, I knew I'd gotten you mixed up where you didn't belong. But mostly you looked unhealthy. I thought I'd be doing you a favor by getting you away from Quarantine for a while."

"Was it doing a favor to report on me to him?"

"By then I thought it would be better to continue. I never told him you were involved. From the first, I said I doubted it. When we met the men on the list, I was supposed to watch you, see if you gave any sign of knowing them. I thought I could get a read on you by seeing how you helped with the investigation, as well. And we calculated it would be an easy way to keep an eye on your movements. But it was obvious you knew nothing about it! He wasn't happy when I let you go off to Kostrihe alone, but by that time I was convinced you had nothing to do with it."

"That was good of you," I said bitterly.

We stood in the half light of the hallway, not looking at each other. I was turning the meaning of what he'd just said over in time with my hand's throbbing, and it almost surprised me when he spoke again, his voice thin and distant. "When I joined the force, Tolya . . ." He trailed off, then picked up his thread again. "When I joined the force, I was younger than you are now. They assassinated Tsar Alexander in Saint Petersburg when I was thirty-one, all those years ago. So in Odessa we dug into our own anarchists. Found out what they'd been saying, sent them away. Then on my fiftieth birthday they made me chief inspector for murder investigations, and I heard everything that happened between violent men and their women, their drinking partners. For fifty years, I was the police. Now I am supposed to be a criminal. It isn't so easy to make the change . . . Closing in on the truth becomes a habit. You see? Then, maybe, a compulsion. So now, seventy-six, I am on Solovetsky. I report what happens among the *zeks* around me. It hasn't felt so different. It's felt like—like a return to my life. Does that sound strange? Twelve years I spent, buried in my daughter's kitchen."

The tone was more hesitant, more uncertain, than I'd ever heard from him. I let him wait for an answer. After a minute he went on, defending himself now: "After all, all I've reported is the truth. A man in the first big cell they put me in would make up misdeeds for you if he didn't have anything to tell when they called him in. That was a slug. Or there are the ones who entrap you, the way you ended up here. That I've never done, not under the tsars and not now. Burrowing in towards the truth, that's all I am good for."

"That is—" I stopped. My anger had receded. "It's what we need. You've taught me a lot. But I can't do the rest alone. I need your help."

He hemmed, a sound from deep in his chest. "We don't even have a pass that will let us move around to make inquiries. What is it you think we can do?"

I told him, as succinctly as I could. First what I'd learned about the accession numbers from Veronika, then what had emerged about Zhenov's acquaintance with the White conspirators during my encounter with Luka. Finally I explained what I thought could be done.

Petrovich listened. "Lucky Vinogradov is coming back to the kremlin this evening," he said reflectively after I was done. "It all depends on your being right about him."

"If I'm not, I'll be the only one in danger," I said. "You'd be in a position to provide the Chekist some information he'd find interesting. That might be worth something to you."

The KrimKab door opened, and one of the faces that had watched us leave peered out. "Yakov Petrovich, are you —?" The man's eyes widened when they fell on my hand. Without my noticing, it had emerged from my pocket again. I maneuvered it back in. "Oh. I—Aleksander Nikolayevich had a question. Just—come in when you're finished."

Petrovich coughed a little. His voice sounded more normal.

"All right. All right. I need to go in. But I will come to the infirmary this evening, when the office closes."

"Wait. One more thing. Why did the Chekist suspect those men? Where did he get the names on your list?"

"I was never sure. He wanted me to find out whether they had anything to do with Antonov's murder. Or really, not whether, but what. We were supposed to learn where they were at the time, whether they had alibis, whether any had seen him recently. Infosec thought they were on to something, I could tell that much. When he turned up dead in the bay, it alarmed them. They had been letting it play out, to see where it led, maybe. Afterwards, they thought there was something going on they didn't understand. I assumed an informant had given them the names."

"Another informant."

"Another informant." The glance he gave me was bloodshot, but its combination of blear and sharpness still unnerved me. Even after all of that, the old man wasn't toothless. "You are sharp as ever. Maybe I was wrong not to let you go by your *detektivy* all along." He opened the door to the office. "All right. I'll come for you this evening. At the infirmary."

The rest I barely remember. Pain and weakness carried me, the way they sometimes do when your strength fails and you still require something to go on with. I'd lost a lot of blood. Somehow I made it out of Administration, and I must have showed my pass to get through Nikolski.

At the infirmary, they did what they could. I remember the rush of agonized sensation into my hand when they removed the tourniquet. After that I recall the smells of blood and iodine, the pricks of a needle.

I believe I dreamed, or half-dreamed. It was like consciousness, but with every thought and perception reconfigured as nonsense. The pain in my hand somehow became a line extending across an infinite, featureless plane, then a series of parallel lines, then one line again. The line was also the men who, I knew, lurked somewhere out in the kremlin's yards. The line had killed Foma, and it was coming for me.

And what was the plane? I don't remember. In the wound dream, these things were meaningful, but I remember the sense of their meaningfulness without having any access to the meanings.

When I came to, I was in a cot, with another patient in another cot breathing on the other side of the room. His back was to me, and I couldn't make out anything about him other than his wheezing gasp. My hand had been wrapped in layers of gauze and yellowed bandages, through which a red blot had already begun to seep.

It was cold and, except for the other man's breathing, quiet. I couldn't have said how long I lay there, drifting in and out, before I heard the voices.

"Bogomolov here?"

"Who?"

I'd been aware for some time that an attendant of some sort was in a room on the other side of a door. I'd come into the place through a vestibule, and I thought he was stationed there as a kind of receptionist. He'd come in to check on me once or twice as well.

"*Zek* named Bogomolov. Anatoly Pavelovich. Thirteenth Company. Got hurt today. Someone said he cut off his finger."

I didn't recognize the other voice at all. For a dim and stupid moment I let myself hope Petrovich had sent someone to check on me.

"Oh. Our new patient. I believe he's sleeping. Should I wake him?"

"Nah. Just wanted to know where he'd ended up."

I heard a door bang shut. Beneath my pain and exhaustion, panic turned over.

Foma's killers had found me.

26

They were saying in the administration building that Comrade D. V. Uspenski had been the one to pull the trigger. The morning after the executions, the man had been seen at one of the hand basins down the hall from KrimKab, still drunk, washing blood from his boots.

So Petrovich told me, when he came to collect me from the infirmary. But information of my earlier visitor forestalled any more conversation on that topic until we were safely away.

Our plan had always called for me to go with him that evening. But we hadn't realized there would only be one way in and out, or that an attendant would be posted on the infirmary door. We'd assumed it would be easy to walk out: *zeks* typically looked for ways to get into medical beds, not escape from them, so why set a guard? And now, with Foma's killers having found me already, the problem had become extremely pressing.

As we hurriedly plotted, our voices dropped to whispers. Along with news, Petrovich had brought me the green cardigan from Antonov's chest, so that I could walk about without drawing attention with blood-covered clothes. The old man went out to handle the attendant, while I changed into the clean sweater, then put the bloody one and my coat back on over it. When I emerged, they were arguing.

"It's a serious injury," the other man was saying. "The order said he was to stay overnight."

"I'll bring him back by curfew," Petrovich lied. "He can sleep here. I only need to take my young friend to his cell."

"He lost a lot of blood. When he came in, he was hardly coherent. I can't have him collapsing out there when he's supposed to be in here."

"I'm feeling much better," I said. "All I needed was a rest."

"For a severed finger?" The medic shook his head and turned back to Petrovich. "I have to account for the prisoners who are assigned here, understand? What if I let him go with you and he goes missing?"

"Where could he go? Neither of us is allowed to leave the kremlin. I told you, they won't let me into his floor to fetch him clean clothes. They said he has to come himself. You see what a mess he's made. He'll be more comfortable with a clean shirt. And maybe your sheets won't be smudged with so much blood."

The man glanced back at my hand, then gave me a knowing look. "You understand, if they see you walking around and saying you're feeling much better in your old group, they may put you right back to work? I don't know how any of this happened. But maybe the whole effort will have been wasted. Do you see what I mean?"

"My axe slipped," I said. "That's all. I need a clean sweater."

He scoffed, then shrugged. "Fine. Do as you like. Only, if they don't revoke your medical pass, be back here by curfew."

Outside it was dark. I waited until we had gone around the nearest corner, then stipped off the bloody sweater and tossed it into the shadows.

We would not be returning to the infirmary. It was a shame: I'd hoped to be able to take to my sickbed again after Petrovich and I had done what needed doing this evening. But if I wanted to stay ahead of the men who were after me, that was no longer an option.

As we passed through the courtyard, Petrovich resumed the subject of D. V. Uspenski. He quickly reviewed what he'd told me already, showing unusual animation: the execution, Uspenski in charge, drunkenness, blood on the man's boots. Whether Uspenski'd shot all the victims himself or let the guards have a turn was debated, the old man declared. Word was the whole undertaking had been as haphazard and unruly as one expected at SLON. Though all agreed that he'd been drunk, opinions also differed as to his reasons for drinking. Some proposed he lacked the stomach to do the work sober. Others considered the man so depraved that his killing mixed smoothly into a single spree with his boozing.

Then there was the question of why Uspenski had been made responsible for the executions at all. As head of the Culture and Education Section, he need not have counted it among his regular duties. Had he volunteered? It seemed possible. By the official account, he had even volunteered for assignment to the island, making him one of the few Chekists who, instead of discharging a sentence, received pay.

According to Petrovich, however, the truth was a weak and horrible sort of camp joke. Rumor had it Uspenski had murdered his own father. His motives for this were lost to hearsay (though of course patricide has its own primordial associations). Since Uspenski-the-Elder was a priest (perhaps only a deacon, according to some), the State regarded his death as a casualty of necessary class warfare, and Uspenski-the-Younger got off. But the Cheka could not help being embarrassed by an agent apparently in the grips of a frenzy more Freudian than Marxist. And so some other pretense was found for shipping him to Solovki, where he would be out of sight.

Hence the joke: "You killed your father as a class enemy, now shoot some real class enemies."

This sort of thing does not have to be funny to be laughed at. A pariah must take on dirty jobs without complaining. Of course he couldn't say he wasn't willing to kill.

KrimKab was nominally a unit within EduCultSec, and their offices were on the same floor as Uspenski's. By listening for activity out in the hall, Petrovich had been able to catch him as he came out his door.

"Sometimes an ambush is what's best. That way you don't give your subject the chance to think about lying. Or refusing. I simply asked, 'Comrade Uspenski, during the events two nights ago, were there coffins for the executed men? Were they painted?' At first he turned to look at me and I thought he'd knock me down, there in the hall. Then a strange look passed over his face and he said there had been coffins, but he didn't know what I meant by painted. I left it at that. I didn't want him to ask why I was asking."

Delivering an explanation of his questioning methods restored some of the bristle to the old man's mustache. He looked more lively than he had that afternoon. "The point is," he continued, "you might be wrong about the coffins being made from Antonov's icons. Uspenski didn't remember seeing them. Then again, by all accounts the man was soaked as the sole of a shoe. It's possible he simply missed them."

He was right: here was a new uncertainty to take into account. I could feel the cold air on my face focusing my mind, but I was still thinking slowly.

"My other piece of news is about Zhenov," Petrovich was saying. "They say he's been drinking in the officer's club ever since he learned about the executions. Making enough of a scene for people to talk, even among my crowd of schoolteachers in Krim-Kab. That's where we're going. I want to talk to him."

"That's good. We have a lot to discuss."

"Yes." He hesitated. "Listen, Tolya. It so happens that I still have that list of Whites the Chekist gave me. Force of long habit prevents me giving up documentary evidence until I'm forced to. But we need to go forward with this carefully. We'll be on thin ice, even if we do find out something we can take to Infosec."

"Didn't you just hear me describe a murderer coming to locate me? And when I don't come back to the infirmary tonight, that orderly will start asking questions. Who knows how long we have? We're past being careful."

He stopped. I had not given him my arm to lean on, but I turned anyway. "You wanted my help, didn't you?" he said. "This is my advice. This is how I judge we solve the case and keep our skins."

The sun had gone down, and the wind that blew in the courtyard was freezing. Anger slipped in with it, under my coat. But no. I had asked for his help; we were allies again.

I shrugged. On we went.

The old man directed us to one of the buildings along the west wall; I hadn't known there was an officer's club. The sun had gone down. He seemed to find the path hard going, but he didn't take my arm.

A short set of stairs led to an exterior door, then another door that opened off an entrance hall. Inside, the club occupied a room that must always have been intended as a parlor. Its wainscoting and greenly arabesqued wallpaper showed signs of wear, but that they were there at all was remarkable. The place hadn't been constructed for the monks, or any life ordered by monastic rule.

A guard stationed by the door jerked his thumb when I said we needed to talk to Valery Zhenov, indicating the other side of an enameled screen. At one end of the room, a little ceramic stove emanated waves of heat, and the perfume of tea wafted from a samovar on a nearby table. Near the stove, a group of men were playing cards and talking. One noticed as we went over to Zhenov. He tapped his neighbor's shoulder and gestured.

"Subcommandant," said Petrovich. "A word, if you please."

The screen sealed Zhenov away from the tea-scented rest of the room, in his own sour atmosphere. He slumped in an upholstered yellow armchair, one elbow on the table in front of him. Next to the elbow a bottle of brandy, two-thirds empty, then a glass. The stub of a cigarette smoldered in an ashtray. We hadn't talked about what we would ask him, but I suppose it was clear enough between us what we were there for.

"Who—?" he said, his eyes swimming into focus. Behind him, a tall bookshelf built into the wall was a deserted city. The volumes that were there showed a disordered mix of gilt-leather spines and paper wrappers. "You two. What do you want?"

"My colleague looked for you at the warehouse this morning," said Petrovich. "We have a few more questions."

"Your questions," said Zhenov, slurring. The surface of the table, I saw, was covered in ash. In places where he'd spilled his drink, the varnish was swollen. "You may think I am a man of no account, but I am a gentleman and a patriot. The devils are in charge. Russia has been plunged from the earth into hell. If I am to be put to death, I will clutch my honor to my heart."

The man was absurd. All he was saying, really, was that he had spent the day indoors, with tobacco and alcohol close to hand. No one on Solovetky could ever summon such rhetoric otherwise.

Meanwhile the place where my finger had been throbbed. "The men who were executed," I said. "They were associates of yours."

Petrovich put a hand on my arm. "You've had a difficult day, Tolya. Why not let me ask the questions?"

"We don't have time to hear about his honor!"

Zhenov squinted at me, his face red and hostile. I was not attempting to conceal my bandage, but he took no notice of it. "That's what brings you snuffing after me now, then? You've heard that every side suspects me of something different, and you want to hang your murder around my neck as well?"

"That's not it," said Petrovich quickly. "Tell me, did you know that Ivan Kologriev was an *urka* before he came to work for you?"

The other man poured a drink, not answering. Only his part of the room was a mess. Across the parquet floor, a piano stood in a corner. There were photographs in frames on the green walls, dozens of them.

When he spoke again it was into his glass, hunched over. "I assumed the murder investigation was done with, when I heard nothing from you after I came back from Anzer."

"Not yet," I said.

"No, not yet," said Petrovich. "Shall we take it that you did know about Kologriev's past?"

"Isn't this a prison? Aren't we all criminals of one sort or another?"

Petrovich shrugged. "Suppose so. It didn't worry you, to have a man like that working under you?"

"Why should I answer any questions of yours?"

The look the old man gave me meant I should be quiet. "We are still trying to find out who murdered Gennady Antonov," he said. "We may find something that vindicates your honor as well. What about Kologriev?"

Zhenov huffed. "He wouldn't have been working with me if he'd still been an *urka*, would he? Decent fellow, Kologriev. Decent. Knew how to do hard work. Where's the thief who does that, eh?"

"You weren't worried about theft?" said Petrovich.

"Insubordination. That's the trouble, not theft. Man like that, with a little competence and the respect of the rabble around him—he'll talk back to his superiors, always. But theft, no. He never was a bad worker. I only came four months ago. He was helpful when I first arrived and was learning how things worked with supplying Anzer. Helped me grasp quickly how things were organized."

"Yes," said Petrovich, "you mentioned that he'd informed you that requisitioning icons was a possibility, didn't you? You want timber, and because the Bolsheviks are Marxists they think it is funny to give you holy paintings to build with. But these things aren't just wood, no matter whether Lenin's ghost says so or not. It would be easy for a little 'timber' to be misplaced in a carpenter's shop, wouldn't it? I think you said you had a system to make sure none of them went missing?"

"There was a system," said Zhenov.

"All right. Good. What was it, then?"

Zhenov sniffed and screwed up his mouth. The brandy had made his features smaller, and they swam in the vacancy of his face. "They'd sent along a diagram—sent it down on the train for me. Simple, two yards on a side—" He stopped himself.

"The diagram was for coffins, wasn't it?" I said.

The drunk man gulped. "Yes," he whispered.

"All right," said Petrovich. "We knew as much already. Tell us how your system used the diagram."

Zhenov was silent, then proceeded in a different voice, haltingly. "Two long, wide icons joined together at one end for the lid, then the same again for the floor. Then two smaller joined at either end, and the walls made of however many it took to make the right length. Fill in whatever gaps resulted from irreg—" He hiccuped. "Irregularities in the painting's measurements with scrap wood. Would have been easy. Easy to count the icons, be sure they were all used up. Only they were ordered down early."

"What do you mean, 'ordered down early'?"

"A telegram. It came while I was still on Anzer. The . . . the finished products were not to have been delivered until much later. Tomorrow, in fact. But the order came to move up the date. I had to make arrangements for the men to bring them directly from the train, deliver them to where . . . where they would be used."

"And the supplies we were looking for," said Petrovich. "You never found any sign of them?"

"No, no."

I looked at the old man, but he was staring at Zhenov, who in turn heaved a sigh and pointed his face away. Into their hesitation, my frustration and fear erupted. What would Nat Pinkerton have done? He wouldn't have let the man's self-pity delay him. He'd have charged forward at the truth. "Tell me, Subcommandant Zhenov. Do you have any idea who they put in those coffins?"

"Yes."

"They were for those late associates of yours, weren't they? Fellow officers, executed by the Administration of this camp."

He covered his eyes with one hand. "Oh God . . ."

"Show him the list, Yakov Petrovich."

"Tolya," said Petrovich warningly.

I went on: "Yakov Petrovich has a list of men Infosec was interested in in connection with our case."

Reluctantly, Petrovich unbuttoned his coat and reached into it. He put the document he withdrew on the table in front of Zhenov. "Are any of your associates' names on this list?"

Zhenov glanced at the paper as though it might scuttle towards him. He couldn't have read every name with such a sidelong glance, but he gave a small nod.

"It's quite a coincidence, isn't it?" I said. "The coffins you helped build were used for your friends. And now those friends prove to be involved in the matter—a murder!—that we had already spoken about to you. Don't you find it odd?"

"Tolya," said Petrovich again.

Zhenov snatched the bottle from the table and drank from it before covering his eyes with his hands again. "Oh God . . . ," he moaned.

"You never questioned what these coffins would be used for?" I said.

Zhenov shook his head. "I should have told you—" He stopped and took his hands away to look at the bottle, but didn't drink any more. "It's predictable. When a special order comes in for coffins, adding to the normal production schedule—it always means that something is planned by the main Administration. They make it a high-priority job. Whenever one of those orders come in from main Administration I—I know that they are contemplating it. Do you see what I mean? I didn't think I should let it be known what they were planning. If you'd been supposed to know about the coffins, you would have already." His eyes swung frantically back and forth between Petrovich's face and mine. "But I didn't know who they meant to put in them! I did not betray my comrades! I have my honor, by God!"

Not seeing what he hoped to see in our expressions, perhaps, he put his fist to his mouth. A gesture of sorrow, yes, but on his reddened, drunken face it was ridiculous, as though he were stifling a belch. He began to cry. On the other side of the screen, the card game erupted in laughter. I couldn't tell whether it was in response to Zhenov, but he released a racking sob and laid his head down on the table. His flattened mustache spread on the tabletop beneath his cheek and lip, where it grew damp with tears.

It stopped me. How to handle this total collapse? After we'd stared at his slumped form for a moment in silence, Petrovich said quietly: "How is the encyclopedia of your scalp progressing?"

"Yakov Petrovich!" The subcommandant's book of lost hairs struck me, at the moment, as worse than trivial.

"Damn it, you've asked your questions, let me ask mine." Zhenov made no move to respond, and the old man went at him again. "Come, I want to hear about your project. What was the German professor's name? Glockenbauer?"

"Gruenewald," muttered Zhenov.

"Of course. Dr. Gruenewald. I see that you're under some stress. I hope you are still maintaining his regimen."

"Not since it happened," muttered Zhenov.

"Not since it happened," repeated Petrovich. "But isn't this one of those times when you should be looking to your hair for guidance? If your record is ever worth anything, it should be worth something now, when your constitution is unbalanced." He frowned down at the other man. "Not to say deranged. The key to general health, you said."

"Go on, mock," said Zhenov, his voice choked. "No one cares how you treat me, so why not?"

Petrovich shrugged. "I am only half mocking. I like to see a thing like your notebook of hairs carried through once it's started. Maybe you've had a break of a few days in your record keeping. You should start again."

Zhenov raised his head. "'A break of a few days.' You don't

understand. Gruenewald's clear on this point. Regularity—it's the only value of such a record. 'How are we to rationalize upheavals in today's follicular headscape without reference to that of the day immediately prior?' That's what he writes. Take it back up now, it means starting from the beginning again. What would be the point?"

I was on the verge of saying something, but a sudden wave of exhaustion overcame me. The urge to sit down, to close my eyes, was very strong. The pain in my hand, improved since being bandaged, had begun to get worse again as well. Let Petrovich talk about nonsense with the man. At least he'd induced him to raise his head from the table.

"A shame," the old man was saying. "Even so, you must start over somewhere, eh?"

"Yes. Yes, I suppose."

"Your friends, the ones on the list I showed you. They were all White officers, like you, I think."

Zhenov sounded dazed. "Yes. Fellow officers. It's not good here, to try to go it alone. We did each other favors as we could."

"How did you come to know those men in particular? There are many Whites in the camp."

"Adrian Albyertovich—surname Batishchev. His name was on your list."

"Yes," said Petrovich. "I spoke to him a few days ago."

"We knew each other in the army. Fighting the Teutons. Artillery commander. Fine soldier—how I admired him! He wrote a letter that somehow reached me, telling me to come and join the Volunteer Army under Kornilov. By the time I was able to join them, Kornilov—Kornilov had been killed—in Ekaterinodar, you know—and Denikin was in command. Well, both of us ended up here. He introduced me to several others. A man of wide acquaintance." He hiccuped sadly, then blinked and huffed, laboring to breathe through his fug of brandy. "Now he is dead and rotting. One of those they killed. And Nail Terekhov! He has been missing for days, they say. He was not one of the executed. He is only gone!"

Petrovich caught my eye and shook his head. I supposed he was right. I could think of little to be gained by confronting Zhenov with what had really happened to Terekhov.

The old man cleared his throat. "The rumor is they were making plans to escape. A plan to leave the island somehow, perhaps flee to Finland. Had you heard about anything of the sort?"

Zhenov nodded slowly, making a face. "Yes. I began to hear of it when I came back from Anzer. The morning after they'd been . . . But all of that's nonsense. Idiocy. They would never have been so foolish. They were bold men, military. Capable. Not stupid. What chance would they have had to escape? In that case why would they have tried it? And if there had been such a plan, I'd have known."

"All right," said Petrovich. "But if someone set up your friends, who'd have known they were all in communication with each other? Could they have been meeting somewhere you didn't know about?"

"They wouldn't have kept it from me," Zhenov insisted. "Anyone—anyone might've known. I do well here, or I used to. I would lay out a table of pickles and herring in my office, if I could manage it. I met them, often, in my office or my quarters. Or here, for a cup of something, tea or vodka. No secret about it. About our acquaintance."

"Did any of your friends ever mention Antonov? Our victim?"

"No. No. Why would they have done? I didn't lie before, when I told you I'd never heard of him."

Zhenov began to sob again. He did it quietly this time, but with little hiccups and embellishments—it was elaborate weeping. The tears ran into the fuzz on his cheeks. At first he tried to wipe them away, but after a moment gave up and cried freely, jamming his fingers up into his hair. Under the assault of whatever grief he was feeling, his mustachioed face creased and distended until it resembled the portrait of an infant.

When the storm of weeping had passed, he appeared to realize what he was doing to his scalp. He removed his hands gingerly from his head and patted the bent hairs back into shape, sniffling. Tears still ran from his eyes.

"Why do I bother?" he said. "Now that my record has been disrupted, it is pointless."

"All you can do is start again," said Petrovich.

The way Zhenov gulped, you could hear the slick muscles of his throat moving. "They'll kill me, too," he whispered. "Soon they'll kill me, too."

It was probably true, but I didn't care to stay and commiserate. We'd heard enough. I could hear the old man's cane thumping behind me as I left. When we had reached the courtyard I felt his grip on my arm, familiar and weak.

"Tolya, wait. You need to listen to me. We won't produce the best results simply by charging forward. Even with these dangers bearing down on us, you won't be able to bully your way to a solution. Tease out information, then put it to use. Understand? If tonight you approach Vinogradov the way you tried with Zhenov, you will be finished."

"I don't need your lecture," I said. "And I thought bullying people into talking was part of your program."

"Of course it is. Only not all of the time. You have to be able to see when someone like Zhenov needs to be allowed to go on about his favorite subject."

I wanted him to be wrong, but what he said made sense. Zhenov was a fool, but Petrovich had kept him talking and gotten us more information—even if it still wasn't clear in what manner it could be put to use.

Nat Pinkerton be damned—Petrovich was who I had. Whether I liked it or not, there was no one to trust but him.

27

The stairwell was dark, but at the top a little light came under the door onto the landing. That meant the usual small group had gathered at the museum. They would be chatting quietly, or working separately at their desks. It had been like this the times I'd come to meet with Antonov. For a moment, it was as if he was waiting for me on the other side of the door. But only for a moment. Under layers of glove and bandage, cold knotted my throbbing hand.

I'd left Petrovich back at Company Ten. The plan depended on his staying safe there while I caught up with Vinogradov. Neither of us knew where the museum director quartered, but it seemed likely he would come directly to the museum upon his return to the kremlin. If he didn't, I hoped I'd be able to get one of the museum's workers to take me to wherever he had gone. If no one would—well, it wasn't an option.

I had to find Vinogradov tonight. My breath came short at the thought of what I would need to do, how I would need to work on him. The plan had seemed straightforward when I'd concocted it that afternoon, but now I wasn't so sure.

It was Ivanov who answered my knock. Again his smallness surprised me. He held a lamp, which he raised to my face as he peered up at me. "You. You were here with the old man the other day. What do you want?" Behind him the room was dim. Light from the lamp glinted on gilt and polished wood. Its beams shone back from the painted eyes of saints.

"Bogomolov. My name is Bogomolov. Your director returns tonight. Is he here?"

He stuck out his chest. "No. His sledges haven't arrived yet." His hand stayed on the door.

"I'll wait," I said.

"There's no time for that tonight. Come back tomorrow."

"No. It has to be tonight. He's going to want to hear what I have to say."

The Anti-Religious Bug. The name had seemed amusing the other day, but popping into my head now, it only aggravated me. He looked me over again. "Where's the old man?"

"I told you," I said. "Vinogradov's going to want to hear. I spoke to him the other day, on Kostrihe."

For another moment or two I could hear the breath in my nose while we stared at each other. Then he took his hand from the door and turned back for his desk. "The director will decide that himself. You can sit. Don't touch anything."

I shut the door deliberately, wounded hand still in my pocket. There were fewer men inside than I'd pictured. The faces that registered my entrance were smudges in the gloom. Two or three more lamps made little pools of light, limited to the desktops they sat on.

Ivanov must have noticed me stepping over to the arched window left of his desk, but he declined to acknowledge it, and took the seat from which my knock must have disturbed him. I stared down into the courtyard, then let my forehead rest against the cold glass. With the light behind me, no one looking up from the dark below would be able to tell who I was. But now that I was inside I could feel my heart racing. The short walk from Company Ten had been harrowing, every silhouette passed on the path outlining a possible enemy. I reassured myself: no one had been watching as I opened the little door to the museum's stairs, there by the Holy Gate. The man who'd asked after me that afternoon would still believe I was in the infirmary.

"I say. Bogomolov, wasn't it?"

It was Sewick, head cataloger and aspirant conspirator. In

his way, the man was guileless. The need to know everyone's business perched on his face like his glasses. I nodded.

"Of course, of course." His gaze darted at Ivanov, whose frown pointedly ignored us. "May I offer you a seat? There is a chair, you see, there, over at my desk."

Sewick's was one of the desks with a lamp on it. A heavy, loden-green coat hung over the back of his chair. Behind that, the catalog's three scuffed cases hinted at geometry in the dim light.

"I see the assistant director continues to throw up obstacles to your inquiries," Sewick said. "That's to be expected from him. He's a personally difficult man, but you must not make too much of his obstructionism. Of course I am not privy to all that you've learned. Maybe from your perspective . . . ?" He trailed off.

"Listen," I said. "I need to check something in your catalog."

He sat to attention. "Of course. I'd be happy to help you find anything. What is it you're looking for?"

"I can't say yet. Maybe I'll know it when I see it."

"Well." He was nonplussed, and for a moment visibly weighed complaining. "Yes, of course. Make free. Do let me know if you locate anything of use."

To my relief, finding 7.38 was not difficult. Vinogradov's collection encompassed more than I'd realized, its thirty-four categories ranging from "1: Manuscripts" and "2: Icons" to "22: Biological Specimens—Flora" and "34: Artistic and Literary Productions of SLON Inmates." "Chapel Paraphernalia" was the seventh. Within each grouping, items appeared simply to have been arranged in the order the museum staff had happened on them. I could have gone directly to the correct drawer, but I was aware of Sewick glancing over his shoulder to see what I was doing. Veronika's accession number would be less valuable with Vinogradov the more people knew about it. To throw him off the track I spent ten minutes flipping through drawers I had no interest in.

When I finally came to 7.38, it communicated little to me. *Rizi. Set of two. Silver. 88 zol. Unident. (smith) Pavel Dmitriyev (assay) Saint Petersburg 1845. Provenance unknown.* An expert might have gleaned more. But this was enough. *Rizi* were icon covers, used to protect and conceal the surface of a painting. Usually they would leave a cutout to show a saint's face, and perhaps the hands as well. I'd asked Antonov once whether he didn't resent having his repairs hidden away, but he'd said it was respectful to protect the holy work. What mattered was that it was there, and revered, not that anyone saw the paint.

I shook my head. No, what mattered was that the things were silver. "Zol."—*zolotniki*—were a measure of purity. I seemed to recall that 88 was a high grade. Item 7.38 would be valuable, even melted down.

I opened a few more drawers in one of the other cases, then made an excuse to Sewick about needing to check on something among Antonov's papers. At his desk, the icon of Saint George was still there. The dragon writhed as it had before, porcine and smoke-tendriled. The princess's red thread still bound its neck.

Finally the sounds of unmusical clinking and men's voices rising and falling came from outside: the expedition's sledges were being drawn up below us. Ivanov rose and hurried down the stairs. Before long he returned, trotting at Vinogradov's heels like a bulldog.

The director stopped when he saw me. "Anatoly Bogomolov, wasn't it?" he said. "From Saint Petersburg University. Mathematics. Ivanov tells me you wish to speak to me."

"I wanted to know about one of the items in your collection." I said it quietly, so only the two of them could hear. "Accession number 7.38."

"7.38?"

"A pair of silver *rizi*."

His narrow mustache twitched minutely while he thought it over. It was not quite as square as when I'd seen it before, and on the whole his face appeared more human, less molded or fashioned, than it had when we'd met on the cape. He looked tired. "All right. Ivanov and I have a few matters that must be discussed, but I will be with you shortly. Wait here."

The two men were shut up in the office for perhaps twenty minutes. When Ivanov came out, he still looked sour.

"You can go in," he said.

Vinogradov's office was, in fact, the chapel's sacristy. A short hall separated it from what had been the sanctuary. Inside, the little room was neat but crowded with objects on every surface: a delicate porcelain cup patterned and blue around its rim; a lion cast in bronze; a minute enameled box whose lid showed a peasant girl on a black field, surrounded by vines with red and yellow leaves. Three high filing cabinets filled one wall completely. Leaning against them was a stack of five or six canvases. They were evidently modern paintings, not icons. I could make out only the topmost, a kind of brown, cubist portrait that was difficult to decipher.

Vinogradov himself sat at a wide desk, on which papers had been marshaled into neat stacks and arranged, along with a few bibelots, around a central blotting pad. Behind him, a window looked out on the dark bay. I'd passed a steaming samovar in the hall, and he held a cup of tea and a saucer.

"So. Bogomolov." He indicated the folding metal chair in front of him. "Tell me again what the number was."

"7.38. The card in your catalog says it refers to a pair of silver *rizi*. Icon covers."

He blew on his tea. "Is that right? And what is your interest in them? Earlier you were asking about requisitioned icons."

"I have it on good authority those *rizi* are not to be found in the museum."

His eyes narrowed. "When an item leaves thc collection, either because of damage or for any other reason, its card is removed."

"But not if you don't want it known that it's gone."

"What do you mean to say?"

"You traded them away. To someone who could arrange a work transfer for a woman named Veronika Fitneva. A favor for Gennady Antonov."

The china clinked as Vinogradov slowly put the cup and saucer down. "I see," he said. His face expressed nothing, as though everything in it had been arranged to balance around the square of mustache on his upper lip. "When we spoke on Kostrihe, you seemed to suggest I was a suspect in Antonov's death. Am I to take it that you are presenting these purportedly missing items from the collection as some kind of evidence against me?"

"You're still a suspect. But no, that isn't what this is." I took a breath. Petrovich knew where I was, I reminded myself. It was go forward, or return to the infirmary and die. "What it is, is a threat."

So much, after all of my straining and thinking, for modeling myself on literary detectives. With this I removed myself from their side of the page. Blackmail existed in the America of Nat Pinkerton, the London of Sherlock Holmes, true, but it was not a tool put to use by protagonists. Rather than a detective, a blackmailer was most likely to be a murderer—or, indeed, a victim. I could remember more than a few publications in which the investigator uncovered a killer, only to overflow with forgiveness when it was proved that the unfortunate had committed her crime (it was usually a woman) against a base extortionist. Pinkerton's visage, with its broken nose framed by its medallion at the top of the page, stared down in disapproval at creatures like myself.

But what, really, was the appeal of such a story? Surely that the reader enjoyed two dark secrets for the price of one? In order to be forgiven, after all, the killer must endure the very fate she killed to avoid. Her first shameful crime must be exposed (at least to the reader) to expiate her later one. Perhaps Pinkerton had more in common with the blackmailers than I'd have liked to believe when I was a boy.

"From you," I continued. "I need a pass that will allow me and my partner to move freely in and out of the kremlin. And a safe place to sleep. Tonight, maybe tomorrow. If I don't get those things from you, I'll tell Infosec I know the number of certain items misappropriated from the museum collection. I imagine their audit will turn up others in addition to 7.38."

His face didn't change. "I understood you to be conducting your investigation under Infosec's authority already."

"We were. We've . . . fallen out of favor. The pass we were relying on is no longer current."

"Why would they change their attitude towards you? Something you did?"

"It doesn't matter. What you need to understand is what I am telling you will happen with these *rizi*, if you don't do what I say."

The cup and saucer clattered as Vinogradov slapped his palm down on the surface of the desk. "Yes. You are making a threat, you tell me. I have chosen not to eject you from my office immediately. Do me the courtesy in return of explaining the situation I find myself in. I want to know why you are no longer working for Infosec."

I could see the intensity in his expression now. It seemed

best to answer. "Something we found out, maybe. The truth is, we don't know. They didn't explain, so now finding out is part of the case. The best guess is that we turned something up that someone with pull didn't like. Someone who could have our patron take us off the case."

"Then you are still pursuing the killer? But without any official sanction."

"Yes."

"Why?"

I tried to think of how much to reveal at this point. "Certain signs indicate the murderer doesn't like how much we've found out so far. Whoever he is, we already know he's capable of violence. If we're going to be secure, we need to finish the case."

"And you are still working with the man who sent you to me before."

"That's right. Yakov Petrovich. His name goes on the pass along with mine."

Strange, the sorts of things you remember about such a moment. Vinogradov held my life in his hands. He might very well have destroyed me. My threat had been real, but it was hardly so dangerous that I could be sure of him. He could have refused. And I? I'd have died.

And yet, when I look back on that hour spent in his office, what I see in my mind's eye is the painting that leaned with the others against his filing cabinets. Cubist, modern, brown: aggressively not one of Antonov's icons, but somehow reminiscent of them. My glance kept returning to it. Behind its refractions and doublings was a face, certainly. The reflected and re-reflected features—multiple eyes, multiple nostrils, a bouquet of narrow mustaches—had a familiar molded quality to them. But this was only on the left side. On the right, curves and rounded surfaces arced through every plane that could be imagined out of the flatness of the canvas. Light coming from all directions at once glinted on some hard substance that could not have been flesh.

I never saw the piece again, after that night. It is certainly beyond my examination now. But I believe the painting was of Vinogradov, half his face obscured by something—a plate, perhaps—he held up to cover it.

"And why do you believe you are in need of a safe place to sleep?"

"I was transferred back to Company Thirteen. Last night there was an attempt on my life there. I expect another tonight."

He paused, thinking, then said: "Won't you be missed in Thirteen, if you aren't there at curfew?"

"No. I'm meant to be in the infirmary. But staying there isn't safe either. They've found me already."

"The infirmary? Are you ill?"

Yes. A plate, hiding a human face. Something ceramic, flat, and round. Or was it flat? The bristling perspectives made flatness hard to tell from depth. Perhaps it was a plate—perhaps an earthen bottle.

I took my bandaged hand from where I'd been holding it in my lap. Placed on the desk in front of us, it looked misshapen, swollen with wrappings and lopsided without its finger. "No, not ill," I said. "Desperate."

Vinogradov looked, then took up his tea again. "This is the result of the attempt on you?" he said over the rim of the cup.

"No," I said. "Self-inflicted. It wouldn't have been possible for me to get away from them, to come to you with this, if I'd been confined to Quarantine. Luckily for me, my work group was using hatchets today."

"You are very determined." He sat back in his chair. Light from the alcove lamp glinted in his glasses' lenses. "But coming to me is not without its risks. I am one of the parties of suspicion in the case. What will happen to you if I prove, after all, to have been Antonov's murderer? I would have to be the one behind your attackers as well, wouldn't I? In that case, you would seem to be putting your head into the lion's mouth."

The cold one feels in moments like this, I've been told, comes from the hormone adrenaline. I tried to ignore it, and watched his face instead. He gave nothing away.

"I am assuming," I said, "that if you killed Antonov, or had him killed, you'll simply refuse my offer. In that case I'll go to Infosec with the information I have about your missing silver *rizi* and do what I can to have you sent off to a penal cell. You will continue with whatever strategies you've already put into motion to rub me out. You wouldn't want me to be done in here, since it would be too easy to trace back to you." That wire of cold adrenaline moved into my chest, inexorable as logic. "However, if you do decide to mislead me, there's little I can do. Then it will be Petrovich who goes to Infosec, with news of my death to add to our information about the *rizi*."

Vinogradov pursed his lips minutely. "A very comprehensive account. You aren't reluctant to carry out such a daring plan? By your account, there is significant personal risk."

"There's nothing daring about it. It's the safest bet I can think of to make. If there were a better one, I'd make that. But the probability of my surviving the night is worse in any other situation. It would be stupid not to face the risk."

He laughed, a neat, bloodless *ha*. "Both determined and admirably pragmatic," he said. He picked up a pile of envelopes, which he began sorting deliberately. Something warned me not to interrupt, and it continued for some time. Eventually he opened a drawer and deposited the greater part of the stack inside, arranging the remaining three or four letters in a neat stack on the edge of his blotter. The face that looked up at me was hard.

"I have not agreed that there is anything at stake in item 7.38 beyond a mislaid bit of cataloging, of course. But you are correct that I would prefer not to have attention directed to our operations here. I suppose no group head wishes to have his work checked by Infosec. At the same time, I have no desire to set myself at cross-purposes with my colleagues in that section. That is what I would seem to be doing, if I were to grant your investigation my authorization after they'd withdrawn theirs. Why should I choose the difficulty of helping you over the difficulty of being harassed by you?"

I exhaled. This I was prepared for. Petrovich and I had discussed the plan at length in between visiting Zhenov and coming here, and had dwelt on this moment. If it came to Vinogradov asking what was in it for him, the old man said, then I had come through the dangerous part of the conversation. There was a ready answer.

"Because I can help you protect the rest of your collection," I said.

"Protect it? What does it need protection from?"

"The icon requisition I was asking about—it was the second you'd had to fill, wasn't it? There's something suspicious about them. If you do nothing, the time may come when you find yourself having to fill a third, fourth, and fifth."

Vinogradov absorbed the idea silently. He said: "We spoke the other day about the missing gold leaf."

"Yes. That focused our attention on it. Antonov had left the kremlin under your orders to recover it when he was killed. But there's more to it than that." The chair creaked under me as I leaned forward. "You've heard about the executions?"

"Ivanov has just informed me of it. According to him, they are saying it was an escape plot."

"Right. And the plotters—the supposed plotters—were all White Army officers, and all acquainted with a man named Valery Zhenov."

"Zhenov . . ."

"He signed your most recent requisition order. He's Anzer Division's subcommandant for supply. He operates a warehouse outside the kremlin, and sent the icons from there up to the cabinetry workshop."

"I recognize the name. What do these friends of his have to do with my icons?"

"The coffins for the execution were built on Anzer by special order of Infosec. Where do you think they got the boards?"

At that his face finally moved more than a fraction of an inch. "Coffins?"

"Right. The requisition only made it through Administration because they needed them ready for the men they were going to take out to the cemetery. Zhenov doesn't seem to have known anything about who was going to be shot. But he's connected to the icons in two ways, you see? Either he's lying, or someone else is up to something."

"Or you've discovered a coincidence."

"But there's still more. Infosec was pushing us to connect Antonov to this escape plot as well. We were given a list of sources to follow up on when we began our investigation. Every one of them was rounded up among the supposed escapees." I paused to consider how much of Petrovich's secret I wanted to reveal. "And my partner and I know that Infosec had Antonov under surveillance before he died as well. It has to have been that they thought he was involved."

Vinogradov sniffed. "Antonov part of an escape? I hardly find that believable."

"I agree. In fact, we weren't able to verify his connection to anyone on the list. Infosec may have been wrong. But just the fact that they suspected him connects him to the icons in a second way. It connects him to them as coffins, just like Zhenov."

"Yes," he said slowly. "That is strange. I wouldn't have expected it."

Vinogradov sat, still undecided, his doll's-head considering atop its gray shirt. I had one more piece of evidence to push him with. But I hesitated, thinking of Veronika. "There's more. Antonov . . . preserved the accession number of those *rizi*. He did it because he thought you might be moved to revoke the woman Fitneva's transfer, or maybe to do something else against him. Something was making him cautious. At least he thought he had a reason to mistrust you. Maybe you have a better idea what it is than I do. To me it suggests he was up to something you wouldn't have liked."

"Perhaps," he mused. "But tell me: how did you come to learn this suspect accession number recorded by Antonov?"

The man was perceptive; he'd put his finger on just what I wished to hold back. And the temptation was there, I could feel it: to give Veronika up would show I was on his side, an ally. That was what I needed, wasn't it?

But I could still see her face, features flying. And she had helped me, when I had no one else.

"That is my affair," I said.

"If you insist," said Vinogradov after a moment. "Exactly what is it you are suggesting, then?"

"I don't know. Not exactly. But there is something off about these requisitions."

More silence. Vinogradov's black eyes didn't leave my face. Finally he said: "All right. I will write the pass in the morning. Tonight you may sleep here, in the museum. We cannot make you very comfortable, but I don't imagine you will mind."

There were not many details to iron out. I'd left it with Petrovich that I'd come to tell him the results myself, so he could be sure nothing had happened to me. He was to have checked at the infirmary in the meantime as well, to see whether Veronika had sent word that we could use the monks' gate.

Vinogradov promised that he and Ivanov would wait in the museum until I returned. As we went out through the sanctuary, I mentioned my worry about being recognized down in the courtyard, and he beckoned to Sewick. "Lend Bogomolov your coat and hat, Johan Martinovich," he said.

"My coat? Now then—well, I mean to say, I don't see—"

"You'll have it back shortly," said Vinogradov. "Do as I say."

With the green collar turned up around my ears and the cap pulled down, I felt safer, but still I did my best to skulk around the edges of the yard. Alleys, walls, high windows, and snow. There were fewer men on the paths now. I passed two, but neither seemed to look at me. Nativity I gave a wide berth, as well as the infirmary.

Petrovich was waiting for me at the door to Company Ten. "Tolya!" he said. His gravelly voice quavered. "You were gone a long time. What happened?"

"It's all right. I'm staying there. I found out what Item 7.38 is. A pair of silver *rizi*."

"That's good. We can proceed, then. There was a note from Fitneva at the infirmary. She says the Fish Gate is all right."

The guard on the door watched while I explained the rest. It didn't take long. We agreed he would meet me at the museum in the morning, and I left.

Sewick accepted his clothing back resentfully. The leading questions he asked about my conversation with Vinogradov were, I thought, cursory, and he left as soon as I made it clear I wouldn't say anything. Soon Ivanov and the director appeared out of the latter's office. They nodded good night and departed down the stairs, taking the lamp and locking me in behind them.

Alone, finally, but blind, I felt my way around the sanctuary, stumbling among the desks. The windows were shut. Twice I checked to be sure Ivanov had turned the outer door's key, then put two chairs in front of it for anyone who came in in the dark to stumble over. I'd watched Vinogradov himself lock the doors to his office and the storage area. When I was sure the sanctuary was secure as it could be, I lay down next to Gennady Antonov's desk. In the cold, pregnant blackness of the museum, I pillowed my head on a stack of books I'd come upon as I ran my hands over the museum's surfaces.

I cradled my wounded hand to my chest, protecting it as best I could from whatever I might do to it in my sleep.

28

What I feared has come to pass. Just as I have achieved a measure of safety in my story, today I find that the book itself, and I the author, are in danger. It is a disaster.

Last night I laid down my pen and fell into bed. Slept. Dreamed. Awoke sweating, tangled in sheets, the sun in my face. Rode the bus to the plant as usual. It was as we filed in that I began to hear the news, first-shift men muttering it to the arrivals as they clocked in. The talk was of the morning's meeting of the Party bureau.

Vasily Feodorovich has been purged from the Communist Party.

Vasily Minayev, the engineer. Yes, they've booted him. He's gone.—No, no. They didn't fire him, only took his Party card.—Isn't he a member of the bureau?—He was. That was why he had no warning of it. They'd have had to write him a summons so he could answer the charge against him, but they knew he was going to be there anyway. That Ehrenburg, he's a slick one with such tricks.—They're saying it caught Minayev completely by surprise. He didn't know whether to argue or to beg forgiveness and promise to do better.—Wouldn't have mattered anyway. The vote on the motion to expel was unanimous. Anyone could see he was going too far.

Just what the charge made against Vasily-my-neighbor is, no one seems to know. Hijacking the struggle for reform for his own ends. Parroting, for personal aggrandizement, the slanderous propaganda with which capitalist powers smear the Soviet state. Violation of Party discipline. It hardly matters.

We have not spoken. I should not be seen with him. Some of the men at the plant were claiming he would be arrested. Others said no, the Party never lets its members be punished, even after they've kicked them out. I cannot tell what will happen.

There was no way to ask for more details without demonstrating I knew him, without attracting suspicion to myself. And it would do him no favors to have Anatoly Bogomolov, class enemy and political criminal, setting himself up as his advocate.

If there is more suppression, I am not safe. I ought to burn all I've written. What's the use of putting down these images that fly up before me in my basement nights? Why risk myself? Vasily Feodorovich's pinched red-haired wife will have told them about our meetings. At any moment I could hear the boot on the stair, the knock on the door.

It was for a book they took me the first time.

And so, here I am at the point of decision again. I did not burn these pages before when I wrote that I would. Can I now? Can I cease producing empty wire spirals for my drawer? Can I forget this account?

No. I hardly need to think about the answer. No, I can't forget. And I will not stop writing.

I will need to hide the manuscript. A place of safety for my story, like my place among the desks and painted walls in that chapel above the Holy Gates.

When the scrape of the door hitting my chairs woke me, I knew I'd survived the night. I roused myself to find Vinogradov regarding my improvised barrier, nonplussed, at the other end of the chapel. Gray light came through the three big windows on the eastern wall.

"Perhaps an excess of caution," he said as I came over to the chairs. "Under the circumstances, I suppose I understand. Put them back where you found them. When your partner arrives, I'll see the two of you in my office."

My hand felt worse. It had been a bad night. Pain had affected my dreams.

Once I'd gathered myself, I went out to visit the lavatory. On the stairs, my gut began to cramp, and when I went for a drink my belly clutched at the icy water pulled up from the cistern. With the dirty bustle of men surrounding me, I brought up another dipper-full of water, but let it splash back into the bucket. Suddenly I felt I would be sick. I turned unsteadily, pushed my way back through the crowd, back to the museum.

On the landing I felt a little better. While I gathered myself to enter the museum, however, a problem I hadn't worked through yesterday reared its head: by removing myself from the infirmary, I'd passed beyond the scope of bread distribution. Was what I was feeling now blood loss, illness, or simple hunger? Being without bread: that's panic. While I watched, the arm I had supported myself with to lean against the wall began to shake. Again my stomach turned over.

The fish and potatoes I'd taken from Antonov were still in my jacket lining. There was no way to cook them in the museum, and I'd been warned against eating raw potato. You could tell when a starving, mad *zek* had gorged himself on discarded green spuds by the stains of diarrhea on the back of his pants. It was one of the signs of a *dokhodyaga*.

Neither of the ones in my jacket looked green, but even when the color hadn't changed, potatoes were said to be hard to digest uncooked. I examined them again, sniffed them. The taste of the one I finally bit into was bitter, the texture slimy. I took another bite, then another, until I'd eaten the entire thing. With some difficulty, I bent and broke off a large piece of fish from Antonov's salted slab, then pressed it in my cheek to soften.

It was a substantial fraction of the food I'd meant to ration over the next weeks, but so what? Who knew what might happen today? If my luck ran out, I wouldn't be able to profit from it anyway. Going off to a penal cell, or dying, would be better with something in my belly.

I began to chew. The hard fish cut my gums, hurt my tongue with its salt.

When Petrovich arrived I still had cod stuck in my teeth, but felt little better for having eaten. The fish and potato were a gurgling mass in my gut. Vinogradov welcomed the old man as we stepped into his office. "A pleasure, Inspector." A ghost of irony played across his face before he went on. "That is the correct title, isn't it? I believe Bogomolov explained that you worked in Odessa's police department before your retirement."

"That's right."

The two of them evaluated each other, while I stood to the side and felt sick. Petrovich looked haggard, his mustache a gnarled fist of hair compared to Vinogradov's neat one. Vinogradov stood calmly, smooth white hands at his side. After a moment he indicated the chairs in front of his desk, and we all sat.

Getting immediately to business, Vinogradov pushed over a paper. "I've made out a pass for the two of you. It will allow you to enter and exit through Nikolski. You should understand my authority does not extend to excusing you from your usual duties. That is for you to work out yourselves, although I suppose the infirmary will not be too troubled by your absence, Bogomolov. Moreover, I do not care to be seen to pit myself against Infosec in this. If I am asked, I will say I understood the two of you to be working on a matter for KrimKab, and that my assistance in the matter of the pass would be a favor to that department. Under no circumstances will I take responsibility for authorizing an investigation to be continued against orders from Information and Investigation. Is all of that clear?"

Petrovich caught my eye. "Nikolski is a problem. It would be better if you just wrote that we were allowed outside the kremlin."

"What do you mean?"

"The guards there aren't friendly. More to the point, when our contact in Infosec canceled our investigation, he met us to say so at the gate. They'll tell him if we start traipsing through again on your say-so. That's if they don't decide to give us a beating and lock us up themselves."

"I see. A problem. But I fear I cannot provide access to any other point of egress. Notwithstanding their passing under the museum, the Holy Gates are not mine to control."

Petrovich shook his head. "Not those. The Herring Gate. Tolya has an arrangement worked out with the monks. They'll let us through there, on the condition we are allowed free movement."

Vinogradov looked to me with some surprise. I nodded, without adding anything. My head had started to swim. Petrovich had covered it well enough.

"All right," he said slowly. Drawing the document back across the desk, he folded it once, then tore it neatly into four pieces. While he spoke, he deliberately wrote a few lines on a new sheet of paper, then stamped it at the bottom. " 'Prisoners Petrovich and Bogomolov are permitted free movement within and without the kremlin.' I trust that will do? But I reiterate: officially speaking, you are investigating without my sanction. I have not taken you on as agents, and you must make your own accommodations with your work assignments. We proceed on these terms?"

We agreed. Whatever was being done in the infirmary, they wouldn't be looking for me at Company Thirteen until the next day. As for Petrovich's situation at KrimKab, that was his own lookout. He'd been able to come this morning, so it stood to reason he'd reached some kind of arrangement.

"Now," said Vinogradov, addressing himself to Petrovich, "at this juncture in our investigative partnership it is usual to share certain information, isn't it? I am naturally most interested in Bogomolov's suggestion that there is something amiss about the requisition orders. But it is hard to see who might have hoped to profit from what's happened."

He went again over what I'd told him the night before, with Petrovich adding comments here and there. I allowed the old man to take the lead. My head continued to swim, and anyway, I'd done my part last night. Let Petrovich bear the burden of the investigation for a while.

"There's one more piece," Petrovich said as Vinogradov came to the end of his summary. "Zhenov's foreman, Ivan Kologriev. Contact of mine, an *urka*, says Kologriev is one, too. Or was. Specialized in armed robbery, apparently. But shortly after he arrived on Solovetsky, the spirit of socialist reform filled him and he accepted a position offered by Administration. My contact wasn't happy about it."

Vinogradov touched his mustache, pinching its edges with his thumb and forefinger, like a man straightening a tiny painting hanging on his lip. "Ah," he said.

I'd been slouching, exhausted, but the tone made me sit up. "What?"

Vinogradov said: "I know that Kologriev."

"Is that right?" said Petrovich. "You knew he was a stickup artist?"

"No. Not that."

"Well then?" I said. "Are you going to tell us, or what?"

Vinogradov gave me a look. The window behind his desk faced west. With the sun still rising, most of the light in the room came from the lamp he'd brought in. The flame reflected steadily from the bright things on his shelves and desk. In his glasses, it quivered.

"I have been a curator for some time," he said. "Before being sentenced here, I worked at the Museum of Kostroma Oblast. A fine regional collection, one I was sorry to leave. The so-called misappropriation for which I was convicted—a matter of a particularly fine set of Persian miniatures, which after all bore little relation to any other part of the collection—I regard it in the light of an unfortunate necessity."

He let out a slow breath before he continued. "The pieces in the collection here, or at Kostroma—weapons, paintings, Stone Age figurines, whatever they may be—they are travelers in time. They pass through the hands of their ostensible owners the way an arrow flies through the air. To treat ownership as something permanent or important is absurd. Objects in a collection belong, at most, to each other. Sometimes the good of the collection as a whole demands that a particular piece be sacrificed. And then—sometimes a piece will exert a special pull on an individual. This is what I call necessity. It can overwhelm even other objects' collective claim. But, you understand, it arises from the intrinsic qualities of the piece. It has nothing to do with any person's so-called rights or prerogatives. I do not apologize for responding in the way I had to. It was all I could have done."

Color had come into his cheeks as he talked, and he took a moment to regain his poise before he said: "Last night you mentioned two silver *rizi*, Bogomolov. Before we proceed I would wish to be certain that you and I take a similar view of these matters."

I looked to Petrovich. "All we care about is who killed Antonov," he said. "What you do with the collection is your business."

"Very well." He paused. "It was almost exactly a year ago that the first requisition came in, asking for icons to be used as lumber.

I believe that this is the only time of year at which such an order would be possible, when so much lumber is going to the mainland. I should explain: Deputy Director Eikhmans held the position I do now before he began his rise through SLON's highest Chekist ranks. He continues to value the museum. My relationships with him and others who are well placed in Administration are usually sufficient to protect the collection from depredation. However, my case is weakened in October, before the final ship of the season.

"At the time, I was more sanguine than I have become about preventing the order's being fulfilled. Naturally I was anxious to stop it however I could. It struck me as a bad precedent—as, indeed, it has proved to be. You've talked to Zhenov, who is now in charge of supply for Anzer. But the name at the top of the first form I received was Prokupin.

"I made inquiries. What I learned was that Prokupin was a doctrinaire Bolshevik, of the type who would be gratified at the icons' destruction. However, he was a drunkard, and incompetent. My sources told me that it was Ivan Kologriev, the foreman, who truly ran his warehouse. For some time I wondered what the best approach would be. In fact I discussed it with Antonov, although he had only been here a few months at that point, and had little to contribute.

"In the end, I tried to bribe Kologriev, reasoning that he would be in a position either to convince Prokupin that the icons were unsuitable for their purposes, or to deceive him about whether they'd been received. I'd selected from the collection a small candelabra, made by an unknown craftsman of the Veliky Ustyug school. An unremarkable piece, indeed mediocre, but with a certain amount of gold. For such a person, I reasoned, it would only be the metal that was attractive, not the craftsmanship.

"He refused me outright, however, without an explanation. Instead of staying to hear me explain how the thing could be turned to rubles on the outside, he interrupted, asking to be shown where the 'timber' was. He remained in the office for less than five minutes." Vinogradov had absently picked up a pen that lay before him on the desk. While he'd been speaking, he'd begun drawing a spiraling shape on a sheet of paper before him. As I watched the nib start, stop, and double back, I recognized it as the outline of a labyrinth like the one I'd seen on Kostrihe. "Naturally I was surprised. In my experience there is always something dubious afoot when someone on Solovetsky won't take a bribe. I didn't know then that he was an *urka*."

"You were suspicious already," I said.

"Yes." In front of him on the desk was a slim folder, which he opened and handed across. "As you can see, when the order came in this time, I required Zhenov to provide me an invoice. It was signed by him here at the kremlin, and then by his agent on Anzer when the pieces were delivered. Unfortunately it did not help me to discover anything out of the ordinary."

"But the supplies went missing. That was out of the ordinary," Petrovich said. "About them. There are some questions I wish Tolya had asked you the other day, when he went to you on the cape."

I looked at him. It was a surprise: he hadn't mentioned anything of the sort to me before. But I suppose there'd been no reason to. Short of going back to visit Vinogradov again on the cape, there would have been no way of getting answers until this morning anyway.

"You don't consider this information about the *urka* Kologriev valuable?" said Vinogradov.

"Maybe it is. There something more you think we should be saying about it?"

Vinogradov paused. "No."

"All right, then. The supplies. Ivanov showed us the records for them the other day. The gold leaf, some alcohol, some mineral spirits. Was there anything else?"

"I believe that was all. Those are the materials whose use I required Antonov to track. Pigment and varnish I simply resupplied at his request."

"How'd you hear they'd gone missing?"

"Antonov reported it himself. He said he thought he'd left them in their normal place in his desk, only to find them missing the day after the men from Anzer Division came for the icons."

"But you'd have had to find out eventually, eh? He'd have had to come to you to get more, and you'd have asked where what you'd already given him went."

"That's right."

"What are you getting at?" I said.

"There's nothing I'm getting at. I'm only making sure I understand the situation." He jutted his chin at Vinogradov. "What made you send Antonov to Zhenov's? Someone else who works here would be more likely to know there was gold in Antonov's desk than some warehouse worker who lives outside the kremlin. Why not check them first?"

"It is possible," said Vinogradov slowly. "Not likely, but possible. I doubt any of my staff would risk their position for something as trivial as a book of leaf. But I will admit I did not consider it. Their desks have not been searched. At the time, I had my expedition to prepare for, and since learning of what happened I have not been back here. Antonov himself was the one to suggest he should go and inquire with Zhenov and his men."

I could tell Petrovich was pleased from the way the words rattled in his throat. "Antonov came up with the idea of leaving the kremlin that night?"

"Yes. Now that I recall it, he seemed particularly focused on receiving a gate pass. In fact, I wondered whether he wasn't intending to take the opportunity to visit the woman, Fitneva, whom I gather you know about. I didn't imagine I would be sending him into danger."

"This is interesting," said Petrovich. "Are we even certain the leaf is gone? Maybe Antonov had some other reason to want to be outside—Fitneva, or something else—and reported a theft as an excuse."

"We didn't find the things in his desk," I said. "And there was nothing like it with his body when they pulled him out of the water."

Petrovich grunted. "True. All right. The woman, then. Tolya was right about your helping arrange her transfer, I take it. But when I had him ask you before whether Antonov had anything to do with women, you said you didn't know."

"Yes. I was hoping to avoid publicizing the . . . matter Bogomolov brought to my attention last night."

"What can you tell us about the arrangement with her?"

"The position I secured for her in the fishery was a desirable assignment. I was able to prevail on one of my contacts in Administration, who handles the monks' special dispensations, to grant it to her. I understood that there was another position contemplated for her, one that would have brought her into close contact with another man. I made no special arrangements to protect her from the other fellow, only had her moved to a different workplace. That was all Antonov requested. Other than that, I can tell you very little."

"Ever meet her?"

"No, never. He would sometimes ask for a pass through Nikolski, and I assumed it meant they had arranged a liaison. It was not the sort of thing he and I discussed." He turned to me. "Perhaps, now that I have written you your pass, you will be willing to tell me how you learned about my involvement in their arrangement?"

I cut Petrovich a look to let him know he should keep his mouth shut. "That's not part of the deal," I said.

Vinogradov frowned, but nodded. "I should not be surprised that Antonov left a record somewhere. He certainly knew the collection well enough to notice anything missing, if he'd cared to look. And I begin to suspect that I understood his motivations less well than I'd thought."

"That's between you and your memory of Antonov," said Petrovich. "For us, only one more thing. That list of icons you two disagreed about. The ones you had him make that you were going to fulfill the requisition with."

"Yes," said Vinogradov. "You found it in his desk."

"Tolya says you were correcting him—that he'd added valuable pieces to the list, things you weren't willing to let go." Vinogradov nodded. "So you crossed those out and added things you didn't care for as much instead. What did he say about it?"

"Nothing I remember."

"He didn't argue? Try to explain what he'd been thinking?"

"No. I had been surprised at a number of his choices. I recall bringing the list with my alterations out to him at his desk. I believe I explained my aggravation at having had to tutor him on his own subject. I'd have preferred to be able to rely on his expertise."

"You're saying he was cowed?" said Petrovich. "He said nothing back?"

"No," said Vinogradov. "Nothing."

29

To reach the Herring Gate, at the north end of the western wall, you turned left from the museum's doors. The cathedral was a white presence on the other side of the courtyard, its burnt towers only half there through the snow that had begun to fall.

"You were quiet in there," said Petrovich.

"My hand hurts," I said. "I didn't get any bread this morning."

Our boots squeaked on the path. "I didn't think going back to letting me do all the talking was what you had in mind when you explained your plan," said Petrovich.

"You didn't seem to like what I said to Zhenov."

"You were a little harsh. But you've handled Vinogradov with the right touch. Seems he almost trusts us. We'll see how much good it does, but it's better than I'd hoped."

I recognized the tone, avuncular and teacherly, from before. But knowing he had been the slug who betrayed me gave his words a rotten, saccharine sound. "It's already done us good. I got the pass."

"You've done a lot. But we're still a long way from solving this case. I can't do the rest on my own."

"I came to you yesterday, remember? You were the one who wanted to continue sitting in the KrimKab office until they'd finished me off and arrived to put a knife in you."

The old man sighed. "Tolya, I *am* trying to help. You came to me for my experience. I've seen young men in your state before. Maybe not with the self-amputation, granted. But police work means late nights, stresses. Time away from the family. Danger. A green officer isn't always ready for it. I see it in you. Feel you're at your limits, don't you? Your friend, your finger, your exhaustion. But you're young, strong. You'll keep working, same as my young men on the force kept working. You've got reserves you don't know about." His voice hardened. "So find a little blood in yourself and buck up. Otherwise it will only be me working this case for us. Frankly, I doubt that will go well. I need you. Neither of us can stop now."

A little blood in myself. I considered informing him I'd found some yesterday, using a hatchet. But he was right. It cost me another sick moment to let myself admit it.

"The supplies," I said through a dry throat. "You asked Vinogradov about them. What were you trying to find out?"

"Good," he said. "You're with me."

"Tell me about the supplies."

He made a noise in his throat. "I don't know what I was trying to find out. Not exactly. Only it occurred to me last night. Alcohol, gold leaf: those make sense. But why take three ounces of turpentine? Who here has a use for it, outside of that museum?"

"I don't know."

"Neither do I. Something to ponder on."

We'd arrived. The gate was down a short alley from the courtyard. Before we approached, Petrovich asked to examine the document Vinogradov had given us. It looked different than the one from the Chekist. That had been a printed form, multiply stamped, signed and initialed in six separate places. Vinogradov, as we'd seen, had only torn a page from a notebook and written a short note on it. At the bottom, beneath his signature, was the stamp we'd watched him use. It read "Solovetsky Museum of Anti-Religious and Historical Exhibits" in indigo ink—nothing more.

"What are we going to do if they don't let us through?" said Petrovich.

"What do you mean? You said Veronika sent word."

"She did."

"What's the problem, then?"

"Maybe nothing. We'll see."

A shaft through the wall, with a set of studded wooden doors at the end: that was the Fish Gate. Its arch was so low that standing was impossible. Only with difficulty did Petrovich move through in the necessary crouch.

A monk waited in the dark space beneath the wall, seated on a stool and wrapped in a heavy blanket. The man was ancient, even older than Petrovich. He had a finely drawn, even noble-looking face. But the teeth in his thin beard had rotted away, leaving brown stumps behind. Instead of a greeting, he made the sign of the cross over us both, but his expression was fearful. When I made to hand him our authorization from Vinogradov, at first he waved it away.

"No, no," he said. "Nikolski for the laity. Not here."

"Brother Kiril was to have arranged for us to be let through," I said. "Kiril, who works at the fishery."

"It's a sin to lie. My door is pledged to brothers."

"I'm not lying, and there's no need for you to lie to anyone either. We're allowed in and out of the kremlin as we like. See? These are our authorization papers." The tunnel was not bricked. The raw stones of the wall hung around our shoulders, huge and cold. "Kiril spoke to you, didn't he?"

The old monk looked sullenly at Vinogradov's note for another minute, but at last he took it. His thin lips moved as he mumbled over the thing until, rising and shaking his head, he pulled a large key from the pocket of his robe.

With the gate thrown open, you could see through to the bay, with the horizon and the sky gray and indistinct behind it. I stepped through and straightened up, Petrovich following. The door boomed shut.

We were out. The snow here moved differently than it had in the kremlin.

"The girl was as good as her word," said Petrovich, clearing his throat. "I have to say, I'm a little surprised."

"What?"

"We need to talk to her again."

"She's saved us. Both of us. It was only what she gave me

about the missing *rizi* that made Vinogradov do what we wanted."

"You have another lead in mind for us to follow, then?"

In truth, the course I'd charted for this new stage of the investigation proceeded only to the edge of the kremlin's walls. Between my exhaustion and hunger, I'd barely given a thought to what we should be doing next. "Kologriev," I said, for lack of any other idea. "We can confront him with what we've learned. What Golubov told us, and the bribe from Vinogradov." It sounded lame, even to me.

"Hard to put any pressure on him that way. He's only going to say he refused. He has nothing to hide."

"I just talked to Veronika. That would be a waste of time as well."

He watched me with all his blue-eyed sharpness. "Listen, Tolya. I noticed you left her out of the story you told Vinogradov. I understand: you're grateful to her. But what she told you—it hardly advances the case, does it? She gave you exactly nothing that would help us discover who killed Antonov."

"Say what you mean, Yakov Petrovich."

"Her note promised something we could use. She'd have known revealing Vinogradov's bribe wouldn't have kept me from going to Spagovsky." Out in the bay, the wind slid tiny ripples over the water's smooth surface, their movement deadened by particles of ice. "There's something she's still not telling."

"She didn't have to help me."

"To you it looks that way. To me, frankly, it looks like she told you just enough to make you go away, the way she's been doing all along. I've told you from the start, she's a canny woman. She knows how to play a man."

I shook my head, but it brought me up short. From the start Veronika and I had struggled over how much she'd say—how much I would be willing to make her say. And she'd had the better of it—of me—throughout, ever since she'd first caught me staring at her. Had our wrestling gone on, even yesterday, as I threw myself on her mercy? I'd let myself believe it hadn't, that it had ended when she told me about her brother.

Another mistake of the literary model, perhaps. Sherlock Holmes made it easy to believe in understanding. Hadn't we figured each other out? I'd taken it for a process of deduction, each of us following a trail of clues that proved the other could be trusted. That is not far from the schema of the mystery story, always finally a tale of insight. Holmes, after all, never fails to know the mind of his criminal by the end of the case.

Or do I portray myself as more high-minded than I truly was? Pinkertons provided more than just cerebral thrills. After he'd finished off the foreign hordes or scar-faced hoods who menaced them, dames regularly swooned into the arms of the King of Detectives. You experienced it all along with Nat. You turned your face manfully away from the frippery of romance with him—nevertheless, you were aroused. Over those pages, a boy could dream his dreams of the love of beautiful women, embarrassing and incomplete, with nothing to challenge the fantasy.

Perhaps I only trusted Veronika because it flattered my childish vanity to believe she'd warmed to me.

Those are not the dreams of a *zek*. A *zek* must learn to dream of bread. What was it Petrovich had said? Investigations were a matter of finding out secrets, and then using them. Nothing else. Veronika hoarded her secrets like the rest. She had used one secret to deflect me from another.

I pictured her bruised face as it had looked while she wrapped the tourniquet around my arm. She and Mitya would practice tourniquets on each other when they were children, she'd said.

"All right," I said to Petrovich.

My voice sounded strained. Snow continued to fall around us, each flake a coordinate in a billowing grid. It came to me that they defined a manifold. The term was a modern one, but it encompassed such non-Euclidean spaces as Lobachevsky had explored in his imaginary geometry. Movement within a distorted manifold of three dimensions would not be the same as within our usual Euclidean space. A straight path walked over the ground, I reflected, would veer and bend wildly in the ideal realm laid over the island by the falling snow.

At the fishery Brother Kiril was making marks in a ledger when we came into the main building. Recognizing us, he smoothed his beard down over his filthy robe. When I thanked him for arranging things at the gate, he only shook his head. With some reluctance, he led us down a set of stairs and beneath the porch that jutted out from the front of the fishery to the pier.

There Veronika was at work, stirring a giant pot over a low fire. The overhanging porch provided some shelter and caught the smoke. For a dozen feet out from shore, the water was a frozen white sheet.

She had tied her hair up in a brown scarf. In my memory, a dark curl hangs prettily out from beneath it beside her face, but whether that image is taken from reality or my desires is hard to say. To be on the safe side, you should picture no curl, only the tight kerchief, severe and dull. I am certain that was there.

After a vaguely disapproving clearance of his throat, Kiril left us. Veronika glared at Petrovich, then turned to me. "Here you are. Both of you. Frankly, bringing the old man makes me suspect I'm going to be sorry I didn't let you bleed all over the floor," she said. "Are you going to make me sorry? Maybe now that you no longer need my help, you've returned to pretending I killed Gennady Mikhailovich."

"Yakov Petrovich thinks you still know something you haven't told me," I said.

Petrovich chuckled, a sound like pebbles rattling. "Yes. Who killed Antonov isn't something we pretend to know. Not yet." He raised his cane, looked at its head as though it were a curiosity that had just caught his attention. It was a performance, a piece of acting done for effect. He could be good at that, when he wanted to be. "But the reason we're here is that I was a detective for a long time. After you've done the job for thirty or forty years, you start to notice that when something connects all your subjects, except for just one of them that's left out—well, it pays to search for that final link in the chain. In this case it's the icon requisition I spoke to you about the other day. Seems to be connected to everyone around Antonov. Everyone but you, that is."

Veronika gave him an icy look. To me she said: "Things must have gone well for you after we spoke, for you to arrive here once again. I see someone bandaged you up properly."

"Nothing does any good if we don't solve the case," I said. "Those men are still after me."

She gave the concoction in her pot a vigorous stir. It smelled of tar. Fragments of bark floated in the dark brown liquid. "If I wasn't at least neutral towards your solving this idiotic 'case,' I wouldn't have prevailed on Kiril to let you use their gate. I don't see why you ought to be so suspicious of me."

"Just answer his questions," I said.

"Oho! Is that how things are to be now?" she said. "By doing you a favor, have I licensed you to be hard with me?"

"The icons," said Petrovich. "You still insist you don't know anything about their requisition? When we got your note, I thought you might want to share something about them. Maybe something dubious you learned through Antonov."

"No," she said. "Nothing like that." Both of them looked to me. She was right, I was hard. My face felt like stone. "It was what I told Bogomolov yesterday. About Vinogradov, the accession numbers."

"Of course. Probably you saved Tolya's life. He's grateful, and so am I. I'd have been sorry to see him killed. My question is, why didn't you tell us before?"

Between her eyes, the crease deepened. "What do you mean?"

"What was it about the accession number that made it so important to you to withhold it? Why not come out with it to start with? We could have been friends instead of enemies."

"It would have meant giving up a bit of knowledge that might have been useful to me. And I thought you were slugs. What was the benefit going to be to me, or to Gennady Mikhailovich posthumously, if I shared all my secrets with Infosec?" She pursed her lips. "Even if there had been a benefit: to hell with the Cheka, and with SLON."

"Perfectly reasonable. But in that case, what changed? Why tell it to Tolya yesterday?"

"You'd already extorted it out of me, hadn't you? I was ready to talk when I sent the note." She glanced at me again, wary. "And it looked like Bogomolov was on his last legs. My heart isn't a stone."

He chuckled again. "You are ready with the most plausible-sounding stories. But the fact is, I don't believe you. Tell her what we know about the coffins, Tolya."

My voice sounded like someone else's. Veronika listened. Petrovich had told her about the requisition order five days ago, but the icons having been knocked together into coffins surprised her. When I explained how Zhenov was connected to both the coffins and the executed men they filled, her face stiffened.

"What do you think this has to do with Gennady Mikhailovich?" she asked at the end.

"The men they shot. They said they were planning an escape." I looked over at Petrovich. My tone was even. "And Infosec had Yakov Petrovich helping them investigate Antonov for involvement with an escape. He didn't know that's what they were doing at the time, but they thought he had something to do with it. You see what it means? The icons and the executed men. They both go through Antonov. And he was out of the kremlin looking for missing repair supplies for icons when he was killed."

Even if I'd aimed to say less, I think I would have had to go on the way I did, just to watch the knowledge progress across her face. She had noticed the change in the way I was talking as well: she listened guardedly, attentively, and then with dawning horror. Her pink nostrils flared. It was like watching a heavy curtain blown by the approach of a storm.

Yes, I watched her closely. But, then, how can I still be uncertain about that lock of hair?

I said: "The escape and the icons are connected. The missing supplies. Something about all of that got him killed."

She shut her eyes for a long time. I was about to say something else—whether it was going to be consoling or bitter, I don't recall—when she swore. "Fuck."

Petrovich gave one of his laughs. "You do know something about it, then."

When she opened her eyes they were dry. "Damn it. An 'escape attempt.' That is the right term. I don't know what it should have had to do with the Whites you mention. Anything I try to do here comes out wrong."

"What have you tried to do?" said Petrovich. His voice was harsh.

"Nothing. Only—only I thought I was covering for Gennady Mikhailovich, when I seem to have been covering for someone else the whole time."

"He was trying to escape?"

"Not a real escape. And I—I wasn't involved. I want you to know that much." She rubbed her face with thin hands. "He never was thinking of himself. I'm not sure he would even have wanted to leave the island if he could. He liked being here. He had his work to do, and he was taken care of. Which is necessary, of course, for anyone to find it tolerable here. But he was, and the place itself meant something to him. How boring he was, describing all the ways our prisoner-lives were like the lives of the pilgrims who used to come here. Boring and charming. And the heretics! Did you know all the monks were heretics here in the seventeenth century? That was when the tsar insisted everyone make the sign of the cross with three fingers instead of two. The monks wanted to stick with two. Antonov thought maybe they had been right. That the Church was wrong and the illiterate, drunken hermits who lived on this island were right. About the number of fingers to use."

She wove her own fingers together in front of her. More than anything, she looked angry. "The idea of dissenting on God's behalf appealed to him. No, it wasn't for himself he was planning an escape for. He wanted freedom for them."

"You mean the paintings," I said slowly. "He wanted to get the paintings off the island."

She stomped her foot in anger, kicked the nearest barrel, then barked a laugh like Petrovich's again, the same way she had when I asked for help the day before. "That sounds ridiculous, doesn't it? You'd think there would be more important things. Even the monks think it's better worth their while to fish than to worry about parading the image of Christ before the people."

I'd have thought Petrovich would be triumphant, finally having squeezed it from her. He'd been right all along, about her keeping something back from us. But he only said: "Start from the beginning."

"It wasn't easy for us to meet," Veronika began haltingly. Her self-disgust—at having made the mistake she thought she'd made, at having capitulated in the end to Petrovich and to me—was still in her voice, but she made an effort to hide it. "I was only once able to get a pass into the kremlin. That was the note you found. From the mighty Vinogradov, he could get passes out fairly easily, but we had nowhere to meet, and that cow Stepnova was always keeping track of me, making sure I didn't go anywhere that wasn't work or the dormitory unless she sent me there with Boris. It became easier after he arranged the transfer to the monks, since my hours were less regular and she had fewer means of checking them. I'd send messages with Brother Kiril, the way I sent the note to you. I did my best to give him the idea Gennady Mikhailovich was my spiritual mentor. Maybe in a way he was. I can never tell how worldly Kiril is."

She shook her head and crossed her arms. "Ugh. It's exciting at first, going through all that for a rendezvous with your lover, but it fades quickly." She looked at me. "One of my lovers. I was meeting with Boris, too. You understand that, don't you? Getting out of the arrangement as Boris's housekeeper kept me from becoming his—his slave-concubine. But it wouldn't have kept him from sending me back to the hospital if I'd refused to see him again. It didn't keep Stepnova from sending me to him every other evening. And maybe I wouldn't have wanted to stop seeing him altogether either. I don't know how to put it. I decided when I was a little girl not to apologize for my desires being bizarre or inconsistent. I—" She flushed, and stopped. "Well, it doesn't matter."

She straightened her shoulders, like someone starting over. "The only reason I am mentioning it is that it affected things with Antonov. Not the way you think. He wasn't jealous. He never wanted to talk about—about us. But my time with Boris—my liking the time with Boris—made me want to see Gennady Mikhailovich even more. I wanted what I thought of as his goodness. His calm, his gentleness. His strangeness. Goodness would have to be strange, wouldn't it?

"It felt as if I was always pleading with him to see me. We couldn't meet as much as I wanted, because of the difficulty of getting a room. In the end he hired one for a few hours at a time from one of the voluntary guards. The ones who stay in the non-prisoner hotel, on the other side of the administration building."

Petrovich had been listening intently, but at this he spoke up. "Where did the money come from?"

"He never said. I know he gave the man paper notes. I'd never seen him with money before, but he pulled a wad of rubles from his coat that first time as if he did it every day. And then there were six or seven times, in the same room, after that."

"All right. Go on."

"The point is—the point is that I always felt there was some piece of him, some piece of his goodness, that was inaccessible to me, shut off in the kremlin. I mean the icons. He talked about them all the time, but I'd never seen his work. I complained about it, that first day in the guard's room. He was explaining something about the provenance of the piece he was working on—whether it was sixteenth or seventeenth century, I don't remember what—and I said it was provoking to hear about these images I'd never see, and what was the point if no one ever got to look at them. I think I was flirting, partly, but he took it seriously, so he must have seen I meant it, really. He said the problem was less that no one saw them than that they were never venerated. That was a point he was pedantic about—they were for worship, not staring at. But he said he had had an idea. Solovetsky had been an ideal home for icons when it was a monastery, but as a prison it was no place for them."

She shrugged, her breath fogging in the air. "When I asked what he meant, he wouldn't say, but he was never any good at keeping secrets. He mentioned it again a time or two afterward. Just in passing, but he would make a face every time, as if he had said something very sly." She shook her head. "Stupid man."

"That made you think he was planning to smuggle the icons off the island?" said Petrovich.

"Yes. He didn't confirm it in so many words, but it was clear. I thought it was probably just as well not to know the details."

"So," he said. "What Tolya told you about the requisition order—Anzer, the cabinetry workshop, the coffins, the missing supplies—Antonov hadn't talked to you about any of it? The first you heard that these things might have been involved with his plan was now, from us?"

"That's right."

"What about who he was working with?" I said. "The men I mentioned—Zhenov, Kologriev. Or anyone else. He couldn't have been doing it alone."

"No," said Veronika quietly. I realized I'd been raising my voice. "But I never heard him talk about anyone."

"If the requisition order is involved . . ." I looked to Petrovich.

"It makes sense of a few things," he said. "The disagreement with Vinogradov about the list, his concern Vinogradov would turn against him. Maybe even the missing supplies. Could have taken them himself, if he meant to touch up the pieces before he sent them off." He stroked his mustache. "Trouble is, how far did the plan get? And what disrupted it?"

"What do you mean?" said Veronika.

"If the Anzer icons were the ones Antonov meant to smuggle off the island," he explained, "something went wrong. They're six feet under ground now, turned into boxes with bodies in them. That can't have been the outcome he imagined."

"Maybe nothing went wrong," I said. "Zhenov could still have made a mistake with his bookkeeping. Maybe they weren't all buried. Maybe the plan all along was to get a few away at the cost of the others rotting. Or —" A sour bubble of laughter burst from my throat. My hand was throbbing. "Or maybe the coffins were Gennady Mikhailovich's idea all along—maybe when he said he wanted a larger audience for the pieces, he meant corpses. They'd be a captive audience, at least."

Veronika's jaw shifted. "Do you think you're being funny? He wouldn't have wanted any of them destroyed. I'm sure that wasn't what he meant."

"Regardless," said Petrovich, "we need to understand what happened with those coffins. That's the key."

Veronika stared down, then turned out to face the sea. Ice bobbed in the low swell. The snow gusted about the end of the pier, crazily. "You really think this was how he was murdered?" she said. "It wasn't the Cheka who killed him?"

"Wouldn't have put us on the case in the first place if the killing had been official," Petrovich said.

"No," she said. "No, of course not. I've been hoping the two of you were wrong—that it might be a trick, a way to stop whatever plan he put in motion about the icons. For his sake, I wanted it to succeed. My first thought, when you came and told me he was dead, was that I hoped he'd pulled it off before he died. I knew he had to have had a partner, who might carry it on if I didn't tell you. But now, if one of these White officers was his partner, he's dead, too. And if it was someone else—maybe I've been protecting his murderer." She turned to me, put out a hand to touch my arm. "I'm sorry. You were in danger. I should have told you yesterday. I only—"

I took a step backward. The hand that I left hanging in the air was her right: ungloved, slightly blue in the cold. Intact. "You don't owe me anything," I said.

Petrovich followed me out from under the porch and away from the water's edge. I let him catch up to me at the road. While we looked out over the bay's ice-thickened water, he drew a hunk of bread from his coat and broke off a piece. Smoke rose from under the pier to disappear, gray into a gray sky.

I looked peaked, he said as he handed the bread to me. I would need to be sharp to help work this out in time.

30

We are coming to the end. You feel it, don't you? The increased speed of revelations, the sense of pieces falling into place, even if you don't know what shape they will make. The conclusion of a *detektiv* is always exciting.

And things are falling into place for me as well. I know, now, who you will be, the reader I have addressed throughout these pages without being able to identify. I have wondered whether anyone would ever read this. I have thought that I was writing for the dead.

Now I know that my reader is you: the idiot, my neighbor, Vasily-the-tank-commander. Vasily Feodorovich.

You know about the loose bricks in the wall behind my bed, where I hide this manuscript every night after I have done working. You have been informed, too, about what these pages contain.

For good or ill, you finally know what I have been writing.

The hollow space behind the bricks is the best hiding place I have been able to devise. It would surely be uncovered in a thorough search, but I allow myself to hope it will do if the searchers are not highly motivated. For some time the idea of secreting my pages next door, in the boiler room, where anyone who came for me might not think to look, attracted me. On reflection, however, such an arrangement would be more dangerous than the one I have in place. Opening my door twice a night, as I would have to do to retrieve and store the pages, would introduce entirely new insecurities. And then, the boiler room is less fully in my control than this one. It is December, and in winter the superintendent moves a chair next to the boiler, there to drink and nap.

So what I write remains close to me. But at least my dresser is no longer filled with evidence. The empty spiral notepads, the ones I ritually saved—now gone. Each found its way into a different garbage bin at the plant, smuggled in one by one beneath my coat. I did not find it easy to throw them away. But the manuscript is safer this way.

All of these arrangements I brought to completion within a few days of your expulsion from the Party. That was three weeks ago. But I have found, in the time since, that I have only traded one danger, of my writing being discovered, for another. It preys on my mind just as the first did, and is what has induced me to share my plans.

It is the danger of the writing being lost, of disappearing.

I found myself imagining, as I lay awake in bed with only a few bricks separating me from the pages, what would happen if they came for me and didn't make a thorough search. They would not need the manuscript to send me back to the camps. They do not need anything at all. And therefore my writing might never be discovered. I would be sent off, with no one left behind to know what I'd hidden. These pages would remain immured, trapped in the wall. Unread.

This is clearly, in some sense, a perverse fear. To have hidden a thing, then worry it is hidden too well, certainly indicates some degree of internal conflict. It means worrying that you might have succeeded at what you set out to do. I have been ambivalent. It is not that my fear of discovery has abated. Rather, a new fear, the fear of oblivion for my book, surfaced at the very moment that I stuck it behind the wall. Now the two fears entwine in my throat.

As for you, Vasily Feodorovich, it may be taken as another illustration of perversity that I have entrusted the location of the manuscript to precisely the man whose change of political fortune made it necessary for me to hide it in the first place. Perhaps it is perverse. I've worried in these pages not only about the danger of being swept up along with you—in which case your knowing the location of the manuscript would be no use—but also about the possibility of your betraying me.

I do not believe I will be betrayed. Perhaps I trust you.

Moreover, a police campaign against us looks less threatening now than it did. During the two weeks you waited to visit me in the basement after your expulsion I was all anxiety, but by the time you did, things had started to settle down.

"My wife is furious, of course," you said. "I think she would divorce me, but the Party frowns on divorce these days." Luckily there has been no interest from the MVD in the case. You report that your appeals of your expulsion to the city and district committees have been allowed to go forward, without much hope of success, but without interference from the secret police. And you were not fired, though of course your prospects for promotion are ruined. All of this gives me reason to hope that the Party's punishment will stop where it is. Expulsion still spells disaster, but not, the way it once did, utter ruin for all those in the vicinity of the expelled. Perhaps things are changing. Perhaps.

At any rate, who else is there? I have no one better. And the book's location had to be told.

These were the considerations that led me to climb the stairs this evening and invite you down to the basement. I was able to supply a little brandy, some radish.

Over this little bite, I told you. It was a *detektiv* I had been writing, I said—but not simply a *detektiv*. A memoir as well. I wanted you to know where it was, in case anything should happen.

You were respectful, serious. You would be interested to read it, you said. It would not be the first such document you've looked at. There is more to your interest in the camps than I thought, perhaps.

You will read it. But I am not ready. Not yet.

Soon I will have discovered the killer. Then my story can go out into the world.

The cemetery was the same as ever, a spillage of graves. The afternoon had grown still; the scene before us might have been poured out in slow layers from a series of jars and bottles. In the middle distance, the monks' chapel, Onufrievskii, hunched on a little rise. Beyond that, the cathedrals' steeples jutted over the kremlin wall, with Transfiguration's towers marked by giant soot stains. And nearer to us, close to where the burial plots began, there was an unpainted wooden structure that might have been a grounds building or a utility shed.

Those were the fixed points. Among them, headboards swirled and eddied.

I gestured at the shed. "Maybe someone there can tell us where the grave is," I said.

Petrovich shrugged. He'd been skeptical of my suggestion that examining the burial site might bring us closer to understanding what had happened to the icons. "Can it be that you still haven't been disabused of the notion that looking for clues means staring at the ground through a magnifying glass? The question is, why were they buried, when Antonov meant for them to be shipped off the island? You're not going to find that out by poking around some pit." But he'd relented; the cemetery was on our way, and Zhenov would wait.

We'd already looked for Kologriev, back at the warehouse. That, Petrovich had insisted, was the correct next step: confronting Antonov's possible partners with what we'd learned, seeing how they responded. Of the two, Kologriev seemed more likely than Zhenov—if the latter's drunken confusion had been a performance, it had been a very complete one. There would be danger with Kologriev, the old man said. No one who'd defied Golubov and the code of the *urki* would be frightened of us. The man would be capable of anything, if he thought we were a threat. But the risk was necessary. For all we'd learned, we still had no proof that would sway the Chekist.

Kologriev had been anticlimactically absent, however. No one we'd asked had been able to say just where he might be found, and it would have been imprudent to wait in the warehouse until he came back. An encounter out in front was one thing. One in a darkened corner of his own den was quite another.

In the cemetery, the shed was shuttered. Snow fell around the edges of the building in fine, straight lines. The door we tried was locked, but voices came from around the rear. Following them, we found a low roof built out from the back wall, where it covered a jumble of tools, several short stacks of weathered boards, and a wheelbarrow. Two men were sheltering in the crowded space as well, one rebuking the other.

"No, Tyomkin. There will be no advancing of the line to a new allotment, no changing of the plan whatsoever. You are to dig where you have been instructed to dig, and nowhere else. Any little problems your platoon may encounter are yours to solve, not mine."

"Fine then," grumbled Tyomkin. "We dig up any more bones, we'll set 'em aside."

He turned to stomp away, and as we maneuvered past each other he gave me an angry look. His face was drawn and dirty, even for Solovetsky. Putting a hand on the stack of boards, I saw they were inscribed with names and dates: fallen headboards, gathered up and laid atop one another here.

"Maybe you can help us," I said to the man left under the overhang. "Your company dug the graves before the executions the other day. Who was in charge of that work? We have some questions for them."

"Why do you want to know?"

"Director Vinogradov has asked us to look into a certain matter," said Petrovich from behind me.

"I don't know any Vinogradov," said the man to me. "And any information about Saturday's burials is strictly restricted, by order of Camp Administration. I'm instructed to report any questions about it to the Information and Investigation Section, and that's what I'll do if you don't leave now." He nodded curtly as he shouldered past. "Good morning."

I half expected Petrovich to stop him, but he didn't. We didn't have that kind of authority anymore; the threat of being reported was real to us both. For Infosec to find out about our resumed investigation before it produced any results would have been a disaster.

"Maybe we'll be able to find it ourselves," I said.

Petrovich cast a glance over the wilderness of graves and snorted. "I wish us luck."

However, out from under the overhang, we found the first man, Tyomkin, waiting for us. He looked a little less angry. "That Golodkin's an ass," he said. "I heard what you were asking about."

"You know who dug the graves for the men they shot?" I asked.

"That, no. Only know it wasn't my lot. And unless you have a good excuse for it you'd best not ask around too much. They've been keeping it quiet. Golodkin would be just too happy to make trouble for you." He looked over his shoulder. "Word is, though, the shooting happened over on the northeast side. Past the chapel. And they bury them where they fall, usually. No point having to carry the bodies around, I suppose. At any rate, you could have a look at it."

"Will it be marked?" asked Petrovich.

"Usually aren't, if they've shot a group."

There was a reason for this. Although the Administration's authority to execute went uncontested within SLON itself, things were not quite so clear outside. The Bolsheviks had been a party-in-exile long enough, with sufficient numbers of them languishing in the tsars' prisons, that in Moscow in the '20s, men who disputed the notion that jailers ought to do anything they wished to those they jailed were still allowed to fill certain positions of power. It would have been inconvenient for Camp Administration to have argued with those position-fillers after every time someone needed to be shot. Thus many such killings were reported as deaths from disease or accident. In what was perhaps an excess of caution, the graves were left unmarked, so that no autopsy-inclined investigator could ever find them to say otherwise.

All of that I only learned much later, of course, from Vinogradov. It was the kind of thing he knew.

"Might be someone out there keeping watch, though," Tyomkin went on. "Type they pick for that work aren't good for much, but if you find someone the grave might be nearby. That's if the fellow hasn't wandered off."

Petrovich shook his head. "Why post a guard? It would be better for there to be nothing, if they don't want it found."

"Too sensible," said Tyomkin, shrugging. "Camp Administration doesn't want it found, sure. But if it is found, my bosses want to be able to say they took precautions. How would it look if someone found the grave and no one was there to turn 'em away from it? Better to do something, even if that makes it more likely you'll have to do something."

"Thank you," I said

"Just don't let on to Golodkin it was me who told you, 'case he hears about it."

We headed northeast. Once we reached the area I thought Tyomkin had been indicating, we left the path and walked among the graves.

There was no wind to blow the snow. It was as if a gale had blown through the ground instead: graves sprayed themselves over each rise, rows of headboards looped and then dissipated. There was no order to anything. Even knowing we were in the approximate area, we spent a fruitless half hour wandering to and fro among the rows. Petrovich traced slow arcs, while I darted off and back to check spots that looked promising. In the quiet we could hear the sound the snow made as it fell.

"Over there," said Petrovich finally. "There's someone there."

A low hump was just visible through the white curtain that hung in the air. As we approached, it turned gradually into a thin man with his head stuffed into a hat and his hands stuffed into a green overcoat with a ragged fur collar. He was seated, with his knees drawn up to his belly, on a grave marker that had been uprooted from its original position, and had one of its ends propped on a rock. He was so covered in snow that we hadn't recognized him from a distance. He must have been sitting there for some time.

Beneath his beard, the man's face was swollen and purple. Raw fissures scored his cheeks, and the skin between them flaked off in scales. He only noticed us when we stood directly in front of him. He stared up blankly from sunken eyes—a *dokhodyaga*, one of the goners.

"You're not supposed to be here," said the sick man. When he raised a hand from his pocket to rub his mouth, snow fell from his shoulders in clumps. The hand was purple, too, its skin horny and rough. "Not here," he said again.

"We just want to ask a few questions," I said.

"Questions . . ." He trailed off, then seemed to regain the thread. "What questions?" His eyes' whites showed starkly above his dark cheeks. The expression in them had turned cagey. "You have some bread?"

I didn't, but Petrovich was prepared. "I do," he said, pulling out the lump he'd given me a piece of before.

The man's gaze tracked the bread passionlessly. "I haven't been too hungry since I got sick. You see I'm sick?"

"Pellagra," said Petrovich. "Ruins the appetite." The distaste showed on his face. "Go on and eat it."

The man took it gingerly from his hand, as though it might be hot, and bit a small piece off. His disease had done something to his teeth, leaving them long and chaotic in his mouth. The gums pulled back far enough that you noticed the wrongness.

Placing the rest of the bread in his pocket with care, he chewed lethargically but at length. The man's jaw traced slow circles while he stared away from us at the falling snow. After some time, it became clear he'd forgotten we were there. Petrovich and I exchanged a glance.

"What are you doing here?" I said. "Weren't you put here to guard something?"

The suspicion leapt back into his face. "Eh?"

"The men they shot. Are they buried somewhere nearby?

"Who are you? What do you want?"

"We're from Information and Investigation," lied Petrovich. He meant to intimidate the man, I suppose. I did not think it was going to work. He looked beyond normal human responses like intimidation. Bribing him had had little enough effect. "We are investigating a murder," Petrovich went on.

"They shot them," he muttered, hunching his shoulders and looking away again. "That's right. Murder. You—you're police?" Some dim memory of what that meant crossed his face. If it hadn't persuaded him to help us, perhaps the bread had revitalized him.

"That's right." I repeated the lie, its pointlessness notwithstanding. "Tell us about the men they shot."

There was a pause. "You're police," he said again, less tentatively this time.

"Yes," I said. "We want to know about what happened here."

"I have to stay. Else I don't get bread. No one's supposed to come."

"When did they place you here?" asked Petrovich. The other man didn't respond, only looked dully into his face. Petrovich turned to me. "This is worthless. He's too far gone. Let's take a look around for ourselves."

Two days' worth of snowfall had covered the ground, but it

didn't take us long to come across traces of the burial. The grave, a rough rectangle perhaps twenty feet long by seven wide, looked like nothing so much as a small vegetable patch left fallow for the winter. Where it had been shoveled back into place, the earth was loose and raised. Around the edges, a few tall stalks of grass stuck up out of the snow, like browned weeds allowed to stand by a careless gardener.

It took a moment to realize this was all there was. The men had all been dumped into the same pit.

"What do you make of it?" said Petrovich.

"Why bury them together?" I said slowly. "After someone went to the trouble of making separate coffins, I mean."

"Less effort to dig one big hole than eleven small ones. Never underestimate a *zek*'s ability to find the sloppiest way to do the most straightforward job."

"Maybe so," I said.

There was nothing else to see, though Petrovich circled the grave slowly and poked at the stalks with his cane. Back where we'd left him, the *dokhodyaga* paid us no mind. He'd occupied himself with holding Petrovich's piece of bread up to his face, alternately peering into its crannies and nibbling at the crust.

"Maybe we can still get something out of him," I said, indicating the man with my chin.

Petrovich shook his head. "We don't have the time to waste, Tolya. You wanted to see the grave and we have. Time to go."

"I thought you'd be pleased there's someone here to talk to. Isn't that better than looking at footprints, according to your system?"

"Talking to that one is the same as looking at a footprint. Neither one can tell you whether you'll learn anything worthwhile from it. What I have been trying to teach you is that investigations, ninety-five percent of the time, are about information passing among people. Do you think our friend here is a person anymore? I doubt he knows his own name, much less anything that will help us."

Perhaps he was right. If there is one truth acknowledged by all *zeks,* it is that starvation is a bright and terrible light, blinding you to anything but itself. It had already occurred to me that the man seemed beyond intimidation. Still, we had come for a reason, hadn't we? Was I really prepared to hand the piloting of the case so completely back to Petrovich already?

I was still vacillating when the *dokhodyaga* called out. "Gentlemen!" He'd risen and taken a step towards us, a look of surprise on his ravaged face. At hearing himself come out so loud and clearly with such a word, maybe? I looked again at the collar of his coat. Who had he been before the pellagra, before Solovki?

He went on, grasping at a tone of civility that had grown awkward with disuse. "Gentlemen. You're police. Tell them to give me my bread. Say I was here. Don't say I went to the kitchen."

When I pointed out that no one had any reason to believe he'd gone to the kitchen, he shook his head rapidly. The swollen fingers of his left hand had begun to scratch his neck above the collar, where the worst of his rash was. "No, no. I've been here. But I couldn't stand it. Not the first morning, not just after . . . I left." His hand stopped, and he looked away. The bread really had revived him: he almost looked ashamed. "I got into the potato peels." His eyes narrowed, and he glanced from me to Petrovich, evaluating us, perhaps, as potential rivals for his kitchen garbage. "Cook throws the bad ones out."

"We'll omit that from our report," I said. I kept the excitement out of my voice. We might still learn nothing. Petrovich's impatience at my shoulder only made me more stubborn. "You can rely on us. But what made you leave the first day?"

"I was hungry," he said uncertainly. His eyes had dulled again. "I didn't get my bread."

"You couldn't stand something," I said. "That's what made you leave, wasn't it? What was it you couldn't stand?"

I watched his face. There was nothing in it that acknowledged my question. The expression that had flickered there for a moment was fading: humanity slid off him like oil.

"Damn it, Tolya, I told you," said Petrovich. "We need to find Zhenov, report what Fitneva told us to Vinogradov. It's already after noon."

I was on the point of giving up when the voice finally said, "The ground. The ground was moving."

Petrovich sensed there was something to it before I did. "The ground—?"

We understood at the same moment. "He means the dirt in the grave," I said quickly. "Something—someone was moving."

The old man scowled. He looked back at the plot he'd just circled, then jammed his cane violently into the snow. "This is a sorry business."

A sorry business. That was true. But I could see that he was thinking. Something tickled my own mind as well.

The man who moved the earth would have been lined up with the others, forced to his knees. They'd have made him face the pit, wouldn't they? To keep from seeing his face when they shot him, and so filling in the grave would cover up any splatter.

He would have looked into it, thinking, perhaps, "This is the last thing I will ever see."

Then, later, waking up covered with earth: he would remember that thought. A moment of horrible understanding: he is in the pit that was the last thing he ever saw. Now it's dark. There are no new sights; sensation is blind now. He's been shot through the neck, or in the ear, or the bullet only cracked his skull and glanced off. He's been shot in a way that made him black out without killing him. The pain is dulled by shock. He's panicked, he's weak. He tries to push against the dirt, finds he can't. Can't turn his head. His thinking is rapid, incoherent—*I am in the pit I was looking at, they shot me, if I could only shout, someone would dig for me, I must just shift my arm*—and simultaneously, in his chest, he feels the unmovable pointlessness of his doing anything at all.

The dirt fills his mouth. There's a hint of beet, of vegetable rot, in the way it tastes.

That grub-like wiggling, as if there is a worm or mouse moving just beneath the soil: that is a man six feet down thrashing with all his might, trying to breathe, to dig his way to the surface. There's no air for him. Each time his lungs heave, the breath is half earth. The blood is still pumping from his neck, and he lies at an angle. Warmth flows past his face, turning everything to mud. After enough bleeding, he not only asphyxiates, but also drowns.

Consider it: officialdom declares a man has been put to death, then, despite the inconvenient fact of his continuing to draw breath, proceeds to treat him like a corpse and tip him into the prepared hole. Few killings are nice, but for one to transpire symbolically prior to its literal taking effect is especially unpleasant. The truth will always overtake fact in the end. It was fact being overtaken in that way, down there, that was horrible.

I wonder: before he quit breathing, was there a moment when even he stopped thinking of himself as alive?

I couldn't stop myself imagining it. The weight of it pressed on my chest, the pain of his bullet throbbed in my hand. Even so, there was something in it, something in my re-creation of his death that seemed not right. What did it mean for him to have tasted dirt as he died?

Eleven shots, one not killing its man. Eleven men, ten dead, one struggling with the earth that covered him. Eleven coffins—

"If the ground was moving," I said slowly, "then the man under it wasn't in a coffin. One of the coffins was missing."

Petrovich looked up from his cane. The blue eyes widened. "That's right," he said. "That's right. At least one of the coffins. And the common grave—there may have been none. Then the icons—"

The *dokhodyaga's* gaze, a dull mirror, followed ours back to the patch of turned earth. For a moment we stood there, the three of us. Each in his way confronting the secret in that grave.

"They're still out there," I said. "Someone has them. If we can find out where they are—"

"Let's hurry," said Petrovich.

Trying to find this place, we'd come from among trackless graves and uneven burial plots. But close to where we were, at the top of a little rise, there was a path that led back to the road. Neither Petrovich nor I said any more. Trying to move quickly made his breath ragged and uneven.

I looked back at the man guarding the grave. The only sign he gave of having registered our departure was to resume his close inspection of the bread Petrovich had given him. He held the crust so close to his face that he might have been tallying its crumbs. Then, while I watched, he opened his mouth wide, wide, wider still—wide enough to show me, again, even at a distance, all those thin, disordered teeth—and pushed the wad in whole. It was not like eating at all. It left him with his fingers caught between his cheeks, and he pulled them out awkwardly, leaving the bread behind.

I did not stay to watch him chew. We were heading on already, moving as fast as we could along the path laid out for us among the graves.

31

The lake was a blank space. That was one side of the road. On the other, the cemetery's last few headboards petered out. Narrow utility transoms reached up into the falling curtains of snow above us, their bundles of cables growing denser as power lines met and joined each other, then, on their way to the nearby plant, crossed telephone wires destined for the cluster of administrative buildings beyond the kremlin.

"It will depend on Vinogradov's pull," I was saying. "With this he'll be able to talk to the Chekist. To Eikhmans. No one knew about the icons being stolen when they pulled us off the case. They can't have. We could have a real search of the warehouse. With enough men, every box—"

"Wait," Petrovich said. He was panting, his cane slipping. "Now wait a minute. There could be an accomplice in Company Sixteen. The best place to hide coffins would be with the sorry bastards whose job it is to dig our graves, wouldn't it? You're right to want to go to Vinogradov, but we've got to be careful. Move too fast, we'll give away what we know. What if someone in Infosec knows all about it? That could be why they tried to kill the case."

I shook my head. "There isn't time. We have to get Vinogradov to act now. Today."

I still didn't understand all that had transpired. It looked as though Antonov's plan to liberate the icons from their captivity on the island had gone forward, even after his death. Whether the coffins had been spirited away from the grave site, or simply never delivered, I couldn't say. It could only have been done amid the secrecy and chaos of a shooting. And if Administration had sent, instead of the drunken Uspenski, a representative with any interest in confirming that the requested preparations had been made—it almost seemed to require advance knowledge of the executions.

Calculating in cold blood on the scheduled passing of bullets through the heads of eleven men didn't seem like Antonov. But where did that leave us with the partners we'd considered for the smuggling operation? Someone from the Anzer warehouse would almost have to be involved. But how could they—Zhenov, Kologriev, or whoever—have known about the shooting before it happened?

We'd reached the kremlin's southeastern tower when we heard the noise. Three long, low blasts, lower than our usual steam whistle, unmistakable. It was the ship's horn.

Petrovich grabbed my arm, but I already knew. "That's the last of the season," I said.

"At Administration they were saying the water would freeze finally, tonight or tomorrow. If they're aboard, if they leave—"

If they left, we were finished. The story could only be corroborated one way. Infosec would never consent to exhume the bodies they'd spent so much effort to blot off the island's face. Vinogradov could help us if the coffins were still on the island, but once the ship had sailed they'd be beyond our reach. There was a wireless station for communicating with the mainland and boats at sea, but with the water expected to become impassable in a matter of hours rather than days, the authorities would never permit the year's last shipment of lumber to be faced about and returned to Solovki. The prospect of coordinating a search of the ship at Kem was little better; too much could go wrong, there were too many ways to slip stacks of paintings past uncaring and ignorant guards. We didn't even know how they had been smuggled aboard.

And the icons would be on the boat. That was certain. The alternative was to store them through six months of winter.

"You go to Vinogradov," I said. "Tell him what we've found. See if there's anything he can do. I'll try to stop the boat."

He hesitated. "I will need the documents. For the monk."

I took them from my coat and handed them over. One of us had to reach the museum. And anyway, papers or no, at best I would be able to delay the ship's launch briefly. Even with Vinogradov's stamp, no one would launch a search of the cargo on my say-so.

Petrovich looked on the verge of saying something—the mustache had begun to bend, the sign of some gruff sentiment about to be emitted—but I left before he could do it. There was no time, and I had no interest in a long goodbye.

As I rounded the southern tip of the kremlin, the bay came into view, smoking in the frigid air. The *Gleb Boky* rode low in the water. It covered more than half the quay on the opposite side of the bay, a hundred and fifty feet. The steamer's telegraph masts and rigging bobbed and swayed before the white administration building, giving the whole the air of a huge, slow insect turned on its back. Men scuttled about the deck, steam rose from amidships. The red star on the side of the funnel was the only color in the otherwise drab scene.

I broke into a run. Along the road, prisoners had stopped to watch the departure, huddled at the water's edge or sheltering in the eaves of what few little structures there were. I saw one of them jerk a thumb at me and say something. His friends laughed, but whatever it was he'd said was lost on the wind as I passed. The huge stones of the kremlin wall flashed by in the snow.

On the quay itself I had to slow down to make my way through the crowd. Work crews leaned against the sledges they'd brought in, with a more active cluster closer to the edge of the water. The gangplank had not been raised—I was able to see that, at least. Halfway up, someone argued with a gray-uniformed guard, gesturing angrily.

"Look," said a voice behind me. "Still room for that stuff, isn't there? Not packed quite as full as they've been making out, I reckon."

Down at the other end of the ship, a crane was lowering a pallet loaded with long, low crates to the deck. At one end was a sailor in a pea coat. At the other, buttoned up to the neck as usual and with one huge hand gripping a guy rope, was Kologriev.

Kologriev. That was who, then. Strange, after so long, to put a face to that enemy. The problem of unwinding the secrets around Antonov had reduced itself to stopping the man on the crane.

Looking back on it, the shock of revelation was surprisingly weak. You expect to be angry at a murderer, to hate a man who's tried to kill you. I looked at him to see whether he resembled either of the figures who'd chased me through the forest that night. His build wasn't right for the one I'd seen up close at the canal, but I thought he could have been the other, the one who'd first appeared before me on the road. But whether he'd tried to do it with his own hand or not, he'd meant to put a knife in me. And Antonov, Foma: he was responsible for both those deaths as well.

But watching him pass above the heads of the crowd there was like looking at a painting of someone you hate, which you can easily turn away from to look at something else. Since my first glimpse of Antonov's body, laid out there on the quay with the pink blood frozen in his face, the case had continually put so much before me that there was no lingering over anything. My attention turned constantly from one detail to another. Always the task was to look past, to see what lay behind. In this way even Kologriev, himself behind so much, slid out from beneath my eyes.

Where were the icons? Had they been loaded into the boxes I'd seen on the pallet with him, or were they still somewhere on the quay? The only way I could think of to find out was to stop him, confront him somehow.

I turned to the man who'd spoken behind me. "They shouldn't be putting those on," I said.

He gave me a surprised look. "What do you mean?"

"I happen to know they're contraband. Prohibited goods."

"Well, what do you want me to do about it?"

"I'm telling you you're right, there's still room on the ship. Maybe if you get this sorted out, you can get your load on."

If the man took my advice it might slow down the ship's departure, but it wouldn't be enough. I didn't wait to see what he'd do. A few more shoves with my elbow brought me to the bottom of the plank.

"—your head on the block when they find out in the Forestry Section that this order hasn't reached the depot in Kem!" The man I'd seen from the edge of the crowd was still yelling. His eyes popped with anger.

"Not my head," said the guard.

When he felt the wood bowing under my steps, the man with the Forestry Section order turned. "What do you want?" he said.

Adding a third person to the plank made it crowded. Below, in the chute formed by the ship and the wall of the quay, the water welled up blackly, more slush than liquid. The gap was narrow.

"Listen," I said, trying to talk around him, to the guard. "This ship can't leave yet. It's an emergency."

"Ship's leaving soon as they cast off," said the guard. The bill of his cap was pulled low over his face. "Horn just blew."

"Not until my lumber's on," said the other man.

I hesitated. Explaining too much would only confuse them and waste time. "Something's been smuggled aboard."

"What are you talking about?" the other man said again, before the guard could speak.

"Something stolen," I said. "They're trying to sell it on the mainland."

He threw up his arms. "There! You see? I've been telling you, the whole process is a bad joke!"

The guard shrugged. "Not my process. Not my job. Told you, I only make sure no one comes on."

"Whose job is it, then? I told you before, I have a writ from Forestry—"

A low guardrail made of pipes, painted white, circled the hull. A life preserver hung on each post, but in the wide gaps between them there were no balusters. The wood of the deck, recently shoveled or swept clear, was already stippled with a slippery-looking layer of snow.

"You two get off now," said the guard, catching a signal from someone further down the ship. "They're going to pull this up in a minute."

"I won't," said the other man. "There was to have been a berth reserved—"

I jumped. My feet slid from under me when I hit the deck. My chin hit the bar—the taste of blood filled my mouth—but

I'd wrapped my arms around the rail, and was able to scramble through underneath.

"Hey," said the guard, "what are you doing, you prick? Fuck! Stop that guy."

Someone crouched in my way, working at something on the deck. I caught a surprised face in a watch cap, a rope in his hands. Before he could stop me, I was past.

Behind, the sound of the argument delaying the guard reached me.

"If he's allowed on the ship, I'm going, too. We'll just see if that hold is as full as you say."

"Oh no you don't. He's not allowed any more than you are. You'd better stay here."

"Listen, the berth, reserved—"

The crane had put Kologriev down somewhere towards the ship's bow, on the other side of the cabin. What I would do when I found him, I still didn't know.

"Hey!" That was behind me. I skidded around the corner. I could hear excited voices raised on shore—someone had seen me running. Footsteps thudded at my back.

Coming around the bow to the other side of the ship, I pounded into a kind of sudden privacy. With the flat box of the cabin blocking out the crowd, the bay's expanse made itself present again, as if it had been waiting behind a door. Even pelting through the snow, I was aware of new quiet and altered distances. I slowed.

Kologriev was nowhere to be seen, but the sailor I'd noticed on the other end of the pallet—I thought it was the same one—leaned on the railing, staring off across the water. Next to him were the crates that had ridden with them.

There were five, one stack of three and another of two, like two stairs leading up and over the rail. The narrow, two-yard boxes were all roughly the same shape, but now that I could look at them closely, I could see that their proportions were off. Here one was a little shorter, another a hand's-breadth deeper, a third squatter. And they were a patchwork, each side made of mismatched wooden panels, attached to each other with what appeared to be tongue-and-groove joints. Where the larger panels were insufficient, gaps had been filled in with new, yellow wood, but most of the grain was gray or beige, worn and old.

Again the shock of knowledge. These were the coffins—these were the icons, hammered together, with the painted sides turned in. I'd assumed Kologriev would have disassembled them after claiming them out of the grave. Instead he'd simply nailed on their lids. Transit papers had been glued to the outside of each.

More thudding from behind—"Sorry, Chief Mate. Sorry."—and a hard arm wrapped around my neck. I jerked, and someone else grabbed me by a flailing elbow. "Crazy bastard jumped aboard. Just now." The man panted in my ear while I struggled. "We'll take care of it. Hand him over to the guards."

"Wait," I said, choking the words out best I could. "Wait. Damn it. Those crates. Shouldn't be here. They're coffins. That is—paintings."

The mate, or whatever he was, raised his hand. "Just a moment. Let him talk."

The arm around my neck loosened. "Those—crates." I hesitated, coughing a little. "They're being used to smuggle paintings—icons—off the island."

"I don't think so. These contain . . . " He made a show of consulting the transit manifest. "Salt in twenty-five pound bags."

"No." I shook myself free of the men who held me. There were two of them, both sailors by their looks. The guard must have been stuck arguing with my collaborator on the gangplank after all. "Kologriev—the man who brought them—it's the boxes themselves he cares about. They're painted—painted on the inside."

The mate considered. "I'll settle this," he said, waving off the other sailors. "You two get back to work."

The one who'd choked me gave me a little push in the shoulder as he left. I caught my breath for a moment. Down at the edge of the bay, I could see the huddles of men I'd passed earlier, the kremlin looming above them. They looked small.

"Now," the mate said after watching the others disappear. He stood before an open hatch, with a set of stairs disappearing down it into the hold. Tall and thin, he was in his late forties or fifties, with a long, grizzled neck. He had a competent look. "Tell me what this is about."

I went over to the stacks of coffins. The lid of the topmost one on the taller, outer stack hung an inch over the side of the box. The nails that fastened it on were small and few.

"If we can open one of these," I said, "I'll show you." I could hear the start of panic in my voice: Kologriev was still somewhere on the ship. I took a grip on the lid and began to pull. The coffin shifted. It was surprisingly light, lighter than it should have been if it had been filled to the brim with salt, but I could feel something shifting inside. "The paintings—they're icons. You see, these panels are the backs. The wood is old. You can see the paintings themselves if you only get the lid off. On the other side they're all gold leaf and saints."

Unfolding his arms, the mate came over to inspect the panel I was yanking at. "Why would someone use something like that to make a box?"

"They're selling them. On the mainland. They were stolen. From the camp museum. Please, it will be perfectly clear if we can only pry off the lid." With the fingers of my good hand under the rim and my elbow against the opposite side of the box, I had leverage. As I spoke, the lid slowly began to separate. A nail creaked out, then a louder creak as two more went.

The mate's hand thumped down onto the lid, knocking it back into place. "And what's your involvement with it all?"

His hooded eyes took me in. For the first time that day, I was aware of my appearance: my stupid cap, my dirty bandage. "There's been a murder," I said. "It's complicated. Please, there must be a crowbar. Something. You'll see."

The chief mate nodded slowly, then looked up at the distinctive sound of boots on metal stairs.

"That spot is fine," said a familiar voice. "Let's get the fucking things moved."

"There you are," said the mate. "What are we going to do about this?"

The face that rose above the deck was Kologriev's. "Anatoly Bogomolov. Fuck your mother. You are fucking persistent."

The wind blew through my coat. I stepped back and bumped into the mate, who'd maneuvered behind me. Between the two men, the wall of the cabin, and the coffins, I was trapped.

"He knows, Ivan," said the mate. "You haven't done much of a job keeping things quiet, have you? How the hell are we going to fix this?"

All of it was surprisingly calm. So often a crisis's nature does not make itself apparent in the critical scene. No one raised his voice, or made a sudden move. The arrival of a new face had simply launched a new phase of the conversation. I'd been wondering where Kologriev was. Now he was here. It was natural. My heart beat harder, but I thought it was slower.

"How are we going to fix this, Bogomolov?" said Kologriev.

"How did you fix things with Gennady Antonov?" I said.

His eyes flicked over my shoulder to catch the mate's. "Yeah. Suppose that is how it's going to be. Don't know why you should be getting your prick up about it, though. Not like it's good news for you." His voice was flat. "We're all going below deck now."

"Just a minute," said the mate. "A hundred men just saw him jump onto this ship. We're going to have to answer for it if he doesn't make it off."

"A hundred men? That's fine. I told you, my friends in the big office already think Bogomolov here has been making plans to escape. Now everyone's seen him jumping on a boat headed for the mainland. They'll thank me for saving the bullet."

"And what if he has friends of his own?" said the mate. "They radio ahead, and we find someone waiting for us in Kem, wanting to search my hold for your damn boxes of salt."

"You don't think I would have radioed ahead before I came here?" I said.

Kologriev's beady eyes hadn't released mine the whole time he'd been talking to the mate. Again, the high reediness of his voice struck me, but it was irrelevant. The wide shoulders, the hard body: the man was a door ready to open, with violence on the other side.

"He's bluffing you, you cunt," he said to the mate, reacting to some expression I couldn't see. "The only friend he has is some geriatric cop from Odessa. Neither one has any pull, and I've got plans to take care of the old man, too. Don't wor—"

I drove my head back without warning, trying to catch the mate in the nose. I only managed to hit the side of his chin, but I surprised him. I twisted as he grabbed at me, and we both staggered against the wall of the cabin.

Then Kologriev was on me. I felt myself lifted by my coat.

His fist detonated against my cheek, once, twice, before I was able to cover my face with my arms. A third blow struck my wounded hand, and I nearly vomited.

My coat didn't fit—that was lucky. With the sleeves above my head, I slipped out of it backwards, leaving him gripping empty fabric.

Reeling, I still had the presence of mind to kick at the mate's groin. He released his hold on my leg as Kologriev threw my coat over the side.

A labyrinth, with all its turns, lobes, and convolutions, presents only one way to go in the end. That was what Vinogradov had said. Well, the mate was pushing himself up already as Kologriev started for me. There was only one way.

I leapt for the rail.

It meant going over the coffins, but Kologriev caught me. We fell hard into them, only saved from knocking the taller stack into the water by its banging up against one of the posts in the railing.

As he pulled me back towards him, I tried to wrap my arms around the topmost coffin. A nail from where I'd loosened the lid tore my hand, and there was a loud squeal as more bent or came free. We struggled for a moment, then toppled over to the side, coffin and all. For a fraction of a second I was aware of paper sacks thudding against the deck near me and breaking, salt hissing over the side of the ship. The lid, I could see now, was two joined panels, and the joint had splintered under my pulling, so that one of them slanted away from the rest of the coffin.

Then he caught my shoulder, and had me. A hand in my face, in my eyes. Heavy pressure on my back. Something slammed the back of my head, and for a moment it was impossible to breathe. I saw black.

I bit, and the hand at my face moved.

I jackknifed. Once, twice, without the leverage to create any force. A knee bore down, a hand found a soft part of my neck. The edge of the deck was close to my face, a drop into the water inches away. My leg had somehow gotten caught under the fallen box.

I bucked again. Somehow that gave me purchase to crawl out from under him a little, towards the bow. As he crawled over me to put his fingers around my throat again, I drove my elbow back hard, and he grunted.

He must have rolled, then. He must have done it at just the wrong moment, in time with the ship's bobbing. For a moment our faces were close together: his nostrils flared as he began to go over the edge of the deck.

He pulled at me to stop himself. Too late.

Our bodies' vectors projected their shared center of mass out over the water, and it dragged us over. I grabbed wildly, held whatever edge my hand touched: the coffin.

It can't have scraped the deck for as long as it seemed to. The mate had no time to do anything.

Then we were falling.

Here is another panel for the iconostasis that stands for Solovetsky in my mind: gray stone and white snow, undergoing the necessary transformation from objects of sense into memorable values, reemerge unrecognizably as a flat ground of gold. Then the trees that rim the scene disappear. The waves harden and sharpen below. The *Gleb Boky* flattens and shrinks, no longer jutting in the water, only tracing its own outline. It's become far smaller than any of the bodies in the scene. Behind us, the towers in the kremlin's wall wheel about and cluster to the front, presenting themselves, all seven in a single row, to be counted and named.

And us, myself and Kologriev? We still fall, but separated now by the golden field. It freezes us in the air, contorts us into abject postures, like Apostles overcome by the radiance of Christ's transfiguration. In a cascade we fall: the *urka*, me. Then the coffin coming after us.

Of course, that's memory, with its imaginations and reconstructions. The moment itself blurred. Only a lurch as the box came over the edge, and my stomach flipping with the feel of the drop.

At that temperature water is a frozen vise. It appalls the nerves. Plunged muscles clench so hard they forget their connection to bone. In my panel, the color of the water's paint is deepest black.

Something hit me as I tried to swim up for air. A roof nailed on the ocean, an event from my nightmares. I'd gasped when I hit, somehow without my lungs sucking water, but now I had no air. The water was cold, too cold. The bulk above twisted my neck, and my knuckles scraped wood.

The breath I finally gasped when I surfaced was half wave, and I coughed, floundering. All that kept me from going under again was the object I'd just blundered out from beneath. It was the coffin, floating lid down. I'd been trapped when I swam up into it, confused by the icon panel I'd wrenched loose from its lid. Now I clutched at the wood with numb fingers. Where my skin was exposed—my ears, my neck, my face, my hands—the wind burned. Already I felt myself shivering violently.

When I could look around, I saw Kologriev had come up a dozen feet away. He was moving towards me, holding his chin above the water. The *Gleb Boky*'s hull loomed above us.

I could barely move, but was able to maneuver the length of the coffin between us. It made a poor raft, and I ended by having to hold it with both arms. But when I looked up again, Kologriev was wallowing. A passing swell covered his head, and he sputtered and coughed as he reemerged.

The shivering rattled every part of me now, but the thought-annihilating panic that had come with first being submerged had begun to pass. I might freeze, but I didn't think I would drown; I'd learned to swim long ago in the Neva, and could tread water indefinitely. Kologriev looked like a weaker swimmer. If I swam around the ship for the quay, I might be able to beat him, and there be pulled ashore.

But then, what awaited me there? I'd leapt onto the boat without permission, eluding the guard. Any *zek* who did as much would be lucky to get five minutes of questioning before being handed over to the Cheka's torturers. Even if I got that, the icons, the proof I needed to show my plunge hadn't been some sort of insane escape attempt, were invisible beneath me in the water. There were still the coffins on deck, yes—but would I get another chance at them?

I glanced up at the ship, but couldn't see the mate at the railing anymore. No, of course not: he would be stowing them away, as quickly as he could. He was in charge on the ship. Only I knew about his involvement in Kologriev's operation, and to anyone who didn't know Petrovich's and my story, the coffins would still be simple crates. If I left this one, if Kologriev sank it—he'd have me then as surely as if he'd wrapped his hands around my throat.

Snow fell into the water between us. My breath came fast

and shallow, in shivering gasps.

"Come here, little fucker," Kologriev gasped as he reached the other side.

I pushed myself up onto the floating wood. (Somewhere the stump of my finger stabbed with pain, but adrenaline and freezing water abstracted it from me.) From above, I hit him as hard as I could with my right fist, twice. He rocked back and slipped under the water with a gurgle.

"Help," I tried to shout. I could not seem to take in full breaths. I could not stop shaking. The only other noises in the world were the hum of the steamer's engines and the slap of waves against the hull. I tried to kick myself and the coffin away from where Kologriev had gone under. "Help."

Kologriev surfaced, coughing and pushing his head up. He'd moved out of reach, near a floating chunk of ice. He seemed disoriented.

"Help," I shouted again.

At the sound of my voice, he moved towards me. I waited, then hit him again. This time he raised an arm to grab at my wrist, but the movement sank him. I pushed the coffin into his face, forcing him the rest of the way under the water. I could hear him knock against the wood as I pulled myself around to the other end, again out of reach.

"The float," a voice called. "Behind you. Take the float."

When I looked around, there was a life preserver in the water.

The man at the railing above shouted again, something I couldn't understand. The ring bobbed on the black water, white with red stripes. When I kicked out to put an arm through it, I felt myself pulled, my grip on the coffin slipping. I looked up to see the man, joined by others, hauling on a rope. Someone gestured, miming madly, for me to put my other arm all the way through.

The water was torture; this was rescue. But if I let them lift me up to the deck, it would be the same as if I'd swum for the quay. The icons would be lost. Petrovich and I would never be able to prove anything before Solovetsky's punishments descended on us.

I let the preserver go.

A gasp and some weak splashing told me Kologriev had come up again. They'd noticed him up at the railing as well—new cries interrupted the swearing they were doing at me. A second preserver splashed down.

"A boat," I yelled up to the men on the ship. "Send a boat!"

Pushing myself up on the coffin gave me a view of Kologriev. He was sputtering, but the preserver had fallen close to him. While I watched, he managed to push his shoulders through it, and they began to pull him in. He dangled as they lifted him up the side, limp and spinning slightly. When he spun towards me, his big face, with its tiny features clustered in the middle, looked gray. He did not seem to see me. Water dripped from his boots. I noticed—oddly, irrelevantly—that the shirt remained buttoned up to his neck, still hiding the tattoos we'd been told were there. By the time they pulled him over the edge of the deck and out of view, his coat had acquired a fine dusting of snow.

By now the first preserver had been pulled back up as well. They threw it back down again, closer to me. The sounds of abuse and encouragement increased the longer I ignored it. I'd wrapped my arms around the coffin, so as not to lose it from crabbing hands. To them I must have looked frightened to abandon my raft.

"A boat," I called. I couldn't tell whether I made myself heard. "It has to be a boat."

The coffin had settled further into the water, and now floated aslant, open end down, closed end towards the surface. It had been well made, tightly joined. Trapped beneath it, and only gradually leaking out, there must have been a pocket of air. Kologriev could only have loaded it with a few sacks of salt to start with, and by now those had fallen out and sunk.

Still, while my numbing feet treaded water, the wood grew heavier and heavier. Long minutes passed. Vaguely I began to worry about it sinking, dragging me under with it.

How can I describe that time? I did nothing, only waited and suffered, hoping dimly they would send someone out for me. Each wave that sloshed up on the coffin left tiny crystals of ice behind. When I blinked, I could feel my lashes stick together. Weakness spread from arms to shoulders.

The wind came through my clothes like wires—but underwater was worse. Spikes of ache drove into my knees, the joints of my hips. The muscles in my abdomen shook like an electric current ran through them. My lungs were fists.

Cold is so basic a feeling, it requires to be related though other things. What happened to my body. What the wind and water looked like and did. How Kologriev and I behaved trying to save ourselves. But these are only signs. They stand like screens before what cold really is. There in the bay, they paled, faded away. What could have been more meaningless than the ache in my knee? I was barely conscious of it.

My consciousness was cold. Cold, the direct experience of being cold. That overwhelmed the rest. If, in memory and on the page, I can only represent it through profusion, in life the cold sucked every reference towards itself, until the single meaning of everything—the sky, the icons, the coffins, my fear, the hull of the ship, the discovery of Antonov's murderer, the giant stones in the distant kremlin wall, the island itself—concentrated in my bones. And that meaning was: *cold*.

Cold contracts, and contracts, and contracts, until all that's left is a unity: single, black, and frozen. A point.

It took their trying to pull me in for me to realize the rowboat had arrived. My feet and legs had gone quite numb by then, which felt almost like warmth and allowed me to drift off a little. I struggled once I understood. The coffin was almost entirely submerged. It would go down without me supporting it.

Three faces stared down at me out of the boat. "You maniac," said the one I'd shaken off. "Come here."

"He's delirious. Get his collar."

The oars knocked against the coffin. One nearly hit me in the head as they brought the boat forward. I slipped and felt my face dip into the water.

"Wait." I choked, then said again: "Wait." Below the surface I could feel the thing bumping my knees.

"Come on, now."

As they reached for me, I took a breath and went under. The cold shocked my eyelids, filled my ears. The opening I'd made was at the coffin's lowest point. I forced myself down. Numb fingers could barely close around the rim, but I held as best I could, pressing the wood to my body with my arms. A hand took the yoke of my shirt and began to pull.

The end I'd taken came up along with me. The other, tilted up, released whatever air remained in it, and I felt it grow still heavier. I could not let it sink. I repeated that to myself as I came up, as I gasped for air: I could not let it sink. I tried to turn the streaming thing so that the paintings would face the men.

"Look," I gasped, "Look."

The man who'd had to reach in after me was wet to the shoulder, and irate. "You want to tip us? I should have let you drown."

"Take it," I said. "Take it, hurry. Look."

I couldn't tell whether the one who spoke next was the one who thought he should have let me drown.

"Is that . . . is it the Blessed Mother?"

One took the coffin from me and held it up, while the other two pulled me in. I couldn't close my fist around the hands they offered. In the end they dragged me over the side by the armpits.

32

All winter, there was talk about them: the icon-built boxes. They'd been constructed on orders from Moscow, you heard, as a way of punishing disobliging Church fathers. That one ended up in the bay was no accident, of course; the deed had needed to be made public somehow.

Or: the whole affair had been engineered by the monks, in fulfillment of a secret ritual, laid down by Saints Zosima and Savvati at the time of the monastery's founding, to keep corrupt boyars from benefiting from the island's spiritual authority. To this it was responded that, even if the Bolsheviks could be considered as in somewhat the same position as corrupt boyars, they had no interest in Solovetsky's spiritual authority to start with.

Sometimes even the truth circulated. During my short time back in Quarantine Company, Genkin informed me in confidence that the crates everyone was so excited about had been part of a foiled smuggling attempt, and that Administration was not quite as good at stopping things coming on and off the island as they wanted us to think. What he thought about that was that a smart boy like me should keep an eye out for opportunities, for partnerships . . .

Of those of us who knew, it seems no one spoke about what the boxes really were. At least the idea of coffins was not widely publicized, and I was never aware of a connection being drawn to the execution of the White officers.

I remember how I stood on the quay and froze, staring down while they pulled the coffin from the bay. Having handed me up, the men who'd gone out in the boat struggled to bail my prize out so it could be passed to those ashore. I was dazed, nearly delirious with cold. With the box floating half submerged, the paintings looked as though they were themselves liquid. Saints sloshed the walls, halos and crosses eddied. Eyes and beards swam like fish. When the men finally managed to tip the thing and pour out the remaining water, it was almost a shock to see it issue forth clear. A mad part of me had expected a flood of images to stain the sea.

On land, there were exclamations of wonder as the coffin came up. My struggles had already pulled back one of the panels of the lid, and when someone pried back the other with a bar, we found ourselves perched on the brink of a shaft of paint. It was the first good look at the requisitioned icons I'd had. I recall, in one of the wall panels, a man. Bearded, seated atop a stair-pierced, crenelated tower. The tower bright blue, his face brown and sorrowful. There was something wrong about the proportions, as though, despite the graceful buttresses and windows, a child had built the structure out of blocks. The man's legs were not visible. Later I determined he was Saint Simeon Stylites, hauling up his food and drink in baskets attached to ropes.

What else? Wet colors shimmered and smeared as they froze. On the coffin's bottom I remember two panels: a sorrowful adult Christ raising a crooked hand above the head of Mary, who held a complacent infant Christ enthroned in her arms. But the panels' orientations were reversed. The hand would have pointed at a body's feet, while Mary cast her eyes upwards towards the heaven of a prospective corpse's scalp.

There was so much to look at that you could barely see. Like dazzling light, which brightens everything, illuminates nothing. An iconostasis produces the same effect. Yes: it was exactly as if an iconostasis had been folded into a box.

I might have succumbed to hypothermia there, standing and staring, if someone hadn't led me away to a room in the administration building. The captain of the *Gleb Boky* came along, talking loudly at me. I'd been identified to him as the one who'd slipped past the guard on his gangplank, and he demanded I explain what had happened. Even as he snapped his fingers in my face, I could feel my mind wandering, my body beneath its clothing pallid as marble.

It took Vinogadov arriving to satisfy the captain. Without changing his expression—the level mustache, those blankly reflecting glasses, remained the same as ever—he explained that I had stopped a theft, then suggested that a guard be posted on the coffin.

"Who was it?" he said to me after the captain had been mollified. "Who brought them aboard?"

I stuttered the name: Kologriev.

I'd learned the secret of Antonov's killer, and I'd told it. What happened after was out of my hands.

Petrovich, moving at a slower pace than Vinogradov, only came on the scene later, once I'd been taken off to the hospital. As a result we missed each other. The old man and I didn't meet again until two months had passed. By then Vinogradov had made my assignment to the museum official, and I'd been transferred back to Company Ten. As it turned out, solving the case had come with more benefits than just saving my skin from Kologriev.

My new cell was in the company's second dormitory, which faced the kremlin wall, rather than the courtyard. Two sets of stairs and a hallway separated it from the one Petrovich and I had shared. The new cell, much larger, bedded six. I remember best a loud-voiced Romanian named Byrsan, who wore an embroidered shirt every Sunday evening. I never knew any of them well.

I'd been there for five days when Petrovich came to me. A pot of groats for my lunch was bubbling on the cell's stove when he appeared in the door. Never a careful shaver, he now appeared to have given in to haphazardness altogether. Hair bristled at different lengths on his cheeks. The unkempt mustache hung over his lips.

"Anatoly Pavelovich," he said, crossing the threshold. "They told me I might find you here."

He must have timed the visit carefully. I'd soon decided I preferred not to compete with my cellmates for time at the stove. Thus it was two in the afternoon, well after the time most *zeks* cooked their midday meal.

I limped over to shake his hand. After my time in the water, my feet had blistered, swollen, and finally begun to rot. Frostbite's final toll amounted to four toes and a half, along with a hunk of my right heel.

"You're well, I hope?" he said. "Happy to see you'd received your transfer here. Still dangerous in Quarantine, eh? This was probably the best outcome for you."

"Probably," I said.

"Vinogradov's taken care of you. Good friend to have, that one." Underneath his gruffness was a whine. His way of talking was the same but with something perfunctory about it, like a man no longer convinced by his own personality. When I didn't say anything, he went on. "Been thinking. Antonov's body. Remember I wanted the remains accessible? Thought I might need to look at them again. Didn't need to in the end, but I thought I might."

"I remember."

"Yes. Well. What happened to him after that? The Chekist had him left out somewhere to freeze, but I never heard of him being taken care of after everything was over." He made a weak gesture, as though he'd been planning some confident motion of the hand, only to think better of it at the last moment. "Wouldn't be the first time they lost track of someone dead, eh? Accidentally, I mean. But someone should see he gets buried. Properly, you know. Antonov—Gennady Mikhailovich deserves that much from us, doesn't he? Wouldn't want to be left out in the snow myself. You've come up in the world and I've sunk down somewhat, but we're still his friends. We made a good team for him before."

My pot needed stirring. "You needn't worry," I said, stepping over to it. "He's been buried."

"Oh." When I looked back, the focus had faded from his features. The blur that had been his face could have belonged to any unkempt, hungry old man, with eyes of any color at all.

"The Chekist took care of the body shortly after they sent Kologriev off. It wasn't too public, but Vinogradov heard."

"Oh."

I knew already: the Chekist had dropped Petrovich, and his position in KrimKab was tenuous. All because he'd defied Infosec to proceed with the investigation, its outcome notwithstanding. That was my doing. The missing toes and finger aside, he was right: my position had improved, and his had gotten worse.

Embarrassment, I think it was, that made me explain. I didn't want to share my groats. I gave him talk instead.

"Vinogradov was irate, actually. It was part of Infosec's saving face. They insisted the requisition was entirely legitimate. Do you see what I mean? Officially, it was declared a matter of a routine order, only subject to interference by an *urka* with corrupt, reactionary tendencies. No one can prove Kologriev's misinformation was what made them shoot those Whites. Even you and I, knowing what we know, I don't think we could prove it. As long as the coffins were delivered to the cemetery with bodies in them, it would make things all right. In someone's eyes, at least."

He looked at me uncomprehendingly, foggily. I concluded lamely: "They buried him in one of the coffins."

"Ah," the old man said. The sound was strangled. "Yes. Yes. Saving face."

We were quiet. The December wind rushed by outside the cell's single window. "Maybe he'd have liked the idea," I said hopelessly. "Surrounded by the paintings that way."

Petrovich stood for a moment, looking at the floor. When he looked up, he was grimacing. An attempt at a smile.

"That's something I taught you, then. You're keeping track of all the little bits of information that come your way now, aren't you? Never know when you'll get to use them." I nodded. "You weren't there when they finally found that bastard Kologriev, eh?" he went on. "Too bad. You deserved it. Nothing more satisfying than seeing them take your man into custody."

"Too bad," I said.

The gnarled fingers picked at his sleeve. "He didn't try to run, you know. Just curled up by a stove in the corner of the ship's mess. No one expected him to stay on the boat. Took some time to find him. He must have been cold, eh?"

"Yes," I said. "Must have been."

Petrovich gazed at me for another moment. "I still picture you turning Antonov over onto his back by his ankles," he said. "You told me he was a lever . . . What kind was it?"

"A lever of the second class."

After he left, I finished cooking and ate my meal. We would nod if we saw each other in the dormitory, but it didn't happen often. After our week of partnership, Yakov Petrovich was no longer part of my life.

That January there was an outbreak of typhus in the kremlin, and I heard he'd died.

Even so, our case kept unspooling its consequences.

Kologriev gave up his side of the story under interrogation. No, call it what it was: he gave it up under torture. Everyone knew what went on in the basements he toured.

By his account, the idea to smuggle the icons off the island had been Antonov's. In fact, Gennady Mikhailovich had approached him at the time of the first requisition order. Naturally Antonov wanted to keep the icons from being broken up for their wood. A buyer had already been arranged. Antonov offered Kologriev two-thirds of the proceeds from their sale if he would make arrangements for their delivery in secret to Kem. (Later Vinogradov admitted to me that he feared he himself had given Antonov the idea of suborning Kologriev. The two had discussed bribery when the requisition first came through, though Vinogradov's goal in broaching the subject was to keep the icons in the collection, not remove them from it.)

It was a deal Kologriev could accept. His then-boss Prokupin took no interest in what happened to the icons. Collecting them for boards had amused him for the way it insulted the church, but afterwards he lost interest. Kologriev had found it easy to "lose" the pieces in the warehouse, and his criminal contacts put him in touch with the mate of the *Gleb Boky*, a man who possessed both access to the mainland and a flexible attitude towards camp rules. The two soon reached an agreement.

That first time they'd hidden the icons in a shipment of processed lumber, among the boards. The buyer's agent, for whom neither Kologriev nor the first mate could give a name, had delivered payment on the spot. The mate took his cut, then duly conveyed the remainder back to Antonov and Kologriev.

Thus thirty-eight icons were spirited off the island and delivered to Kem, before Petrovich and I ever entered the case. It was done smoothly, profitably, calmly.

In the year that followed, problems arose.

First, the buyer objected to the condition in which his purchases had reached him. Evidently the paint of certain panels had suffered scrapes, likely as a result of their being stacked up against one another. Kologriev wasn't able to say how the message had reached Antonov, but it had, and the restorer was irate. He would not, he declared, participate further in any scheme that might allow harm to come to the sacred works of art. Moreover, the buyer refused to pay full price for damaged goods.

Kologriev reassured him as best he could: next time they'd do better. Soon afterward, however, Prokupin lost his position. The replacement of the Bolshevik's neglect and inattention by Zhenov's system of careful record keeping and audits made everything more difficult.

Kologriev's solution was ingenious. But, it had to be admitted, sending the icons to the cabinetry workshop to be hammered into coffins seemed at least as serious a threat to their integrity as stacking them up had been. Antonov, then, could not know what the plan entailed. At the same time, Kologriev was mindful that delivering the paintings in the best possible shape would maximize his profits. Without explaining why, he suggested to Antonov that there might be some extramural restoration work to be done. He should prepare what he needed and wait for word.

No explanation was ever found for what Antonov did next. Instead of waiting for word, he took gold leaf and other supplies from his own desk as soon as the requisitioned icons had been collected. Reporting to Vinogradov that they'd been stolen, he acquired a pass out of the kremlin, ostensibly to investigate. Then he presented himself at the Anzer warehouse, demanding to see Kologriev.

He must have assumed he would be able to see to any necessary repairs, then report to Vinogradov that he'd been able to recover the majority of the supplies. Should it have been surprising that this appearance had not been reported to Petrovich and myself in our inquiries at the warehouse? Whether through bribery or intimidation, Kologriev had the men he worked and lived with under his thumb—that had long been clear.

At any rate, he and Antonov met. The *urka* could only conceal for so long the fact that the pieces had already been sent to the cabinetry workshop. When Antonov learned what lay in store, their partnership at once dissolved. He announced that he would rather have the whole affair exposed than to see his icons hammered into boxes. He intended to go to Vinogradov immediately, that night, and confess all.

Kologriev, for his part, did not waste any words announcing his intentions. Instead he simply waited for his erstwhile partner to turn away, then hit him in the base of the skull with a pry bar. Once he was sure Antonov was dead, he waited for darkness, then dragged the body to the bay and threw it in the water.

It was not what Kologriev had planned, of course. It was hurried, it was a risk. But perhaps Antonov's fate was already sealed. Perhaps it had been ever since it proved necessary for payment to be made on delivery in Kem, instead of being sent by mail to Antonov himself. After that, it was only a matter of time before Kologriev figured out a way to remove the restorer from the loop. By the time he killed him, he'd already given Antonov's name to the Chekist as a conspirator in the rumored escape. Details of this part of his scheme were never revealed to us. Infosec proved reluctant to discuss with Vinogradov or me exactly how Kologriev's status as an informant had allowed him to defraud the camp authorities. Instead, they pressed us to fill in a different gap: who was the final buyer for the stolen icons to have been? The concern was less to punish this individual, assumed to be a foreigner anyway, than to discover how Antonov had made the arrangements. It suggested a much freer channel of communication with the mainland than they liked.

In fact, Vinogradov had been able to tell me immediately what the channel was. "I am afraid I facilitated the arrangement myself," he said with a small frown. The museum, as an independently administered entity within the camp, came with a number of privileges for its director, of the same kind as those enjoyed by grander creatures, company commanders or production-section coordinators. One of these was the right to send and receive sealed mail, bypassing the censors' normal review. Vinogradov had permitted several of his favored subordinates, Antonov among them, to include in his packets letters of their own. It was a courtesy: he had not insisted on reading what they sent.

Thus negotiations for the illicit sale of his collection had been carried out directly under his nose, even with his assistance—naturally not a fact he was anxious to have widely known. He needed to be seen to make inquiries.

And so I was sent to Veronika.

This was February, four months since I'd last seen her. Vinogradov would have given me a pass to the fishery earlier, if I'd asked. Something had stopped me.

"Anatoly Pavelovich," she exclaimed when I found her. She pushed a strand of hair behind her ear. It was longer than it had been, I thought. She was thinner. "I never heard from you. I thought—" She trailed off. Whatever she'd thought, she didn't say it.

The sea was frozen solid, and out on the ice two gatherings of bearded men bustled with ropes, visible sign of nets moving beneath the surface. The monks were fishing. We leaned on the fishery railing and watched them, bundled against the wind, while I explained a little of what Vinogradov and I had learned. Of course, she had no idea who the buyer had been.

"Maybe you overheard a word or two about his contacts," I said. Vinogradov had emphasized the desirability of telling Infosec we'd found out something new, whether it had anything to do with the smuggling or not. "Any name might help. Someone among the Germans, maybe. He mentioned once there were respectable collectors in Germany."

"I don't know any Germans." The sky that day was unseasonably clear and blue. The wintry sun shone on the monks, and she laughed shrilly, happily. "Having once kept a secret from you, I suppose now you'll never again believe I'm innocent of these schemes."

I shrugged. The sun glittered in her eyes, and they gave back a black reflection of the day, the way an animal's do. I suppose she saw that I did not really care what I was asking her.

"So," she said. "This is how it is for you now, is it? You're the museum director's man-of-all-work?"

Yes: she knew that there was nothing I wanted from her. But still there was something in her voice, in her manner.

"Mostly I'm in the archives," I said. "Some date or other is always missing from the catalog."

"But you track down other loose ends, too. You got his icons back for him. Anyone would respect you as a tracker-down of ends, after that."

I didn't correct her about what had happened to the icons, how they had been buried. And there was no point pretending I didn't understand what she meant. I was wearing a new watch cap, a new coat—both provided by Vinogradov. "That's right."

The monks' raised voices drifted towards us from over the ice.

"I heard they'd ended up in the bay. They say someone jumped in after." She raised an eyebrow at me. "That would have to have been you, wouldn't it?"

"It turned out all right," I said.

I hadn't jumped in after, of course: I'd gone for the rail to escape Kologriev, with the coffin falling in behind. But it was true that I'd saved it. And that had been the right choice: if I hadn't endured the water as long as I did to keep the coffin afloat, the mate would have denied us our proof. While Kologriev and I gasped and struggled, he had been stowing the remaining coffins away in the *Gleb Boky*'s belly, just as I feared. When they came for him, he was urging the captain to launch despite the disruption, desperate to make his escape to the mainland.

Veronika watched me, waiting for me to say more. At last she looked down.

"I don't need to know all the details," she said. "You say you caught the murderer. Fine, I'm happy you did. But these coffins you say you found . . . Tell me, did I misjudge him?"

"Misjudge him? Antonov?"

"Yes, yes." She sounded exasperated. "It would be a misjudgment, wouldn't it? You aren't telling me everything about the plot. Fine. But even so, I can see there would have been no way to get the paintings off the island if those executions hadn't happened at the right moment." Her voice could change so quickly. It trembled now between emotions, from frustration to sorrow. Or was it to pleading? "Did Antonov know what would happen to those men? Did he have a part in it?"

"You mean, was he ready for them to die to save his icons?".

Veronika shook her head, a quick, tight shake. "Just tell me."

How had the smuggling depended on the executions? Vinogradov and I had not been able to sort it out entirely ourselves. Kologriev, obviously, had set himself up as an informant. It was only in such a position that he could have arranged for the executions to take place at the time he needed them to. Given this, we reasoned that he must also have been the one behind Petrovich's and my investigation authorization being revoked at the crucial moment. He'd have said—what? Something about my untrustworthiness, no doubt, and about our clumsy investigation threatening to throw the conspirators' suspicion on him.

But why had he ever been believed? Knowing, as we did, that any information he'd provided had been pure fiction, it was easy for us to ask. But you could ask equally: what reason did they have not to? From the Chekist's perspective, at worst a few reactionaries would be disposed of. A reformed *urka*, coming to them with information about a plot among the Whites? As a story, it was irresistible. What a success to report for the project of SLON!

He must have been talking to the Chekist and Infosec for a long time, then, long enough for the narrative he'd fed them to be well established. Since the victims had all been associates of Zhenov's, we hypothesized that his tale had involved a plan hatched at Zhenov's gatherings, with the military men planning to seize supplies and cross the ice as soon as it became solid enough to walk on. How Kologriev had accounted for his knowledge of these meetings was as unclear as everything else. (For instance: how had he transported the painted coffins from the train to his warehouse, and thence to the ship? With Zhenov absent on Anzer when the shipment took place, he might simply have relied on the executioners to be too intent on covering their work with dirt to notice anything else, and never delivered them to the cemetery.) He could, of course, have claimed they'd recruited him, knowing he'd managed to pull off escapes in tsarist camps. He had not implicated Zhenov, but that might simply have been a matter of it being more convenient to continue with a known supervisor, one who'd proved exploitable already.

But whatever the other details, we knew Kologriev had connected Antonov to the escape plot, whether intending for him to be rounded up with the Whites or simply to have something to use against him later. (Indeed, that was Kologriev's first mistake: if the Chekist hadn't been interested in Antonov already, he never would have sent for Petrovich to investigate his death.) And surely, being implicated falsely in that false conspiracy cleared him of implication in the real deaths that followed?

"No," I said. "No, he didn't have any idea, never even found out about it. When he learned what Kologriev meant to do, just to the icons, he tried to back out. That's why he was killed."

She nodded. "Good," she breathed. "That's good. It's reassuring. I'd have hated to have been wrong about him. I always thought that he was good. I'd never heard of someone able to keep his life so much the same, after being sent to Solovki. It was one of the things that struck me, when we met in the hospital. For everyone else, prison is a demarcation, a—a sharp inflection in the line of your life. But he managed to keep on the same way afterward as before. That made him seem good. You are saying I wasn't wrong."

"You weren't wrong," I said.

Veronika was quiet for a minute. "His whole life, here and in Yaroslavl," she said. "All colors, brushes, candles, and God, then see what happens in the end? Schemes, counterschemes, and betrayal. But even the good and the very straightforward develop schemes on this island. Everyone gets tangled."

The way she said it, I couldn't tell whether the idea pleased her or made her sad.

For a time we were quiet, gazing out at the sea. While I watched her still body out of the corner of my eye, I thought about Antonov, about the two of them together. At last she let out a long breath, pushing air through her lips, and turned to face me. Her lips pursed, not quite a smile. "You aren't straightforward, are you, Tolya Bogomolov? I ought to be frightened of you."

"Frightened?"

"Four months ago you showed up here missing a finger. Unknown men were after you, and you'd run afoul of the Camp Administration to a point where I wondered whether I'd regret tying your tourniquet. I recall that not all the blood you were covered with was yours, but it didn't look promising. Now, today, you reappear with a new coat and hat, new boots. Your deadly foe has been sent off to Sekirnaya, or shot, and you work for the man I thought you were investigating."

"That frightens you?"

"Who knows what you might do on this island, if you can do all that? And now you want me to tell you a name I don't know. You might think I was crossing you, if I don't."

She didn't sound frightened. The music that dropped out of her voice while we talked about Antonov had returned. It was the first thing I'd noticed about her, back when she was denying all knowledge of him to Petrovich: she could talk the way other people danced.

"I am still missing the finger," I said.

"Are you? You haven't removed your hand from your pocket the whole time we've been talking."

I did, bending back the finger of my glove to show it was empty. "It still hurts. The cold makes it worse." I didn't mention what had happened to my feet. By that time I didn't limp as much anymore.

"Well, even so. I wouldn't want you for an enemy."

I said: "Vinogradov did the most, in the end."

"That only means you have pull." I'd been waiting for her to gaze into my face, and now she did. Black sardonic eyebrows pulled up the black eyes that met mine. "Influence. You understand this as well as I do. For people like us, power is simply pull. Someone, somewhere, probably in the Cheka, pulls, and that is how we all end up in prison in the first place. Someone pulls—a new work assignment for you. Someone pulls—your ration is worse, or better. Pull—a good spot in the hospital. If I still wrote poems, it would be a poem: everyone caught in one of these nets I've been making for the monks, and the only way we can affect anything is to drag on the ropes in our gills. Or, better, get some fish in a better position to drag on our behalf. You, I perceive, are a favorably enmeshed fish."

That made me laugh. "It doesn't sound enviable."

"All a matter of who you're next to. You—"

She broke off. A figure had left one of the groups of monks and was facing us, waving a hand above its head.

"That's Brother Kiril. I need to take this load out to him. Don't leave yet. I'll be back in a minute."

A few thuds and scrapes said she was working at something beneath the pier. After a minute, she appeared out on the ice, carrying a large load in both arms.

Even with the sun shining, it was cold standing still. As I watched her cross the ice, I thought of Petrovich. There was a connection I'd had, an example of my favorable enmeshment. I'd convinced him to pull on my behalf. And Foma, Foma had pulled, too. I kept my eyes on the girl, but my feet burned and itched with unmentioned wounds.

It didn't take her long. As she came back up to the top of the stairs, she said: "They're stupid fish. When they're running you just cut a hole in the ice and lower your hook in to pull them up, one after another. So they tell me. With the nets they do much more. But that only lasts while they're running. The season is almost over." The wind and the effort of hurrying across the ice had put color into her face.

"How do they work the nets, under the ice?" I said.

I could tell from her expression that my voice sounded strange. "There's a system. It's complicated. There's a pattern of holes, with ropes attached to the net through different holes. I tried to understand it when I first began work, but the truth is, I don't care."

I looked at the bare birches along the shore. Their trunks, bent inland by years of wind from the sea, seemed to shine in the sun.

"When they're done with these *navaga* for the year, they won't have any more use for me," she said. "I'll need to be reassigned."

I waited for her to say something more. I suppose she was waiting for me. "What will you do?" I finally asked.

"You mean, will Stepnova send me to Boris, without Antonov around to stop it? It isn't something she's discussed with me. But I haven't heard of Boris getting a different housekeeper."

The band that had been closing in my throat tightened. "You still see him."

It wasn't what she'd been hoping I'd say. "Sometimes," she said.

"You would never tell us whether you loved him."

"No," she said. "I wouldn't."

I kept looking at the trees. After a minute, her voice moved again quietly: "Have you ever been in love, Anatoly Bogomolov? I thought I had. You read my file, didn't you? I'm sure my lovers in Petersburg were there. All of that was romantic enough. There were the requisites under the flowering bird-cherries, and tremendous fights, too, with them and their other women. You wouldn't call it passionless. But when I look back on that period, all I see is myself wishing to be a bohemian. At least not to participate in being a virtuous and crude youth of the new Soviet age. I took a part of my life and carved something I thought looked like a woman out of it. It was—it was sculpture in the stone of my own existence."

I waited. She shook her head. "Now I am not sure I could tell you what it is to be in love. Boris beats me. That's hateful. But he can be sweet, too. Not gentle like Gennady Mikhailovich. But it isn't always gentle you want, is it? I—"

She stopped herself. The look in her eyes was an appeal. I held my face still, and she went on.

"I'd never have said I could have loved one man for the way he stopped love for another from running away with me. Yet that was what I felt, for both of them. It would have been a lie if I'd answered your questions about who I was in love with, as if I knew." Taking a step closer, she put her hand on my sleeve. Below her touch, I felt my mutilated hand inside its intact glove. "A person never feels just one way, do they? But you and I—we like each other." She smiled. "Not just like, I think. I will admit I thought you were a boy when we first met, but the difference in our ages isn't so much, not really. We could help each other. You have the same pull with Vinogradov that Antonov did."

What was she offering me? Not herself. She did not propose to give up Spagovsky. *We have come through, both of us*, I thought. And whether that meant *we've come through, why go back?* or *we've come through, and only you can understand* was not yet certain.

There was the column of her throat as she raised her face to me: graceful, the source of speech. I remembered the sound of shots while they were executing the Whites; I remembered holding the coffin up, so cold in the water; I remembered what it had meant to skulk under her window and hear her talk, and later to watch her face go through its transformations.

What she offered was a glimpse of something, that was all. A glimpse of her wrist, every so often, for as long as it stayed lovely. A turning, for who could say how long, off the singular path of the life I was laying down in the camps.

"It isn't as easy for me as you think," I said.

"Nothing is easy here, Tolya Bogomolov," she breathed.

After the bay, I think there was always a core of cold in me. I never warmed up again. Since then, I have been hard instead of soft. Instead of trembling, I shiver. That must be why I said what I did.

"If we'd met in Petersburg," I said. "Things would have been different, then."

She did not back up immediately. First she touched the lapel of my coat. Then, in a different voice, she said: "Yes. Things would be different anywhere but here."

On the way back, the kremlin's amputated towers thrust themselves into the air, higher and higher the closer I came. In the sunlight, the soot and burned timbers where the domes had been showed raw as broken teeth. They rose above the green terraces of the pines.

Then, as I came out from among the trees, behind a scrim of telegraph poles and power lines, it was there. *Zeks* tramping like toys before it, the outbuildings huddled to its lichen-and-snow-crusted stones. The wall. With each step, it approached like the appalling future.

Of the three years on Solovetsky Island that remained to me, I spent most in the museum. I was not transferred away until the place itself was closed, the collection dispersed. By that time Vinogradov's sentence had ended. After a period of overseeing us as a free employee, he'd moved on, who knew where.

SLON, too, had moved its base of operations away from the island. It now administered penal colonies all over Karelia, with inmates of the old kremlin spread among them. The connections I'd made on the island, along with my background in mathematics, allowed me to secure an accountant's position upon my transfer to Belomor. I lived out the remainder of my sentence without having to starve too much, without handling a pick or a shovel. It was different for others.

And the wall still rises: Solovetsky is what always lies before us. The future that lay beyond that wall? More walls, surrounding zones of imprisonment scattered across the country. They would be built on SLON's model, even if their barriers were done, for reasons of economy, in barbed wire and posts instead of in stone. A negligible difference: as Antonov knew from his icons, all that matters is that the essential configuration be preserved.

I saw Kologriev again only once. It was in the summer, with insects buzzing, the sky blue and hot. I must have been on an errand for Vonogradov. Near the little complex of buildings north of the kremlin, I had to step to the side of the road to let a work group go by, some thirty men or so. They were dirtier even than the usual for *zeks*, and stank. Two bored guards came along behind, driving them along. The men looked worthless, spent. If the guards hadn't been there to prod them, they might have dragged to a halt.

I almost didn't recognize Kologriev. When I did, it was only because his features had that quality of being miniature, pinched together in the middle of his face. He walked at the back, head down, teetering like an old man. How can I say it? The features themselves had changed, wizened. The smallness was the same.

I made no effort to hide my staring, but he never noticed me. His body, still giant, was gaunt now, fractured, as though pieces might shear off under their own weight. While I watched, a tremor began to shake his arm. Starting in his hand, it twitched up past his elbow and into his shoulder, until he jerked like a fish. Then it subsided, without the *urka*'s ever having seemed to acknowledge it.

What did I feel? Surely I knew already that the man had been destroyed. He'd spent a year at the punishment cells to the north of the island, the ones called Sekirnaya.The converted church they occupied sat atop a steep hill, and the place was known for two punishments. The first involved guards tying a prisoner to a heavy log at the wrists and ankles, then rolling both, man and log, down the two hundred stairs that led up to the church door. This Kologriev appeared to have been spared.

The second punishment was this: they would force prisoners to sit for days atop high, narrow poles. It was said there was a great hall fitted for the purpose, so that a dozen or more inmates could experience this penal regime at once. You can picture it: a roomful of men teetering twenty feet in the air, contorting themselves, day and night, to keep from falling. It is the exoticism of such cruelty that impresses. They would have been unable to sleep, starving. Holding yourself there, your tendons would weaken, your bones would twist: every integrity sacrificed, in the end, to balance.

The essential configuration preserved: when I picture Kologriev now, I picture him along with the image of Saint Simeon Stylites I saw that day on the quay, on the coffin's interior wall. The blue tower, the brown face, the altered proportions. Kologriev's ravaged, guilty features. His tremor.

Of course, the Church teaches that Simeon sat on his pole for forty years, while my *urka* was only at Sekirnaya for a fraction of that time. But, then, I understand the saint had a platform. Perhaps he could lie down.

The platoon shambled by. I didn't watch for long. After he was gone, I never heard of Kologriev again.

But did I have to? No, I had what was essential. And this is the matter of mysteries, and icons. Maybe it is the matter of prisons as well. Petrovich and Antonov had it in common: both thought they could look at the flat surfaces presented to them by the world and see through them to something truer, something on the other side. The paint flakes, the clues are faint, but if we can only put them into the right relation, something new, something important will emerge . . .

Deeper and deeper, truer and truer, more and more secret—always inside our painted box.

EPILOGUE

It has been months since I wrote the lines on the previous page, lines I thought were final. With the story of the murder complete, my frenzy for writing subsided. I no longer fetishize the wire spirals from the tops of my notebooks. I do not now work into the small hours of the night. My hand creaks around the pen, the familiar gesture of writing grown stiff.

But I find that I must add one last thing. It comes, of course, from Vasily, with whom the whole undertaking began. Vasily-the-tank-commander, Vasily-my-neighbor. He has read the story now. Perhaps, as I wrote when I first revealed the nature of this manuscript to him, I was writing it for him all along. Perhaps, or perhaps not. He has had the tact not to insist on discussing it at length, at least. But it seems he has not stopped considering the topic.

Months have passed, and there have been no further ill consequences of his expulsion from the Party. His appeals to city and district committees duly rejected, his red-haired wife initiated divorce proceedings—but at the plant the situation has settled. If he will never again occupy the position of respect he did, he is still less a pariah than I.

And so he has resumed a correspondence that, it transpires, he had already begun keeping up before we met. There are others like him, a network of them, interested in accounts of the camps. They must be secret, of course: such accounts are forbidden. But via this network he has received a packet of writings from Siberia. It is a sorry sort of publication, each piece either copied out by hand or reproduced by carbon. But, he said, it contained something he thought would interest me.

And so there sits on my table a poem . . . I will copy it again here, by hand.

Its title is "On Solovetsky Island." The anthologist identifies the author as "a lady prisoner who, having entered the camps quite early, later found herself married to an administrator in Magadan."

Her initials are given as VFF.

VFF. It means that she survived, doesn't it? Veronika Filipovna Fitneva survived the camps.

Survival is a surprise. You do, after all, know how the stories of so many *zeks* end: they end in death. In this way camp stories are much like my *detektivy*, which take their course and inevitably conclude with the crime solved, the criminal punished.

Of course, when the camp story has been written into a memoir, like mine, the ending is not the same as the one you must expect for the average *zek*. Anyone who lived to tell the tale must, by that very fact, have a tale that is a standard deviation or two away from the mean.

You knew I would find the killer. You knew that I would live. My own ending is no less confined by necessity than the unwritten stories of the dead.

But Veronika—her survival was not so sure. It was not to be inferred from the structure of things, was it?

A year ago, drunk, I wrote that I wished her dead. But now, whatever her miseries and compromises, I am glad—glad for her to have outlived my story.

Let her poem of survival end this book.

On Solovetsky Island

A hundred miles of gray cloud out to sea,
where the pines came down to the water.
When an old man inquired officially,
I said: "Why should I believe in lovers?"

It was the kind of lie you tell in jail,
where they pass you on yourself as sentence.
Heart, if you fret, I tell you: shiver, crack, go unhealed!
I'll not-not-not do one more ounce of penance.

Do not remind me now what you were for,
Or of gulls heard through a rented window crying.
We must thread this century's corridors,
and exercise the choice that's left us—to refuse.

ABOUT THE AUTHOR

James L. May holds an MFA from Florida International University, along with a BA in English from Cornell. He grew up in New Jersey, lived in New Orleans, and now resides in New York City. His short fiction has appeared in *Tigertail*, and he reviews fiction for *The Florida Book Review*, *Gulf Stream Literary Magazine*, and the *New Orleans Review*.